Revealed

Berkley Sensation Titles by Kate Noble

COMPROMISED
REVEALED

Revealed

Kate Noble

BERKLEY SENSATION, NEW YORK

THE BERKLEY PUBLISHING GROUP
Published by the Penguin Group
Penguin Group (USA) Inc.
375 Hudson Street, New York, New York 10014, USA
Penguin Group (Canada), 90 Eglinton Avenue East, Suite 700, Toronto, Ontario M4P 2Y3, Canada
(a division of Pearson Penguin Canada Inc.)
Penguin Books Ltd., 80 Strand, London WC2R 0RL, England
Penguin Group Ireland, 25 St. Stephen's Green, Dublin 2, Ireland (a division of Penguin Books Ltd.)
Penguin Group (Australia), 250 Camberwell Road, Camberwell, Victoria 3124, Australia
(a division of Pearson Australia Group Pty. Ltd.)
Penguin Books India Pvt. Ltd., 11 Community Centre, Panchsheel Park, New Delhi—110 017, India
Penguin Group (NZ), 67 Apollo Drive, Rosedale, North Shore 0632, New Zealand
(a division of Pearson New Zealand Ltd.)
Penguin Books (South Africa) (Pty.) Ltd., 24 Sturdee Avenue, Rosebank, Johannesburg 2196, South Africa

Penguin Books Ltd., Registered Offices: 80 Strand, London WC2R 0RL, England

This book is an original publication of The Berkley Publishing Group.

Cover art by Aleta Rafton.
Cover design by George Long.

PRINTING HISTORY
Berkley Sensation trade paperback edition / March 2009

Library of Congress Cataloging-in-Publication Data

Noble, Kate, 1978–
Revealed / Kate Noble.—Berkley Sensation trade pbk. ed.
p. cm.
ISBN 978-0-425-22174-7
1. London (England)—Social life and customs—19th century—Fiction. I. Title.

PS3614.O246R48 2009
813'.6—dc22

2008048320

PRINTED IN THE UNITED STATES OF AMERICA

10 9 8 7 6 5 4 3 2 1

To my father and brother, the two wisest and most unflappable gentlemen I know.

Prologue

THE setting sun reflected off the inn's bronze door knocker, blazing orange light like a beacon to the weary traveler. He had been on the road for days, on the trail of his enemy, and at last, the inn at the end of the road beckoned him as if to say, "This is it. The final place."

It would end now. He was certain of it.

The building sat on the jagged edge of land and sea. He felt, he feared, it was the right place. His sinking stomach told him it was. He took a swig of water from the leather pouch he kept hooked to his waist. Squaring his shoulders, he ruthlessly combed his fingers through his hair, willing himself out of exhaustion. Then, as he approached, the building came into focus.

His instincts had been right, and tonight there would be bloodshed. But would it be his or his enemy's?

His contact's information was very good, he thought, as he read the choppily carved text beneath the inn's name on its masthead. Fin de Rue Poisson. Literally translated, End of Fish Road. His contact had told him that the encoded communiqué they had intercepted had been translated to say "fish fin." And thus, he had been searching every stall, every ship, every pub in every small coastal village in this northern region of France for a "fish fin." The Fin de Rue Poisson may not be a literal translation, but as an amalgam of English and French, it fit the bill.

The sea lapped jawfuls of water nearly at the base of the inn. If he looked hard enough, stared long enough, could he see England? Could he see home?

No. All he could see was the water and the looming building, beckoning him closer.

It was time to find the man who had eluded him for so long.

The Frenchman stood at the window in the westernmost room of the uppermost floor of the seaside inn at the end of the rue Poisson. He faced the cobbled street that led from the village to the seashore, the farthest corner of the structure, yes, but it was strategic. Here, he could see what was coming. The copper sun burned his eyes, but he had to remain vigilant, had to stay aware, had to stay alive.

He knew the man they called the Blue Raven was due to arrive. He knew, because he had leaked the clue to the safe house whereabouts himself.

Tonight he would prove his worth.

The Frenchman glanced at his pocket watch. Who knew it would take so damned long?

Movement on the street caught his eye. The Frenchman squinted into the sun and leaned into the glass, searching. His heartbeat quickened, the blood rushing to his temples, his muscles tensing, ready for fight or flight.

The clacking of horse hooves on cobblestones reached his ears as a carriage came into sight, a large, burly man driving the team. His face was shaded by an oversized leather hat, his form covered by a heavy cloak. The Frenchman watched and waited as the carriage approached . . . and turned a corner, out of sight.

A breath held too long fell from his lungs in a staccato rhythm. The Emperor had waved the white flag at Waterloo nearly a fortnight ago, but he knew the loyal were still being hunted. He was still too used to that rush of noise in his ears that woke him up in the dead of night. They would come together again. They would not surrender as easily as their leader. But for now, he kept his hand on the beautifully scrolled pistol at his waist, squeezing its cold, hard length for comfort.

"That will not help you now," said a deep, rasping voice from the door.

The Frenchman turned, his hand remaining still on his belt, and took his first look at the Blue Raven.

He was dressed in the worn oilskins of a local fisherman, but the ornate pistol leveled at the Frenchman's fair head was not part of a fisherman's costume. That deadly weapon, as a matter of fact, was an identical match to the one he held at his waist.

"So," the Frenchman spoke in perfect if accented English, "the little pigeon has arrived. Finally."

"I apologize if I kept you waiting," the Englishman replied in perfect if accented French.

The Frenchman leaned back in the comfortable, leather, winged chair. "I must say, you look different than I expected."

The Englishman's eyes narrowed. "You look exactly as I expected."

"Do I?"

"Yes, but then again, I have the advantage. I saw you once at a distance." The Englishman cocked the pistol, the metallic click echoing in the small room. "You were slitting the throat of one of my countrymen."

A sudden flash of feeling ran down the Frenchman's spine, so unfamiliar, it took him a moment to identify it as panic.

He knew, in that spare second, that he had greatly miscalculated his adversary. He had neglected to factor in the hate he saw burning in the Blue Raven's eyes.

"You've been tracked through cities and across battlefields," the Englishman said, his voice breaking with bitter spite. "And too many lives have been taken or destroyed by you."

"Monseiur," the Frenchman said, managing a cold smile in spite of the wildness of his heartbeat. "Surely we can settle our dispute as gentlemen."

The Englishman regarded him, his arm and gaze steady and strong. "No," he replied. "I tire of being a gentleman."

The Frenchman's hand came up in a blur of movement, and the air rang with the sound of gunfire.

The Blue Raven remained standing in the doorway until the weight on his leg gave out. The hole three inches above his knee leaked smoke, then a warm red spurt began trickling down his calf. But the Frenchman, the adversary he had hunted for the better part of a decade, who had seduced secrets from England's top leaders and spilled the blood of those who weren't so easily charmed, remained seated.

He wouldn't be getting up any time soon.

The red stain grew and spread on the white lawn of the Frenchman's shirtfront. His eyes were opened in surprise.

Until the end, he had believed he would win.

The Englishman hobbled over to the Frenchman's body and removed the pistol from that man's limp hand. He stuffed it ruthlessly into the waist of his trousers, reuniting it with its mate after so many years. A small glint of metal from around the dead man's neck caught his attention. He pulled it free of the bloody shirt: a crucifix. Quietly laying it back on the man's chest, the Englishman took a moment and then gently closed his enemy's eyes.

The Blue Raven straightened, wincing as his weight fell on his wounded leg. He didn't have much time; the English had won the war, but he was still on French soil. He could hear the innkeeper's boots on the stairs already; there was only time for one last detail.

From the pocket of his oilskin overcoat, he pulled out a black feather and laid it gently on the dead man's lap.

As he departed the inn via a window, he couldn't keep the elation from flowing, adrenaline overcoming his injury and powering his escape.

It was over.

Finally.

One Year Later

"Will this work?" the first man asked, more nerves in his voice than he liked. He prided himself on maintaining an air of nonchalance, but the jostling evening crowd at the Bull and Whisker and the company of the man next to him had him slightly on edge.

"But of course. While your English imagination is lacking, I see clearly," his companion answered, his French accent smoothing over the cruel bite of his words. "But I'm counting on your English prejudice." He rapped his knuckle on the bar once more, and the beefy man behind brought over the bottle and refilled his glass again.

The first man held up his hand, refusing to let his own drink be refilled. "I don't think imbibing so much is good for our . . . operation."

"*C'est la difference*. England seems to have better French brandy than France. Even in this"—he gestured at the crowded, common merriment about them—"place. I will take my share of its pleasure. The pigeon robbed me of much, but he did not rob me of that."

"But when—"

"When it is necessary that I be sober, I will be. For now, we are nothing more than two *commoners* meeting for a drink. So I suggest you have another," the Frenchman bit out. "*Non?* Fine. As for our arrangement, I am prepared. I suggest you prepare as well."

And with that he stood, picking up his silver-handled walking stick, and turned, perfectly balanced. He loped to the door with the grace born to those of his nationality, and exited.

The first man turned back to the bar, signaled the man for another drink. He let out a low, unsteady breath.

He knew what he did was for his good and the good of England.

But damned if he wasn't making a pact with the devil.

Outside the Bull and Whisker, it was a generally quiet evening, as evenings down at the docksides go, Johnny Dicks thought, chewing the stub of his cheroot. He watched as the sober went into the pub, nodding as they doffed their caps to him as they passed, and then watched them leave, drunk and sloppy. Sometimes he had to stand up off his somewhat comfortable stool and keep the rougher sort from entering the Bull; sometimes Marty would poke his head out and bring him inside to remove someone who became a bit rougher with drink than Marty liked.

When he and Marty were mates in the Seventeenth Regiment, he was a rum one for a good fight, but ever since he bought the Bull, he'd said the cost of replacing all the broken chairs and crockery made the fighting a touch less the crack.

So it was that Johnny Dicks was contemplating the last time Marty had bemoaned a splintered chair and how his brother-in-law the carpenter was like to bilk him, when the reedy gent came strolling out the Bull and Whisker, swinging his stick like he owned the world and the sky above it.

"Have a good evenin', Cap'n," Johnny Dicks called out and nodded as the man passed. The man swung around wildly, his cane connecting with Dicks's shin.

"Hey!" he called out. "That hurt, that did!"

"What did you call me?" the reedy man spat out, his Frenchy accent slurred by drink. The man held himself together when walking well enough, but with his temper up, the drink showed through. Johnny Dicks gained his feet. The height and weight that made him an imposing doorman was put to work now, leaning over the Frenchy. But the Frenchy's face took on a peculiar sheen, a glint of anticipation in his eye.

"I am not your captain," the Frenchy bit out. He swung out with the stick, like a cricket bat. Johnny caught it in his hand and swung with his meaty fist. But the Frenchman was faster, ducking and landing two quick blows to Johnny's body, one to his liver and one to his spleen. The silver-headed cane clattered to the ground as Johnny Dicks fell to his knees.

"The pigeon did not end me; neither shall you," the Frenchy spat out, and with one swift, vicious motion, his heavy Hessian boot landed on Johnny Dicks's jaw.

Johnny fell back, tasting the grime of the cobblestones. He lay on his side, breathing heavily, his jaw on fire, and watched as the Frenchman picked up his cane and, easy as you please, strolled down the way and disappeared around the corner.

"Oy! Johnny!" came a high, soft voice. Johnny rolled over and saw Miss Meggie, a local "lady"—couldn't be more than twenty years old, but long since initiated in her professions of part-time prostitute and full-time pickpocket.

"You all right? That bloke just felled you like you was made o' sawdust!" Miss Meggie said, helping Johnny to sit up. Johnny felt his jaw, happy to find it unbroken, but he found it necessary to spit out a small bit of blood and a tooth or two.

"What'd you say to 'im?" Miss Meggie asked.

"I said good night."

"Yeah, and I reckon he said it right back," Miss Meggie snorted.

"Actually he said somethin' odd—somethin' about a pigeon." Johnny's brow furrowed, only a little painful. "Meggie, you think you can follow the gent? I have a mind to find out more about 'im."

"No worries, Johnny; there ain't been a gent yet that Meggie could'na track down."

And with that, Miss Meggie left Johnny sitting on the ground, ducking into the alley after the gent and disappearing in the shadows.

Fifteen minutes later, Johnny was installed back on his stool outside the door of the Bull and Whisker, two teeth fewer than before and developing three good-sized bruises, when Miss Meggie came walking out of the shadowed alleyway.

"What happened?" he asked.

"I caught up to 'im in the high street, but he hopped in a hansom that was waitin' for him. It took off too fast for me to follow."

"Which way did it head?" Johnny asked.

"West."

"Well, that's somethin' at least."

"Yeah," Miss Meggie said with a smile, "and so is this." She pulled out of her skirt pocket a folded-up bit of foolscap. "Ah, ah, ah!" Miss Meggie said with a smile, holding the paper out of Johnny's reach until he produced a coin and traded her for it.

"What's it say?" Miss Meggie asked, leaning over Johnny's shoulder as he unfolded it. Johnny was not the best reader—his talents lay in other areas—but he knew Miss Meggie was no reader at all. Willing to satisfy her curiosity, he concentrated on the slanted, educated writing.

"Its . . . it's a list," Johnny replied.

"What's it a list of?"

"I dunno," Johnny said. His mind knew he had pieces to a puzzle. A Frenchy who spoke about a pigeon; who hit with the precision of a sharpshooter, even when in his cups; and now this list. He had the pieces, but he didn't know how it all went together.

He turned to Miss Meggie. "But I know a gent who might."

One

EVERYONE agreed that Mrs. Phillippa Benning was a beautiful young woman. Stunning even, with her cornflower blue eyes and cornsilk hair. One poetic gentleman had likened her teeth in shape to perfect corn kernels, but that perhaps was taking the metaphor too far.

Mrs. Benning simply sparkled. Her wit and humor and gay joie de vivre, gave her entrée into the most exciting crowds in the Ton, a place that lady enjoyed and intended to stay. So, if she was occasionally seen as being too forward in her thoughts and too ambitious in her flirtations, it was easily forgiven as the capricious combination of youth and beauty, for when Phillippa Benning smiled—a sultry pout known to cause married men to forget their wives' names—no one could find fault in her.

Indeed, everyone thought well of Mrs. Phillippa Benning. And they certainly would have done so even if she were not so rich and so conveniently widowed.

All the world knew Phillippa Benning's short marriage had been the stuff of fairy tales, merely lacking the ever after. And after mourning her husband of five days for a full year, Phillippa had discovered it was exceedingly pleasant to no longer require that smothering protection unmarried ladies lived under, and took to her life as a young woman of independent means with verve.

She liked all the same things other women liked but made them artlessly hers. She read the latest gothic novels by M. R. Biggleys and Mrs. Rothschild, but whenever she commented that the hero of one was far too bland for her taste or the setting of another was spine-chilling, it was automatically taken as fact and quoted by scholarly ladies and gentlemen alike as such. She could affect sales of fabric as much as a drought or rainy season would affect a crop: If Phillippa Benning declared lilac watered silk to be déclassé, sales of such material would plummet; conversely, if she was seen strolling the park in mint green sprigged muslin and butter colored walking boots, two dozen such costumes would be on order at the best modistes the next day.

It was uncommon for someone so young to rule the Ton (she was just one and twenty), but when it came to Mrs. Phillippa Benning, it was unquestionable. Her favor could make or break a novel's success, a modiste's reputation, a hostess's event, a young debutante's popularity, or a young buck's heart.

And she knew it.

"I absolutely refuse to attend Mrs. Hurston's card party. She insists on wearing that feathered violet turban, and I have taken the trouble twice to tell her how it does not suit her," Phillippa said as she looked through her opera glasses, scanning the crowd lined up along the parade route.

Phillippa's best friend, Nora, clucked her tongue and shook her head, supressing a delicate giggle beneath a tiny hand.

Nora was an adorable little creature Phillippa had picked up this year. She was eighteen, in her first Season, and could have turned out disastrous if not for Phillippa's intervention. Miss Nora De Regis was very rich, born and raised English, but suffered from a touch of dark coloring inherited from a Greek grandfather and from a mother who refused to allow the child to dress in anything other than eyelet cotton and stiff corsets. Phillippa simply made certain the world saw Nora's dark eyes and olive skin as exotic and steered her mother to more expansive modistes. Now mother and daughter alike would not be caught dead in anything but the latest fashions. Nora, at the beginning of the season, also had a rather innocent and open nature, which Phillippa was teaching her to suppress.

Nora was proving a very apt pupil.

"No Phillippa Benning at Mrs. Hurston's party?" Nora replied archly. "She'll lose more face than if Prinny himself failed to appear. Maybe that will shock the good Mrs. Hurston into taking your advice more seriously."

"Really," Phillippa replied, lowering her opera glasses, "you would think they would know by now."

Normally, Phillippa was not one to partake in organized outdoor activities before noon. But then again, there were very few social events whose express purpose was the ogling of men, and a parade of militia was one of them. Patriotism was all the rage. Her companion, Mrs. Tottendale, could not be roused to attend, but Nora was always game for assessing young men's attributes. And besides, Phillippa's other best friend, Bitsy, her Pomeranian, could use the fresh air.

The red woolen coats slashed with gold epaulettes glinted brilliantly in the sun, but none of that distracted Phillippa from her view of a dashing gentleman in a dark green coat watching the processional from the other side of the thoroughfare.

"Did you spot him? The Marquis of Broughton?" Nora craned her neck, trying in vain to see over the throng gathered at the park.

"He's just across the street, to the right," Phillippa replied, never looking directly at him but always keeping him within her view. After all, she did have all of these dazzling redcoats to look at. Bitsy shook delicately in Phillippa's arms, his emerald collar jangling with the dog's nervous energy.

Nora went up on tiptoes and leaned over far enough into the

thoroughfare to nearly be knocked over by an outside fife player. Finally, she spotted the object of Phillippa's intensely purposeful inattention.

"Oh! He's simply delicious!"

"I know," Phillippa purred, letting a small smile play about her mouth, soothing Bitsy with long, gentle strokes. "Where has he been keeping himself? The past few seasons would have been so much more interesting if he had been around."

"The past few seasons have not been dull for you, Phillippa; admit it," Nora replied, wide-eyed and mocking.

It was true. Phillippa had thoroughly enjoyed her first season as a widow. Oh, she had enjoyed her original season, too, but it had ended rather abruptly with Alistair's death, and as such, Phillippa had been determined to regard her emergence from mourning as a fresh start. She knew she would marry again—the hazy vision of a quiet country life with rug rats loomed over her like a cloud threatening rain—but her first season as a widow had been such an overwhelming success, she refused to settle down before giving herself another. She was accountable to no one. Her funds were her own, having inherited her trust upon her marriage. There was something unbelievably luxurious about being untethered. She could flirt with no dreadful repercussions. She could dance until dawn.

Oh, her parents, the Viscount and Viscountess Care, were hopeful that she make a match, of course, and provide them with a few grandchildren to dote upon and make heirs. But Phillippa informed them she required the perfect specimen of man for her to even consider marriage: rich, titled, a leader of the Ton. And until that man arrived, her parents could do nothing more than throw up their hands and go back to their own lives. Her father to the estates and playing the market, her mother to Bath or Brighton, where the waters were as invigorating as the men, she'd say.

But her parents would be very pleased when they learned of the Marquis of Broughton's arrival on the scene, and how very perfect Phillippa had found him thus far.

"Rumor has it, Broughton's been locked up at his estate, poor thing," Phillippa pouted saucily.

"Which one?" Nora asked. "They say he has a dozen."

"Does it matter? It only matters that he wasn't here before, and now he is." A small, satisfied smile lifted the perfect bow of her mouth.

"Well," Nora conceded, "if he's as *delicious* up close as he seems to be from a distance . . . Have you been introduced?"

"Not yet," Phillippa said, as the last of the militia trooped past, leading cheering revelers in their wake (luckily, the parade had been horseless, else the revelers might suffer a misstep and a smelly fate). "But he'll introduce himself shortly."

Nora's brows shot up in surprise. "How can you know that?"

"Watch."

As the last of the revelers passed, Phillippa let go of her coyness and turned, catching hold of the Marquis of Broughton's hawklike gaze and holding it.

One . . . two . . .

She arched a brow, slightly, allowed the faintest upturn to the corner of her mouth.

Three . . . four . . .

Never did his eyes lift from hers. Never did she allow the heat of his gaze to cause more than the faintest of blushes to paint her cheek.

Five.

With one last fractional brow raise, Phillippa pointedly turned away and addressed Nora.

"He'll introduce himself shortly," she repeated. She didn't even attempt to hide the smugness she considered well-deserved. "In the meantime, shall we get some ices? Its unbearably hot among all these"—she flitted her hand—"people."

Phillippa handed a squirming and eager Bitsy to his liveried attendant for walking, and taking Nora's arm, she gently steered her toward the shops that lined the park. Out of the corner of her eye, she saw the Marquis of Broughton approach them. He was still a good twenty feet away but moving like a hunter stalking his prey. Surreptitiously, Phillippa reached over and grabbed one of Nora's gloves out of her hand (she certainly wasn't about to let her own glove get muddy) and dropped it, all without Nora noticing. The Marquis was behind her now, out of her line of sight.

She slowed, and then counted.

Five . . . four . . .

He would be a few feet from the glove by now.

Three . . . two . . .

Bending down, he'd have picked it up.

One.

"Excuse me, madam?" an unfamiliar, deeply masculine voice addressed them, a warm drawl coloring his expression.

Phillippa turned, sly smile and coy look at the ready to lay claim to . . .

Someone who was not the Marquis.

"You seem to have dropped this," the incredibly tall man with the deep voice said, holding up Nora's small, now-soiled glove.

"Thank you," Nora said, accepting the glove with a polite smile. "I hadn't realized I dropped it, Mr.—"

"Mr. Worth," he replied before tipping his hat.

"Mr. Worth," Nora repeated, doing the conversational duties Phillippa had abdicated.

Abdicated, because her gaze had narrowed and locked onto the Marquis of Broughton, who, like them, had attracted his own barnacle of sorts, as she watched him hand a reticule back to a vaguely pretty female who lightly touched his arm at discreet intervals.

It seemed he had "accidentally" been bumped into by none other than that treacherous harlot herself, Lady Jane Cummings.

Two

THE rivalry between Phillippa Benning and Lady Jane Cummings was of such long standing, no one knew its origin. Some were certain that a young buck must have, at one point in time, favored one over the other. Others with keener memories knew they had been rivals at Mrs. Humphrey's School for Elegant Ladies, ruling opposing factions of adolescent girls with strong hands, witty remarks, and imaginative pranks, which would have been unbecoming of young ladies of their station . . . if they had ever been caught. Still others thought the rivalry had begun in the womb, as both their mothers were notorious in their own exploits in their beautiful youth. Whatever the cause, Phillippa Benning's hatred of Lady Jane and vice versa had the effect of setting every tongue in London wagging.

Phillippa, of course, had thought herself removed from Lady Jane at her coming out; Phillippa had debuted at seventeen, and Lady Jane's mother, the Duchess, would not hear of launching her only daughter into society until she was eighteen. But, while Phillippa married, then mourned, Lady Jane had debuted, and then was shocked into nursing and soon mourning herself, when her own mother took violently ill and suffered for weeks before finally succumbing. And so, the seasons had passed, and Phillippa and Lady Jane found themselves again staring each other down in society.

It was highly annoying.

Phillippa had the advantages of the freedoms of widowhood, but Lady Jane, although the exact same age as Phillippa, had the impression of youth and newness. And there was nothing so alluring to the Ton as something new.

Every lady of marriageable age was either in Phillippa's camp or Lady Jane's, and every gentleman knew what it was to walk the line between them. So when one gentleman caught both Phillippa and Lady Jane's eye, it was certain to cause a commotion.

But due to her great advantage in height, Phillippa was absolutely certain she had seen him first that day in the park.

"The Marquis of Broughton," announced the imperious butler at the door of Lady Plessy's parlor.

She also had the good luck to be the only one of them invited to this dinner party.

Lady Plessy's dinner parties were entirely Phillippa's arena. The people who populated them were fashionable, eager, and determined to have their fun. Lady Jane would be wholly welcome in that circle, if not for Lady Plessy's allegiance to Phillippa.

Phillippa Benning was nothing if not determined. They were gathered in the parlor before walking in to dine, milling about talking of the eventful nothings of the day. As Broughton made his bow to their hostess, Phillippa walked directly up to him, extended her hand, and spoke.

"Good evening. I'm Phillippa Benning. And you are . . . ?"

Sometimes the direct approach had its advantages.

Broughton blinked once, then twice, then let out a short guffaw and bowed over her hand, saying, "Broughton, Mrs. Benning. Terribly pleased to see your gloves are none the worse for wear."

That earned a brilliant and knowing smile from Phillippa.

Having sweetly bribed Lady Plessy with promises of an introduction to her famed mantua maker, Madame Le Trois, Phillippa earned the honor of sitting a mere seat away from that good lady, and therefore opposite Lady Plessy's other favored guest, the Marquis of Broughton. He was certainly making a splash in society, a mere three days introduced.

Phillippa let him lead the conversation, her clear blue gaze finding his a dozen times throughout the meal. As he spoke of his exploits hunting, his fencing prowess, his pride in Britain's victories abroad (although he had taken no part in them), and his homes and estates (careful to gloss over their net worth in the way of polite people), he kept turning to her, seeking her out in the flow of words between them. Phillippa couldn't help but smugly think, *Lady Jane doesn't stand a chance.*

He led her to the floor after dinner, his hand lightly brushing the back of her neck and sending a delighted frisson down her spine, causing a small hitch to her breath and curve to her lips. She felt a greater willingness to hold on to his hand through the turns of the quadrille, the effortless stepping of place to place, his movements graceful and perfect.

Lady Jane who?

When the party broke up to go on to others, Broughton leaned over Phillippa's hand, this time lingering, the heat of his thumb caressing the tips of her fingers.

"I do hope to see you again," he said in a deep rumble. "At Almack's, perhaps?"

"Almack's?" Phillippa replied on a cough.

"Almack's," he repeated, a decided twinkle in his eye. "Should I wager for you or against you?"

And at that, all she could do was smile.

"But you hate Almack's! You always say the patronesses look down their noses at you," Nora said in a rushed whisper. They were seated in the ladies' retiring room of the next party—was it the Hurstons? No, Phillippa had refused to attend that one—they were at the Winters', enjoying the small luxury of gossiping in the relative privacy provided by a number of screened-in alcoves, allowing several ladies the necessary privacy required for the secrets of beauty.

Or just secrets.

"They look down their noses at everyone, but they have never denied me a voucher," Phillippa replied nonchalantly.

"But—"

"Nora, I'm well aware of my feelings about the place." And so, apparently, was the Marquis. But he had nearly dared her, nay, *challenged* her to go. What would he think of her if she were not up to the challenge?

The happy, melodic hum of other women chatting, gossiping, laughing in their own alcoves kept their conversation private, but slowly some voices became more easily distinguished than others.

"Did you *see* the Marquis of Broughton at the parade? So tall and elegant! He was practically more beautiful than every man in uniform!" spoke a young lady who could only be Miss Louisa Dunningham, by her high-pitched, girlish squeaks.

"Yes, my dear," spoke her surprisingly deep-voiced mother, "he eclipsed them all."

"Did you see him after the parade?" another young woman, likely Miss Sterling, said. "Practically *mauling* Lady Jane Cummings!"

"Now, now," Mrs. Dunningham replied, "I saw no such thing. You shouldn't spread such gossip, Penny."

"But I saw—"

"What you saw was a man fetching a reticule, nothing more."

That quelled the young debutantes into silence. But only for a moment.

"Oh, he fetched her reticule! How *romantic*!" Louisa squeaked, causing Phillippa to roll her eyes in a thoroughly exasperated and most unattractive manner. Louisa's youthful outburst of vicarious emotion was followed by Penny Sterling's artfully wistful sigh, and "Oh, do you think he'll fall madly for her? That he'll be whisked away by her endless beauty?"

"More likely frightened away by her endless nose," Phillippa whispered to Nora, who unfortunately giggled and then covered it with a snort.

Nora, as much as Phillippa enjoyed her company, had a rather distinctive snort.

The overheard conversation ceased. Then, instead of taking up some other topic with delicacy and grace, the curious Louisa stuck her head around the privacy screen, treating Nora and Phillippa to a view of her eyes going wide.

"Oh! Mrs. . . . Mrs. Benning! How do you do?" Louisa stammered. "Miss De Regis," she turned to Nora, and in doing so, dropped to a curtsy, forcing Nora and Phillippa from their seats to do the same. They emerged from the private alcove (no sense hiding any longer) to greet Mrs. Dunningham and Miss Penny Sterling.

After a moment of stiff bobbing up and down, Penny elected to speak first.

"We were just talking of—"

"Something that would never happen in a million years!" Nora burst out, much to the shock and surprise of everyone, including Phillippa. "I mean to say," she continued, "that the Marquis of Broughton is not going to fall in love with someone like Lady Jane Cummings simply because she dropped her reticule, especially not when he has since danced with Phillippa. Twice."

The shocked and delighted gasps that statement elicited from their audience covered the shocked and appalled "Nora!" that escaped from Phillippa's mouth. For the first time in many many months, Phillippa felt a faint blush spreading across her cheeks. She would be deeply angry at Nora, if she didn't look so well when blushing.

"Where! When! How!" Louisa and Penny were squealing, while Mrs. Dunningham was far more silent but still just as interested in any piece of gossip.

"Oh, its so romantic!"

"Was it at a party? Was it as if you were the only two people in the room?"

"What is the Marquis like? He must be incredibly dashing!"

Phillippa smiled. She was more than willing to expound upon Broughton's virtues. "Dashing is an acceptable word. *Delicious* is far more appropriate."

And he was. Phillippa thought back to their long-delayed introduction, only hours ago. His gorgeous blond hair, falling over his forehead in perfect fashion as he bent over her hand; he never took his eyes from hers, lingering slightly overlong but not in a leering way. It was rare that Phillippa was affected by anyone, but Broughton certainly piqued her interest. And then when he asked her to dance, it was a challenge, a dare. Phillippa doubted Lady Jane would prove such a tempting partner.

"Oh!" Louisa sighed, snapping Phillippa back to reality. "Do you think he'll ask for your hand?" Mrs. Dunningham joined her daughter in delight, "I hear he's worth half a million pounds."

"Well, it will match Mrs. Benning's half a million pounds tidily!" an aptly named Penny Sterling added.

"Ladies!" Phillippa cried, unwilling to let the innuendo go any further. "Goodness, you'd have me married by morning, wouldn't you? All I can say is that if I choose to bring the Marquis of Broughton to heel, I would do so."

"But what of Lady Jane? She's set her cap—"

"Lady Jane?" Phillippa trilled. "Do you honestly think I consider her a threat in any way?"

Nora snorted beside her. "Lady Jane couldn't catch Broughton with armed gunmen and a net. Phillippa will win him, you'll see."

"Nora," Phillippa said quickly, her smile faltering slightly, "I only said if I *wished*—"

"Is that so, Mrs. Benning?" A throaty voice, sharpened by wit and edge, said from behind a screened alcove to their left. "Do you really think you can best me in anything?"

Lady Jane Cummings emerged from behind the screen, a few

of her closest minions behind her, forming a wedge of pretty, fierce scowls.

An undercurrent of electricity cut through the room. Before Phillippa could open her mouth with a smarting reply, Nora's mouth got the best of her.

"Of course she can," Nora said, turning her small body to block Phillippa from onslaught, in a move that Bitsy, her Pomeranian, had performed for Phillippa countless times. Against the foe of squirrels, but still a protective move, nonetheless.

"Why?" Lady Jane answered. "Men only want you for your money. And Broughton *has* money."

A sudden chill descended upon the group. No one spoke. No one breathed. Lady Jane had said what no one ever dared. At least, not to Phillippa's face. Phillippa's eyes narrowed; her expression turned to marble. She thought it only fair to answer in kind.

"Meanwhile, men only want you for your connection to a title. And Broughton *has* a title. I don't know how you think to catch his eye by relying solely on your sparkling personality."

"Lucky for me, my personality sparkles a bit brighter than yours." Lady Jane shot back, cool as the Thames on a December day, as she and her entourage floated toward the door and out.

"Oh!" Nora scowled at the now-shut door, "that Lady Jane thinks since she's the daughter of a Duke she can do and say anything!"

"True," Phillippa replied, then took notice that she still had an audience of Louisa, Penny, and Mrs. Dunningham, all waiting for her to either crack or cry. Phillippa refused to do either.

"Do you know, I've recently read a little Chinese text. Most adorable thing, filled with just the most useful observations," she said with an easy smile to the crowd around her. "And it says that if someone who is engaged in words leaves before the thing is finished, he has absolutely no ammunition with which to fight."

The three ladies blinked at each other, until Mrs. Dunningham piped up with, "She's right, girls! Imagine that! Lady Jane left the room so quickly, before Mrs. Benning had opportunity to retort!

She must have been terribly afraid of what Mrs. Benning could say!"

"Absolutely!" "Oh goodness, you're right!" the younger girls gushed.

"Mrs. Benning, where would one acquire that Chinese text? It would be so useful in guiding the girls through society!" Mrs. Dunningham asked, her face flushed with the anticipation of being able to tell her friends of Mrs. Benning's recommendation. Phillippa graciously supplied the name of a bookseller, and she and Nora made their exits.

"That was neatly done," Nora whispered, as they made their way back to the Winters' drawing room, where several card tables had been laid out in anticipation of a night of genteelly deep play.

"It's the truth." Phillippa shrugged.

"But what are you going to do about Lady Jane and Broughton?" Nora asked right before they chose their table for a rubber of whist, playing four with Phillippa's friend and companion Mrs. Tottendale, who cornered Mrs. Winter and a bottle of sherry to be her partners that evening.

"Its simple, Nora," Phillippa replied. "I'm going to win."

Three

When Phillippa Benning entered a room, it was an event. People stopped their conversations midsentence, craned their necks to see. The favored rushed forward to greet her, usher her to the best spot in the room, the one with the most advantageous views, to see and be seen. The unfavored—well, they wouldn't be invited in the first place. And the admiring throng would part like Moses's sea as she swept past. It was always the best moment of hers or anyone's evening.

Yes, Phillippa Benning knew how to make an entrance. It was an incredible show. That was why, upon entering Almack's, it was so terribly disconcerting to discover that the Marquis of Broughton had yet to arrive.

"But they close the doors in twenty minutes!" she whispered to Nora through a deceptively placid smile.

"How definite was his intention of coming?" Nora whispered back, while nodding to an acquaintance.

"Wholly certain!" Phillippa shot back. Then, musing, she added,

"Well, he never did say definitely if he'd show up; he just wondered whether he might see me here."

"That is difficult to ascertain," Nora agreed.

"Well, I refuse to be put out by his not seeing my entrance."

"Bravo!"

"This . . . delay gives me time to greet the patronesses and fix my gown."

"Is your gown amiss?" Nora worriedly scanned Phillippa's rather demure gown, a higher-than-normal silk bodice and a chiffon and lace skirt that skimmed her body as it flowed to the floor, all of it the color of a blushing rose, setting off Phillippa's skin tone delightfully. "I see nothing wrong. Do you want me to send for my mother?"

Phillippa rolled her eyes. "No, Nora, your mother can't sew worth three shillings, and I don't require any stitching in any case."

"Then why did you say your dress required repair?"

"I said I was going to fix it," Phillippa said with a mock-innocent stare. "Who said anything about repair? Ah, Countess Leivin, how wonderful to see you . . ."

❧

"I should have known. You always have something up your sleeve." Nora said with an admiring smile as she passed Phillippa in the turn of the quadrille.

Within ten minutes of their arrival, Phillippa was already on the dance floor, causing a stir.

It must be some sort of record, she thought. Delicious.

In fact, she was causing such a stir that she and Nora both grinned deeply when they saw (and heard) Mrs. Hurston, in her offensive purple-plumed turban, say to Mrs. Markham, in similarly nauseating yellow feathers, "I cannot *believe* what Mrs. Benning is wearing; it is so incredibly over the top, and beyond calculation, that I can *not* countenance . . ."

But there Mrs. Hurston's rant ended, as the wild gesticulations that accompanied her speech caused her cup of orangeat to pour down the front of poor Mr. Worth's shirt, who's only offense had been that he had been there, he had been overly tall, and he had been in the orangeat's way.

Nasty stuff, that orangeat.

Phillippa momentarily felt sorry for Mr. Worth as she watched him leave the ballroom, hunched and coated in orange liquid. Then she recalled he was the man who had been so rude as to pick up Nora's glove at the parade, and decided orangeat was just punishment for it. Then, just as quickly as the notion had entered her head, she let it flit away, turning her mind to more pleasantly nerve-racking topics.

She had spent the last ten minutes constantly flitting her eyes back to the main doors, all the while dancing and being admired and appearing uninterested and blasé about the attention. Truly exhausting work. But her observational devotion paid off, for just as Mr. Worth passed through the main doors, the massive portals swung open again, this time admitting the Marquis of Broughton.

Phillippa couldn't help it; she audibly sucked in her breath. Her dance partner, a Mr. Green, looked at her askance but wisely kept his countenance. Luckily, Phillippa was too graceful a partner to let a little thing like the entry of her new conquest cause her to miss a single step.

Broughton was a glowing, golden god. Light seemed to reflect off of his achingly beautiful self, let alone from the diamonds at his cuffs and neckcloth. It was rumored one young lady fainted at the sight of his glowing, golden hair, certain she had seen an angel's halo. But the reason he attracted so much of Phillippa's attention was that dastardly twinkle in his eyes. As if he were bored by what he saw and longed for trouble.

And it seemed that she attracted his eye, Broughton having wound his way through the throng of admiring people to her side just as the dance ended. She curtsied politely to Mr. Green, who, seeing the lay of the land, again showed his intelligence and took himself off without another word.

"Mrs. Benning." Broughton spoke, his voice a throaty rumble. "I'm pleased to see you here."

She let his voice run down her spine in that pleasant little shiver only Broughton seemed able to produce and gave him a sultry smile. Even better than his voice, even better than his presence, was the fact that the entire hall had begun buzzing like bees roused from their nest.

"Is that Broughton?"

"Aye, I believe so. He's bowing to Mrs. Benning!"

"Did he kiss her hand?"

"He'll kiss more than that if he can—the utter rake!"

It was quite impossible to not hear this last exchange, as it was voiced by the shrill Mrs. Croyton, who, having three daughters out in the dangerous waters of society (and none with much hope of prospect, Phillippa thought wryly), felt it necessary to voice her disapproval of unacceptable behavior at a high, loud pitch.

Broughton smirked, amused, and then brought Phillippa's gloved hand to his mouth, holding it there for such a length of time, until he heard a gasp of "My word!" from Mrs. Croyton, and the inevitable shuffling of her and her gawking daughters' skirts. But his eyes—his eyes never strayed from Phillippa's.

Then, without another word, he smoothly tucked her hand in his arm and led her to the floor.

Almack's had only recently allowed the waltz, it being seen as scandalous for a good number of years due to the contact it allowed men of women's bodies and the proximity in which the dancers stood. But as the dance grew in popularity, standards became relaxed, until grudgingly, the patronesses had to allow it, if only because there was so much popular music written in its three-quarter time.

But scandal could still be awoken from a three-step rhythm.

For, as Broughton laid one hand high on Phillippa's waist, its size and strength wrapping around to her spine, his eyes widened in surprise.

Phillippa's lovely white dress was completely backless.

From the front and side, the dress looked perfectly respectable, with a front neckline one would even call demure. But the neckline at the back was now closer to a waistline, the fabric coming down in straight lines over her shoulder blades and ending at the waist belt. Broughton's ungloved fingers had landed squarely on the warmth of the valley of her spine.

Phillippa looked up with sinful innocence into Broughton's suddenly intense icy blue eyes, and she knew that all the extra money she had paid Madame Le Trois to have a removable panel installed had been worth it.

The music began, pulling the couples into spinning swirls of black and white, Phillippa and Broughton along with them. Once he had recovered his surprise, Phillippa was again shot with a thrill of pleasure; Broughton danced marvelously. His pace was strong but not too fast, and oh! His ungloved fingers on her unclothed flesh made it so the slightest bit of pressure moved her according to his whim.

Reveling in the dance and musing on how well she and Broughton must look together, their matching blond hair and crisp blue eyes, their individual beauty combining to outshine the stars, Phillippa almost did not hear Broughton speak.

"I'm glad to find you accepted my challenge," he began, his voice pitched just above a murmur, for Phillippa's ears only.

"Challenge?" she replied innocently.

"To come to Almack's tonight." He smiled sardonically. "Rumor has it you despise it almost as much as I do."

Phillippa smiled, blushing prettily as she gave the slightest of shrugs. Broughton's hand tightened ever so slightly on her back, drawing her barely closer.

"I find Almack's confining, don't you?" he said, his voice conversational again.

"Somewhat," Phillippa replied, arching her brow, "but most Society likes a little confinement."

"And you do not count yourself among them," Broughton stated.

"How do you know that?"

He leaned in, his voice caressing her ear.

"Because you're not wearing a corset."

Phillippa sucked in her breath and felt his fingers flex and resettle against her skin. Broughton's touch, the air around them, all of it crackled with electricity. Phillippa was very good at this game, the cat and mouse of flirtation, but rarely had it been as exciting to play as it was with Broughton. Impulsively, she decided to play a little deeper.

"I don't require one." She spoke breathily. "Besides, its impossible to wear with this dress. Its impossible to wear almost *any* undergarment with this dress."

Now was Broughton's turn to suck in his breath. Phillippa gave him one of her half smiles and followed him through the turn. His eyes turned positively black, like a hawk about to swoop in on its prey.

"Mrs. Benning, I find your conversation refreshing. I do hope we have the chance to continue it. Perhaps this evening?" She held his gaze. "Perhaps at the Iversons' ball?" Broughton spoke, his voice pitched low and calm, the perfectly polite gentleman. But still it caressed her skin more intimately than his hand was allowed. "I understand their library is very exclusive. And very private."

Was he . . . was he suggesting what Phillippa thought he was suggesting? Oh goodness! But that sparkle in his eyes—that deep-down wickedness—he *did* court trouble, and he knew how to have the best time with it.

Perhaps . . . perhaps she could play a little deeper. She was a widow, after all. Perhaps it was time that she partook of *all* that widowhood afforded.

But it would be on her terms, of course.

"Oh, my lord, I am engaged at the Fieldstone affair after Almack's," Phillippa replied, aiming for a note of palpable sorrow in her voice.

"Your plans can be changed, surely. Nothing is ever set in stone," he growled.

"My plans are as readily changed as yours, my lord," she countered with an arched brow.

"Now, now; you responded to my invitation to meet me here. Why not follow me to the next step? Have a little adventure." As the music finished, the whirling couples came to a stop on the floor, polite applause masking his next words from all ears except hers. "Phillippa, am I not worth the chase?"

Phillippa's mouth went slack for the barest of moments. Then she set her expression and gave him a long, cool assessing stare.

"You ask the wrong question," she said after thoroughly grazing him from toe to head. "You should inquire whether or not *I* am worth the chase."

Broughton smirked, opening his mouth to answer, but Phillippa boldly held her fingertips to his mouth. "The answer to which," she said, her eyes never leaving his, "can be found in the Fieldstone library at midnight."

Then, with a low curtsy, prompting an automatic bow from Broughton, Phillippa turned, walked into the throng of the Ton, and refused to look back.

Her heart going a mile a minute, Phillippa allowed herself a secret smile. *How's that for a little adventure?*

Four

"WHAT on earth have you done?"

Nora pulled her best friend aside in the Fieldstones' receiving line, shocked white by what she had just been told.

"Its nothing, Nora. Just a rendezvous." Phillippa shrugged off her friend's horrified reaction, which only prompted further horror from Nora's petite form.

"No. No, it's not. I know that you flitter and make suggestive comments—every move calculated to pique a man's interest, as you've taught me—but you have never been so bold as to arrange a tryst!"

Nora's whispered protest was abruptly cut short as their chaperones had reached the head of the receiving line and signaled for Nora and Phillippa to join them. After perfunctory curtsies and polite murmurs to the hosts, the girls moved into the main gallery, where Nora took the first opportunity to force Phillippa into a private corner no bigger than a broom closet.

"You cannot mean to meet Broughton—do you?" Nora questioned, the bleak hope in her voice unmasked.

But Phillippa merely gave her friend a raised eyebrow and an elegant shake of the head. "If I were to leave him waiting there, he would be embarrassed—and worse yet, likely to never believe I can play deep."

"You shouldn't play so deep!"

"Shouldn't I? Nora, you will come to understand that men have different expectations of different women. The rules are different for me. And Broughton cannot stand missishness; he's made that clear. If ever there was a time to play deep, it's now. Besides, I can do as I like . . . Who's to say anything against me?"

Nora knew her friend was right. Extreme beauty and extreme wealth had gifted Phillippa Benning with an overwhelming sense of entitlement, assisted greatly by the fact that she had been widowed. No one questioned her behavior.

And yet it was a very daring thing to do: rendezvousing at a party! Nora could not help squealing with a little girlish delight. "Oh, Phillippa, it is so exciting! Promise me you'll tell me everything! And should we inform Totty?"

Phillippa shot a glance toward Mrs. Tottendale, her erstwhile companion, who had wandered over to a liveried servant bearing a tray of glasses. "No," she replied, "let's leave Totty to her amusements. She'd only worry."

"Maybe rightly so," Nora ventured, chewing her lower lip, "Phillippa, do be careful. You are walking a line."

"Luckily, no one walks a line as well as I. And now, if you'll excuse me, I have an appointment to keep."

"I knew you'd come," he said, a greedy smile spreading across his face, deepening his sole dimple.

"I knew you'd be waiting," Phillippa replied with a saucy wink. Their prescribed meeting place was dark; only the light from under the door that led to the ballroom illuminated their faces. Phillippa could see his was flushed with the anticipation of (she thought wryly) getting what he wanted.

"No one saw you?" he asked, his eyes flicking warily to the source of the muted babble and music of a fete in full swing.

"No one saw me." She looked up into his face, into those sparkling eyes she was quickly coming to adore. "Except, of course, for the servant who brought me these."

And with a flourish, she revealed a tray of sweetmeats and marzipan pastries, a sight that had ten-year-old Reggie Fieldstone nearly apoplectic with delight.

"Shh! Reggie! Do be quiet! If your mother finds out, she will have your head," Phillippa scolded.

"No, she'll have your head," Reggie countered, as he reached through the banister of the elegant staircase, trying desperately to reach an apricot tart.

"No one will ever have my head, Reggie. I'll sell you out in a heartbeat," she said with a smile.

"Oh, Mrs. B, you're the absolute ultimate—such a cracking good lady. All my parents' other friends would tell me to go to bed."

"Well, I shan't make you go to bed. However, I make two requests."

Reggie nodded for her to continue, his mouth too full of whatever he managed to grab to answer vocally.

"First, don't tell a soul about how you showed me where the library is."

"Kwosh—" Reggie swallowed, allowing freer speech, "excuse me, Mrs. B. Cross my heart. Only my papa uses that room in any case. I'm not allowed in; only grown-ups are." Reggie was the eldest son in the Fieldstone family, a full decade old, and therefore, he considered himself quite adult. However, his youth was still in enough of a bloom that petulance occasionally surfaced.

"Understandable. Now, secondly, I request that you don't sneak down here again."

"But, Mrs. B, you said I should enjoy the party, too!"

"Yes," Phillippa replied, soothing Reggie's scowl off his face, "but I meant from the balcony on the third floor; you can see the ballroom very well from up there."

"How do you know about the balcony on the third floor?" Reggie frowned.

"A very complicated procedure," she countered. "I went into the ballroom and looked up. There it was."

This was met with an adorably puzzled "Oh." Reggie might not be the quickest ten-year-old on the square, she thought, but he was terribly cute.

"And . . ." Phillippa lowered her voice, "I'll give you a shilling if you make note of everyone the Marquis of Broughton dances with while I'm not in the ballroom."

"A shilling . . . and a slice of cake?"

"Bargain."

Phillippa extended her hand. Solemnly, Reggie accepted it, and then, plate of sweetmeats in hand, fled as silently as a loping ten-year-old can, presumably to the third-floor balcony. Pleased with her small bit of espionage, Phillippa turned, intent upon attending the ladies' retiring room, where she had decided to have supposedly been for the past ten minutes, before returning to the ballroom. However, she was not three steps down the dark corridor before bumping soundly into the surprisingly rock-solid form of a very tall, very eavesdropping man.

"Mr. . . . Mr. Worth!" Mr. Worth, the gangly gentleman who had managed to recover his evening from the disastrous orangeat incident at Almack's, had caught her at her waist as she turned directly into his path.

"Mrs. Benning," Mr. Worth said, before removing himself to a safe distance of three feet and assuming his characteristic hunch. Or perhaps that was what he thought was a bow.

"I did not intend to intrude—"

"How much did you hear?" she asked, her normally light, sweet voice suddenly sharp with fear.

"Only from young Mr. Fieldstone bemoaning that only

grown-ups are allowed somewhere." Mr. Worth replied, an eyebrow going up.

"Oh!" She said and then gave a perhaps too-bright trill of laughter. "He meant the ballroom. No, sadly, Reggie cannot attend the dance, else all the ladies will be in love with him. I do hope you'll keep my giving the boy sweets a secret," she went on, giving Mr. Worth her best beguiling smile, her eyes wide with innocence. "I've a great fondness for young Reggie, and I do recall being of an age where nothing would be so exciting as attending the festivities and due to nothing more than youth, finding oneself excluded. Why, this is a different shirt than you were wearing at Almack's, isn't it? Identical shade and style to what you were wearing, of course, but not cut for you. Although it is close."

And with that comment, Phillippa laid a small, gloved hand on his shirt and brought her eyes up, shyly, to meet his, which were a dullish brown, with perhaps some hazel in them. His hair was a similar shade of dullish brown, uninspiring, not worthy of a single swoon. Indeed, aside from his height, Mr. Worth fell into the category of most men: pleasingly formed, handsome enough in an unobjectionable and totally uninteresting way.

Now, most men would have fallen into blushes and stutters, entranced at the notion of having her undivided attention, not to mention the intimacy of her hand placed lightly on their shirt-front. Unfortunately, Mr. Worth chose this particular moment, for likely the first time in his life, to distinguish himself from the category of Most Men.

A small smile crept up the left side of his mouth, setting his generally boring brown eyes to a twinkle.

"Mrs. Benning," he said, not a blush or stutter in sight, "you speak as if you showed that child a great kindness."

"You speak as if surprised that I am capable of such kindnesses," she replied, puzzled.

"Oh, I think you capable! Of many things. Including coercing a child through bribery into being your spy."

A bucket of cold water would have been less shocking.

"Did you think I missed that part of the exchange? Or if I hadn't, found it lighthearted and forgivable due to your lovely form and even more lovely attentions?" Mr. Worth caught her hand against his chest and held it there.

Really, who would have thought bland Mr. Worth would dare scold Phillippa Benning? Such a jolt was his behavior that Phillippa could only stare and gape.

"Mrs. Benning, do not mistake me," he said in jovial tones with a complacent smile, "if I cannot admire your kindness, I am well capable of admiring your resourcefulness."

"Well!" Phillippa wrenched her hand away from his chest as if it burned her skin.

"By the bye, Broughton is currently dancing the reel with Lady Jane Cummings. And quite the pair they make, too."

And with that, Mr. Worth bowed and withdrew, folding back into the shadows like some demon of the night, all before Phillippa could pick her jaw up off the floor.

One deep breath later, Phillippa placed a placid smile on her face and headed down the hall to the ladies' retiring room, putting thoughts of Mr. Marcus Worth out of her head. He had eavesdropped poorly, luckily for her, missing the most crucial part of her conversation. And besides, Marcus Worth was a nobody in the eyes of the Ton—and therefore a nobody in total. And Phillippa Benning did not concern herself with nobodies.

She instead turned her attention to Broughton. Delicious, desireable Broughton—and the one thing she knew she had that Lady Jane Cummings didn't: a midnight appointment with the object of both their attention.

Five

HE had to show, he simply had to.

Forty minutes later, after a obligatory dance or two and an obligatory curious glance from Nora, Phillippa slipped through the door of what Reggie had assured her was the Fieldstone library and, after a heart-stopping moment where the door didn't seem to want to unlatch (luckily it did), slipped through.

After lighting a nearby candle, she blinked for several moments as her eyes adjusted, certain she was in the wrong room.

Because this—*this* was the most insane library she had ever seen.

But she was certain she counted the number of doors in the hallway correctly, and it had been the room with the ivory door handles. It had to be the library.

But it certainly didn't house books.

Phillippa had heard tales that the Fieldstone library housed Lord Fieldstone's pride and joy: his collection of Classical antiquities—a very fashionable hobby. But she expected there to be at least a few staples of the common English library, a desk, maybe a book on British history or two, but the entire room was covered in bas-relief tiles, paintings, statuary, even a massive sarcophagus in the middle! It was highly possible, knowing Lord Fieldstone, that an ancient Egyptian mummy was currently in residence.

Oh, the statuary itself was lovely, the paintings amazing (although Phillippa decided she would not be the one to inform Lord Fieldstone of the fraudulent nature of two of his four Caravaggios), but the space had been so cramped, so uncomfortable, that no one could appreciate the decor. Phillippa decided that Lady Fieldstone must have wisely limited her husband's enthusiasm for his collecting to one room of the house. But oh! What that man could fit into one room!

It was the most uncomfortable and most unlikely place for a romantic rendezvous.

"Well," she said aloud, hearing her voice reverberate dully off the multitude of stone objects, "it was meant to be a short visit in any case."

Truly, she only had ten minutes or so to spare before she and Totty were due to leave for their next engagement. So Broughton had best hurry and arrive, she thought with a small pout. Ten minutes was a worthy timetable, wasn't it? Nothing truly scandalous could happen in only ten minutes; she couldn't even unknot her garters in ten minutes, for goodness' sake. She was safe, wasn't she?

The room was warmer than she had expected of a small, high place completely done in marble. But perhaps that was her imagination.

Or her nerves.

"Nonsense," she said aloud again. "Phillippa Benning does not become nervous over a man."

No, it was she who made men nervous.

Still, whatever her collected outward appearance, whatever the world speculated as her private activities, she was not given to rendezvous with men in libraries. The situation at hand was . . . uncharted, in her experience.

And uncharted territory always revealed a certain extra sensitivity to her surroundings.

So was it her imagination, or did she hear . . . breathing?

Was it her own?

But such a thought was quickly tossed aside, as the trickiness of the door handle lay prey to another victim.

Ducking into the shadows, Phillippa held her breath, watched wide-eyed as the door opened and Broughton revealed himself in the doorway.

And what a sight he made.

"Mrs. Benning," he whispered, drawing out each letter like satin over her skin. "Phillippa?"

She stepped into the light, knowing full well that she made a stunning entrance, and she received the small thrill of watching Broughton grin with anticipation.

"Close the door." She spoke, surprised to find her voice—normally schooled into seductive huskiness—slightly thready and weak.

Once the door had been shut, they were plunged back into darkness. Alone at last with Broughton, Phillippa found herself at a small loss. She had only intended to have him meet her there, to show him her ability to take risks; the actual meeting itself was not so well thought out.

"I accepted your challenge, as you see," Broughton spoke in a deep rumble.

"As I accepted yours earlier this evening," she countered, happy that her voice was resuming a normal pitch.

"Although," he said, stepping closer to her, "I'm afraid I do have to question your choice of locale for a tryst. There's barely room for one person to move freely here. We shall have to stand very"—he took another step toward her—"very close."

A delicate hand came up to his chest, gently pushing the approaching Adonis back on his heels—although such a gesture of protest only made his smile deepen.

"Why, Broughton, who said one word about a tryst? We are simply friends who have met in this secluded space for . . . conversation and enlightenment."

Broughton caught her hand against his chest, held it there. For a moment, Phillippa's mind flashed back to a similar warm hand, holding hers steady against a man's chest. But a different man. Very, very different.

"Enlightenment?" Broughton spoke, his voice a near growl. "Well, in the hopes of honest conversation, allow me to enlighten you what it means to invite a man to a library at midnight."

And he plunged forward, taking her mouth, her neck, her jaw.

Would she allow his kiss? Certainly. She was Phillippa Benning. She was one and twenty; she had, discreetly and sometimes publicly, kissed and been kissed by several gentlemen. But as Broughton opened his mouth, inviting her to do the same, she wondered if she would allow more than this kiss.

She would have to think on that.

Gathering her closer, Broughton broke away, placing his mouth by her ear, all the while his hand flexing over the exposed flesh of her back.

"I'll chase you," he growled, sending low shivers to her toes, "but know I always catch my prey." And with that, he captured her mouth again.

Phillippa felt her head swimming. She was enjoying Broughton's skillful assault on her senses tremendously—no one could say the man's reported practice hadn't paid off—but more than that, she was enjoying the notion that she could catch Broughton. Snare him, allure him to her will. Certainly she would have to stop this lovemaking before it became the actual act instead of the precursor, but for the time being, she would just relax into his embrace.

She did, until she suddenly felt her bare back touch the cool stone surface of the sarcophagus lid.

Maybe she had become too relaxed.

"Eek!" Phillippa yelped, having been brought ruthlessly to her senses, and she sat up quickly. So quickly, in fact, that her forehead hit Broughton's temple with a solid *thwack*!

"Ow!" was the reply that reverberated off the statuary, as Broughton stumbled back, nearly upsetting a collection of knee-high Venuses rising from the foam.

"Oh! I am sorry!" Phillippa cried, once she had recovered from her own head injury, her contrition genuine (as well as a certain amount of unexpressed relief; she was, perhaps, getting in over her head). "The . . . the stone was so very cold, it startled me, you see."

"Yes, well," he grumbled, "er, perhaps you'll allow me the privilege of choosing the location of our next tête-à-tête?" He chuckled at his own joke.

Phillippa smiled slowly, a purr entering her voice. "Why, my lord, where in the world did you get the idea there would be another meeting?"

A frown creased Broughton's brow. "Mrs. Benning, I have been locked away at my estate for so long, with no one to play with. It was terribly dull. I simply cannot abide dullness, you know? But now I've come to town and met you. You accepted my challenge, and I accepted yours. Do you intend to stop now?" His scowl took on a tone of petulance. "Just when we were beginning to have fun? I should have never thought you so boring."

"You are correct, my lord," she let the words slip off her tongue, her voice taking on its most demure, most innocent, most seductive tone. "I did accept your challenge. I should hope to never be so boring as . . . as some dull dish like Lady Jane Cummings."

"Lady Jane?" An eyebrow went up.

"I heard you danced with her earlier. A girl like her—surely she would not be so bold as to play the game on your terms. Surely, she is too insignificant to be worth your time."

"Ah. I see," Broughton replied, his brow clearing.

"I would hate for anyone to think that she and I are on the same level in your eyes." She again laid her hand upon his chest, assuming a posture of vulnerability, and began to play with the buttons of his shirt.

"Oh dear, I've undone one. Drat, that's two buttons gone. How do you keep these together? They're so very small and slippery." She allowed her gloved hand the freedom to roam over the exposed flesh of his chest. His breath hitched.

"You," he gasped, "are far more worth my time than any other female."

"Every other female? Including Lady Jane?"

His grin deepened as he removed her hand from beneath his shirt. "I choose our next gambit."

"Of course, my—" But her practiced demureness was never to reach its full effect, because at that moment, the distinct sound of the door latch catching against the wood frame echoed through the space.

"Someone's at the door!" she whispered.

"Quick!" Broughton grabbed Phillippa by the arm and swiftly lifted the lid of the sarcophagus. It seemed hydraulic hinges had been installed for just such an occasion.

"Have you gone mad?" Phillippa cried under her breath. "Why should I be the one to hide?" But Broughton didn't respond, so she tried a different tack. "What if there's a mummy in there?"

"For your sake," he replied, "I sincerely hope not."

And before she could open her mouth in protest, Philippa found herself unceremoniously tossed inside.

Much to her relief, she did not land on a mummy.

Much to her surprise, she landed on something else entirely.

Six

WHEN he thought about it, Marcus Worth decided he was having a rather eventful evening.

First of all, he had attended Almack's, which is not a terribly eventful occurrence, other than the fact that he rarely attended any such societal gatherings. Unfortunately, it was a necessary component to his plan, one that had forced him to gad about town for the past week attending every dance, soiree, and dinner party he could wrangle an invitation to. His sister-in-law, Mariah, was keen to assist with the wrangling. Also the occasional public gathering, an opera or a parade. It was important to look like he was sociable, providing cover for his real intention. Luckily, his elder brother, Graham, and Mariah managed to include him in many of their outings. But those were smaller, less auspicious affairs than the Fieldstones' or Almack's. The fact that he had managed a voucher for Almack's was a feat of bribery, good luck, and subterfuge unlikely to be repeated.

Once at Almack's, of course, he had orangeat spilled all down his shirt.

A singular experience.

It was a turn of events Marcus hadn't minded, really, as it allowed him to depart early with a memorable and worthy excuse. Again, luckily, Graham's house was within walking distance (however uncouth walking in London may be), where he procured a spare shirt from Graham's nonplussed valet.

Next, of course, he arrived at the Fieldstone affair, the party he had been waiting for all week, the party during which he had requested a private audience with the director of the War Department. While waiting for time to tick by, he walked in on Mrs. Phillippa Benning—millionheiress, and locally revered as some sort of goddess, apparently—while she bribed a child with sweets to spy for her on that fluffed-up idiot, Broughton.

Then, while idly waiting for the director to come through the Fieldstone Library doors (no easy feat, considering the director was possibly as wide as he was tall), the door was opened by someone who didn't know that the lock tended to stick, whose shadow was unexpectedly narrow, and so he hid in the only hiding place available in the overstuffed space: the sarcophagus.

Then Phillippa Benning landed on him.

While individually the events of his evening were not terribly impressive, taken together, they amassed to be very eventful indeed.

The conversation that Marcus had been subject to, between Mrs. Benning and her prey Broughton, left very little to the imagination. What landed on him shortly thereafter, well, that left very little to the imagination, too.

Phillippa Benning's left ankle landed squarely on his head with an audible *crack*! And as such, Phillippa Benning's head landed on his calf, twisted as his long frame was into the sarcophagus's cramped space. When he had first occupied the sarcophagus (thank heaven for the historically inappropriate hinges Fieldstone had installed!), he was very happy to find that it housed only a few spare antique yards of cloth, softening his landing. No ancient Egyptians in residence.

However, ancient Egyptians were obviously smaller than

modern Englishmen, and as Marcus himself was a good head taller than said modern Englishmen, the space was not terribly accommodating. Add another person to the pile, and space became extremely dear.

She wore silk stockings—not much of a surprise, as most ladies of wealth did—but still rather disconcerting against his cheek. It was nearly pitch-black in the stone tomb, but what little light filtered through the crack between the sarcophagus and its lid showed a very fine embroidery of ivy winding over Phillippa's ankle, which for some reason made Marcus smile, just a little. However, her soft rear had landed in a somewhat inopportune spot. Or opportune, depending on one's outlook.

Looking down the length of himself, Marcus silently sought out Phillippa's eyes, and when he found them, the faintest sheen in the deep dark, they were wide with bewilderment.

Silently, desperately, he brought his finger to his mouth, pleading for her not to emit an admittedly justified scream. After a moment, she nodded, allowing Marcus to exhale that breath he hadn't realized he was holding. It caused the hem of her dress, some floaty, lacy material, to flutter. However, before her eyes could widen at the sensation, a new conversation outside of the sarcophagus had begun.

"Wha . . . oh, Broughton, is it? What the devil do you do in my library?" The booming baritone of Lord Fieldstone, owner of the house, the library's collection, and host of the party, sounded muted and dense through the thick stone.

"Lord Fieldstone! I was looking for . . . well, I guess it hardly matters now, does it?" Broughton began. Marcus could almost hear the affected charm, the sheepish smile in that man's voice. Since he was encased in darkness, he didn't feel it necessary to hold back his eye roll.

"It seems I became lost," Broughton continued, "and found myself in this remarkable room. It's quite the most marvelous collection, sir. You are to be congratulated."

"Thank you very kindly; I am rather proud of it." As evidenced by the pride in his voice. "But you should be careful. Good heavens, did that Venus get knocked over?"

"Hmm? Oh, no, I . . . I may have nudged it a bit, but it stayed upright."

"Nudged it?" Fieldstone sounded panicked. "But she's priceless! You can't go nudging something priceless! Come with me; I'll show you the way back to the ballroom." And then, lower, as if under his breath, "Nudged it!"

"Oh, that's too good of you, Lord Fieldstone, but I can find my way back, surely. Don't worry, I'll stay here, and . . . and set the Venus to right . . ."

"No!" Fieldstone's voice was barely masked panic. "Don't touch it! Come, my good man, I'm certain there are any number of young ladies eager for their dance . . ."

Their voices faded away with their footfalls. Then, with a solid click, the library door must have closed, leaving Marcus and Phillippa all alone in their quiet, tight space.

He sought her eyes once again, and, finding them, held up a hand, signaling her to wait, just a precautionary moment. Just in case.

But Mrs. Phillippa Benning did not hold precaution in high regard.

Or him, apparently.

"Would you . . . Ouch!" She squirmed. "Get off me. Lift the lid, please!"

"You—ow!"—he exclaimed as the heel of her dress slipper connected with his eyebrow—"are on top of *me*, ma'am. You push from your end, and I'll push from here. Ready?"

"Stop staring up my dress! Ready."

"Watch your heels. One. Two. Three!"

The lid came up, and two dusty, disgusted figures emerged, scrambling to get as much space between them as possible.

Which, in that library, was not terribly much.

After a few deep breaths and a small amount of coughing and sputtering, they regarded each other.

Or, at least Marcus regarded her. She seemed resolute in her determination to not regard him.

"I cannot imagine what you think you were doing in that sarcophagus," she finally said, still not looking at him.

"No," he replied, not able to suppress his reply or the smile in his voice, "but I can well imagine what you were doing on top of it a few minutes ago."

That earned him a look. A deeply outraged one.

"A *gentleman* would not mention such a thing to a lady," she sniffed.

"True." He grinned, having too much fun watching her turn red. "But a lady would not have engaged in such an activity in the first place. Perhaps we've both been mislabeled."

The light was dim, but he would swear she had gone from red to purple. "You . . . you did hear!" she spoke in strangled tones, her face mottled with horror. "You . . . knew I was coming here! Did you lie in the coffin to wait for us? To *overhear*? That . . . that's disgusting!"

Marcus stared at her, bewildered. "What on earth are you talking about?"

"Reggie Fieldstone!"

"What has that child to do with anything? Good God, he's not here, too, is he? Where would he hide?"

"No, you . . . you *overheard* him telling me how to get to the library, and . . . and you followed me!"

Marcus took a deep breath. "First of all. I technically could not have followed you, since I was here before you, as evidenced by the fact you landed on me. But"—he said, cutting her off before she could speak—"I take your meaning. However, I can assure you that I did not overhear anything Reggie said beyond what I told you before, and I am here for my own purposes and certainly did not expect anyone to choose such a dusty, crowded space for a tryst. I promise, I am more surprised by you than you are by me."

She bore herself up to regal height, her color returning to normal from its mottled, enraged shade. "Phillippa Benning does not engage in trysts."

Well, what could a man do but shrug? "As you say."

Her chin went up. If it weren't so imperious, it would be charming in a girlish sort of way.

"I find no need to explain myself to you, Mr. Worth. No, indeed. You may or may not derive pleasure from lying in coffins, listening to other people's romantic assignations. I assure you, it's of little interest to me."

She then swept to the door, certain in every step, and placed her hand on the doorknob.

"I wouldn't do that if I were you," he said, taking a moment to wipe the smudges from his spectacles.

"But you are not me, Mr. Worth. Thank the heavens."

"No, but we do share a common trait at the moment."

"And what is that?" She sighed.

"We are both covered in dust."

Phillippa pulled her hand off the knob and looked down at herself. Even in the darkness, she had to see she'd become distinctly gray. Her skin, her dress—

"Even my hair!" she cried, as she patted the now-gray stands, only to engulf herself in a cloud. "Oh goodness! Imagine if someone saw me this way!"

"Yes, yes, imagine if someone saw *me* this way!"

"Mocking is only good for eliciting humor, Mr. Worth, and right now, no one is laughing," she snapped at him.

"I'm quite serious, you know," he took off his coat and began to shake it out. "Imagine if someone saw you covered in dust, and then me covered in dust. What would they think?"

"Oh!" her hands shot to cover her dropped jaw. "Oh, they would think—Oh, how appalling!"

"Thank you ever so," he said drily. "Turn round, I'll see what I can do about your skirt."

He knelt beside her and began beating the folds of fabric of her skirt as if he were beating out a rug.

"Do be careful! This is imported lace; the design is one of a kind," she said as she took off her left glove and shook it out as much as possible. "If you didn't come to spy on me, why were you in that sarcophagus?"

"I thought you didn't care," he grunted as he continued thwacking the skirt free of the dust, albeit a little more gently.

"I . . . I don't," she said primly. "I asked for the sake of conversation."

"Well, for the sake of conversation, and to assuage your apparently nonexistent curiosity, I will say that you are not the only one who had a scheduled meeting this evening."

"Hmph," she harrumphed in a not very ladylike fashion. "Some mousy little thing, no doubt, dared by her friends to meet a man—any man—at midnight, and turning coward before she even left that ballroom?"

"Hah!" he laughed aloud, surprising Phillippa into looking down at him. "Mrs. Benning, I told you, no one sane would chose such an awful space for a . . . romantic interlude," he concluded, aware of her narrowed eyes on him. "No, contrary to your mindset, not every midnight assignation is romantic in nature." He rose, causing her to shift and look up at him. "Yours wasn't, for example."

Her mouth dropped open in shock. "It most certainly was!"

"Really? It seemed far more businesslike to me. You maneuvering to acquire an asset and to outpace your rivals in that acquisition. Tactical, and brilliantly so, if I may proffer my admiration."

She narrowed her eyes, obviously not unfamiliar with the idea of a backhanded compliment.

"I am sane," she said, her chin still higher than her nose.

He raised a brow. "No one claimed otherwise."

"You said no one sane would chose such a spot for . . . Anyway, I've never been here before. I didn't know it looked like this."

He smiled wryly. "Fair enough. But next time you should do

some reconnaissance. Check your surroundings in advance. Find a library with some cushioning. A sofa is just as easy to dive behind as a sarcophagus is to hide in."

He meant it in a chiding, fun-mannered fashion.

It wasn't taken that way.

"Mr. Worth," she began, hands on her hips and all simpering artifice dropped from her frame for perhaps the first time that evening, "this is not how I planned for my evening to end. I am meant to be dancing in the great hall right now, before going on to any number of other parties. Not stuck in here with, among other things, fourteen knee-high Venuses, four Caravaggios, two of which are fake, six bas-relief panels, forty-two alabaster nymphs, one Egyptian sarcophagus, and you! And as cramped and horrific as these surroundings, the only one of my company I find wholly objectionable right now is your person. Now, would you be so good as tell me what you want in order to never mention the circumstances of our meeting *ever*, or give your odious opinion of it, else I will take my leave."

She swept past him, but before she could reach the door, he took hold of her arm. Much to his surprise, she didn't pull away, just turned to face him, blue eyes blazing in the darkness. Beneath the spectacles, his eyes blazed right back.

"Mrs. Benning," he said, his voice pitched to a low growl, "make no mistake; this is not the ideal situation for me, either." At this she snorted, expressing her disbelief. His hand tightened imperceptibly on her arm, a sort of subtle massage. "I have been teasing so far in an effort to make light of our circumstances. However, if you think I give a bloody damn about you and your carryings-on, you are more self-absorbed than I took you for—which is not an easy feat."

An eyebrow went up. "What are you saying? That you can't be bought? I have heard that before, and inevitably it is not true."

"I have no use for your money; I have no use for you. What on earth do you propose to purchase me with?"

She flinched, as if struck. "I . . . I . . ."

He took the opportunity to lean barely closer. "I have a short lesson for you, and take note. The easiest way to assure my silence—"

But at that moment, the now-familiar sound of someone fiddling with the sticky door handle reached their ears. Marcus's eyes shot to the base of the door, where an unusually wide shadow had blocked out most of the outside light.

Marcus blew out the lone lit candle.

"Quickly!" he breathed, pulling her back to the center of the room, back to the sarcophagus.

"What? I'm not going back in there!" She pulled at his grip, futilely.

"I'm afraid you have very little choice in that matter," he whispered as he lifted the lid.

"But . . . but my dress! 'Twill be ruined!" she whispered, but to no avail. Before she could protest further, she was thrown into the familiar dusty, musty confines of the sarcophagus.

"As if a girl like you would ever wear a dress twice in any case," he delivered his parting shot in a whisper and brought down the lid, just as Lord Fieldstone (incidentally, director of the War Department) opened the library door for the second time that evening.

Seven

"Hullo? Who's there?" Lord Fieldstone asked in a stage whisper, groping in the darkness.

"Marcus Worth, my lord. Thank you for coming." Marcus stepped past Lord Fieldstone and shut the library door quietly behind him.

"Worth! Thank goodness. I came in here before and found the Marquis of Broughton nosing around my treasures."

"Yes, I know. I asked you to meet me, because I—"

"You know?" Lord Fieldstone asked, interrupting Marcus. "How?"

"Oh. Um, I was here, actually. In hiding. I must say you got rid of him marvelously."

"Where did you hide? You didn't knock anything over, did you?"

"No!" Marcus held up his hands in protest. "No, I, erm, was in the sarcophagus. I was very pleased to find it vacant."

"Vacant?" Fieldstone looked momentarily puzzled. Then his

brow cleared. "Oh, that's right, we took the mummy out last week to have it repaired. A limb fell loose."

"Hmm," was the only reply Marcus could give and the only one innocuous enough to cover up the muffled groan he was certain emanated from the interior of the sarcophagus. Luckily, Lord Fieldstone did not seem to notice.

"I do hope you didn't nick anything on the inside, Worth. How was the fit?" Lord Fieldstone made for the coffin and almost had his hand under the lid before Marcus reached his side and ever so gently held the lid down.

"The fit was tight, sir, but everything is intact, I promise. Both of mine and the sarcophagus. I asked to meet you here for a very specific reason, but now, I must wonder if you wouldn't recommend somewhere more spacious. I should hate to be responsible for breaking any of your Venuses or nymphs. How many nymphs are there, by the bye?" Marcus asked casually as he tried to maneuver Fieldstone to the door. Unfortunately, Fieldstone was not easily moved.

"Forty-two. And somewhere more spacious would be nice; however, I've got a houseful of guests, a wife with four glasses of punch in her, and absolutely no time to dillydally. So tell me what it is you want."

"Are you sure you wouldn't rather—"

"Out with it! Now!"

Marcus frowned, hesitating. On the one hand, it had taken too long to get face-to-face time with the director. On the other, a pair of prying ears was not three feet away. However, time was the most crucial factor, so Marcus squared his shoulders and pitched his voice low, hoping it was too quiet to hear through stone.

"Sir, I have received some information from trusted sources that perhaps an old enemy has found his way to London and is plotting . . ."

"Plotting what?" Unfortunately, Lord Fieldstone's voice remained at normal pitch.

"I'm not certain, sir."

"Ah, I see. And who is the old enemy?"

"I hesitate to say, as he's meant to be dead," Marcus replied.

"Ah, I see," Fieldstone repeated. "And who are the informants?"

"A workingman who has been of use in the past. I trust his information."

Lord Fieldstone set his jaw and took a moment to digest this. Marcus held his breath and knew all too well that he sounded a right blockhead. A street informant tells him a dead man is plotting something dire? And with this, he decided to accost the head of the War Department? Maybe he was boxing at shadows, but his gut, the one thing he never doubted, told him different.

"Worth," Lord Fieldstone began, as he paced the room as much as his wide form and its limited space would allow, "you did incredible work during the war. Hell, I can name half a dozen times that the Blue Raven was the sole cause of any victory we could claim. But the war is over, twice now. You should be out having fun, dancing; or else, find a young thing and settle down in the country. Getting out of the city might be worthwhile at any rate. Visit your brother's estate, breathe some country air. Don't go hunting old ghosts."

Lord Fieldstone looked up at him with fatherly sincerity, and for a moment, Marcus wished he could take his advice.

"Sir"—Marcus pushed his spectacles back up his nose as he spoke—"my instincts tell me this old ghost is no such thing."

Fieldstone sighed deeply and resumed his pacing. After a moment, he stopped, turning to Marcus. "I imagine there is some reason you went outside the offices, directly to me with this, not to Sterling or Crawley or any of your collegues."

"The information I received: I have reason to suspect it was generated inside the Security section."

That piqued the older man's interest.

"What is this information you speak of?"

Marcus produced a small scrap of neatly folded paper from

his pocket and handed it to Fieldstone, who looked it over for interminable seconds.

"Did you write this list?"

"No, it came into my hands."

"What makes you think this originated inside the section?" he asked gruffly.

Marcus took a deep breath. "The ink and the paper . . ."

"Neither is distinctive."

"Yes, but both are the kinds used by the Security section. I know; I stare at them day after day. And do you see this small edge of wax? It's the same as we use in the offices," he continued, knowing he sounded ridiculous at best, delusional at worst. It was the thinnest possible evidence, and if it had been someone else, he would have likely been disbelieving as well. "My lord, I have a gut instinct about this. And I trust it." He drew Fieldstone's attention to his face. "And so have you."

Lord Fieldstone exhaled as he looked over the list again, seemingly considering his options. Then, "Your information is spotty, at best, you know."

"I know it."

"I cannot sanction any action you would choose to take in this matter, you realize." He handed the paper back.

"I understand, sir."

"Do you?" Fieldstone sighed and looked up at Marcus, who stood rigidly at attention. "Worth, if I promise to look into this matter, discreetly, will you fall back and allow me to do the inquiry?"

"For as long as I can, sir." Marcus replied. "Some of the events on the list—they are set to occur within a matter of weeks."

"Fair enough." Fieldstone said, turning to the door. "Now, I'm going back down to the party. In five minutes' time, I am sending a footman up here to lock this door from the outside. I suggest a good night's sleep for you, Worth."

"Yes, sir."

But by that time, the door had already swung shut behind

Fieldstone, allowing Marcus to ease his stance and chance exhaling.

His actions would not be supported. Well, he had guessed that. And the minister of the War Department thought he might do well with a respite at Bedlam. Disappointing, but not wholly unexpected. But Fieldstone himself promised inquiry, and he was not barred from investigation, which was all he needed.

Before he'd taken over the War Department, Fieldstone had been a cracking good investigator. He'd ask the right questions of the right people. And, if something unfortunate should occur to Marcus in the meantime—well, he wholly believed in being prepared. He never operated without a backup in place. Without someone he trusted knowing his intentions.

Unfortunately, in this instance, he had been forced by circumstance to also reveal them to someone he suspected was less than completely trustworthy.

Stalking over to the sarcophagus, he wrenched it open easily, revealing Phillippa Benning lying with her hands crossed over her body, eyes closed tight, newly covered in more dust. She looked almost innocent and, of course, slightly dead. But God bless her, Marcus thought, he could see her listening.

"It's just me," he said, his voice a little gruffer than had been intended. "Overhear any good conversations recently?"

Her eyes opened, found his, and locked to them. She stared at him somewhat weirdly, as if she was trying to memorize something. But he couldn't be bothered to ask what.

"For heaven's sake, it's just me. Get up now; we haven't much time." He offered a hand, pulling her up and out. "I fear your dress is beyond saving now. We'll sneak you out the back. And Mrs. Benning, it goes without saying that you would do well to forget what you saw and heard tonight."

"Why? Because if I tell anyone I'll be arrested as a French sympathizer?" she said with a queer sort of smile.

An eyebrow went up. "It's a possibility. But I was warning you against the implications of having to explain how you came across such information. I fear far more people would be interested in how you came to be in that sarcophagus than in what you overheard while inside."

"Oh," she said, looking momentarily downcast, her brow furrowing, obviously stumped by the rightness of his assumption. Then she looked up at him with a smile. "Fear not, good sir, I am well willing to forget what I heard. And I could merely hope that you do the same, if you please."

"I'll forget yours, if you forget mine?"

"Seems fair, reasonable. Polite, even."

He had just reached for the door handle, but her words made him turn and smile. "Do you see? That was simple enough. I told you the best way to assure my silence—"

"Was what?"

"Why, to ask me, politely."

Three minutes later, at about the same time one of Lord Fieldstone's footmen arrived at the library door to find it not only ajar but with a long trail of dust leading from it down the corridor, Phillippa found herself bundled quickly into a hired hack at the back gate of the Fieldstones' garden. But suddenly it didn't matter to her that her dress and her hair were an awful mess or that the hack was not her own soft, velvet-upholstered carriage. She was still too stunned by the very idea, the implications of what she had overheard.

Was it true?

Could it be possible?

Was unassuming, unnoticeable, surprisingly affable Marcus Worth . . . the Blue Raven?

Eight

His exploits were legendary: During the war, the papers had been crammed with details of his heroics. His prowess. His renown. He was rumored to have "removed" as many French from power as the guillotine had some twenty years before. And his cunning, his guile, unmatched. It was said he could slip into a bedchamber and steal a wife's jewelry and her virtue all without waking her husband.

He was the Blue Raven.

The most infamous spy in all of England.

Generally, infamy is a negative in the career of a spy, but luckily, anonymity was preserved in that no living soul knew who laid claim to the sobriquet.

Until now, that is.

Phillippa could keep her countenance, she told herself several times over the course of the morning. (For indeed it was morning, having been sent home the night before and fallen asleep at an unprecedentedly early hour, she, therefore, was awake in similar fashion. Her maid nearly died of shock.) Yes, she was well able to hold her tongue. She could keep a secret as safe as a tomb. And did so.

For a whole hour.

Luckily, for herself as well as others, her chosen confidant was sworn to secrecy.

"Could he be? Is it even possible?" she whispered.

Bitsy, her Pomeranian secret keeper, didn't react much to Phillippa's question. He seemed far more interested in the breakfast ham.

Phillippa obligingly fed him a piece under the breakfast room table and was rewarded by a sympathetic nuzzle. Bitsy was wearing the rubies today. Phillippa thought them less impressive than the sapphires, but as Bitsy wasn't to leave the house today (sadly, he could not stay away from the Warwicks' déclassé basset hound when it was in heat), it was permissible if he dressed down.

Only occasionally did Phillippa regret naming her male dog Bitsy, but to be fair, she had been unaware of his gender until it made itself clear, and by then, Bitsy was already becoming more of a Bitsy by the moment. He seemed to really respond to the jewelry.

After that brief interlude of pet fashion, Phillippa's mind returned to the subject at hand. If Marcus Worth was the Blue Raven, it would be nearly impossible to prove. The Blue Raven moved like mist, it was said, and was nearly as difficult to take hold of. However, it would be relatively easy to disprove, would it not? Simply fix the location of Mr. Worth when it was known the Blue Raven was elsewhere. He had been involved in the war, she knew that much.

"But then again, so was just about every young man not lucky enough to be firstborn or sermon-minded," she said, receiving a quizzical look from Bitsy. "If we can place his regiment in, say, Spain, when it was known the Blue Raven was in Paris, why, that could be very damning evidence against!"

"What could be damning evidence?" came a voice from the doorway of the breakfast room.

Phillippa turned to find her inattentive companion, Mrs. Tottendale, garbed in a dressing gown and looking all the blearier from the night's festivities.

Mrs. Tottendale was a dear friend of Phillippa's mother, who, when Alistair died so suddenly, had been happy to stay with Phillippa when her mother could not. The Viscountess Care had pressing social obligations that the death of a son-in-law could not abate. Phillippa understood.

And Totty had been a great comfort to Phillippa. Totty, in turn, found her lodgings (and the well-stocked cellar) in Benning House to be very comfortable, so she simply never left. Phillippa was glad of it. She knew it was invigorating for Totty to have found a new purpose in life as her companion after suffering the disappointments of a son and husband who both died too young. And much like Bitsy, Totty needed Phillippa as much as Phillippa needed her. Totty was harmless, and she was delightful in her way.

Just not in the mornings.

"Good God child, what makes you so bright at this hour? No, Leighton, no toast, just the tea and a tomato juice, if you would be so good." Mrs. Tottendale seated herself opposite Phillippa, and visibly winced when she looked at her. "Child, can't you do something about your hair?"

"My hair?" Phillippa questioned, arched voice and eyebrow.

"It's far too shiny. The reflection is hurting my eyes. Oh, thank you, Leighton." Once the requested fluids were placed down, Leighton, a man of such high thought and morals that his nose was perpetually stuck at an upward forty-five-degree angle, was quelled by one small look into wheeling over the sideboard tray to Mrs. Tottendale's elbow. This was established routine.

After selecting her chosen decanter and pouring a decidedly liberal amount of liquor into her tomato juice, Mrs. Tottendale kicked back her morning constitutional and addressed her young hostess.

"You were saying something about evidence?"

"Well, I—"

"And where did you get off to last evening? I was halfway to the Norriches' card party before I realized you were not with me."

"I had a headache—decided to call it an evening and left from the Fieldstone affair."

"The Fieldstones! So early! Not even Lady Draye's?"

Phillippa shook her head and was once more thankful for lack of chaperonage. Before she was married, Phillippa's mother would have been apoplectic had Phillippa left a party early, ruining a dress with dust in the process. Now, her mother was off somewhere with a Spanish Count, and Phillippa's mistakes were hers to make.

Yes, more often than not, Phillippa was thankful for her freedoms. For every time she would have welcomed a supporting presence and the wisdom of her elders, there had been a dozen others that the restrictions a mother or chaperone wrought would have hampered her most unduly.

She liked being able to do as she pleased, no matter how lonely it became.

But she wasn't alone, she thought, shaking off such a ridiculous notion. She had friends, like Nora, to keep her company. She had rivals, like Lady Jane Cummings, to keep her occupied. She had Bitsy, who relied on her completely—except for those times Bitsy had business to attend to, wherein his walker took him out—and she had Totty, who pinched Phillippa in the arm to bring her attention back to the table.

"Ouch! Totty!" Phillippa jolted back, rubbing her arm.

"Well, stop thinking while I'm talking. Who gave you such license? I was telling you all about the commotion at Lady Draye's!"

"Why, what happened at Lady Draye's?"

"I cannot believe you were not there! It was madness. That Marquis you've got your eye on, he gave his dance with Lady Jane away to Mr. Worth! He did the reel with your friend Nora instead."

Phillippa nearly spat out her tea. "Marcus Worth! How did *he* get to Lady Draye's?"

Totty looked at her charge with an expression of astonishment. "Carriage, I expect. Much like the rest of us."

"Of . . . of course," Phillippa said coolly, delicately dabbing at the corner of her mouth. But all the while her mind was reeling: How did dust-covered Marcus Worth recover his appearance enough to go to the Draye affair after being encased in a sarcophagus with her? Maybe he really was a spy. Such quick-change abilities certainly warranted a mark in the pro column.

"So . . . how did Lady Jane feel about having her circumstances so reduced?" Phillippa tried to maintain coolness in her voice.

"Hmph," Totty said, gulping her tea. "To watch Lady Jane, you would think that dancing with a second son instead of a Marquis is no step down at all. Rarely have I seen anyone so gracefully cool." At Phillippa's eyebrow, her chaperone added, "Excepting you, of course, my dear."

"Lady Jane's too insipid to lay any claim to grace. Still, she could not have been happy with Mr. Worth's dancing abilities."

"Actually, I believe he acquitted himself rather well," Totty said on a yawn. It was still very early for her.

"Really? But he's so tall; it must have been awkward," she mused.

"Truly, darling, I have little idea. You can't expect me to pay attention to Lady Jane's dance partners all evening, you know."

While Totty, having finished with her hearty breakfast of tea, tomato juice, and alcohol, turned her attention to the morning's stack of invitations, Phillippa tapped her teeth in what she knew to be an unbecoming fashion.

But in times of truly deep contemplation, teeth-tapping tended to occur.

Really, she shouldn't care as she did. Who gave a fig if Marcus Worth was England's premier spy against the French? The war had ended twice over, and his name—or pseudonym—no longer graced the papers. She had no reason to pay any attention to his movements.

But what *had* he been doing dancing with Lady Jane?

Stop it, Philly! she told herself harshly. Her concern was not whom Lady Jane had danced with; it was whom she hadn't. Namely Broughton. He had done as she bade and refused a dance with Lady Jane. That brought a slow, sure smile to her face. Broughton had played the game admirably, and the next challenge would be his to issue. Phillippa felt a small twinge of fear as to what the challenge could entail, but all in all, this season was going wholly according to plan. So she should not allow her attention to be diverted by someone of no importance and no proven secret identity.

"Your mother writes," Mrs. Tottendale said with a raised brow as she scanned a letter, "to remind you not to book the same musicians as last year; they were the only dim spot in an otherwise bright party."

"Party?" Phillippa replied quizzically, her attention dragged back to the breakfast room.

Totty looked up, placing the letter to the side. "The Ball, dear." At Phillippa's blank stare, Totty slapped a hand to her forehead. "The Benning Ball! Phillippa, it's less than two months away. Don't tell me you forgot! You never forget anything!"

Phillippa felt color stain her cheeks, shame mingling with horror at her own thoughtlessness.

She had forgotten. The Benning Ball was one of the premiere social events of the year. Wellington and Prinny vied for invitations. When she first reemerged in society, her mother had insisted that Phillippa throw a ball—and she had been right to do so. The Viscountess was of great assistance then. But as Phillippa's popularity grew, it seemed her mother felt quite confident to cease meddling and leave the entire business up to her. On a fixed date, all of her family and the rest of the world descended upon town for the occasion, and Phillippa was in charge of it all. From the theme to the napkin color to the entertainments, she chose every last detail. Except, apparently, the musicians.

"Of course I didn't forget, Totty. I simply expected mother to be in town by now, to . . . add her judgment to the precedings."

"Yes, your mother said something to that effect," Totty replied, as she picked up the next correspondence in the pile. "But it seems she's enjoying herself far too much. She leaves everything up to you and is wholly confident you will outdo your success of last year."

Oh God. Oh God. Phillippa bit into a piece of ham and furiously began chewing. So little time—the best caterers and florists will be overbooked for the end-of-Season events already! The theme had to be decided, decorations made accordingly. Invitations, engravers, musicians, entertainments—if she failed in this, she would be mocked mercilessly. What would Broughton think? Lady Jane would use this to her advantage for certain, make no mistake. She would have to have something, something truly spectacular to outdo last year, something—something people would be in awe of, something that would make the papers the next day. And here, she thought with a laugh, she had been idly, sillily, mulling over how to reveal Marcus Worth as the Blue Raven!

Reveal the Blue Raven.

Phillippa stopped still, mid chew. What if . . . she swallowed her food loudly.

She would need proof, of course. Hell, she would need to be able to present him on a stage. But a theme began to emerge in her mind. Cloaks and daggers. Bravura and derring-do. All she needed was to be certain, to have physical evidence of Marcus Worth's secret identity. She had to be sure. But how would she gain access to his life? How was she to find out?

"Oh!" she exclaimed, shaking her head. It was no good. The chances of him being the Blue Raven were slim, and she would be mucking around in someone's life for her own gain. Generally, when she did this, she at least received that person's tacit permission. She should forget the idea entirely. She should forget him.

"Dear Lord. Lady Worth just will not give up, will she?" Totty said with a snort.

"What?" Phillippa nearly overset her teacup, she swung round so quickly.

"Lady Worth has invited us to a dinner party—again."

"Let me see!" she grabbed the small ivory card out of a startled Totty's hand.

"Its nothing, darling. Lady Worth throws these twice a month. Dull as dishwater, I'm told; it's all so she can attempt to recruit new investors for her charity."

"What's the charity?" Phillippa tried (and admittedly failed) to inject nonchalance into her voice.

Totty, looking at Phillippa as if she had grown an extra head, answered, bewildered, "Some orphanage, I believe. Goodness gracious, what do you care? You can't possibly think to *attend*?"

Lord Worth was Mr. Marcus Worth's brother. Chances were, this was a dinner party he was forced to attend often. And even if Mr. Worth was not present, clues about his life would be.

"Darling, no!" Totty pleaded. "It's ridiculous! The Worths are not *our* kind of people. They are so reprehensibly goody-goody, they wouldn't know fun if it shot out of their noses! How can you expect them to throw a supper party that's remotely enjoyable on any level?"

She did have other things to do, didn't she? Win the hand of Broughton. Defeat Lady Jane. Plan a ball to end all other balls. Go to her modiste after nuncheon. Oh, she shouldn't care about Marcus Worth. She shouldn't be curious about his activities.

But, God help her, she was.

She examined the note again. "It's for tomorrow a week. A week from tomorrow, we shall have to dine somewhere."

"You didn't come down with a fever last night?" Totty asked anxiously. "Are you feeling nauseated?"

"No."

"Well, I am. Leighton! Another tomato juice, if you please!"

"Perhaps I'm feeling charitable. Accept the invitation, Totty." Phillippa handed the ivory card back to Totty, who merely shook her head.

"Oh, Phillippa, please reconsi—"

"Accept the invitation, Totty."

Goodness, Phillippa thought. Normally, her friends didn't have to be told what to do more than once.

Nine

"MRS. Benning, Mrs. Tottendale! I cannot tell you how pleased I am you accepted my invitation to dine!"

Marcus entered the drawing room just in time to see (and hear) his sister-in-law greet her latest arrivals.

Mariah had been glowing for a week now, positively alight, saying that this supper party would be the best yet. Honestly, Marcus had no idea how it could be any better or worse than the others; a change of menu altered very little, and every party ended with Mariah either triumphant in luring other people to her way of thinking or disappointed in her efforts.

It was far too often the latter. Marcus was continually surprised that Mariah kept doing these.

But now, Marcus understood her sister's nerves for this particular evening. Her insistence on the best courses, the polished and repolished silver, the best tallow for the chandelier. Mrs. Phillippa Benning, her considerable influence and her astounding wealth, would be a catch, indeed.

Marcus leaned against the doorjamb and regarded Mariah's prize quarry.

She looked stunning, but that was nothing new. Phillippa Benning was dressed at the height of fashion, although in what, Marcus had no idea. A blue silk. But it was a very nice silk and a very nice blue. Something about the way she wore clothes made them . . . better? Marcus shook his head. As if that made any sense. Or mattered to begin with.

Her companion was dressed well, too, but everyone knew Mrs. Tottendale was naked without a glass in hand. Which a servant promptly remedied.

Greetings done, and Mariah welcoming the next arrivals, Phillippa was free to move about the room, nodding to a few people she knew from someplace or another. As she passed his station by the door, her gait slowed, just barely, but all she did was give him the same cool nod as she had doled out to others. He returned it, and when he did, their eyes met for the briefest of seconds.

He'd be damned if he read any recognition of their last mutual adventure in her eyes.

It was hard, very hard, to reconcile this cool, prepossessed creature who was the queen of every room she entered with the dusty girl in a sarcophagus or even the cheeky lady who bribed a child with marzipan.

Still, all of those women had one thing in common: They were all looking out for their own interests.

Marcus shook his head ruefully. Mariah had her work cut out for her, if she was determined to have Phillippa Benning consider the orphans a worthy cause.

He'd bet all the money in his pockets that Phillippa Benning rarely considered anyone but herself.

Halfway through supper, Phillippa had decided conclusively on two things.

First, she had no *earthly* clue if Mr. Marcus Worth was the Blue Raven.

Second, Lady Mariah Worth was insane.

The first, more inconclusive conclusion was arrived at through a week's worth of research into the matter. None of her subtle (and she could be amazingly subtle) inquiries into Mr. Worth's rank in the army, or his division, current occupation, *anything*, had yielded fruit.

In fact, no one—not even a general—could confirm that Marcus Worth had even been in the army!

Perhaps she had been too subtle.

But he had been in the army; she was sure of it. She recalled he wore his red coat to a gala event in the spring, held by the Prince Regent. All the officers in London were invited, and all wore their uniforms.

And he had been there. She knew it. One thing Phillippa never doubted was her own memory.

Plus he had attended the parade. Not in uniform, but he had attended. He had some level of love for the military.

Since her own discreet inquiries had gone nowhere, she was forced to rely on direct questioning, which was facilitated by the fact that she was seated directly across from Mr. Worth.

And hindered remarkably by the fact that she was seated at the end nearest to Lady Worth.

Who, as it turned out, was insane.

The evening began thusly: Once everyone had arrived and greetings done, they proceeded to the dining room. Unfortunately, Phillippa was not matched with Mr. Worth; he, as a member of the family, was escorting somebody's aunt. Therefore she was forced to make small talk with an uncle to someone, twice removed, who had an eligible son. It was the only topic of conversation the man ventured, and he did so repeatedly.

Once the first course was served, Phillippa thought she could safely begin her inquiry. Alas, she was wrong.

"Mr. Worth," she began, over a spoonful of turtle soup, "I'm pleased to see you here this evening."

He looked up at her. If he was startled, he didn't show it. "And you as well, Mrs. Benning. I did not know you were acquainted with my sister-in-law."

"Oh, I'm acquainted with a great many people, Mr. Worth," Phillippa replied, "but I—"

"I can think of a few people you're not acquainted with, Mrs. Benning," Lady Worth jumped in. "Their names are Jackie, Jeffy, Michael, Rosie, Malcolm, Roger, Frederick, Lisel, oh, dear little Benjamin . . ."

At the odd look Phillippa gave her, Lady Worth clarified. "They are orphans, Mrs. Benning. Students at the school I fund."

A quick glance at Totty only earned Phillippa her companion's raised brows. *I told you so,* they said.

"There are dozens and dozens of others," Lady Worth continued, unmollified by Phillippa's stricken expression, "and new children in need every day. Bright children, talented children, whose misfortune—no fault of their own—has lost them all opportunity in our cruel world."

She paused for breath, obviously expecting a response to her impassioned plea. Phillippa opted for a noncommittal, "Lovely soup, Lady Worth," and proceeded to focus her attention on consuming it in a leisurely manner.

Phillippa was used to people wanting her money. She was one of the richest heiresses in Britain and had been since birth. When she was seven, she almost fell prey to a man who swore to save the puppy population of Surrey from the painful death of a cruel winter with her pocket allowance. But even he saved the hard sell for later on in their conversation.

Determined to pursue her own line of questioning, Phillippa gave her attention once again to Mr. Worth. "I wondered if your work would have kept you from attending," she said.

That did startle him, his spoon pausing halfway to his mouth.

"You are often absent from society, is all I mean. Until recently, that is."

A wry smile lifted the corner of his mouth. "Work does not hamper me. The offices at Whitehall close before dinner, just like everywhere else."

"So your sporadic attendance in society is due to . . . ?"

An eyebrow joined the upward tilt of the mouth. "My prospects for enjoying an evening, of course. For instance, last week I thought to attend Almack's, but I did not enjoy it, so I left. But then I went to the Fieldstones' and had a most interesting time."

It was Phillippa's turn to pause and meet his eyes. They twinkled with amusement—far too much for her liking.

"I imagine your social schedule is dictated by the same whims, Mrs. Benning," he drawled.

"Marcus is very involved with the school as well, Mrs. Benning," Lady Worth, having recovered from the previous slight, found her tongue and employed it once again. "I daresay it takes up a lot of the time used by more frivolous people in more frivolous pursuits. Not that I think you frivolous!" Lady Worth stammered. "No, no, its just, of course, you don't have work to attend to daily, and . . ."

She trailed off lamely, her face beet red. Phillippa almost felt sorry for her. She was trying awfully hard.

"What kind of work do you do, Mr. Worth? It must be very prestigious if you're at the Whitehall offices. Unless, of course, it's secret."

"No secret at all—and not terribly prestigious, I'm afraid," he answered, as the soup bowls were taken and the next course, a cold lamb roast, was brought round. "I shuffle papers in the War Department. There is an immense amount of paper generated when there's no war to fight, and it all requires shuffling."

She smiled at that. Who said the Blue Raven could not have a sense of humor?

Even if he was blithely sidestepping her question's intent. Such it was for the remaining four courses. Phillippa would attempt a seemingly innocuous and yet slightly probing question, Lady Worth would interject in a ham-fisted manner, and Mr. Worth would barely answer her query.

Never had Phillippa been so relieved to have the ladies remove to the parlor. It signaled a quickly shifting end to the party; another half hour, and she and Totty could make their escape back to the mad whirl of a *real* Ton party. One with people she, if not liked, then at least knew, and saw all the time, and danced with regularly, who were all interested in the same things. And eventually, someone would do something scandalous—sometimes her—to enliven the festivities, and . . .

Then again, after tonight, she would likely not be afforded the opportunity to uncover information about Marcus Worth with impunity. Perhaps it would be worthwhile to spend more time here.

"And then Jimmy—he was the fourteenth orphan the school gave a scholarship to—he told me how it was the first pair of socks he'd ever had that didn't have holes," Lady Worth declared from across the room, in sharp, carrying tones.

Worthwhile to spend more time here, yes. In the same room as Lady Worth? Perhaps not.

Gently leaning over, Phillippa whispered in her companion's ear. Mrs. Tottendale seemed to have frozen herself superbly in a gesture of self-defense, as if the charity-minded ladies wouldn't see her if she remained still.

"Totty, see if you can't tear your hem."

"Hm? Wha—?" Totty replied, coming out of a glassy-eyed reverie.

"Tear your hem," Phillippa reiterated while keeping a placid smile on her face.

Totty looked down. "No I haven't. Phillippa, what on earth are you talking about? And where is my wine? I can't fault the cellar in this place, certainly . . ."

Rolling her eyes, Phillippa shifted casually, pinned a bit of Totty's hem with her heel, and—*riiiiip*!

"Oh, Totty! Your hem, look!"

❧

"I understand the need for a break from insipidity. But why did you have to ruin my dress?"

Having successfully excused themselves in search of a place to repair the torn hem, Phillippa and Totty left the parlor and easily found a retiring room, where Totty whipped out her miniature dress repair kit (God help Phillippa if she ever left home without it) and quickly went to work on the seam.

"Because it was your dress or mine, and I certainly wasn't going to tear *my* dress, Totty. Don't be silly. Will you be all right here?"

"Of course," Totty replied intent upon her sewing. Then she looked up, just when Phillippa's hand was upon the door latch. "Phillippa . . ."

"Yes, Totty?" she replied, all innocence.

"Where are you going? Back to the parlor already?"

Phillippa paused a moment before pasting on her sweetest smile.

"Yes, Totty."

And she slipped through the door.

She had no idea where she was going. This wasn't even Marcus Worth's home; it was his brother's London house. Marcus maintained bachelor quarters in town. But he must have spent time here as a child; there must be something from his youth that would indicate a future interest in subterfuge. Perhaps a book on spying techniques, or a diary with an entry entitled, "Dear Diary, I have recently taken a surprising interest in subterfuge . . ."

Although that might be too much to hope for.

But she had to know. She had to. Something about him—that is, about the idea of him being the Blue Raven—picked at her brain like a woodpecker on a tree. It annoyed the tree, certainly, but what if a beetle was hiding under that bark?

Shaking off any doubts (and bad metaphors), Phillippa opened the first door she came to.

Well, her hasty search had to begin somewhere, and the library seemed as a good a place as any.

Unlike the last library she stole away to during a party, this one actually contained books.

Tons of books. Yards of books. *Miles* of books. Shelves stretched to the double-story ceiling, ladders on rollers allowed access to the highest. A desk by the large bay windows was in a state of efficient disorder. Obviously someone knew where everything was on that mahogany surface—and that someone certainly wasn't her.

But it was the least dusty section of the room, and given the amount of square footage to cover, the least dusty place, and therefore most recently used, seemed the place to begin.

Carefully, carefully, she began to leaf through the papers and books on the desk. She learned very little, except that Lord Worth seemed to have an unhealthy obsession with crop rotation. What a man in London was doing thinking about cabbage growth was beyond her, but she didn't have time to care. Nor did she care about his investment portfolio, which seemed marginal and not particularly exciting, nor his notes to his secretary and valet, requiring new dress shirts, a possible acquisition of a painting for his wife's birthday, and a detailed list of grouse recently shot to be mounted.

Frustrated, she reordered the desk into its original appearance. It certainly didn't help that she had no real idea of what to look for: something incriminating, something worthy of note; a letter from the war department; a medal of commendation, a—

"Oh, I'm going about this all wrong!" Phillippa whispered into the pale blue light of the empty room. After all, she was blindly looking, hoping to find something, anything, when what was wanted—nay, what was needed—was to think like *him*.

"Now, if I were the Blue Raven, where would I hide incriminating evidence in my brother's library?"

It felt a little silly to say out loud, she thought as she allowed her eyes to scan the shelves. Especially that name. "Blue Raven?" she said again, testing the sound of it against reality. Honestly, she thought, if I were a spy, I would pick a better name. Something menacing. The Destroyer. The Snake.

Was there even such a bird as a blue raven?

Her eyes flitted automatically to the farthest wall, where a section of the library was dedicated to the natural world. Then it hit her.

"Of course!" she cried. Grabbing one of the ladders, she wheeled it along the shelves to that side of the room. What better place to hide evidence of the Blue Raven than in a book about birds?

She slid the ladder as far as the rails would allow, entrenching herself in titles such as *Zoology: A Catalogue of Animals* and *Wild Beasts of the West Indies.* Whether blue ravens were wild beasts found in the West Indies she did not know, but she guessed not; if they existed at all, it was likely closer to home and somewhere in the *B* for *Birds* area of the shelves.

So up she went. Higher up the ladder, past *Elephants: A Remembered History*, past *Small Dogs* and *Large Cats* (Bitsy would surely be featured in one and scared to pieces of the other) until she found, far to her left, several volumes labeled *Birds*, volume A, volume B, and so on. They were merely marginally dusty, bespeaking use in the past year or so. And Lord Worth's passion for shooting grouse notwithstanding, she doubted the gentleman himself had much true interest in starting an aviary.

She reached over and pulled the second volume, *Birds*, volume B, off the shelf. It was a slim, brown leather book that had been published approximately twenty years previous. Unfortunately, it contained no reference to Blue Ravens. She replaced it carefully, and leaned over even farther, reaching for *Birds*, volume R. Reaching, reaching . . . almost there . . . her finger was *just* on the spine—

"Why is it I always find you skulking about other people's libraries?"

Phillippa nearly jumped out of her skin and turned. Unfortunately, being so precariously balanced on a ladder while out-of-skin jumping has the most predictable of Newtonian effects.

She fell.

Right into the waiting arms of Marcus Worth.

"Hello," he said cheerfully, his mouth twisted into a wry smile. "Just me."

Cradled in his embrace, staring into his eyes, Phillippa knew one thing.

It was going to be the challenge of her life to talk her way out of this one.

But when she opened her mouth to speak, something at the corner of her vision caught her attention.

She had not been the only thing to fall from the shelves. *Birds*, volume R, lay on the floor, splayed open. It contained no reference to ravens. Nor did it contain any references to rheas, rock pigeons, or red-throated loons. Indeed, it contained no pages at all. The book had been hollowed out, and in the place of information, there was only a handful of feathers.

Raven feathers.

Ten

"I knew it."

Marcus had to admit, having the long, lovely body of Phillippa Benning in his arms temporarily made him foggy on what it was that she thought she knew with such certainty.

But he remembered quickly enough.

Her eyes—ridiculously blue, even in the dark of the unlit library—were wide and fixed on his face. The corners of her slack mouth tilted and crept upwards, as if she were amazed, nay, *awed* by what she beheld.

Very rarely were women awed by him.

He almost smiled back. Almost.

Marcus felt curiously reluctant to put the beautiful Phillippa Benning down. But really, prolonging the moment was foolish, as he had no reason to keep holding her.

"You should be more careful," he said, his voice surprisingly soft as he set her on her feet. Her gaze remained on his face, unflinching, almost rapturous.

Really, it was becoming disconcerting.

"I can't believe no one ever guessed," she said, her hand still on his arm. Marcus looked at it. Then at her. Then he assumed his most bored tone.

"Guessed what? That you have a passion for mischief in libraries? True enough, I would have never guessed that at all. Mischief yes, libraries, no."

He expected a reaction from her, hoped for a superior look, like she gave Mariah at the table—anything to stop her staring at him as if he had grown a second head more handsome than his original.

But, as it was, she refused to comply.

"You hardly seem the type," she spoke conversationally, "which is, I suppose, what makes you the perfect type. Unassuming, blends in, except for your height, but of course you can stoop when necessary—"

"Mrs. Benning—"

"And I cannot fathom the training you had to undergo." She continued blithely, as if she were discussing something as mundane as a new riding habit. "Those spectacles, are they real?"

Caught off guard, he answered automatically. "They're for reading. Mrs. Benning—"

"But you wear them always . . . Oh, I understand, it's a sort of counterdisguise—"

"Mrs. Benning!" he said firmly (all right, yelled). After a deep breath, he continued more calmly. "What is it you think I am?"

"Why, a spy, of course." She leaned down and picked up one of the black feathers. "Specifically, the Blue Raven."

For a moment, he could only blink at her.

Those stupid feathers. They were put there so long ago, he'd almost forgotten they existed.

Trust *her* to find them.

"Mrs. Benning"—he sighed—"have a seat. We're lucky to be in a library with a sofa."

"I am not the Blue Raven," he said after folding himself next to her on the couch.

In response, Phillippa simply raised an eyebrow and waggled the feather in front of his rather astonished-looking nose. She almost giggled. He really had no idea who he was dealing with, did he?

"Those could be uncut quills, you know."

She responded by simply giving him look number five. The one that said, *You have erroneously come to the conclusion that I'm an idiot.*

He sighed. "You do realize that this is not my home. It is my brother Graham's home, not mine. Any evidence found in this establishment to support your theory would incriminate him, not—"

At times, Phillippa found the best way to stop someone from talking was to slap a hand over their mouth. Since this was a practice she wasn't allowed to engage in often, being a lady, she relished the opportunity to do so now.

"Mr. Worth. I know. And I know you know I know. And I can't stop knowing what I know, no matter how much you deny it. So, in the spirit of gratitude, for all of the—whatever it was you did during the war, I would like to show you my appreciation."

An eyebrow went up. He calmly pulled her hand down from his mouth, and asked, "How would you show your . . . appreciation?"

"Why, by throwing you a party, of course!" she replied, beaming her most ingratiating smile at him.

Suffice to say, he seemed shocked.

"You wish to throw a party. For me," he repeated dumbly.

"Absolutely! I know the whole of London would love to thank you for your service, and what better way to do it than at the gala Benning Ball?"

Phillippa knew very little of Mr. Worth, his mind-set, his habits. But one thing she did know was that he had at every turn surprised her. He did not fail now; he placed his head in his hand and began making the muffled noises that one could only associate with crying.

"I know, I know," she said consolingly, "you think it excessive. But I assure you, it's not! Why, the Blue Raven is a hero, a legend in our own time! No amount of festivities would ever be enough!" Gingerly, she placed her hand on his jerking shoulders, smoothing her palm over the fine cloth of his coat. A conciliatory, soothing gesture. "There, there," she murmured in time with her ministrations.

However, her ministrations stopped abruptly when Marcus Worth lifted his head, revealing his muffled, racking sobs to instead be a full fit of laughter.

"Oh, Mrs. Benning, leave off, I beg you!" he said in between chuckles.

"Leave off?" she spat back, rising from the couch indignantly.

"Yes. Stop this pretense of selflessness. You're so much more engaging when you're yourself."

Phillippa stopped cold, her mouth gaping like a fish. Then, suddenly, as if all the wind had left her body, she fell onto the couch next to him, her posture relaxed.

"Most men enjoy playing the game, you know," she said, somewhat amused. "Most men, they respond to a flittery innocent or a coquette or—"

"Most men are too blockheaded to realize only you know all the rules to this game." He sighed and shook his head. "Mrs. Benning, why not simply tell me what you want?" he said, a half smile playing across his face.

"Fine." She leaned back, crossing her arms. "I want to reveal the identity of the Blue Raven at the Benning Ball. It will be the most spectacular event in the Ton, and it will take place at my party. A tremendous triumph."

"And you will no doubt be cited in the papers the next day," he said, nodding along.

"I'll be cited in the papers for years! It will be fabulous—a full masquerade, all the men and women masked alike, and then, each person strips off their mask one at a time—the entire hall will be done in capes and shadowed corners, espionage, the thrill of the hunt—"

"How very gothic you are, Mrs. Benning," he said wryly. "However, if I were the Blue Raven—and I refuse to confirm that assumption—you would be exposing me to the world and all my enemies. Revealing my identity would very likely get me killed."

Phillippa had to admit, he had a point.

"But . . . the war is over, sir! Your enemies have been vanquished."

"Not entirely."

"But surely—"

"Not entirely." He repeated firmly, standing. "Don't play coy, Mrs. Benning. I know that you could hear perfectly well in that sarcophagus. Hence your whole . . . maddening curiosity. By the bye, I told you to disregard that conversation."

"Which only made me regard it more," she retorted.

"In any case," he said, firmly returning to the subject at hand, "you know that I believe my, er, the Blue Raven's enemies are still active. Why on earth would I agree to your scheme?"

At this, Phillippa stood toe-to-toe with him. She looked him dead in the eye and played her trump card. "Because you want something from me."

Phillippa held her breath, watching his brow darken. He leaned in to her. "And what could you possibly offer me, Mrs. Benning? A nod and hello? A spot on your . . . guest list?"

"Exactly," she said, choosing to ignore his idiotic if somewhat startling innuendo. "You're correct, sir, in that I could hear very well in that dusty sarcophagus. I heard you have a list of social events that are possibly under attack. May I venture a guess as to what was on that list?"

At his nod, she continued. "The Whitford Banquet?"

He nodded again.

"The Hampshires' Racing Party?"

A nod.

"The Gold Ball at Regent's Park?"

He nodded a last time, then eyed her speculatively.

"How did you deduce—"

"They are annual events," she interrupted. "They are exclusive. And the people that throw them . . . really, it wasn't all that difficult to discern." Phillippa took a step forward, closing the space between them. "I can get you into all these parties. I can make certain you're on the guest list."

"What makes you think I don't have invitations already?" he inquired.

"You're not good Ton," she replied matter-of-factly.

An eyebrow shot up. "Please Mrs. Benning, don't spare my feelings," he said drily.

"Oh, you're not bad Ton," she shrugged, "not by any means. But you're not the best Ton. You're the second son—"

"Third, actually."

"Even worse. No title and no possible hope of one. Your prospects are modest at best. Your brother's a rather minor Baron and your sister-in-law's fervent charity work does not grease the wheels of Society in your favor, does it? These parties—they're not everyday type things like Almack's. I wager a thousand pounds that you have no earthly idea of how to get into any of these exclusive events."

She smiled. "You need me."

He glowered.

She stepped up to him. Delicately, she placed a hand on his shirt, felt the rise and fall of his chest stutter. "You once told me that to sway you, all I need do is ask you nicely. So, *please*. Just consider it?" She batted her eyelashes. "That's all I'm asking right now."

His hand came to rest on top of hers. And then, deftly, he cast it away.

"Is that your sole trick? One would think you'd have a more expansive repetoire."

Phillippa recoiled as if stung. Haughtily, she stepped back. Looked down her nose at him. As best she could, at any rate.

"I'm sure I don't know what you mean."

"I'm sure you do," he retorted. "Your plan is ridiculous, and yet you try to persuade me with coy looks and a hand on my shirt. You tried this ploy on me before, if you recall, and it didn't work that time, either. Perhaps you're confusing me with your much-sought-after Marquis?" He leaned back languidly against the shelves as she stood straight, holding her ground. "After all, that little maneuver seemed to work wonders for you in your competition to entrap the poor sod."

Phillippa felt her smile falter. "You are aware of a . . . competition?"

He snorted. "My congratulations. As of our last meeting, you were making great ground with Broughton. I doubt Lady Jane could possibly be faring as well."

She stared at him, unable to countenance this hard talk with the mild man who presented it. "I daresay I am making great strides with Broughton. Not two days ago he took me on a private picnic; we got to know one another better. It was very pleasant."

"I'm certain it was. The dewy grass is far more pleasant for getting to know someone than the lid of a sarcophagus."

Phillippa almost smiled. In point of fact, the picnic with Broughton had been an exercise in her own agility as a flirt. Oh, she made certain that Broughton did not tempt her to feel that dewy grass, but every syllable of conversation was so loaded with double and triple meaning that Phillippa herself didn't know what was being said half the time. Such discourse was the Ton's stock and trade.

So she had to admit: Speaking frankly to Marcus Worth was so refreshing, it smacked closely of being entertaining.

But that didn't mean she wouldn't defend herself against his playful taunting.

"I can assure you, Mr. Worth, that my . . . meeting with Broughton on the sarcophagus lid was perfectly comfortable. Why, he almost made me forget the cold. And I'll have you know, I never forget anything."

At that, Marcus shouldered himself away from the shelves, and with easy, lazy shuffling, came to stand directly in front of her. His hand playing on his chin, and a twinkle in his eye, he asked, "You said he *almost* made you forget the cold?"

She nodded.

"Well then"—he smiled—"you're, er, meeting, didn't go as well as you think."

"My meeting went very, *very* well," she retorted, watching his every move suspiciously.

"I don't think so. You see, if it had gone well, you would have burned through that sarcophagus lid, never mind its temperature at the start."

"Oh, and you would know, would you?" She narrowed her eyes, cocked her head to the side.

"I would. But more's the pity," he whispered, leaning into her, "you don't."

It was the smallest thing, really. No reason that this little taunt should have gone any further. Except—her eyes flicked to his mouth, that wry corner lifted, the hint of white teeth shining through. Curiosity flickered in her belly. But he was watching her intently, she knew, so she would just step back, remain passive, cool.

But she didn't. Suddenly, the gap closed between them, and his lips were on hers.

This was new.

This was different.

Because this kiss she felt to her toes. This kiss hit every single one of her senses with its delicate force. And this kiss made her forget that she shouldn't be kissing him.

Whereas Broughton had felt the need to press her back, Marcus Worth did not overpower her. In fact, he didn't touch her, except for his mouth on hers. But she could feel everything. His strength, his warmth. His arms remained at his sides, in his pockets, but she knew that had he touched her, his hands would run through her hair, graze her jaw, follow the length of her collarbone.

A shiver raced down her spine. Unknowningly, she parted her lips, let him inside. As his tongue danced with hers, she leaned into him, put her silk-covered length against his wool. Her hand found its way to his hair, ran through it, the other grazed his jaw, followed the length of his collarbone—and all Phillippa wanted was to feel more.

But just as surprisingly, as suddenly as the kiss had begun, it ended.

He pulled away, slowly. Phillippa followed, at first, until he broke their connection, the cool air filling the space between them. She opened her eyes, slightly bewildered, her heart beating at an alarming rate. His face reflected her wonder, as he let out a long, slow breath. But then that corner of his mouth slid up, arrogant and taunting, letting her know that he knew every single feeling that had coursed through her body in those last few moments.

Want.

Need.

Desire.

So, considering the time, the place, and position she found herself in, Phillippa did the only thing she could think of as situationally appropriate.

She hauled back and slapped him.

Eleven

WELL, to be fair, he'd deserved it.

Marcus didn't know what had come over him. They had just been talking—flirting, really, as he turned the conversation away from her ridiculous plan, and suddenly, her voice had become a siren's call, the candlelight played off her skin, and he was thinking about things he shouldn't.

And then he acted on those thoughts. Impulsively. And Marcus Worth was many things, but he was never, ever impulsive.

But Phillippa was such a different person than he expected, Marcus thought, as he shivered against the cold, standing in a narrow winding alleyway in one of the less desirable sections of Whitechapel, a patched and threadbare coat his only protection from the unseasonable chill. He was waiting for the signal from the broken slit of a window across the street, and until he got it, he was unfortunately apt to let his mind wander. And it was unfortunately apt to wander to his activities the previous evening.

Phillippa Benning looked, from afar and within the constraints of Society, like one of the meaner, slyer women with lucky advantages of birth and fortune to propel them to their current status and allow them to be provocative. Women who wouldn't normally give him the time of day, and he wouldn't normally give a second thought to. But then their conversation let out her surprising sense of humor, and her wit proved . . . seductive. Oh, he couldn't deny she was a singularly beautiful young lady, but he had thought her beauty a bit hard around the edges, as if polished to a point. But some of his opinion had been chipped away during their interlude in a sarcophagus, and the rest fell free when she had, without intending it, leaned into him and opened her mouth to his.

He smiled at the memory—until it was quickly replaced by the memory of a well-placed slap across the face.

Well, as he'd said, he'd deserved that.

After he restored Phillippa Benning back to the ladies, she stayed another few minutes before taking her leave, giving excuses that she and Mrs. Tottendale were late for another engagement, leaving Mariah to go into raptures of Mrs. Benning's grace and dress and manners, and fearful aspersions regarding how she herself acted and if she gave any reason to offend and wonder if her orphanage would benefit. Marcus, meanwhile, was left to determine his next course of action. That led him here, standing outside in this unnaturally cold spring day and waiting for a bloody lamp in a window in a part of town no respectable person cared to venture.

Overloaded carts carrying the skinned carcasses of fatted lambs trundled down the street, their blood dripping off the back, bleeding red into the groves between the cobblestones. Women lost to liquor and time plied whatever was left of their wares in broad daylight, taken up by men who used them for mere minutes to forget their own lack in life. Marcus could have stood in this alley for the first time or for the thousandth, but the view would never change. Absentmindedly he rubbed his thigh. That damn desk they gave him at the Home Office—he kept bumping his knees against it most painfully. No matter what Fieldstone said, he was not hard up for adventure. He did not crave this life. He would like nothing better than to lay it all down and rest.

But just when they thought they could stop looking over their shoulders . . .

Johnny Dicks had sent him a message. Said the Frenchy had ambled in again. And maybe Johnny could provide a better description this time.

Marcus needed confirmation; he need to know who he was dealing with and reassurance from his contacts that the information they had given him was solid, because he was too far out on a limb to be boxing at shadows. He'd lose his balance, if that was the case. So here he was, having signaled Johnny Dicks in the Bull and Whisker to meet, waiting for the all clear. Waiting. And waiting.

He shook his head, stretched out his stiff legs. Suddenly, out of the corner of his eye, he saw a flicker of movement from the window across the way. It wasn't the signal he was waiting for—that was the lamp in the window—but it set Marcus's spine tingling.

In an affected, loping walk, Marcus shuffled across the alley, dodging carts and drunks, and into the building across the way. Climbing the creaking, narrow steps to the third floor, Marcus quietly removed the dagger from the under his long coat. Approaching the door of Johnny Dicks's rented room, dread trickled down his stomach to find it not only open but the latch busted and lying in pieces on the floor.

Moving swiftly now, silently, Marcus swept into the cramped room. Careful to keep his back to the walls, he gripped his dagger as he peered around corners and found nothing.

Nothing but Johnny Dicks.

He was a burly man, no more than thirty, who looked like he earned extra money pummeling teeth out of men's heads in amateur tournaments, and he did on occasion. He'd enjoyed being out of the army and had added a layer of padding to his gut—the effects of solid meals and less necessary marching. He'd always been an affable chap with a keen eye and better brains than some officers.

But now he lay at odd angles on the dirty cot, his fingers mangled and bloody, blood pooled beneath him, running from the long, clean gash across his neck.

Marcus stared for what felt like an eternity into those cold, lifeless eyes, left open and horrified by whatever had ended him.

"Damn and blast," he whispered, lowering his dagger.

A sound from the staircase jolted Marcus into movement. Footsteps, light and quick, running down the stairs. Marcus darted out into the hall. He looked up, then down, only managing to catch a glimpse of a mud-colored cloak before it disappeared out the door.

Bounding down the stairs, four at a time, threatening to break the spindly structure with the force of his running, Marcus reached the bottom in record time and bolted out the front door.

Looking left and right down the street, Marcus searched in vain for the cloak he saw, only to be confronted by the sight of dozens on the backs of every man, and sometimes woman, in the street.

"Look out, ye nit!" A barrel-chested man cried, startling Marcus just before he was run over by a horse drawing a fish cart. It whinnied and went up on its hind legs as the driver of the cart cursed at him.

"Watch it, ye blind geek. Feckin' fool!"

"Sorry! Sorry!" Marcus said, backing off the thoroughfare.

Damn. Damn and blast.

Johnny Dicks, his main contact, was dead. And his killer was gone.

Going to the constable proved useless, but Marcus did it anyway. He did not mention his association with the government, but he wanted it recorded somewhere that Johnny Dicks had died by means of foul play, even if the Whitechapel constables didn't see it that way.

"Maybe the bloke cut hisself, coulda been accidental," the reed-thin patrolman said. He was missing three teeth, and the rest were black. It was better that the man didn't smile; it would have been like looking into a cavern to hell.

"Cut himself? How? Whilst shaving? Then what? Bled out, died, and only then got rid of the knife?" Marcus crossed his arms over his chest.

"Listen, bub," Constable Black-Mouth said with a sneer. "Moren' like he got hisself knifed by a doxy looking to take more than she earned. I got a dozen people died today, in ways worse than this. I got too much to do without some swell comin' down to my turf and tellin' me which dead body is more important than the next. Now, I'll ask around, but you got no weapon, and my guess is, nobody seen nothin'." With that, the officer tipped his cap to Marcus and trolled his way down toward a group of young prostitutes who would either likely be run off by the presence of the law or bribe him to remain. Marcus didn't wait to find out which. To his mind, he had far more solid evidence than anticipated that Johnny Dicks's information had been correct—and worth killing for.

Marcus walked into the Home Office of the War Department, his massive, determined stride making pounding footfalls that could be heard from the other end of the fastidious building in Whitehall. He was so direct in his movements that he nearly knocked over two uniforms in his path, both too young and too well bred to do anything other than get out of Marcus's way. He wound his way through the labyrinth of offices and hallways of the different sections of the War Department—Strategy, Planning, Defense—before walking through the door affixed with the nameplate Security. It was an innocuous enough title, the Security section of the War Department—seemingly used to secure locations for meetings of the other section leaders, official state visits, treaty signings, etc.—but little did most people know—including the higher echelons of Parliament—that the Security section chief's office connected directly to the director of the War Department's.

Any time someone from the Security section needed to speak

to the director, Lord Fieldstone, he could, without having to make an official appointment. They simply needed clearance from the section chief, which Marcus hoped to bypass if he could, but if he couldn't, he would lie his way in. There was no time anymore for subterfuge. No time to arrange a chance meeting at a ball.

The offices beyond the door labeled Security were rather nondescript. A large room with a number of desks, all in neat rows, the section chief's office door beyond. Only the keen-eyed would notice that every desk was fitted with heavy locks, and the main door had a core of iron.

Since the end of the war, more and more of those desks had become empty, as men who had worked so diligently for their cause found there was not enough cause to go around anymore. Papers sat in neat stacks on those desks that were still occupied, booklets neatly ordered on the shelves. A few men looked up as Marcus marched past, mumbled greetings, and then returned to the draining occupation of doing nothing. He subconsciously rubbed his thigh as he passed his own too-short desk—the only somewhat cluttered one in the room—and headed straight for the section chief's door.

"Hold on, Worth!" the squeaky voice of Leslie Farmapple, Section Chief Sterling's secretary—and indeed, the tiny dictator who ran the entire Security section with ruthless order and efficency—stopped Marcus midstride.

"Worth, I need to speak with you about your monthly ink allotment."

Marcus really did not have time to pause or patience to discuss the necessities of quill and ink, and so instead, pointing to Sterling's door, said, "Is he in?"

"Yes, he is," Leslie replied, as he sorted Sterling's correspondence into piles. "Now, if you are going to exceed two jars of ink a month, please fill out a request for more, don't just take another pot from the stores. I don't care that you need it, I just need to know who's taken it—"

"I put in that request three days ago, Leslie. Now, is he alone?" Marcus interrupted, again indicating Sterling's office.

"He went in alone," Leslie replied and, unable to be deterred from his intended subject, continued, "and if you put in that requisition, I have not received it. Also, your desk. May I please request that you attempt to maintain some standard of organization—"

"No." Marcus said abruptly.

"No?" Leslie squeaked.

"We've been over this, Leslie. It is in order—my order. And in this manner I can tell if anyone has been rifling my desk."

"Oh," Leslie replied, obviously thinking over messiness as a security measure. "But everyone else—my word!"

Unfortunately for Leslie, Marcus had finished the conversation. Feeling his business with Fieldstone to be of the utmost urgency, Marcus discovered he had the capacity to knock Leslie rudely to one side and barge through the section chief's door. And as such, he did so.

Closing the door behind him and lowering its shades, Marcus had barely turned around as he said, "Sir, I need to speak with the director—on personal business."

Sterling sat behind his wide desk, a cigar poised at his lips. At one time, Sterling was likely a trim, athletic man with a healthy tan and a full head of hair, but a decade inside this building and a fondness for his cook's rich dinners and a brandy afterwards had left him doughy, balding, and in the middle of his life. Now he wore a startled expression as he blinked at Marcus, before laying the cigar down in the tray before him.

Folding his hands over his growing stomach, Sterling spoke. "What personal business?"

"Yes, what personal business?" came a voice from Marcus's behind left.

Turning, and admonishing himself for not checking his corners (where had his battle-readiness gone?) Marcus laid eyes on

Lord Fieldstone, squeezed into a deep leather chair in the corner, companionably puffing on a cigar.

"Oh, sir—as I said, it's—it's personal." Marcus stammered. Both men kept their seats, eagerly looking to Marcus in anticipation. "I . . . I found a vase. I think it must be ancient, and since you are such an avid collector . . ." He hoped his lie did not sound so implausible. But the skeptical look he received from Sterling told him otherwise.

Fieldstone, however, raised an eyebrow. "Did you bring it with you? I could take a look, if you like."

"Uh, no. It's still at the shop. Are you free? Perhaps you could accompany me. The shop's purveyor is, I fear, trying to get more than it's worth."

"Worth." Sterling's voice came from between cigar puffs. "Do you expect me to believe you barreled Leslie over for a vase?" He looked genuinely saddened as he said, "You're chasing a new theory, aren't you?"

Marcus's eyes flicked to Fieldstone in the corner, who sighed and shook his head. "I simply asked Sterling here for his opinion on how his section had transitioned from wartime to peace. He's been most enlightening."

"You're not the only one who boxes at shadows," Sterling said with grave sincerity, "but you certainly do so more than most."

At Fieldstone's questioning look, Sterling continued. "There was an incident at Vauxhall in the fall—also the demand for extra plainclothesmen to patrol the docks in February. Hell, just last month, you took an old woman into custody because you mistook her for a Frenchman in disguise!"

"I had reason to suspect that a ship bearing French enemies was going to dock in February, and to be fair, that old woman *was* a Frenchman in disguise." Marcus replied, holding his posture at attention.

"Monsieur Valéry was going to a fancy dress ball as one of Macbeth's witches, and that's besides the point," Sterling replied.

"Worth, we don't have French enemies anymore! You cannot go through life always suspicious."

Marcus knew he had to hold his ground, even as he felt it slipping out from under him.

"Sir, I must remind you that I am paid to be suspicious; and previous incidents aside, this time, the threat is very real. I just came from my informant, who—"

"Oh? What is the threat?" Sterling asked. "Who is the threat toward? How do they plan to carry out their deeds?"

"I . . . I do not yet know, sir, but I—"

"Damn it, Worth!" Fieldstone stood up from his chair. "You can't expect action on so little information." Then he paused, flicked a glance to Sterling. "The desk—it doesn't suit you anymore, does it? Maybe it never did."

Having received the silent message from Fieldstone, Sterling stood and moved to the door, saying nothing, leaving them alone. After the door closed behind him, Fieldstone said in solemn tones, "I'll make certain you get your full pension."

Marcus felt himself go very pale, then flushed with checked fury. But he kept his voice and his temper under control.

"Sir. My contact is dead. His throat slit." He handed Fieldstone a card. "This is the constable who took the report." And then, leaning close, his voice low, his back straight, his eyes locked with the Lord Fieldstone's, "The list came from this very section."

"Because the ink was the same? The drop of wax?" Fieldstone whispered, his expression sad. "Or do you suspect your coworkers because they have blithely disregarded you?"

"Sir, I—" Marcus tried, but Fieldstone held up a hand.

"It has to be very aggravating, not being believed, time and again. It makes trust difficult, and unfortunately here, trust is necessary."

"What are you saying?" he asked warily.

"You no longer trust anyone, and they in turn will not trust you." Fieldstone replied in hushed tones. "The Blue Raven is retired. Perhaps Marcus Worth should retire as well."

There was nothing more to be said. Marcus, too shocked to feel other than numb, clicked his heels, bowed sharply to Fieldstone, and opened the door.

There, Sterling very nonchalantly stood very close to the doorjamb, obviously trying desperately to not look like he was listening.

Marcus refused to meet eyes with Sterling or Leslie, who had just come in from the hall, or any of the other men diligently doing nothing at their desks, as he passed them and turned out of the Security office's door.

Did everyone think him gone round the bend? He passed Crawley in the hall and caught his eye. Crawley, always one of the more logical if mundane members of the section, looked away sheepishly, confirming that it was known what would happen today.

Marcus wanted to scream. It was true what Fieldstone had said; the war had been hard on him. But he knew for a fact it had been harder on others. He was too used to being suspicious—and had been embarrassed by it in the past—to not acknowledge that it could color his judgment.

But he knew in his gut he was right.

Shaking with rage as he exited Whitehall, Marcus surveyed his options. There were few people left to trust, even fewer resources available to him. The desk no longer suited him. Perhaps it never had, really.

It had begun to rain, a soft drizzle that coated London in gray. People on the street shrugged deeper into their greatcoats, huddled in packs underneath frail parasols meant for sunshine but suddenly tested to prove their mettle. They congregated under eaves and awnings, waiting for this slightest of inconveniences to pass. Suddenly, the soft gray drizzle opened up to a punishing downpour. People ducked into open buildings or dodged their way to the street to hail an available hack but never finding one.

Marcus let the rain pound down on him, wash over him, clean his mind. With Johnny Dicks dead, Marcus couldn't track the man from whom Dicks had stolen the list. Dicks's friend had disappeared, too, likely dead, in his estimation. Without Fieldstone's trust and assistance, he could not investigate anyone from his department. Make that former department.

He had to find proof, to get Fieldstone to listen to him.

He briefly considered consulting his brother, but he rejected the idea immediately. It would kill him, Marcus knew, to find that the whole Blue Raven mess had started up again. Best to endanger as few people as possible.

A sudden flash entered his mind: a lithe body, pressing up against him in a most delightful manner. Shining hair, angelically golden in the moonlight. Lush lips, parting and offering him a deal with the devil.

Marcus shook his head. He'd be damned if he took Phillippa Benning up on her insane proposal. He'd be exposing himself to extreme scrutiny, not to mention involving her in a business far more dangerous than a dizzy social butterfly could possibly imagine or he could hope she'd take seriously. If he told Phillippa Benning the extent of what he suspected, she'd probably gossip about it over tea, like it was the plot of her latest favorite novel, and then go purchase a new bonnet.

But worse than that, she was an innocent in this business. She could get hurt.

No, he thought, plodding along in the downpour, he would have to try a new tack. Go back to the East End, see if he could track Johnny Dicks's last days, see where his path crossed with anyone from the Security section or with the Frenchman.

The ghost.

Dicks told him what the Frenchy had said about a pigeon when he exited the Bull and Whisker, and it was a bucket of cold water to his face.

The sudden heavy downpour let up just as abruptly as it had begun, the clouds parted, and suddenly sunlight shone on the wet cobblestones, making the city seem fresh-scrubbed and clean. Marcus rounded the corner, crossing the invisible line into Mayfair, and was immediately surrounded by that world of fashion and sophistication that Phillippa Benning existed in. The world that would flock to those events on the list.

Marcus did a quick mental check. The first event on the list, the Whitford Banquet, was four days away.

He would retrace Johnny Dicks's steps. He would find some way into the Whitford Banquet. He would hunt the ghost. He would *not* take up Phillippa Benning on her devil's deal.

Because it was dangerous. Because it was lunacy.

Certainly not because that devil was far too tempting for his peace of mind.

Twelve

"It's going to a fabulous affair, Nora, don't doubt it." Phillippa said airily, as she paraded down Bond Street in her new plum-colored walking costume, with lavender suede gloves and a silk bonnet. Bitsy panted, companionably held in the crook of Phillippa's arm. Totty, on her other side, blinked blearily into the afternoon sun, flushed from the exertion of following Phillippa from store to store to store to . . . the entire length of Bond Street, New and Old.

"I would never doubt it!" Nora exclaimed, hurrying to soothe any feathers she may have ruffled. "But did not Lady Cambridge give a party with a similar cloak-and-dagger theme during the little season?"

"Hah!" Totty guffawed. "Not one the likes of which Phillippa is going to have! Lady Cambridge will find herself shamefaced for even attempting to throw an event similar to, albeit before, the Benning Ball."

Phillippa blinked a moment, for Totty had not strung such a number of words together all afternoon, but it looked like the afternoon's exercise was doing some good, leaching out last night's excess. "Quite," she finally replied, taking Totty's arm and smiling at that good lady. Far be it from her to admit it out loud, but she had a decided fondness for her companion, even more so when she trudged half of London with her, her complaining moderate, as they searched for the perfect color table linens for her ball.

"Totty is correct, Nora; no one is going to remember Lady Cambridge's little ball after they see mine."

And indeed, if she managed to get the ingredients she required, it would be The Event of the Season. Unfortunately, her last encounter with Mr. Marcus Worth, the man who was to be the centerpiece of the affair, did not go as well as hoped, but that did not give Phillippa cause to abandon it. Men tended to come around to her way of thinking.

Pausing in front of the next shop's windows, which featured bolts of fabric in every available hue, Phillippa's mind turned to the details of that last encounter with Mr. Worth.

He had kissed her. Really kissed her. To be fair, men had tried in the past to steal kisses from her, and occasionally she allowed them to succeed. And when she did engage in that intimate contact of lips that the opposite sex seemed to enjoy so much, Phillippa was always the one who had control of the situation. Her husband, Alistair, used to write passable poetry about plucking down the moon for a kiss from her lips. She'd suspected he cribbed from Shakespeare. And Broughton seemed ready to dance attendance on her for the mere possibility of where a kiss could lead.

But when Mr. Worth was involved, it seemed she had no control whatsoever.

There had been a moment—nay, a full minute—when it was she who was kissing him. He had set off a spark of intensity in the deep center of her being that caused her to veritably *nestle* into his embrace. That is, if he *had* embraced her. Phillippa had the blush-inducing memory of being the one to embrace him.

She could have turned that to her advantage, of course. She

could have used what she'd felt, and was certain he must have felt, too—after all, he did initiate the encounter—to get him to do as she bade, allow her to continue with her schemes for the Benning Ball, assured of his cooperation.

But instead, she'd slapped him.

Which, when looked at objectively, was actually his fault. If he hadn't, er, stirred her, she would not have been so unsettled as to forget herself and turn back into offended prim propriety.

"Phillippa—" Nora hissed, pulling at Phillippa's sleeve, obviously stepping up her attempts to get her attention. Poor Bitsy nipped at Nora's hand for unsettling his comfort.

"Bitsy, darling, be still. Nora, stop pulling; you'll ruin the line of my cuff. Now what do you think of this deep blue color for the Ball? It looks sinister and luxurious, but is it sinister and luxurious *enough*?"

"No, Phillippa—Broughton! To your left!" Nora said in a rush of breath, her wide eyes glowing with the anticipation of encountering the man Phillippa had marked to conquer.

Phillippa coolly turned her head to where Nora indicated. Thirty yards up the street, strolling with ease of being and greater ease of living, was Broughton, surrounded by a small group of young men who all had humor, fashion, and wealth—and all obviously looked to Broughton as their leader. Phillippa and Nora watched as the group tipped their hats in greeting as they passed a group of tittering young nobodies, each girl staunchly held fast by their mothers. After they passed the girls, Broughton made a comment too low for Phillippa to hear, but the entire body of men burst out in laughter.

They were twenty yards away now, really nothing at all, and so Phillippa made her gaze direct and gave her slow, saucy smile, reserved for those occasions when meeting an interesting man on Bond Street. Broughton caught her smile and knew it was directed at him, as he raised an eyebrow in return.

"Oh, Phillippa," Nora said breathlessly, "he's headed this way!"

"Of course he is," Phillippa replied. Although the group was proceeding at an annoyingly slow rate. "Totty, take Bitsy, please."

"Does the Marquis not like dogs?" Nora asked, concerned.

"Hmph." Totty replied, taking the fluff ball into her arms. "There ain't a man alive who likes this dog."

"Totty, shush. I have no notion as to Broughton's opinion on dogs. I simply wish to spare Bitsy any censure if it's negative."

"I daresay the Marquis is walking very slowly," Nora said, a frown crossing her brow. "Really, if he doesn't get here before five minutes are out, you shall have to ignore him, so he'll know he's being punished."

Fifteen yards now . . .

"Nora! How very cruel. You're catching on well." Phillippa smiled.

"Watch your back, ladies, looks as if we're to be attacked from both sides." Totty said, her eyes fixed in the opposite direction.

Phillippa risked a glance to their other side, and saw Mr. Marcus Worth strolling toward them, arm in arm with his sister-in-law, Lady Worth.

More accurately, Mr. Worth was being pulled down the street by a very determined Lady Worth, whose aim was directly for them.

"God save me," Totty said, and gripped Bitsy tighter to herself, causing the poor pup to whimper. "That woman will talk about orphans and good deeds and *needlework*. I simply cannot take that much wholesomeness."

"Now, Totty, be kind. Perhaps she has hidden vices that will make her far more likable." Phillippa replied, her eyes unaccountably locked onto the form of Mr. Marcus Worth. She had not taken notice of him before, but ever since she had been pressed up against him in that sarcophagus—and wound around him in his brother's library—she had to admit he was very well-formed. He was as strong as a boxer, certainly, but it was stretched out on his long frame, making him lean and—

"How dare she!" Nora exclaimed, drawing Phillippa's attention back to her other side.

"You look away for three seconds," Nora continued, "and that magpie sweeps in and tries to steal him away!"

For indeed, Lady Jane Cummings and a friend were now immersed within the group of young men, all of them smiles and laughs. She must have been lying in wait, Phillippa thought, in the shop the group had stopped in front of. Indeed, Phillippa saw a footman in Lady Jane's livery loaded down with boxes emerge from said shop.

"Clever girl," Phillippa said under her breath. Then, after a quick glance in the other direction, she leaned down to Nora.

"Isn't that Thomas Hurston in Broughton's group?"

"Why, yes!" Nora replied. "But oh, I'm supposed to be angry with him. He fetched me punch instead of champagne at last night's fete. Can you imagine?"

"Oh, the horror," Totty said with a shudder.

"See if you can bring him to you."

"How?"

"Count to five," Phillippa answered in a rush, glancing behind her to see Lady Worth and her companion bearing down on them, thirty yards away . . .

Nora obeyed instructions, and, catching Thomas Hurston's gaze, held it for a count to five.

He started walking their way before she got to three.

"Marvelous. He's coming over."

"Good! Now go and meet him halfway."

Twenty yards . . .

Nora's brow puckered for a moment, then cleared. "Oh, I understand! You'll join me, and then Broughton will be able to excuse himself from the group to fetch Thomas—and incidentally greet you."

"Actually Nora, I'm going to speak to Mr. Worth for a moment."

"Mr. Worth?" Nora exclaimed. "Why? Are you still peeved at Mrs. Hurston's turban? Because I assure you, Thomas thinks it horrid, too—"

Ten yards . . . Lady Worth moved at a speed far more keen that Broughton did.

"Nora, please, Mr. Hurston's almost halfway; go to him. You'll seem to be forgiving and . . . just do it!"

Phillippa gave her friend a little shove and turned just in time to drop a curtsy and say, "Good afternoon, Lady Worth. Mr. Worth."

If the pair was astonished by Phillippa's quick and kind greeting (and her hasty removal of her friend) they made no comment on it and bowed and curtsied in return.

"Mrs. Benning," Lady Worth gushed immediately, "I cannot tell you how delightful it is to run into you today. I have just come from the orphanage, and you will not believe what has occurred!"

"Indeed? I hope nothing tragic. Oh, I trust you remember Mrs. Tottendale?"

Lady Worth nodded quickly to Totty, who returned it. Mr. Worth silently reached over and tickled Bitsy's chin in greeting. Bitsy leaned into his hand as Lady Worth continued.

"Yes, of course, Mrs. Tottendale. I'm sorry, I'm in such a state. And it's nothing tragic! Far from it! Mrs. Benning, I don't know what you did or how you did it, but my orphanage has received more donations in just the past week than it has since its inception!"

"I assure you, Lady Worth, I did very little." Phillippa said, gently removing that good woman's hand from her sleeve and just as gently transferring it to Totty's free arm. "Mrs. Tottendale was just telling me about how much she admired your good works, weren't you, Totty?" Totty looked stricken for a moment, but seeing Phillippa's pointed look, forced herself to smile and nod. "Might I entreat you to tell her how you began your philanthropic endeavors?"

"Er, yes," Totty added through her strained grin. "I . . . can't imagine why—I mean *how* you did it."

Lady Worth latched on to Totty with a mighty grip and began to stroll with her and Bitsy down the street. One last glaring look over her shoulder, and Totty found herself well ensconced in a conversation far more wholesome than she was accustomed to, and Phillippa found herself alone with Mr. Worth.

And for the first time in quite a while, she found herself without comment.

"You sell yourself very short, you know," Marcus said, cocking an easy eyebrow.

"Do I? How so?" Phillippa replied, doing her best to not fidget. Really, what was wrong with her?

"Mariah claims you anonymously donated upwards of twenty thousand pounds. That's enough to keep the orphans in coal, shoes, and schoolbooks for the next decade. And yet you claim to do very little."

Phillippa brushed this off with a wave of her hand. "Mr. Worth, I assure you, my anonymous donation was no more than a thousand pounds."

"A thousand?" he questioned. "But what of the other nineteen?"

"I fear my man of business was so moved by my generosity that he may have mentioned my anonymous donation to a friend or two. It must have gotten around." She gave a little shrug. "This sometimes happens."

"Ah. And people discover you've done something and simply . . . follow your lead?"

"More often than not," she replied honestly. "Besides, a thousand pounds is nothing; so I shan't purchase that diamond lavaliere I've had my eye on until next week. I'm certain Jackie, Jeffy, Michael, Rosie, Malcolm, Roger, Frederick, Lisel, oh, dear little Benjamin will make better use of the funds."

Mr. Worth looked at her queerly for a moment but then shook his head. "Mrs. Benning, you plot your mischief like a field commander, but do good so casually, almost accidentally . . ." He let his voice drop off.

She blushed awkwardly, surprising herself. "Mr. Worth, it was nothing. And your sister-in-law's intentions for the money are far more noble than mine would be, I assure you."

"Yes," he replied, looking askance. "Mariah is eager for improving the world. The world simply has to catch up with her." He cleared his throat, obviously gathering his courage. Then he came out with it. "Mrs. Benning, the last time we met was . . . unconventional, to say the least."

Phillippa was horrified to feel her face warm again, and it was turning not a lovely blush but what she was certain was an unbecoming red.

But Marcus, seeing her reaction, smiled self-consciously and looked at his shoes. "Uh, yes," he said, scuffing his toe on the ground, "my actions, one action in particular, was highly out of character for me."

"The action you are referring to being kissing me," Phillippa said frankly. If he thought to make her blush, well, let us see if she could do the same.

But she was to be disappointed, because, instead of blushing an unnatural color as she expected, Marcus Worth's gaze shot up and met hers, a challenging glimmer in his eyes.

"Yes. My kissing you. And your kissing me."

"I did *not*—"

"But never fear, Mrs. Benning, now that I'm aware of your astonishing right hook, I can assure you that such an occurrence will not be repeated."

"We . . . we were not boxing, sir. I have no right hook. I did not hit you!"

"I beg to differ. I recall quite well the imprint of your palm on my cheek." Marcus replied, no longer attempting to suppress his smile.

"Aha!" Phillippa exclaimed, taking a step closer to him. "Impression of my *palm*! I struck you with an open hand, which is the definition of a slap, not a hit."

"But most certainly a strike. Really, I had no idea that young ladies of fashion were so physically abusive. Do you take lessons at Jackson's Saloon as well?"

"Mr. Worth, you are the only man of my acquaintance who has ever inspired me to violence." Phillippa narrowed her eyes, stepping up to him, toe to toe. She stared into his eyes, and he stared right back.

And suddenly they both burst out laughing.

"All right, you win," she said with a smile. "This time."

"Forgive me, Mrs. Benning," Marcus said, once his chuckles had subsided. "I couldn't resist teasing you a bit, as you seemed so ready to goad me."

"Yes, well . . ." Phillippa's voice faded, her gaze lost in his face. He wore his spectacles again, but as unfashionable as they were, they seemed to suit him. Lent him gravity and hid his obviously cheeky sense of humor.

"Mrs. Benning?"

"Hm?" she replied, coming out of her reverie.

"You were staring. Do I have a smudge on my face?"

"What?" She blushed, startled. "You . . . your sideburns are uneven, do you realize?"

He self-consciously brought his hand to his right sideburn, then the left, feeling the difference of where they skimmed his jaw.

"How do you go through life with your sideburns uneven? I cannot countenance it. Your valet should be sacked."

"I haven't a valet."

"No valet?" she burst out in disbelief. "My goodness, how do you manage to tie your neckcloth? Or press your clothes? It boggles the mind!"

"Mrs. Benning," Marcus replied on a grin, "I, amazingly, can tie my own neckcloth. And as for pressing my clothes, you would be surprised at what one learns in the army. But never fear, I will do my best to be groomed appropriately during our association."

Phillippa's eyebrow shot up. "Our association?"

Marcus glanced over his shoulder and then over Phillippa's. She followed his gaze. Lady Worth spoke at a rapid pace, gesticulating to a stricken and frozen Totty, as they strolled up the street, and to her other side, Nora was leaning most coyly on Thomas Hurston's arm. Broughton had not yet left his group, but he kept shooting looks her way.

"I have been reviewing the bargain that you laid before me at our last meeting," Marcus said, pitching his voice low and moving a step closer, keeping his eyes on passersby on crowded Bond Street. "Circumstances have changed and—can you really get me invited to all the events on my list?"

"Those and every other ball, card party, and musicale this Season," Phillippa replied. She saw a black look cross his features, and suddenly a cold line of dread shot down her spine. "Something happened, didn't it? You would not have come within ten feet of me otherwise."

Marcus looked at her, shocked. "Mrs. Benning, yes, something happened. I would not have come within ten feet of your proposal otherwise. You are a different matter entirely."

Her frame, unknowingly tense, relaxed.

He continued. "The first event, the Whitford Banquet, is tomorrow, I believe."

"Plenty of time to wrangle you an invitation," she shrugged but then regarded him speculatively. "You'll agree to be the guest of honor at the Benning Ball?"

"Against every common sense I have, yes. But on a few conditions."

"Conditions? Come, come now, Mr. Worth, surely you can trust my discretion. After all, I could have revealed you as the"—she pitched the next words at a whisper—"*Blue Raven* at any time to anyone since I first suspected you."

"Yes, but without proof—"

"I have a feather from your brother's library."

"A feather is a feather, not absolute proof. No, Mrs. Benning, without proof, you would be rumormongering. And I may know little about you, but I do know that you do not go about starting rumors."

"Heavens no. Other people do that enough in my stead," she replied smartly.

"Mrs. Benning, my conditions are as follows: Keep your council until the Benning Ball."

"That's not a hardship; the success of the Ball depends upon your identity remaining a secret."

Marcus impulsively placed a hand on her elbow. "I am hunting someone. Mrs. Benning, if it is who I think it is, he's a very dangerous individual. If I am not successful in apprehending him before the Ball, you are to cancel the Benning Ball entirely."

"What?" she exclaimed, staring at him openmouthed. Indeed, her cry had attracted no small amount of attention, for Totty and Lady Worth had begun to walk toward them, Totty wearing a look of concern, until Phillippa held her at bay with a small shake of her head.

"I will under no circumstances cancel the Benning Ball! It would be disasterous!" she said in a rushed whisper.

"It would be far more disastrous should I not capture my man before then."

"Why?" she challenged.

"Two reasons: First, if I am revealed as the Blue Raven before he's caught, I will be a marked man. I'd prefer to avoid that."

She chewed on that for a moment.

"And second?"

"Second is quite simple: The Benning Ball is the last event on the list."

For a moment, Phillippa forgot to breathe.

Oh God, she thought. She looked into his face, the utter seriousness there, and felt her stomach drop.

"You're not teasing me anymore, are you?"

His thumb massaged her elbow, soothing her. "I shocked you,

I see. I apologize. But you need to understand—to be aware of the seriousness of the situation. I'm not playing some game; one man has already had his throat slit in this business."

If it was possible, Phillippa went paler. She felt his hand tighten on her arm. Was it possible her knees were buckling under her?

"Mrs. Benning, I'm sorry, I forgot myself, but I simply refuse to allow any harm to come to you if it can be avoided."

Phillippa gained her ground and, with all the strength she could muster, found her balance and removed her arm from his grasp. "Surely . . . surely Lord Fieldstone will assist you now. I know he could not promise to help your quest previously, but given this latest development . . ."

But Marcus just shook his head. "Lord Fieldstone is no longer an option."

A grimness overtook Phillippa. Part of her simply wanted to run away. Run to her family's country seat and hide. What had she gotten herself into? But she couldn't. Phillippa Benning did not run. Phillippa Benning was a force unreckonable. The Benning Ball was going to be The Event of the Season. And she didn't need to look over her shoulder to see Lady Jane Cummings fawning over Broughton.

"Well," she said, squaring her shoulders, "you could be chasing the wind, you realize. What if this, this *man* you hunt is no longer in London? I could end up canceling the Benning Ball for no reason."

"You want reason?" he growled. "Get me invited to the first event on the list, and I'll show you."

Now Phillippa did look over her shoulder and did see Lady Jane fawning over Broughton. But more to the point, she saw Broughton leaning into her solicitously. *Very* solicitously.

"Mr. Worth," Phillippa said brightly, putting forth her most pert smile. "Do you see that, er, rather large woman on the opposite side of the street? Wearing that very, er, patriotic blue and red ensemble? That is Lady Whitford."

"Of the Whitford Banquet?" he asked.

"The one and the same. Now, give me your arm, thank you," she said, and as he did so, "and lean down to me."

When he did, she whispered in his ear, "Trim your sideburns."

And then, leaning back, she let out her loveliest peal of laughter, turning heads from one end of Bond Street to the other. Pulling him gently, they promenaded toward Totty, Bitsy, and Lady Worth, strolling slowly, Phillippa giving a kind nod to Lady Whitford, beckoning that good lady to come and join their group.

"Totty, Mr. Worth was just telling me the most amusing story about a boxing match he had at Jackson's Saloon." Phillippa smiled, addressing the group.

"Marcus!" Lady Worth exclaimed. "Such tales surely would not be for a lady's ears!"

"Oh, I don't know, Mariah, I have the feeling Jackson could learn a thing or two from Mrs. Benning," he replied, just before Phillippa's elbow landed smartly against his rib cage.

As Marcus launched admirably into spinning a story about a sparring match he saw with the great Jackson himself, and Lady Whitford nimbly made her way across Bond Street, Phillippa chanced a coy look over her shoulder. There she saw Lady Jane trying desperately to get Broughton's attention, and failing. For Broughton's attention was fixed on Phillippa, the challenge glinting in his eye.

As well it should be, she thought, leaning a little closer into Marcus Worth.

Farther down Bond Street, seemingly letting his eyes graze over a display of watch chains, the man watched as Mrs. Phillippa Benning took Marcus Worth by the arm and guided him toward her friends, laughing throatily.

He nodded to an acquaintance, who tipped his cap as he strolled past. It was so easy to walk along and follow Worth as he and his sister-in-law did that day's shopping. He had followed them down Brook Street, across Oxford, and now Bond, all without any incident. Indeed, he was beginning to think his associate's fears about Worth were exaggerated, as he again followed Lady Worth into some milliner's or haberdashery, a look of utter boredom on that young man's face. The only time the Worths paused for any length of time to speak with anyone was when Lady Worth had spotted Mrs. Benning and bore down on her like a hound on a fox. Mrs. Benning spent some minutes in private conversation with Worth. Phillippa Benning, the unequivocal leader of the Ton, speaking at length to Marcus Worth. The man shrugged. Maybe they had developed a tendre for each other, but how or when he could not imagine.

As the lady let out a trill of laughter, he decided the entire errand was fruitless and turned away.

Marcus Worth was paranoid, yes. But whatever he suspected, it seemed he was more concerned with earning the favor of ladies than pursuing his hunch.

It was almost disappointing to find Marcus Worth was harmless.

Thirteen

Mayfair during the height of the Season was, on an average day, awash in the well-dressed and the well-to-do, moving back and forth between houses and parks as if they were migrating birds, flitting from one end of St. James's Square to the other. But in the evening, everyone in Mayfair had an absolute destination, whether it be Almack's or a card party or a masked ball. Where there was movement, there was purpose.

And tonight, everyone who was anyone was headed toward the Whitford Mansion.

An enviably large house in the center of London's fashionable district, the mansion was a freestanding structure in the elegant Palladian style, sitting snugly on a few acres of well-manicured gardens.

One would assume that such a large house, with such extensive private parks, would very easily accommodate several dozen of the Whitfords' closest friends for an evening of drinking, dancing, and best of all, eating. And one would be correct.

However, when the number topped several hundred, the fit became a bit tighter.

It was an elite several hundred, mind, but one could easily become lost in the sea of faces, coats, gowns, and jewels.

Unless of course, one were Phillippa Benning.

There was something remarkably comforting about being half a head taller than the rest of the female population, Phillippa decided. Not only could she see over the majority of heads in the crowd, but she could be seen by everyone else.

And everyone else would then be able to get out of her way.

"Goodness, what a crush! I thought this event was meant to be exclusive," Totty said, having barely managed to follow Phillippa through a packed hallway into the ballroom.

The Whitford Banquet was laid out in such a way that you had to pass through all the other rooms of dancing, cards, and of course, the great hall, which housed Lord Whitford's impressive collection of firearms (some of which were of his own design) before entering the banquet hall. Servants wended their way through the crowd with silver trays of small bites and champagne, but the main spectacle of the evening, the banquet itself, was not served until midnight, when the Whitfords' revered French chef, Marcel, revealed his famous Dove Pie.

It was a take on the nursery rhyme, "Four and twenty blackbirds baked in a pie," but Marcel, in typical French fashion, had determined that white doves were far more asthetically pleasing flying out of the wafer-thin piecrust, than "ugly black birds." Lord Whitford was, of course, more than willing to go along with just about anything Marcel decreed, as long as he produced the sumptuous feast year after year that made the Whitford Banquet one of the most celebrated events of the season. Once the doves were released, the banquet began: the resplendent courses of quail and pheasant, duck and truffle sauce, roasted candied ham, goose stuffed with currants, and curried lamb, all dressed with every fruit and vegetable imaginable, whether from out of this season or out of this hemisphere.

Marcel the chef was known to celebrate the exotic, and so the very brave were impressed upon to try the alligator stew or the shark fin flambé. The tarts, pies, cakes, bonbons, ices, marzipan, and meringues that made up the after courses were enough to pop even the staunchest woman's corset strings. If one were intelligent, one would not eat the entire day before in preparation, and if one were successful, one would not need to eat for the entire day after.

Of course, one had to actually manage to *get* to the banquet hall to partake of any of this.

"I assure you, the Whitford Banquet *is* exclusive." Phillippa replied, gently smoothing her perfectly coiled and curled hair. "Look about you; there's no one here we don't know."

"That you don't know maybe," Totty grumbled. "I swear, I don't know how you keep them all straight. You remember to an eyelash every person you've ever met."

"While I regard it as far more remarkable that others find it such a difficulty," Phillippa remarked. They were currently in the ballroom, where dancing took up too much of the space. She scanned the turning sets of couples in rows on the floor, banked by the matrons, older married gentlemen, wallflowers, and less-than-courtly young bucks that made up the sidelines of any party. Indeed, she recognized every face, could pinpoint where they had met, who their parents were, and how much they had in holdings at the Bank of England. Which alternately comforted her and terrified her.

If Mr. Worth was correct, and some threatening force would perpetrate mischief tonight, it would be done with the assistance of someone here. And since there was no one she did not recognize . . .

Unless, of course, it was a servant of some kind. That thought cheered Phillippa, until she remembered that Lady Whitford was notorious for her high wages, as a reward for staff loyalty. Not to mention the kitchen's requirement of secrecy to guard Marcel's culinary godliness from the average human. Indeed, even at a crush like this, the extra staff hired would have been well-known to them, likely the same people they used last year. And the year before.

Mr. Worth should be made aware of this, Phillippa thought, her mind moving as quick as lightning. He should know as much as possible about the circumstances he would walk into tonight.

"Where is he?" she muttered, alternately scanning the crowd and flicking her eyes toward the narrow hallway through which they had entered. They moved forward into the main ballroom, finally having enough elbow room to settle into an advantageous spot.

"Where is who?" an insipid voice came from behind them, causing Phillippa to cover a groan before she turned.

"Don't tell me you lost dear Broughton already," Lady Jane Cummings sneered at Phillippa. "Amazing. I've already danced with him. I do hope he hasn't left yet. Pity you didn't arrive earlier."

"Lady Jane"—Phillippa gave the slightest possible curtsy—"you and I both know that no one leaves the Whitford Banquet without sampling some of the delicacies, which are served later. Indeed, I strive to not arrive too early, since it would be taken as being far too overeager for the treats that await. Dare I say unfashionable, too?"

Lady Jane's eyes narrowed as her cheeks took on a mottled reddish hue.

"Speaking of," Phillippa continued, "I must take it upon myself to counsel you to not wear this particular shade of green again. Ginger curls are hard to downplay, and this gown simply makes it look as if someone lit your head on fire."

Whereas average young ladies would cower and cry from such words from Mrs. Phillippa Benning, Lady Jane Cummings was not so easily daunted. "Indeed? I do thank you for your counsel. You must know that I am a champion of taking unsolicited advice to heart. Not many are, understand." Her eyes narrowed. "For instance, I could tell you that the amount of beadwork on your bodice is an obvious and poorly done attempt to emphasize an area of your person that is severely lacking, but unless you asked me my opinion on it, I'm certain you should pay no attention."

Phillippa quirked up a brow. "You are correct, Lady Jane. I pay you no heed whatsoever."

"To your detriment, I'm sure," she snapped back.

"Very possibly. I don't know how I'll survive."

"Phillippa, look, I see Nora; let us join her," Totty broke in, before the claws really came out and ruined their gloves.

"Oh, do excuse me, Mrs. Tottendale. I see my next dance partner coming to collect me. And I see a waiter with a tray of champagne coming toward you, so I'll get out of your way."

With that, Lady Jane gave the most perfunctory curtsy possible, slighter than Phillippa's, and headed to the floor for the quadrille with an exceedingly handsome young colonel.

"Well!" Phillippa exclaimed, once Lady Jane was safely on the floor and out of earshot.

"That certainly was a delightful skirmish," Totty said, downing her glass of champagne in one go before reaching for another.

"She has always been mean to me, ever since school. That I'm accustomed to. But she's never been so low as to insult you before!"

"Insult me? How?" Totty asked blankly, causing Phillippa to simply shake her head.

"Nothing, dearest." Phillippa's eye was caught by an extremely tall man (Was it Mr. Worth? But no, it was just Lord Forrester standing on a chair, looking for his wife.) as she mused on her nemesis's recent change of strategy. "So, Lady Jane steps up her game, becomes more vicious. I wonder why."

"Perhaps she knows she is losing Broughton to you," Nora's voice came from behind them.

"Hello Nora, Lady De Regis!" Phillippa kissed Nora on the cheek gave a happy nod to her mother, who nodded regally back before seeing a friend beckon her from the other side of the room.

Since Nora was safely deposited with Phillippa and Totty, Lady De Regis excused herself from the group to join the other.

"Nora, what a lovely gown. Is the pattern the same as the gown I wore to the Winters'?"

"Yes, I sketched it out for Madame Boudreaux, and she managed to adjust it for someone my height. Do you like it?"

"Very much; the color couldn't suit you better."

Indeed, Nora did look lovely in the lightest of lilacs, which set off her pale olive skin and made her seem to glow. Phillippa was used to having her dress patterns copied, and even though she would prefer if Nora would try to be somewhat more original, she couldn't deny that the cut of the gown worked on her small frame very well.

"But what did you mean, Lady Jane is losing Broughton? She's the one who managed to wrangle the first dance with him. The little cow must have been waiting for him at the door."

"Yes, but why else would she be so cruel? If she were winning, she wouldn't need to be. She must know that Broughton prefers you."

Phillippa looked at Nora suspiciously. "An interesting theory. But if that's the case, where is he? I've been here five whole minutes, and he has yet to seek me out."

Nora smiled slyly and pointed discreetly toward the far side of the room, where Broughton was weaving his way through the masses, two glasses of champagne in hand.

"He came up to me before you got here, obviously wondering as to your whereabouts. Why are you so late, anyway?"

"I simply couldn't choose a gown, the ones that arrived this week are all so fine." It was the truth as far as it went, but the reasoning was so much deeper. How did one dress to encounter a world-famous spy? Especially when action on his (or her) part would possibly be called for. Do you wear your most stunning, fitted satin creation imaginable? Or do you aim for wider cambric skirts and practicality? In the end, Phillippa had decided on her latest Madame Le Trois, a jewel-toned satin, with a fuller skirt, facilitating movement, and a bodice elaborately adorned with gold beads and sapphires. Best of all, Madame Le Trois had given the gown discreet pockets at Phillippa's request. It was the best compromise she could imagine.

Phillippa caught a glimpse of Totty rolling her eyes, as Nora continued. "I spotted you first, but that odious Lady Jane was with you, so I sent Broughton off to gather some champagne. And now, here he comes."

Phillippa had to smile at her friend's quick thinking. "Well done, Nora."

"I thought so," she said, self-satisfied. But then a sneer contorted her lips. "Ugh, I do hope he doesn't get waylaid by Penny Sterling. She had the gall to ask me where she could get ices near Westminster Abbey. Can you imagine? As if I would go to Westminster, ever."

Phillippa indeed saw Penny Sterling, who, with her friend Louisa Dunningham, had been witness to her fateful encounter with Lady Jane in the Winters' retiring room. Penny wore a dress cut just barely wrong for her, and Louisa should not eat so many sweet things, Phillippa thought objectively. The girls nodded sweetly to Broughton as he passed. He, of course, did not notice, such was his intention. But Penny just giggled into her hand and said something to her friend. Penny Sterling was young and silly, yes, but there was no harm in her. Taken under someone's wing, she'd do quite nicely.

Phillippa was about to say as much to Nora, when Broughton, glasses of champagne in hand, appeared directly before her.

"Miss De Regis, you are a naughty little thing," he drawled. "I am sent at your direction to the punch table and come back to find you gone. I was left all alone." He languidly handed a glass of champagne to her, and she giggled coyly in response.

"Indeed, my lord, but as you see, I found something you were looking for," Nora replied, indicating Phillippa to her right.

"Mrs. Benning," Broughton said, bowing with offhand grace and offering her his second glass of champagne. "I quite despaired for you. I hoped against hope you would save the quadrille for me, but alas, it has passed."

Phillippa took a bare second to allow her gaze to rake over the Marquis of Broughton. Was there a finer specimen of masculinity in existence? His clothing was impeccably tailored, his blond hair rakishly styled, the cold glint of his blue eyes projected a calculated boredom, and his every movement was casual. No man in the Whitford Mansion, nay, no man in London, was so perfect an example of what it was to be Ton.

And he was Phillippa's for the asking.

If only her mind wasn't so keenly occupied by someone else.

Surely she could at least try to forget Mr. Marcus Worth and his prophecies of danger just for a moment and enjoy Broughton instead.

She took a small sip of the champagne, and with a slight quirk of her brow, replied, "A pity the quadrille has passed, but the waltz has not, I understand."

His quirked brow matched hers. "Indeed, it has not."

"Is that the chord of the waltz being struck now?" Nora interjected. "Dear me, I must go find Lord Sterling; he has this dance. I believe I saw him upstairs earlier." And with that and a secret smile, Nora handed her half-drunk glass of champagne to Totty and bowed her way to go search for her dance partner.

"Well, Mrs. Benning, will you do me the honor?" Broughton asked, a cold glint of challenge in his eye.

"Happily," Phillippa replied, handing her glass of champagne to poor Totty, who now had to contend with three half-filled glasses. She did this admirably by emptying one into another, and emptying the third into her mouth.

And with that, Phillippa allowed the Marquis of Broughton to lead her to the floor.

The music surrounded them as they stepped into the circling, swirling couples. People made room for them. People who were before invested solely in each other now watched Phillippa and Broughton as they danced. People gave them the light and the lead.

And they were cool, calm, and perfect.

His hand at the small of her back exerted the gentlest of pressure, pulling her to his rhythm and command.

"Now, the last time I had you in my arms like this, the experience was rather . . . invigorating."

He flexed his hand over the cloth at her back, obviously recalling the dress where such cloth was missing.

"Indeed?" she replied. "Such a statement implies that you are not finding this dance particularly invigorating. I do hope that's not the case." She tried, she truly did, but she could not stop herself from scanning the crowd for Mr. Worth. It was getting late. Surely he was coming?

"I would never presume to consider dancing with you anything other than stimulating," Broughton replied easily, coolly. "But I would imagine we could find ways to make the evening . . . noteworthy."

Noteworthy? Phillippa nearly harrumphed in reply. To her mind, the evening already had the hallmarks of noteworthy. If only Mr. Worth would arrive and . . . and allay her fears. Let her know she wasn't being silly to believe him. Suppose he had been stopped at the door. The invitation Lady Whitford issued was verbal; it was possible she neglected to inform her major domo of the addition to the party—

"There has to be a corner of this house that's unoccupied. That's waiting for us." Broughton continued, his blue eyes forcing hers to steady on him, to fall into their depths.

She didn't find the depths very deep.

"My lord," Phillippa began, a pretty blush spreading delicately over her cheeks.

"Please, call me Phillip," Broughton replied.

His name was Phillip? She paused a moment to digest that before continuing smoothly. "Phillip. Surely we'd be missed. Everyone here is watching us—"

"No one missed us at the Fieldstone affair. Besides, a packed house like this? No one will notice if you and I are missing for fifteen minutes. They'll simply assume we're in one of the other rooms." He leaned down to her ear, allowed his warm breath to dance over the curls at her temple, the line of her jaw. "Which we will be."

Phillippa wasn't about to leave the room, not when she still didn't see Marcus Worth, not when she was certain Broughton's intentions did not include a hand of whist or a game of chess. He must have seen her skepticism, because the wolfish smile he wore at the edges of his mouth suddenly faded into his usual cold facade. "Losing heart in our little game already? Tsk tsk. I had more faith in you."

Phillippa cocked a brow. "Fifteen minutes?"

"Fifteen minutes is all we'd require," Broughton replied, that cool smile coming back to his eyes as the music ended.

"All you'd require maybe. I would want *hours*," she breathed, her gaze never leaving his, and she had the pleasure of watching those eyes go dark with want, smolder with anticipation.

"Mrs. Benning—" he began, as he led her slowly off the floor.

"Phillippa, please," she smiled back at him.

"Phillippa, next weekend is the Hampshires' Racing Party. You are planning to attend?"

"Of course," she replied, her ear to him and her eyes to the crowd. "I enjoy a good house party. So pleasant to get out of the city."

"Indeed." Broughton took a step closer, pitched his voice low. "It occurs to me that at a weekend house party, we would have *hours*. To ourselves. To do as we pleased."

"Hmm," was the noncommittal reply. Phillippa smiled like a cat that swallowed the cream. "That's certainly a possibility. In the meantime, why don't you call on me for tea tomorrow?"

"Call?" Broughton's brow creased. "For tea?"

"Come now, Phillip, have you never called on a lady for tea before? Never fear, we don't bite." She leaned up to his ear and whispered, "Should I wager for you or against you?"

And with that, she dropped an elegant curtsy and turned away from Broughton, leaving him gobsmacked, staring after her with his jaw on the floor. Phillippa sent him a smirking glance over her shoulder as she walked away, before she allowed herself to take a deep, steadying breath.

She had done it. She had enticed Broughton further, kept his interest. But she was playing so deep now that he might actually expect her to make good on her chits.

A nervous thought.

But she let go of it with a slight shake of her head and crossed from the ballroom into the card room. She would ponder that little difficulty later. Right now, she wanted to find the ladies' retiring room and put a little water on her face before she began to scour every nook and corner of the Whitford Mansion for that impossible, unbelievably tardy—

"Please tell me that scowl you wear is for someone besides me. Otherwise, it's a very daunting greeting."

Mr. Marcus Worth.

❧

Marcus could see she was shocked, as he suppressed the urge to touch the ends of his sideburns. He could only hope that shock did not portend displeasure from Phillippa Benning.

But she recovered from her surprise and assumed the air of sophisticated breeding that marked her as the Queen of the Ton. "You are late," she scolded.

"No, you were late. I was exploring the upstairs," he countered. Indeed, he had been carefully, quietly getting the lay of the house and its occupants when he saw her enter from the balcony above the ballroom, and she was immediately swamped by people. First Lady Jane Cummings, followed by her friend Miss De Regis, then Broughton, who looked at Phillippa like an African game hunter stalking a lioness. They were on the dance floor by the time he had made his way downstairs, and he couldn't help but watch, just for a moment, and damned if the lioness didn't turn the tables on the game hunter, for by the time they left the floor, Broughton was completely in Phillippa's power.

He had to admire her skills, even if he didn't particularly like who she chose to use them on.

"Mr. Worth," Phillippa interrupted his thoughts, "I simply cannot stand it another moment. What on earth did you do to your hair?"

He knew she was shocked. Now he did let his hands go and self-consciously ran them over his temples.

"I take it you do not approve then?" he asked, unaccountably curious as to her answer.

She continued to stare, and then let out a short sigh. She looked over his shoulders, then hers, obviously keen for some privacy.

"Come on," Marcus said, anticipating her thoughts, "there's a bit of space this way."

She followed as he led them out of the ballroom, through the card room, down the hall, and up the stairs. There he turned a corner and counted off doors, three to the left, and escorted Phillippa into the upstairs linen closet, a long space lined with shelves and drawers, smelling strongly of starch. With the door closed it was pitch black and confining. He groped around the walls by the door until he found the tapered wall sconce.

"I made the rather questionable decision to tell Mariah about your comment regarding my sideburns," he began as he struck a match and lit the sconce, lending the room enough warm, yellow light to finally see (and work, if one were so employed) properly. Closing the glass door, he continued. "Mariah then commanded that my brother Graham lend me his valet tonight, so that I might be polished up enough to look worthy of your company."

"Sensible of her," Phillippa said as she stepped toward him, "but your hair."

What once had been a rather shaggy, nondescript head of hair, worn parted to the same side that it had fallen as a child, had been transformed by Graham's valet into a bold, strikingly short

Grecian style. Brushed forward, it swept across his brow rakishly, grazed his temples.

Mariah told him it brought out his eyes, his strong, square jaw. He wasn't certain of any of that, but Phillippa's continued gaze told him the change was certainly dramatic.

"I'm told this is the latest style. And I promise you," he said with some chagrin, "my sideburns are perfectly even now."

"It is the latest style, sort of," Phillippa replied. "At least you had the good sense to leave off your spectacles tonight. Let me see . . ." She quickly unbuttoned and removed a glove, placed it to the side. Then she went up on her toes and reached out her hand. Marcus, wary of her intention, jerked his head back, slightly out of her reach.

"Oh, for heaven's sake," she said exasperatedly, "it's just me."

Then, before he could protest, she threaded her freed hand through the hair on the top of his head. Then she shook her hand as she pulled it through, mussing his hair to perfection.

Gently she brushed the short locks back into place, her fingers dancing over his temples, the nape of his neck, her thumb falling on the line of his sideburn. Her hand stilled for the barest of seconds, her gaze moving from his hair to him. He thought he could see something, some spark of something new in those eyes as blue as the sea under cloudless skies. But then her eyes hurried back to his hair, and she pulled her hand back.

Phillippa's eyes sparkled as she pasted on a bright smile. "I shall declare it all the kick."

Marcus chanced a look down and saw Phillippa's gloved hand resting lightly on his chest. He hadn't even known it was there, but he felt it all the same. She hadn't known it was there either, judging by how she reacted once she'd followed his gaze, pulling her hand back as if it were on fire.

"Sorry," she mumbled, her face gone hot. She picked up her glove from the shelf of linens and concentrated on getting it back on and buttoned.

"Does that mean you like it? Er, my hair?" he asked.

"Mr. Worth, once I'm finished, you'll have a hundred young bucks copying your hairstyle."

"Mrs. Benning, that still doesn't answer my question." He smiled as she looked up, bewildered, from buttoning her glove. "Do you like it?"

"It's very stylish. And it does suit your face," she replied with a shrug. "Truth be told, you look marvelous. Its just not how I'm used to you."

"Nor I," he admitted. "We'll grow accustomed to it, I imagine."

"Well," Phillippa said, squaring her shoulders, signaling a change of subject. "We have a great deal to do. The Banquet's official start is within the hour. Everyone will gather in the banquet hall for that, so if something were to happen, it would likely be then. I wanted to tell you," she continued, her face flushed with the rushed importance of her speech, "Lady Whitford is notorious for her loyal staff, so its likely the perpetrator has not entered the house belowstairs. Of course, I have yet to see anyone I don't recognize among the guests, but that doesn't mean—"

"Mrs. Benning," Marcus interrupted, once he managed to catch up with her conversation. "Thank you. I discovered the fortresslike zeal her household lives under when I tried to infiltrate as an extra member of the serving staff two days ago. Her mad French chef spotted me at twenty paces. Accused me of trying to steal his recipes."

Phillippa gave a high, adorable laugh. "Yes, no wonder you felt agreeing to our bargain the only recourse. That was Marcel. He is the reason this whole banquet is possible. And temperamental zealot that he is, you will taste his genius this evening. He bakes four and twenty white doves in a pie, and they all come flying out in the most spectacular fashion."

"However," Marcus continued, unwilling to let himself be derailed from the subject at hand. "*We* do not have a great deal to do. I want you to stay as far from me and this business as possible."

For a moment Phillippa looked . . . dare he say hurt? But she shook that off as easily as water off a duck's back.

"Don't be silly," she said with a wave of her hand. "You have to at least dance once with me. And hopefully at least once with a few other young ladies."

"Mrs. Benning, I have no time for dancing, I have to—"

"You have to what? That's the problem; you don't really know. And how do you hunt what you can't identify? You simply stay alert and armed—"

At that he quirked a brow.

"You did bring a pistol or some such thing, correct?" she asked, catching his questioning look.

"Do gentlemen usually arm themselves for a banquet?"

"No, but . . . but you're not a gentleman!" she protested.

"Regardless of previous assumptions, I am. I assure you," Marcus smirked at her.

"That's not what I meant, and you know it." She stuck her hands on her hips, looking for all the world like an adorably peeved child. Then she sighed, squaring her shoulders. "Well, then you are lucky that I at least have some foresight," and she produced a lady's one-shot pistol from somewhere within the folds of her skirts.

"Are you mad?" Marcus exclaimed, grabbing the pistol from her. He checked the barrel; it was loaded. He took a deep breath, ignored the impulse to dig his fingers into his temples. "Mrs. Benning, what is it that you think to do with this?"

"I . . . I don't know. I thought it might be useful—for you—in case you spot trouble," she stammered. "You can give chase and capture the villain; it will be exciting and properly heroic. Isn't that what spies do?"

Marcus swallowed a laugh. "Actually, in my experience, spying is mostly about watching. Not proper heroics and excitement. And it's certainly not a good idea to pull a pistol out of my coat in a ballroom full of civilians." He smiled ruefully. "Not only is it a dead giveaway, an innocent could get hurt."

Phillippa sighed, conceding his point, thankfully. She held out her hand to take back the pistol. "Fine. I won't use it."

But Marcus simply shook his head in the darkness and placed the pistol in the waistband of his knee breeches, under his coat.

"You'll ruin the line of your coat," she sniffed, which made him grin in spite of himself.

"That's a chance I'll have to take," he replied, the cold metal of the pistol palpable through his shirt. "Now, for your information, I did think to arm myself this evening. There is a dagger in my coat. But I hope not to use it, because you're correct. I do not know what will happen tonight, and I'm not willing to take any chances. This is my mission, Mrs. Benning."

"You're not going to use the pistol?" she asked.

He shook his head. "I'm not fond of firearms."

"But why?" she asked.

"Mrs. Benning, have you ever shot anyone?"

"No . . . but—"

"I have, and its not something I'm proud of. I would spare you the experience."

There was nothing more to be said on the subject. While Marcus watched, Phillippa blew her hair out of her eyes in frustration, defeat, and acceptance.

"Well, while your mission is to track your ghost, whoever killed your friend and you feel is a threat"—she thrust out her chin, moving her mind to the next thing to be done, back in control—"my mission is to get you invited to the next event on the list, so you can continue to do so."

Well, she had him there. And by that triumphant little smirk, she knew it.

"Which is why we are now going to exit this linen closet, cozy though it may be, and you are going to escort me to the dance floor. If there's time, I'll find another young lady to dance with you, while I talk you up to Lady Whitford, who would probably like my head on a platter for having her squeeze you in. I have no notion how she managed to juggle the seating arrangements to accommodate you, but I'm big enough to admit when someone's skills exceed my own.

"Then," she continued without pausing for breath, ticking off each requirement on her fingers, "we go into the banquet and commence the feast. You will converse with the people to your right and left, and hopefully, I'll be able to corner Lord or Lady Hampshire or their daughter Sybil—she's a lovely little creature, married to Lord Plessy, you know—and get you invited to the Hampshires' Racing Party. It's a weekend party, so their guest list is far more limited. Of course, if they cannot accommodate you yet, I'll have to find someone else to cancel and allow you room. But we'll worry about that if it comes to pass. And for heaven's sake, call me Phillippa; its more comfortable for me and will make you seem amongst my circle of intimates."

He simply blinked at her for a long moment. Then, struck by impulse, he saluted her smartly. "Aye aye, sir." He fell at ease, with a sardonic smile, folding his arms over his chest. "And when do I do what I have to do?"

"Whenever," she replied with a dismissive wave of her hand. "Now, shall we?"

"Wait a moment," he said, catching up to her before she turned the knob of the door. Turning her to him, he lifted an eyebrow and then scrutinized her hairstyle.

"Is . . . is my hair somehow amiss?" she asked, worriedly. She lifted her hands to it, but he gently pushed them down. Then, with painful delicacy, he brushed his fingers over the curls at her temple, pulling one down, and sproinging it, so it bounced back up.

"Well," he sighed. "It'll have to do."

He enjoyed seeing the little moment of confusion. He knew that he shouldn't have done it. He knew, too, especially considering the circumstances, he should try to keep his distance from her. But it was a heady thing, being able to tease Phillippa Benning. Being able to unsettle her. It was small payback, he realized now, for the ways she unsettled him.

He whistled a nonchalant tune as he reached behind her and

opened the door. Gently edging her to the side, Marcus stuck his head out and, seeing that the coast was clear, stepped out into the hall.

"Why, you annoying man!" came the cry behind him, as Phillippa followed immediately after. "My hair is perfect! How—"

But the quip died on her lips, for in front of Marcus, just turning the corner into view, was Mrs. Tottendale—Phillippa calls her Totty, he reminded himself—a glass of champagne in hand and a shocked expression on her face.

All three stopped dead, and the only sound was Phillippa skirting out of the way of the linen closet door as it closed.

Totty recovered herself first, and with a shake of her head, she examined her half-filled champagne glass.

"I must have drunk more than I thought."

Fourteen

REALLY, when looked at objectively, the only thing Marcus could do at this juncture was keep out a watchful eye. He had already scouted the mansion to the best of his ability. None of the guests stuck out in his mind as anything other than what they seemed (although his adversary was masterful at disguises and had slipped through British fingers more than once because of it), and every attempt he made to enter the servants' domain of the household had been met by a blockade of staff and flying cutlery, protecting the top secret secrets of the culinary god housed within. He supposed his adversary would have just as much trouble hiding there as he would. That left the bare option of simply keeping wary and looking for danger. And hoping it showed up.

So, really, what else could Marcus Worth do, other than lead the bewitching, bewildering Phillippa Benning to the ballroom?

Upon seeing Totty in the hall, Phillippa latched onto her with great verve and made that good lady accompany them down the length of the floor to a second set of stairs. A knowing look from Phillippa to Marcus told him what she was doing. If anyone should happen upon them, at least now Mrs. Tottendale would be with them, and things would not look improper. But they could not go down the main staircase, as Mrs. Tottendale had just come up it, and if anyone were watching, they would know that Totty had just joined Phillippa and Marcus, not that she had been with them any length of time.

Social subterfuge was an exausting business.

Marcus led the two ladies down the stairs and into what he knew was the Lord Whitford's gallery. Not of paintings—no, it would be too simple for anyone to have a room used to its intended purpose—but filled with rifles, pistols, lances, spears, bayonets, and swords. Lord Whitford was an enthusiastic devotee of all things weaponry. So much so, that he had made a small fortune outfitting soldiers during the war with weapons of his own design. But Lord Whitford was not an arms dealer—oh no—he'd tell anyone who would listen he considered himself an artist and a collector. Given Marcus's dislike of firearms, he nearly groaned when he saw the man himself giving just such a lecture to a small group of patient listeners at the other end of the long hall.

"And this is the oldest matchlock rifle in my collection. As you see, it has a spring loading feature, here. It comes from China, fifteenth century, at least. Ah, Mrs. Benning, Mrs. Tottendale, Mr. Worth! Have you been enjoying the festivities?"

Lord Whitford was a jovial fellow, a little shorter than average, so perhaps he thought having a gun at the ready made up for any height deficiency. He looked up at Marcus as one would size up an opponent but then let his mustached face split into a grin, since obviously, Marcus Worth had never posed a threat to anybody.

Whitford made his way over to Phillippa and Marcus, and the little group that had been held captive by his conversation took the opportunity to float away in pairs to different objets d'art in the long gallery.

"We're enjoying the banquet very much," Phillippa replied with that innate smoothness that never faltered for her. "I simply cannot wait to taste Marcel's accomplishments this year!"

"Er, yes," Marcus added, when he felt Phillippa tug ever so discreetly on his arm. "We've been admiring your collection while we . . . build up an appetite."

Whitford's round and shiny face burst into a grin of unfathomable delight. "It is the most marvelous private collection of weaponry in England, the curator of the British Museum told me so, when he came by to beg to display it. I couldn't have that, of course, not while I'm alive at least; I enjoy it too much. And everything has a history attached to it, and I'm the only one who knows them all. What would I do if it were all at the British Museum? Go over and give tours there?"

Whitford guffawed on this last, forcing Phillippa and Marcus into placid smiles and placating noises.

"These look too new to have a history," Totty said from her position across the gallery. She was peering through her monocle down at a glass box on a polished table. Whitford, Phillippa, and Marcus made their way over to her. "What story do they tell?" she asked as Lord Whitford, whose eyes lit up as he regarded what she was looking at: a pair of silver pistols, beautifully scrolled, lain on a bed of richly colored velvet.

"Ah," Lord Whitford said, gently easing open the lid of the glass box. "These I purchased just last year from a broker who swears on his own grave the story I'm about to tell you. These pistols—beautiful work, I could only wish I designed them myself—were the property of none other than the Blue Raven."

A sudden hush descended on the great hall. Those couples that were strolling idly started to drift toward Lord Whitford. Phillippa had gone entirely still, her hand resting on Marcus's arm with no weight whatsoever, while Marcus did all that he could to keep his breath steady and his face schooled into only mild interest.

Totty, however, due to an unknown number of glasses of champagne consumed, was unaware of the currents around her.

"The Blue Raven? The spy? I always figured the *Times* made him up, to make the war a better read."

"I thought that, too," Mrs. Frederick whispered to her daughter, who replied with a gasp.

"Mother, of course he exists! Oh, he's so *heroic*, so handsome—"

"So you know he's handsome, do you?" Mr. Cuthbert spoke up from their left. "You've seen the Blue Raven with your own eyes?"

"Well, no . . ." Miss Frederick was forced to admit, as everyone else in the now good-sized group began to murmur their opinions about the Blue Raven's existence, level of beauty, and acts of derring-do.

"I heard he works as Wellington's secret bodyguard—"

"He's gorgeous, has blond hair and eyes that could pierce the soul!"

"But he died, didn't he?"

"I was told by an army colonel that the Blue Raven is stationed on St. Helena, just to make certain Boney doesn't escape again . . ."

All the while, Marcus could only quirk his eyebrow and chance a surreptitious look down at Phillippa, who had apparently discovered a small embellishment on her gown that was suddenly very interesting, while she fought to keep her shoulders from jumping with laughter.

"Well, Mother," Miss Frederick asked smartly, "if he doesn't exist, then where did the pistols come from?"

All eyes turned back to Lord Whitford, who cleared his throat expectantly, obviously relishing the chance to finally tell his story.

"Legend has it," he began, for it seemed the Blue Raven had transcended the stuff of rumor, "that these pistols originally belonged to a French aristocrat who, instead of fleeing when the guillotine became populated by his brethren, was certain that no harm would befall him. And when harm did befall him, he hid his young children with a baker in the city, with only these pistols to protect themselves, and if it became necessary, to sell for food. Well, the oldest son refused to sell the pistols, and when Napoleon came into power, he put the pistols to use serving the French cause. He had been in hiding most of his life, and used the skills he acquired then to his chosen profession, that of subterfuge. His name was—"

"Laurent!" Miss Frederick piped up, unable to hold her tongue in the excitement of the story.

"Yes," Whitford agreed, a sharp warning eye on Miss Frederick to keep her interruptions limited. "The Comte de Laurent, who, as the papers have told us, was raised by the baker and therefore in league with the peasants' cause, but knew he was an aristocrat and felt himself far above anyone else. He was a trickster, a sneak, bloodthirsty and mean."

Some ladies shuddered at this, but everyone was riveted. Whitford continued.

"One day, and no one really knows how, the Blue Raven, who had heard of Laurent's reputation, happened upon him down a dark alley. He saw Laurent murder a man who was discovered to be a fellow English spy and chased that treacherous Frenchman back through the maze of narrow streets in Paris. He lost Laurent, but in the chase, Laurent had lost one of these pistols. The Blue Raven took it and swore to end Laurent with it.

"But from that moment on, Laurent also swore to destroy the man who had stolen his father's pistol. And so, Laurent became the archenemy of the Blue Raven and vice versa. They tracked and plotted against each other, until one fateful day, they faced each other—and the fact that both these pistols are on English soil can be taken as proof of who won."

Lord Whitford finished his story to a round of enthusiastic applause. The crowd, which had been a good number of people originally, had grown to be rather substantial. Suddenly, a bell chimed throughout the house, marking the half hour.

"Goodness, half past eleven already? Ladies and gentlemen, I must make my way to the banquet hall to prepare for the feast. You have pleased me greatly with your attentiveness. But now, please my wife and my chef by working up your appetites on the ballroom floor."

A smattering of chuckles followed that remark, as the group disbanded and headed for the ballroom. Marcus and Phillippa, however, held for a moment, utterly still. Marcus's attention was locked on those pistols. Perfect scrolling carved into the handles and barrels, polished to an unearthly shine. He couldn't tear his eyes away, until Phillippa gave his arm a delicate tug.

He looked up and around. The great gallery was empty. Even Totty had wandered away, conversing with Mrs. Frederick as they slipped through the doors that led to the gathered throng of beautiful people having fun.

Then he looked down into Phillippa Benning's blue eyes. Strange. Sonnets had been composed about her blue eyes, but from here, he could see bits of green. He wondered briefly if any of those poets had ever stood this close. Amazingly, in those blue green eyes, Marcus could also see calm. For all her tempestuous activity, there was calm in those eyes.

"Come along," she said. "You have to dance with me, remember?"

It wasn't the waltz, more's the pity, as Phillippa was just bursting with information and questions for Marcus, and the waltz would allow them some level of conversational privacy in which she could relay them. No, it was a maggot, a dance to an almost fuguelike tune that, to Phillippa, had always sounded melancholy and yearning at the same time. In this particular version, by a Mr. Beveridge, the violins rose and fell as the dancers came together, broke apart, rounded, and came together again. The cello provided the dignity but also that low thrumming that felt like a pulse of desire.

Marcus and Phillippa took their places in line across from each other. The music began. Until their cue, they simply stared at each other, lost for a moment to the rest of the world. Then they moved.

Totty had been right, Phillippa thought, as he took her hand in his and executed a turn. He does acquit himself well enough on the floor. More than well enough.

Certain that she should say something eventually, Phillippa decided it best to remark upon the decorations.

"Lady Whitford is rather fond of her country." She spoke, her voice markedly graver, not as smooth and melodious as she was accustomed to.

"Yes," Marcus replied sardonically, "that much is evident."

Thematically, the entire ballroom—indeed, the entire house—had been done up like one great big Union Jack. Boughs of Roses were of the purest reds and white, with rich blue velvet tying the boughs together. The British flag hung from various points on the walls in between the garlands and portraits of the King, the Prince Regent, the Duke of Wellington, and Admiral Lord Nelson, who looked remarkably well for a man without an eye and an arm.

"Lady Whitford has hung those portraits every year in the hopes that one or all will attend the festivities."

"She does realize that Admiral Lord Nelson is unavailable as he's dead, and the King as he's . . . at less than full capacity?"

A smile danced over Phillippa's mouth as he took her hand in his, and they executed their steps. "I'm certain she is aware of the King's illness and Lord Nelson's permanent lack of a pulse. But from what Thomas Hurston was told by his mother, who happens to be very good friends with Mrs. Markham, who is Lady Whitford's sister-in-law, Lady Whitford didn't want to seem as if she were only honoring Wellington and the Prince Regent in the hopes they'd attend, and so put up the portraits of our country's other leaders who could not possibly attend. You see?"

Marcus looked at her askance for a moment and then tentatively nodded as he released her hand and went by once more.

"Good. Now obviously, Wellington was unavailable until this year, but the Prince Regent popped in three years ago, and since Lord Whitford was such a supporter of the war effort—"

"To his own financial gain," Marcus commented, recalling

how Whitford's own rifle and pistol designs had been prevalent among soldiers.

"Since he was such a supporter of the war effort, and he and Wellington belong to the same club, it's possible that this year her hopes will not be in vain."

He took her hand again, and she held on through the turn.

"Possible but not probable," Marcus replied, "as it's almost midnight, and that's when the feast begins."

"Yes," Phillippa agreed, and unable to come up with any more to say without the benefit of privacy, she let silence fall as they continued the dance.

It was the oddest thing, but Phillippa was beginning to think there was something wrong with her hands. Whenever Marcus took her hand in his as they stepped through the turns, she felt it.

Which is ridiculous, because of course she felt it, she did have a sense of touch that would tell her whether or not someone had taken her hand. But it was stronger than that. It was as if her hand, without consulting her own thoughts, was especially attuned to being held in the hand of Mr. Marcus Worth. And as such, whenever he released her hand, it felt the lack of his.

And Phillippa, who had danced with a thousand partners, not to mention waltzing twice with Broughton, had never reacted thus previously. Curious, indeed.

Stop it, Philly! she told herself, giving herself the smallest little shake, which of course Marcus sensed, and which caused him to grip her hand with more feeling.

And that did not help.

No, indeed. It did not help to the point that Phillippa missed the next step and bumped into Miss Louisa Dunningham, who was dancing next to her.

She was certain she heard a gasp from across the room. Then a titter. Then a sweeping wave of voices. Phillippa Benning miss a step in the line? Surely not! Impossible!

"Are you all right?" Marcus asked, breaking into her head with genuine concern on his face.

She looked up and about her and was nothing short of shocked to find that no one else, save Louisa, Marcus, and herself, had noticed her blunder.

"I'm fine." She smiled, brightly, perhaps too brightly. "It's—it's just awfully stuffy in here."

Marcus shook his head, but instead of issuing a placating comment and continuing with the turn, he moved out of the steps and took her hand, pulling her out of the line. And considering her hand was just so terribly pleased to be in his, Phillippa had no choice but to follow it.

Once they were out of the dancers' way, Marcus stopped and turned to her, peered down into her face. "You're flushed," he said sternly, which only made her flush brighter.

"Come along," he spoke with greater gentleness, placing her hand in his arm, "let's find you a breeze."

She could have protested or reminded him of his mission, but she didn't.

He was guiding her toward the terrace doors, where cool night air awaited. While the idea of breathing space sounded lovely, the thought crossed Phillippa's mind that to truly recover herself, she might need breathing space *from* her escort. Having him close by was doing odd things to her hand. What other limbs would be affected should his presence be maintained?

Phillippa had to admit, she was curious on that point.

But no! Going out on the terrace was merely a step away from going out to the gardens, where dark shadows could hold a man and a woman, but only if they stood very, very close.

Her demeanor may have looked calm, but her mind panicked at the idea while her blood thrummed with it, until she remembered one material point.

Surely, she was safe with Marcus Worth. His one kiss aside (for which he had been soundly punished), he was too proper, too stodgy by half, to take advantage of her hand's strange affection for his. Besides, going out on the terrace would afford them some privacy, and she desperately wanted to question Marcus about the legend of the pistols in Whitford's gallery. About who he was hunting. And she knew he suffered her only for what she could offer him; entrée into society.

Certain that Marcus was merely concerned for her welfare, she quickly scanned the room before lifting her eyes to his.

The room was filled with twirling people, some of whom were paying attention to her, she knew, but none of whom seemed to think it odd that she step out of the line or out on the terrace. It was terribly hot in the crush; as the kitchen's ovens must be at full blazes, it invariably warmed the house a few dozen degrees. Add that to all the people in attendance, and more often than not, young ladies were employing their fans with vigor. Indeed, she caught no sight of Broughton, Totty, Lady Jane, or Nora, and everyone else seemed happy enough to be placid in their regard of Phillippa Benning.

Marcus Worth, however, was not.

It was a simple glance up to his face, meant to be a cool, grateful acceptance of his platonic offer to escort her outside. Then she saw it, just a moment. A flash of appreciation in his eyes. A spark of heat as his gaze flicked to her mouth. Then, just as quickly, it was gone, shaken off as he schooled himself back into that teasing, brotherish demeanor he took with her.

A quicksilver grin shot toward her. "Now, Mrs. Benning, you have to promise to protect me from strangers out on the terrace."

"I have to protect you?" she asked, recovering her voice and her sarcasm.

"Of course; you're the one with the right hook."

And with that he had her laughing again, and she would have happily let her hand in his follow him outside if not for the loud chiming of the bells.

Midnight.

"Ladies and gentlemen," the Whitfords' major domo announced in a booming voice that bespoke years of training, "the feast is served!"

Shuttled into the banquet hall on the swelling tide of hungry connoisseurs, Marcus cursed himself silently. He was supposed to be here working, tracking the enemy, and instead, he had been distracted by the thoughts of taking Phillippa Benning onto the terrace on a cloudless night. Of her suddenly feeling the chill in that excuse for a gown and finding it necessary to stand that much closer to him, to use his warmth.

And letting him feel hers.

Damn it all! He needed to keep his head in the game. It was already midnight; if something was going to happen, it was going to happen soon.

And if it didn't . . . maybe he really had gone insane.

The crowd swept them up, no space or time for a formal procession to the dining room, the guests—some of whom had been starving themselves in anticipation of this event—were far too ravenous for anything as tedious as decorum. Marcus kept Phillippa's arm in his, certain that if he didn't, they'd be torn asunder as they entered the dining room.

It was almost medieval in its vastness, if not its decor: a great hall, laid out with rows of long, polished cherry tables, silver candlesticks lighting the room from in between the yards of unencumbered silver trays. There was not a morsel of food in sight. Needless to say, this anticipation just made the rabble's collective stomach grumble louder.

At the far end, on a raised platform, was Lord Whitford, his astonishingly patriotic wife Lady Whitford (who had somehow managed to create a gown with so many pleats and folds, she looked like Winged Victory without the wings), and Marcel, the temperamental French chef that had created this entire banquet.

"He's looking in better humor than when last seen," Marcus commented to Phillippa.

She smiled and leaned up to Marcus's ear, the only way they could hear one another in the crush. "Well, when you last saw him he was a dictator, ruling his kitchen with an iron fist. Now he's an ambassador to be celebrated, with all the smiles and graciousness that goes with it."

Indeed, the wiry chef, whose dignified and unsmiling face held little reflection of the work he did or the praise he was about to receive, stood in a pristine white jacket and toque, his nose high in the air and his hands idly behind his back. Once all of the guests had entered the room, and their scuffling muted to a dull hum, Lord Whitford addressed the guests.

"Ladies and gentlemen, friends all. Thank you for gracing us with your attendance and your patience. Now, Marcel, if you would please."

Marcel gave Lord Whitford a sharp bow, veritably clicking his heels as he did so. Then with a flick of his wrists, the footmen at the double doors surrounding the room opened said passageways as dozens and dozens of trays of food, carried on the shoulders of footmen and kitchen boys, flooded in.

The audience gave a collective gasp, a smattering of applause, and then everyone started talking as one.

Something was wrong here. He could feel it. While the rest of the assembled guests exclaimed over pulled pork consommé and jellied trifle, the hair on the back of his neck began to stand up. There was something . . . off. Something uneven.

And Phillippa, at his side, sensed it.

"What is it?" she asked, worry practically bleeding out of her eyes.

"Maybe nothing. Just a feeling," he replied in clipped tones as his eyes scanned the room, the dishes, and the maddening crowd around them, until her felt her tense beside him.

He didn't need her scared.

"Would you do me a great favor, Mrs. Benning?" he asked, and she nodded mutely in response, "Prattle on about something."

"Prattle on?" she inquired, a brow going up.

"Yes. I need to look around but don't wish to seem to be doing so; it will make it seem as if we are having a conversation." And it will serve to give her an occupation and hopefully calm her down. But he kept that part of it to himself.

"Um, yes, well, the decorations—well, we already commented on the decorations. And yes, I think you're right, I doubt Wellington will be making a show this evening; he's in greater demand than me these days. Although I'm rather surprised Prinny isn't here; he's never one to miss a good roasted apple flambé. Oh, and there are the bread puddings; they have seventeen different varieties, you see? My personal favorite is the American peach, but Totty prefers the brandywine. The braised length of veal looks marvelous, don't you find, as does the lobster curry. Indeed, I remember last year, Lord Sterling ate almost the entire lobster by himself. One hopes that this year he thinks to wear a handkerchief tucked into his shirt. That was simply disastrous, made him the butt of every dining-related joke for a full week—"

"This year?" Marcus interrupted. "Lord Sterling is here?"

"Of course," Phillippa replied, her voice now modulated and relaxed, "at least, he was earlier; he danced with Nora. I haven't seen him since you arrived. But Penny—his daughter—is here." Her eyes flitted through the room and found her quarry. "There she is."

Marcus, who had been scanning the room to no avail, allowed his gaze to follow Phillippa's direction and landed on a brown-haired girl of adequate beauty and apparent good humor, wearing a slightly ill-fitting gown, standing with a friend and their chaperone.

"Are you particular friends with Miss Sterling?" Marcus asked, narrowing his eyes.

"No," Phillippa replied with a feline smile, "but I can be."

Just then, all of the crowd's attention, excepting Marcus's, was caught and held by the arrival of the pie.

It was a practice in contradictions. Monstrous in size, six feet in diameter with a high mound of crust in the center, it was also delicate and light, the pastry puffing up into a flaky structure that looked as if it could be swept away on a light breeze. The pie was placed on the table set on the raised platform, next to Marcel and Lord Whitford.

Marcus kept his eyes on Miss Sterling. Or rather, behind her. For behind her was the only set of doors that had not opened fully. Indeed, they were only open a crack. They could lead to a closed room, a servants' hallway, or any number of innocuous things. However, Marcus didn't think so.

Then, he saw it.

In the tiny gap of the ajar door, a falling shadow, as if someone moved quickly away—someone who had been spying on the festivities. Then the door snapped shut.

"Stay here," he instructed Phillippa. For once she seemed happy to obey him, if simply because the jostling thicket of humanity kept her in place as he maneuvered through them. His face set in determined, grim lines, his mind keenly aware of his dagger and Phillippa's pistol pressed against his body, he managed to wind his way past Penny Sterling and reach the door. Wrenching it open, he found . . .

Nothing.

No staircase, no hallway, and no one lurking. It was the silver cupboard, and as most of the silver was being laid on the long cherry tables behind him, it was mostly empty.

He quickly, ruthlessly began pushing on the walls, the shelves, the floor, looking for a trap, a priest's hole, anything that could let someone in and out unseen.

He didn't find it.

Maybe he really was chasing shadows.

But just when he was about to give it up, he found something else, something unexpected. Hidden within the folds of gray velvet that encased the silver service when it was not in use, his fingers fell around the stem of a feather. Not a quill. It was too fine, too delicate. Too broken in the middle.

It was a feather from the sleek head of a raven.

"Lord Whitford," Marcel addressed the crowd in a thick

French accent. "My country and yours have spent a great deal of time at odds."

"Indeed, they have, Marcel," Lord Whitford replied in what was obviously a rehearsed joint speech. "But I am certain that now that peace is declared, we will live in harmony. Shall we show the guests what peace and harmony between our countries looks like?"

The guests applauded, likely more out of hunger than affection for international relations.

Lord Whitford beamed, and Marcel bowed sharply, and with a flick of his wrist, two manservants handed Marcel and Lord Whitford a beautifully wrought gold knife.

The gold knives plunged into either side of the pastry, ripping a large seam in its fabric in spectacular fashion to mounting applause, from which arose . . .

Nothing.

Lord Whitford and Marcel wore equal looks of confusion, as murmurs began to rise out of the expectant guests.

They sawed at the pastry crust, until a large enough section could be lifted away, and they looked inside.

"What the—" Lord Whitford exclaimed, before shooting angry eyes to Marcel. "You moron! There are supposed to be white doves in here—*live* doves—not massacred blackbirds!"

"But . . . but . . . it iz impossible!" Marcel squeaked, his voice unaccountably high in his throat.

The crowd's murmurs rose to full voice as questions abounded, feet shuffled, and feathered heads bobbed, as word was passed through the assembled guests that something was very, very wrong.

Lord Whitford, meanwhile, had turned purple.

"*This* is how you choose to embarrass me, you damned insolent Frog!" Lord Whitford raged from the dining room, as Marcus stepped back into it, wending his way back to Phillippa's side. "When I found you, you were a gutter rat in Paris!"

"*Oui*—and you still pay me like one!" Marcel snapped back,

his face agog with bewilderment and anger. "You pasty *Anglais*. You make me sick. Thinking you have the world on your strings!"

"Why you little ungrateful—"

"You have no taste! You'd eat *merde* if I told you it was *Français*!"

Lord Whitford went for the jugular. But Marcel, while of a height, was quicker, ducking Whitford's hands and slamming himself forward into Whitford's body, the force of which knocked not only the brawling couple off the platform and to the floor, but the now-mangled, open, massive pie.

The ceramic pie dish crashed and fractured as it hit the hard surface of the floor, sending shards, pastry, and blackbirds sliding across the polished wooden surface. One such bird came to rest at the feet of Lady Whitford who, upon seeing its broken neck and charred form, promptly fainted.

Then the melee truly began. Female voices shrieked and fell, several more women fainting dead away, as if in sympathy with poor Lady Whitford. Those women who did not faint began crying out for help for their friends, beckoning men to their sides to assist them, those that weren't involved in attempting to either end or prolong the fight between Whitford and his famed chef. Marcus shot a look to his side, but Phillippa looked as if fainting were the sole thing she was not capable of.

"This is madness," she said loudly so he could hear above the chaos. "The Whitfords will never live this down. I cannot imagine anything worse."

That, of course, was when they heard the gunshots.

The crowd stilled. The noise continued, from out of doors, as if they were merely firecrackers on a cloudless night. Women who had fainted sat up and looked around, before remembering their prone positions. Then the real hysteria began.

Everyone began running for the exits, overturning plates and tureens of diligently prepared cuisine as they did so. Bumped and jostled every possible way, Marcus threw his arms around Phillippa and moved with the crowd.

They were swept to the front of the house and through the foyer, where startled coachmen quickly climbed up their rigs, and frightened aristocrats dove into them.

"Phillippa! Phillippa!" came a voice from behind them. It was Totty, being led out of the Whitford mansion by Broughton, who, while bewildered, seemed determined to keep his charge safe.

"Go," Marcus breathed in her ear, "go with Broughton and Mrs. Tottendale. Let them get you to safety."

"But what about you?" she asked, her eyes searching his face as another rushing individual bumped her further into Marcus's protective arms. But he held her firm and then, with strong hands on her shoulders, gently levered her back.

"I have to . . . Phillippa, let Broughton be your hero." And with that, Marcus let her go, turned against the tide of humanity, and felt her keen gaze on his back as he fought his way back inside.

Phillippa kept looking, long after Marcus had disappeared from sight. The fashionable world's beautiful people spilled out around her, more than one threatening to shove her out of the way and into the trampled dirt that used to be the Whitfords' front gardens. In fact, Mrs. Croyton nearly did, landing an elbow in Mr. Crawley's stomach instead, so determined was she to get her three precious daughters to the safety of the tangle of carriages. Phillippa's form would have connected with the ground had it not been for the saving presence of Totty and Broughton.

"Move on!" Totty barked, elbowing Mrs. Croyton out of the way, as Broughton pulled Phillippa to his side.

"Mrs. Benning, are you quite all right?" he asked solicitously.

"Phillippa, Mrs. Croyton would have killed you!" Totty said in sharp, admonishing tones.

"Totty, are you all right? Where's Nora?" Phillippa asked worriedly.

"Never fear, Miss De Regis is with her mother," Broughton answered.

"And Lady De Regis was the first person out the door," Totty harrumphed.

"I found Mrs. Tottendale scouring the ballroom for you," Broughton began, before he was rudely shoved from the back to get out of the way. "Mrs. Benning, we really should be leaving. My carriage is this way."

Unable to resist the flood any longer, Phillippa, with one last look to the doors of the mansion, allowed Broughton to guide them through the crowd to his carriage and assist them inside.

Marcus moved like lighting through the corridors, now in complete disarray from the trampling of the party. He wove his way beyond the ballroom, back to the gallery, where less than an hour ago, a calm and composed Lord Whitford was proudly pontificating on his collection of firearms to Marcus and Phillippa. He located the case that contained Whitford's most recent acquisition.

Or had.

Marcus knew what he saw. He had expected it and dreaded it. It was his proof.

Laurent was alive.

And the scrolled, silver-handled pistols belonging to the Blue Raven were gone.

Fifteen

In the wee hours of the morning, by a fire that was under strict orders not to die, Phillippa sat waiting and getting more and more annoyed with each passing tick of the clock.

He just left her there and ran back inside without so much as a by-your-leave. Now she had the off-putting sensation of actually *worrying* about the man, so much so that she had found her all-important beauty sleep impossible and was instead sitting in her downstairs salon by the fire, waiting for either a knock at her door or the sun to rise.

He would knock on her door, wouldn't he? He wouldn't leave her in this awful, distracted state. Oh, she was going to look horrid tomorrow. Even if she slept into the afternoon, she would have dark circles under her eyes and very possibly a small crease where her brows came together. If she had such a wrinkle, she'd hunt him down, and if he was found in good health, kill him.

Tired of sitting, she stood and began pacing the Aubusson carpet its whole length, distractedly following the patterns in the woven wool, sort of dancing lethargically along to its colorful tune.

She loved this carpet. She loved her pink marble fireplace. She even loved that damn rosewood clock on the mantel whose ticks echoed off the rose-patterned wallpaper.

She loved her house. Rarely did she indulge in a full day at home, but when she did so, it was as if she had the fantasy palace all to herself and she could savor its delights. She danced behind the tall hedgerows, in between the blue hydrangeas and bright marigolds she'd ordered put in. A more cheerful garden one was not likely to find. She luxuriated in the massive claw-footed ceramic bathtub she had installed in the tiled and painted antechamber to her own mistress's bedchamber. She was the one who had the entire interior of the house refurbished when she, upon inheriting it, found the entire second and third floors to be in complete disrepair. And she was the one who had decorated it flawlessly, when she discovered that those downstairs rooms that were not in use had been pilfered of their beauty for a few extra pounds.

She liked to think that she would have redecorated in any case, if Alistair had been as solvent as he had claimed, and she was setting up house as a woman who intended to make the grand, austere mansion on Grosvenor Square her home. If he had lived. But this was not Alistair's house. She had never seen him here, they had never lived here as man and wife. Alistair Benning was a footnote in this house's history. No, it was her home, exactly to her specifications. It merely bore his name.

While listening to the overwhelming tick of the clock, Phillippa almost didn't hear the discreet tapping on the salon's door. While contemplating the intricate carpet patterns, she almost didn't notice that door slip open, and a dark-clad figure slip inside.

And she almost didn't scream like a possessed banshee scared out of her wits.

"Holy Mother, woman, make the noise stop!" Mr. Marcus Worth said, his hands clutching at his ears, and then, when the noise did not cease as required, he braved further damage and moved his hand to her mouth. Finally, quiet reigned.

"It's just me," he whispered. "You'll not scream again?"

She nodded.

He removed his hand. No sound emanated. Marcus relaxed.

Which turned out to be a mistake.

Unbeknownst to most people in her social circle, but as Marcus Worth was well aware, Phillippa Benning had an impressive right hook.

Luckily, she aimed it at his shoulder instead of his jaw, hitting him in solid muscle with an ineffectual thud and only minimal pain. He broke out in a grin, even as he exclaimed in a hushed voice, "Ouch!"

"Oh, shush," she said, shaking out her hand from the impact with his shoulder. "That was for scaring me like that. I likely felt that punch more than you. The next time, I'll aim for your stomach."

Marcus shook his head. "No good hitting a man in the stomach, unless he's got a soft belly." Which Phillippa had to admit, he did not. "You'll do greater damage if you hit lower or higher."

"I'm well informed about the pain of a lower blow, but higher?" she asked, curious.

"If you can manage the neck, a solid shot could crush a man's windpipe."

"Hm. I'll bear that in mind," she replied, suddenly proper. Marcus took a few steps farther into the room.

"Your, er, scream did not wake Mrs. Tottendale, or the servants?" he asked, his eyes shooting to the parlor's various doors.

"Totty could sleep in a battlefield. Very useful in a companion," Phillippa answered, a bit more inclined to be kind to him. She was still peeved, of course. How dare he scare her first by running back into the Whitfords' and then by appearing like a ghost (or infamous sneak) in the night, but she was too relived to see he was all right to stay flustered for long. "And as for the servants," she continued, "apparently they can sleep through their mistress's distress with ease, as well."

"Good," he said wearily and then collapsed onto a delicate pink chintz sofa next to the fire.

He was tired, she noticed, concerned. Deeply tired, bone weary. It was only four in the morning; oftentimes she came home at this hour. But obviously the excitement of the evening and the lateness of the hour had lent itself to an exhaustion that caused Marcus to drop the facade of good humor he normally wore. His eyes became lost in the fire, as the light drifted across his face and the small lines at the corners of his eyes.

She would commit suicide before she allowed herself wrinkles so plainly on her face, but Phillippa had to admit, even exhausted, those small lines looked strangely becoming on Marcus Worth.

"What happened?" Phillippa asked quietly, lowering herself to the chair opposite him.

He looked at her then, and on a great sigh, turned the length of his body toward her and decided to tell his story.

"The pistols were gone."

She regarded him blankly for a moment, then she remembered. "The pistols—the ones from the gallery? The Blue Raven's pistols?"

"Actually, they were Laurent's initially. I suppose he has a right to them," Marcus said with a shrug, his sense of irony peeking out from his weary frame. "Of course, he was supposedly shot dead with one of them, so ownership might be in contention."

"So the legend Lord Whitford spoke of is the truth?"

"More or less," he answered. "And Whitford obviously decided it was more so, else he paid too much for them."

"Marcus, please," Phillippa said, a hitch of worry in her voice, "be serious. This isn't about the weapons. What happened next?"

"After I discovered the pistols were missing, I offered my services to Lord Whitford, to assist in regaining order."

Actually, he'd had to pull the still-brawling Lord Whitford off the pudding-slathered mongrel that turned out to be the chef, Marcel, and called for the constable. Lady Whitford was found sobbing hysterically in the corner of the ballroom. She was covered in the detritus of a banquet gone bad and babbling to herself; Marcus could only make out a few words, mostly "ruined" and "laughingstock." Once the constable had arrived, Lady Whitford was escorted up to her rooms by her faithful lady's maid, who petted and soothed the poor creature like a mother hen, while Marcel was questioned by a relatively calmer Lord Whitford and the constabulary.

As it was, Lord Whitford proved rather incapable of question-asking, and therefore, left the brunt of the conversation, rather remarkably, to Mr. Marcus Worth, and if he found Mr. Worth's presence odd and his manner too authoritative for a younger son and legislative clerk (although hadn't he heard he was no longer employed in that position?), he did not speak up. It was far too useful to have a man of sense involved.

Marcel, it seemed, had been as perplexed as anyone to see the dead, mangled blackbirds in the pie. "I do not know what has happened," he said, sputtering. "I put ze doves in ze pie fifteen minutes before the crust was cut; my sous-chef and ze pastry chef assisted *moi*. Someone must have switched the pies!"

"Two identical six-foot pies?" Whitford scoffed, sneering down at the traitorous Frenchman he had allowed into his kitchen. "Not bloody likely, you, you . . . Frenchman!"

"Lord Whitford, please," Marcus began calmly and indicated the constable, who stood placidly by, taking down every word that was said, all the better to sell his notes to the *Times*. Lord Whitford proceeded to hold his tongue, and Marcus continued.

"You think the pie was replaced," Marcus began, and again shot a quelling look to a sneering Lord Whitford. "The piecrust and dish are right here. Do you see anything that could support that theory?"

Marcel, seizing the opportunity to reclaim his innocence and his superiority, stood and went to examine the remains of the pie splattered on the dining room floor. The shards of the massive red ceramic dish he found uninteresting and moved on to the crust. Picking up a large chunk, he examined it closely, tested its weight in his hand. He held it aloft to the light of a candle. Then he snapped his fingers.

"Send for Mademoiselle Quinn!"

One of the footmen at the door snapped to attention, bowed smartly, and headed quickly to the kitchens, bringing back moments later a bewildered young redhead, perhaps twenty, who wore the dough-crusted apron that bespoke her role as the pastry chef.

Marcel went directly to her, handing her the piece of crust.

"Mademoiselle Quinn, what is this?"

"It . . . it is crust from the pie, Chef."

"Are you certain?" he asked in clipped, authoritative tones. "Look closely."

She did. She peered at it, also holding it up to the light of a candle. Then shock came over her features, as she exclaimed, "This is not my crust! Who has done this?"

Marcus immediately came forward, a warily curious Lord Whitford and the constable in tow. "How can you tell?" he asked.

"This is layered dough, folded over again and again to make it puff and rise when it bakes," Miss Quinn answered, her thin, nimble hands moving quickly as she spoke. "This crust only has eight layers. My crust always has sixteen."

"Always?" Marcus replied.

"You dare to question my pastry chef?" Marcel responded, his nose again at its rightful place, high in the air. "No one in my kitchen makes a dough with less than sixteen layers! No one!"

"Lord Whitford, are you satisfied? Someone must have switched the pies."

Lord Whitford's eyebrows went through the top of his head. "But . . . but how? Why?"

"Two very important questions, but I think I can answer one of them," Marcus said, and drew Lord Whitford aside.

"Lord Whitford," he said in a low voice, "have you done a thorough search of your home?"

"A search?"

"It's possible that the entire point of this disruption was to cause . . . a disruption." And then, with only the smallest moment of hesitation, Marcus told him of the missing pistols from the gallery.

Lord Whitford took off like lightning, forcing the constable, Marcus, and Marcel the chef to trail in his wake. He thumped through the halls with such wakeful terror that all the servants he passed automatically joined the growing entourage behind him.

Lord Whitford reached the gallery of armaments, came to a halt in front of the case that Marcus knew to be empty, and seemed astonished to find it so. After going very pale, then purple, then swallowing his rage and returning to a normal shade, Lord Whitford addressed the assembled staff with the authority of the master of the house and ordered a search of every crevice of his home.

Then, with a swift eye to Marcus, he marched off toward a staircase. Marcus followed, leaving the befuddled note-taking constable behind to handle the various napkin rings and flowerpots the servants discovered missing.

Lord Whitford led Marcus to a private study on the second floor, obviously his personal space, as it was dressed in masculinity and strewn with open books and sheaves of paper. It had also been ransacked. Lord Whitford, however, did not look concerned at the mess. His look of concern was reserved for the painting on the wall, a landscape done in cloyingly romantic tones and the only level picture in the room.

"What was missing from the safe?" Phillippa asked, perched raptly on the edge of her delicate chair.

"Beg pardon?" Marcus asked, snapped out of his story and back to reality. He must have fallen silent without realizing it, for Phillippa wore an expression of impatience that was oddly endearing.

"The safe? I assume that was what was behind the painting."

An eyebrow went up. "Why do you think that?"

A small, superior smile flitted across her features. "First of all, Lord Whitford prefers his art more representational than pastoral. In the entire Whitford Mansion, I saw dozens of portraits and twice as many canvases depicting glory in battle, but not a single landscape. And as you said, it was the only level picture in the room, which makes me think it was attached to the wall. On hinges perhaps, so it could swing away, revealing something hidden. And thirdly," She paused for a moment, preening visibly. "I believe paintings have been hiding safes since paintings and safes began. Not particularly original on Lord Whitford's part, but he never struck me as a particularly original man."

Marcus took a moment to regard her. Not to see her as other people saw her, but perhaps as she saw herself. She knew herself to be beautiful—she must—half the gossip columns were devoted to her lovely visage. She was confident, but that confidence was not borne out of her beauty. It was part of her very core, a product of her clever mind.

And she worked remarkably hard to keep it hidden from society but, surprisingly, not from him.

He must have taken too long in his regard, because she resorted to snapping her fingers to literally snap him out of his reverie.

"Mr. Worth! You still haven't answered my question," she spoke with patience.

"I'm sorry," he apologized, "I'm . . . still not used to these hours."

"Shall I call for tea?"

"No . . . I would prefer not to disturb the servants . . ." His voice was sharp as he tried to infuse his speech with energy. Wake up, Marcus, he mentally slapped himself. You're not home yet.

A small, wry smile played bitterly across her features. "Afraid to be seen with me?"

Marcus smiled in kind, replying, "Not at all, but I should think you would rather avoid being seen with me." When her eyebrow went up, he explained. "Entertaining a gentleman . . . at night . . . in your home . . . ?" Of course, the longer he went on, the paler his argument sounded. "I . . . I slipped in through the gardens. I don't think anyone saw me . . ."

A soft laugh lifted through the air as Phillippa replied, "Worried about your reputation?"

"Mrs. Benning, you yourself told me I have no discernable reputation." But what was left unsaid hung between them: *I was worried about yours.*

She must have felt his thoughts, suspended in the air, because she held his gaze in the firelight and then took a deep breath before she spoke.

"Well," she replied, seeming to brace herself with cheerfulness, "you have one now, since you spoke with me on Bond Street, and everyone saw it, and you danced with me this evening—oh, and I spoke to Lady Hampshire; I have hope that you should receive an invitation to the Racing Party within the next few days, and if you don't, I'll take it upon myself to cut that good lady out of my calling rounds until she obliges me—but you shouldn't worry about being here; my servants know better than to gossip about whom I do or do not entertain in my home. However, you are not being entertained, nor am I. We are conducting serious business, which leads me back to my original question of what was missing from the safe."

It took Marcus a moment to work through her speech, but upon reaching its conclusion, he reluctantly handed over the answer she required.

"Schematics."

"Schematics?" she repeated incredulously.

"The only thing missing from the safe, according to Lord Whitford, was a set of technical drawings—schematics—for a new pin barrel firing system he was developing for his arms manufacturers."

"No money? No jewels?"

"This thief was very specific. He tore the room apart but took only the schematics. The housekeeper and head butler reported that nothing else was missing from the Whitfords'." He paused, ran his fingers through his unexpectedly short hair. "The thing is . . . the pistols' case—the lock wasn't broken, the glass wasn't marred by so much as a finger smudge. But the study . . ."

"Was a complete mess, you said," she finished his thought for him. "Why would he make such a mess in the study but not the gallery?"

"He wanted us to know," Marcus scowled. "For some reason, Laurent wanted us to know he had taken the schematics. It's important."

"Or maybe . . ." But her voice trailed away, uncertain.

"Or maybe what?"

"No, it's stupid. You're the expert; you know better what we speak of than I," she dismissed his inquiry with a wave of her hand.

"Mrs. Benning, you have never in our association hesitated to give your opinion; pray, don't stop now," he answered wryly.

"Well," she began nervously, "it seems to me there wasn't much time to get from the gallery to the safe upstairs and then escape with the crowd. What if there were two men? One who stole the pistols and one who rifled the Whitfords' personal study?"

As Phillippa hedged and hesitated with her theory, Marcus's mind was filled with new ideas. He had never even considered that it was two men; he had only seen Laurent. All this time he had thought the information from the department was leaked casually, almost passively, and that was the end of the traitor's involvement. But of course that man could just as easily have been active in his treachery, although it was the height of danger to do so. If caught, the traitor would have no easy excuse for his behavior, while merely leaking information was far, far easier to deny.

One other thing occurred to Marcus, and it was a thought that filled him with equal parts fear and warm anticipation: Phillippa Benning was quick, useful. Maybe indispensable.

"Mrs. Benning you may have a surprising future in espionage."

She blushed at that. "Why, Mr. Worth, what a compliment, coming from you."

They let the fire crackle between them, Marcus enjoying the comfort of the surroundings far more than he should. He could sit here forever in this lovely and yet not overbearing pink room, the lady to his left tatting something—although he doubted Phillippa Benning tatted anything—and, granted, he could use a more accommodating chair, the sofa was a bit spindly on its legs . . . but maybe it was his weariness, maybe it was the company, maybe it was the warmth from the steady fire. Marcus soon realized that in that moment, there was no place else he would rather be.

And that thought made him sit up rather quickly.

"I should go," he began, getting to his feet. "I need some rest before tomorrow."

"What's tomorrow?" Phillippa asked, also rising.

"More . . . more looking," he replied, his eyes catching her face and ultimately regretting it. Her eyes shone with anticipation as they looked up at him, her soft coloring glowing in the firelight.

"You should come call," she burst out abruptly. "Not in the middle of the night, of course. By the bye, what would you have done had I been asleep in my bed? I know the Blue Raven has a reputation for stealing into ladies' bedchambers, but . . ."

"I told you not all stories are true, Mrs. Benning." He reached the door of the salon and turned to face her. "I knew you were awake in this room because I could see the candles burning from without. It's safe to say I would have never entered your home unless I saw the candles. I would have"—he paused with his hand on the doorknob—"likely sent you a note in the morning."

"Oh," she breathed. Then, taking a step closer, "You should come call in a day or two. Lady Hampshire makes her rounds on

Wednesdays. If you're here then, it could help secure you an invitation to the Racing Party."

He nodded and turned to open the door, but she held him once again.

"One last question, Mr. Worth . . . Marcus," she said in a voice that, while strong, trembled slightly, hesitantly. "If you felt you could just as easily send me a note in the morning, why come here at all tonight?"

Marcus turned once more and stepped up to her. They stood so close they could have been dancing.

"I could ask you why you were awake by the fire." He indulged himself for the briefest of moments and lifted his hand to her hair, brushing an errant lock behind her ear.

His fingers felt electric as they slid down her hair to her neck. To the neckline of her nightdress, her dressing gown—remarkably modest attire for someone so fashionable as Phillippa Benning. Thick, warm cotton, draping her from her collarbone to her stockinged toes. It made her look innocent, childlike, except for the curves that the cloth skimmed.

And her wide, unjudging eyes never left his face as he pulled his hand away and slipped through the door, swallowed by the darkness of the hall beyond.

By the time Wednesday arrived, Phillippa was a complete bundle of nerves. She had of course had half a dozen meetings regarding the Benning Ball, from auditioning new musicians (although she had considered hiring the same orchestra as last year simply to peeve her mother, but instead decided that the lady had been correct that they were not the crème de la crème) to the men whom she had hired to construct a maze of mirrors in the long gallery, forcing all her guests to pass through it before they could arrive in the ballroom.

And of course, she and Totty had to attend two luncheons, a musicale, and the botanical exhibition of the Prince Regent's latest paramour, Lady Hertford, and fawn politely over tea cakes and watercress sandwiches over the course of the last few days, and uncounted balls and dinner parties in the evenings.

All of this—all of it—without one word from Marcus Worth.

She shouldn't let herself worry, she knew. In fact, he had visited her home that night to assuage her worry. But then she made the mistake of reading the newspaper, and in between articles about the weakness of the franc and the rabble's continued chafing at the English occupation of Paris, Phillippa found a hearty piece of gossip.

It seems the expatriate French residing on our shores are becoming more and more unhappy with our hospitality. Take the recent disastrous W——— Banquet, which yielded more than a French chef's revenge on his English employer. This reporter has exclusively learned that more was taken than Lord and Lady W———'s pride that night. A pair of pistols supposedly belonging to the infamous spy, the Blue Raven, were removed from their place of honor in the W———'s home, along with other valuables personal to Lord W———. This reporter heard it suggested that the whole affair was a nefarious scheme to remove those objects of such English pride and French shame. Could this be the case? And one must ask, with his famous pistols now missing, where is the Blue Raven? Rumor has it he's been patrolling the lower class of this fair city, looking for answers, a raven's feather the only proof he's left behind.

Phillippa was incensed. How could such claptrap have made the papers? But then she laughed at herself. The answer was obvious. Claptrap always made the papers. She herself had been the object of any number of inches of set type, which could be gracious, ingratiating, infuriating, or just plain false. But while his speculation was wild, in this instance the reporter's facts were more or less true, which set Phillippa's nerves even further on edge.

But now it was Wednesday. An at-home day for Phillippa, where she received calls instead of making them, and this morning, the calls she received were in the dozens.

Which, she reminded herself, was not abnormal.

They surrounded her in the downstairs pink salon, the one where only a few nights ago Marcus Worth had nearly surprised her out of her wits. Nora to her left, with her mother, chatting amiably with Lady Hampshire by the window, while Totty sat guard by the tea tray, her own special tea in a pot by her elbow. Half a dozen others milled about the various bouquets sent over that morning. Two of her favorite gentlemen, Freddy Hawkes and Sir Reginald Ridgeway, charming gentlemen more interested in impressing each other than impressing her, were seated down the couch from Mrs. Dunningham, Louisa Dunningham, and Penny Sterling.

But none of these people were who she wished to see.

Penny Sterling had turned out to be rather delightful, if a little naive. But perhaps one informed the other. She was a pleasant thing, still wearing her youthful flesh, and pink all over, excepting her dark brown hair, which, while the color was unexceptional, was thick and shiny enough that it could be worn fashionably. She again wore a dress just marginally the wrong color for her; the person who selected it obviously had no eye. Phillippa determined to have a word with Penny's mother, but then she learned from the awed Mrs. Dunningham that Lady Sterling had such troubles with the air in London that she had been forced to forgo Penny's coming-out to take the waters by the sea.

"It would be so difficult to be without one's mother during this time, wouldn't it, pet?" Mrs. Dunningham patted her own daughter's hand. Louisa looked as if nothing would please her more than to be without her grasping, needling mother, but she nodded all the same. Phillippa looked to Penny, whose face was a battlefield of emotion. On the one hand, she likely felt like Louisa, wanting to test her wings away from parental supervision. On the other side of it, sometimes a mother came in handy, especially when faced with the new and unknown.

Phillippa could empathize.

"Still," Mrs. Dunningham continued, "her father, Lord Sterling, is in town. He's very influential in the military you know; he has a dozen shiny medals across his uniform! And I am more than happy to take dear Penny around with Louisa and me; she's been Louisa's best friend since school."

And with that, Louisa shot Penny a look, who rolled her eyes, covering a smile. Phillippa suppressed a smile just watching them.

"And what does your father do in the military, Penny?" Phillippa asked, keeping her voice cool. Oh, if only Marcus were here for this, he would know exactly what kind of information to look for!

"He doesn't do anything in the military—not anymore, that is," Penny answered, her cheeks pinking up even more as she answered. "He works at the parliamentary offices, says he does 'strategic planning.' Whatever that is."

"Well, we women do better not to ask," Mrs. Dunningham interjected. "Men go off and do all sorts of things that I have never been able to make heads or tails of—the 'change, shipping and trade, conquering savage countries. It's all so unfathomable, I find it simpler to sit at home, mind the children and their upbringing. We ladies need know nothing more than what concerns us." And with that, she took another cucumber sandwich.

And Phillippa decided the less Penny Sterling had to be around Mrs. Dunningham, the better for her. Louisa would be harder to remove from her mother's influence, but as Phillippa was plotting different ways to make Mrs. Dunningham disappear, Nora, obviously a bit put out with having to endure anyone she considered beneath her notice, interjected.

"Indeed, Mrs. Dunningham. And what a perfect mother you must be. Why, I can tell that Louisa and indeed, Penny, have benefited from being sheltered from the outside world."

"Nora . . ."

"After all, country fashions—" But Nora was cut off by Bitsy yapping at the salon's door.

"Bitsy, shush!" Phillippa admonished her Pomeranian loudly, shooting a dark glance to Nora, who resolutely looked back with an expression of nonchalance. Phillippa stood and collected her fluffy friend, just as Leighton opened the salon's wide double doors.

"Mrs. Benning, a gentleman for you."

Phillippa's eyes lit up. Finally, Marcus was here. He could bow over Lady Hampshire's hand and question Penny Sterling with far greater accuracy than she.

She nodded to Leighton, who bowed and admitted . . .

Someone who was not Marcus Worth.

"Mrs. Benning," the Marquis of Broughton bowed, his voice mellifluous and seductive. And then, stepping closer, raising his hand to her lips, whispered, "Phillippa."

Suddenly, every conversation in the room hushed to a low buzz. Phillippa wasted not a moment to surprise and allowed a warm smile to spread across her face. "Lord Broughton," she said, and then lower, a whisper for his ears only, "Phillip."

"So *this* is what it is to be respectable," he growled in her ear. "Very interesting."

Then, walking past her with the smoothness borne of his upbringing, Broughton bowed to the assembly, and after Phillippa had taken her seat, took the one next to her, vacated by Freddie Hawkes and Sir Reginald Ridgeway.

That afternoon, Brougton would bow and flatter her, would charm the other ladies in the room, and would even have Bitsy eating out of the palm of his hand. But then again, Bitsy was notoriously standoffish, until a berry tart was offered as enticement. (Once the tart was gone however, his affection would be, too.)

That afternoon, Penny Sterling would invite Phillippa Benning to tea, much to Mrs. Dunningham's surprise, after Phillippa had taken the young lady aside and expressed kinship over their mothers' dislike of London air.

That afternoon, Totty would be forced into conversation with Lady De Regis over the best hemstitches. Both women would drink copiously from Totty's special tea.

And that afternoon, Marcus Worth would never show his face.

It wasn't until the next morning that she would find out why.

"Mrs. Benning," Marcus's note began—and Phillippa again questioned how long it would be before that annoying man would take to using her Christian name—"I regret I could not call on you this afternoon"—for indeed, she had received the note late that night after dancing so much her feet ached—"but would you be good enough to meet me in the park tomorrow morning? Ten o'clock, at the north end of the Serpentine?"

Ten o'clock! He might as well have asked for dawn! She fumed, snitted, and then eventually settled down to write her reply.

Which, much to her chagrin, and after several drafts of highly acerbic writing, was in the affirmative.

And as such, she found herself in the park, at ten o'clock, at the north end of the Serpentine, her phaeton, driver, and manservant waiting idly along the path nearby. She suspected the driver was napping. Phillippa was dressed in her newest walking costume, a sage green dress with a dropped forest green velvet spencer embroidered with delicate vines in gold threads. What could have been taken for a muff was actually Bitsy, curled into her arm, snoring away like the little turncoat he was. Her kid gloves and walking boots were of the same rich brown leather, and the latter were destined to be ruined by the dew that still clung to ground.

Totty remained abed, as did everyone with manners or good sense. And just as she was wondering where her good sense had fled to, Marcus Worth came and stood beside her.

"It's just me," he said, his voice flat and sardonic. "Close your mouth, else you'll catch flies."

"But . . . but your eye!" As she spoke, her hand reached impulsively for his face. He drew away when she made contact, sucking in his breath in pain.

"I'm sorry, I'm sorry!" she said. "It looks horrid. Does it hurt much?"

Indeed, it did look horrid. The greenish yellow bruise at his temple webbed out to his eye, in its epicenter a cut about an inch in length, healing nicely but still rather ugly.

"It hurt a great deal more yesterday. Just don't touch it, please." He caught her hand as it went involuntarily toward his temple again.

"I . . . I apologize, again," Phillippa replied sheepishly. Then, "I imagine that is why you found it impossible to call and impress Lady Hampshire yesterday, and hence I had to do it for you."

"Precisely," he replied. "I found when I awoke that it was already past the dinner hour, and, therefore, I had missed the opportunity to see you. I regret it most sincerely."

"Its all right." She said softly, a hint of humor in her voice. "You have expressed your excuse most sincerely. And I managed to secure an invitation for you to the Racing Party."

"Did you? Your powers of persuasion are faultless. Dare I ask how it was accomplished?" He smiled and then winced slightly. It seemed apparent that his bruise was more painful than he was letting on.

"Believe it or not, you have Broughton to thank for it," she replied tartly.

"Do I?" his eyebrow shot up.

"Yes," she said, petting Bitsy as he fussed for a moment, waking himself up. "Lady Hampshire mentioned the number of young unmarried ladies she was inviting, and he bemoaned the fact that she had invited only a fraction of that number of single men. He said he needed more bachelors there as protection."

"Oh, well, I'm terribly happy to serve as a bodyguard to His

Highness, the Marquis of Broughton." Marcus said snidely, eliciting a smile from Phillippa.

"Lady Hampshire was very eager to correct her mistake and provided you an accommodation." She looked at him then, watched him as he stared down the length of the winding body of water the planner of Hyde Park had long ago named after the slithering reptile it so resembled.

London was a lot like the Serpentine, she reflected. Lovely on the surface, but winding, changing, and slippery. Hard to navigate. And Marcus stood at its head like a rock. And just as obscure.

"Is this what you dragged me out of my warm bed for? To show me why you missed yesterday?" she asked curtly, returning her attention to the green, opaque water. "How did it happen?"

"Stupidly." And that seemed to be all he was willing to say about his appearance. "But it's not the only reason I asked you to meet me."

"There's more?" she perked up.

"I thought you might like to try an exercise with me." He said, and for the first time, he smiled without pain.

"An exercise?" she queried skeptically. "Mr. Worth, I haven't attempted exercise since a particularly sadistic governess thought it healthful for young girls to practice swimming."

"Swimming?"

"It was horrid; she made me go in circles until my arms ached. I became so brown and my hair such a tangle that my mother saw my appearance and fired her on the spot." Phillippa smirked. "Now, what torturous exercise are you trying to inflict upon me?"

"Nothing quite so horrific as swimming," he promised. "Would you care to sit down?" He guided her over to a nearby wrought-iron bench overlooking the footbridge that was banked by willow trees. The sun was rising higher into the sky, evaporating the offending dew and forcing open the budding lilies that turned to face its powerful rays.

"I was wondering," Marcus began, folding his long frame

down onto the short bench, and leaning forward on his knees, "how good your eyes are."

"My eyes?" she inquired. "My eyes are fine. I've never needed spectacles like some people I could mention."

"Yes, yes, your eyes themselves are perfect," he replied, "but I meant to ask how well you remember what you see."

"I remember everything I see," she said matter-of-factly. "I do not brag," she replied to his unspoken skepticism. "It's the truth."

"Prove it," he said and covered her eyes with his large, warm hand. "Tell me what you see."

"I see the inside of your hand, you annoying man."

He laughed aloud at that and removed his hand. "All right then, try this. Look out at the lake for ten seconds, then close your eyes and list every man that you see."

"But it's ten in the morning!" she protested. "No one I know is awake. All these people are unknown to me . . ."

"Precisely why I chose such an obnoxious hour. You don't have to name them, just describe them," he coaxed, his voice a singsong of delightful coercion.

Since she was awake anyway, and in the park, and it would only take ten seconds, Phillippa decided to oblige him.

Normally, she never tried to memorize things, she just did. Information that had been said to her once or a coat someone had worn would pop back into her memory precisely as it had been when she first encountered it, and she was invariably always correct. But now, she concentrated. She watched the young ladies, middle-class by the looks of their neat poplin skirts, as they carried baskets of market goods behind their mother. She watched as young men of means on horses indulged in early morning rides before the fashionable hour took over the entire length of the Serpentine. She looked on as an old man sat across the water, reading a newspaper and smoking a pipe.

"Ten seconds," Marcus stated, interrupting her concentration and promptly leaning over to cover her eyes with his hand.

"Right," he said, so close to Phillippa's ear, he only had to breathe his words. "Tell me; how many men did you see?"

"Fourteen," she replied promptly.

He paused a moment, obviously surprised at the speed of her response, and possibly doing a quick count. (Phillippa couldn't be sure, as her eyes were covered.) "Nay, there are thirteen," he replied.

"Nay, there are fourteen."

"Fourteen—describe them for me."

"There are two young men on horseback, although they are likely out of view now; they went beyond the willow tree about seven seconds into my watching. There is the gentleman seated to our right, across the footbridge, reading the newspaper and smoking a pipe. There are the three clerks, who by their speed I think had taken a short break from their work and are now late getting back. Two men of the guard are behind us, but that's not surprising, as Lancaster Gate is behind us. Two footmen crossed our path, a young boy with his mother—not a man, I know, but I count him as he's male—my driver, my manservant, both riding the box of my carriage, and you."

He uncovered her eyes, and Phillippa blinked in the new sunlight and smiled brilliantly up at a nonplussed Marcus Worth.

"Fourteen," he conceded.

"You didn't count the boy, did you?"

"No," he replied somewhat sheepishly, "I neglected to count myself."

"Oh, Mr. Worth," she said consolingly, patting his hand. "I promise you, you are as much a man as that boy." Her eyes glinted wickedly. "You shouldn't sell yourself so short."

"Ha-ha," he replied, but she noticed he didn't draw his hand away from hers.

She grinned. "This is fun, but I have to ask, why are we employed in this exercise?"

Now he did draw back his hand, ran it through his hair as if he still expected there to be more of it. Then he caught her gaze with his and held it.

"Because I want you to be prepared," he intoned seriously.

"Prepared?" she repeated, her voice more quiet than she'd like, a product of a small sensation of dread.

Marcus stared out at the water, refusing to face her questioning eyes. And when he spoke, it was in flat monotones, uninflected, unfeeling.

"What are my chances at convincing you to come down with a cold and having to forgo the Hampshires' Racing Party?" he asked.

"Nil," she replied. "Lady Hampshire would never forgive me, especially when I've already made entreaties on your behalf, and if you think I am going to sit back and watch Lady Jane Cummings get a leg up with the Hampshires . . ." Her voice trailed off when he shot her a quelling look, just before he went back to staring at the lake.

"I don't suppose locking you in your house for your own good would work either?"

"Not if you mean to attend the Gold Ball at Regent's Park as well," she intoned a little heatedly. If he was trying to scare her, it wasn't working. So far, it had only served to make her angry. But still, she snuggled Bitsy a little closer to her chest.

"Precisely," was his calm reply. "I cannot remove you from the danger at hand, particularly when I don't know from which direction it will strike."

"And particularly when I am your ticket into the places where you think the danger will occur," she pronounced archly.

"So I want you to be prepared," he spoke seriously. "I know your memory is good; you have surprised me with it more than once. But I want you to be able to ferret out the necessary information from the rest of the noise surrounding it."

For the first time, Phillippa swallowed some of her anger and allowed a teaspoon of fear to creep in. But then she straightened her spine and her resolve. "All right, then," she said brightly. "Teach me. What should I be looking for?"

He turned to her then and apparently saw nothing in her countenance that bespoke hesitation, for he allowed the smallest of grins when he held her gaze.

"Come on," she coaxed, "what am I looking for? Sly looks between political enemies? Dirty French expatriates trying to sneak into the party via the garden? Whether or not Lady Hampshire's silk is imported or hand-sewn?"

"Tell me"—and the entire time he held her gaze, his brown eyes darkened to brooding, thanks to his wound—"how many ladies here are wearing aprons."

She did not turn her head, his eyes locked with hers would not have allowed it. Without looking out over the moving population of the north end of the Serpentine, she replied, "Three. Two maids crossed our path, and there's a woman with a fruit cart at the park's entrance."

Pleased with that answer, he proceeded to ask her rapid-fire questions, and she proceeded to answer them, without checking her surroundings to see if her answers were correct.

"How many men wore gloves?"

"All of them, except the boy and one of the clerks."

"How many pieces of paper did you see?"

"The old man's newspaper, the boy had a scrap in hand, and there was a pamphlet sitting alone on the bench opposite."

"Which of the men is carrying a knife?"

She sucked in her breath at that.

"Ah . . . the boy," she replied, for the first time unsure.

"Why do you think that?" he asked gently.

"I . . . I don't know. I guessed that out of all the men we've seen, the boy would be the most likely to have a pocketknife or some such thing. The guards have swords, of course, and my driver a whip, but those aren't knives."

"Mrs. Benning—Phillippa. I need you to be sure. You cannot guess. Understood?"

She nodded, and watched as he leaned back against the bench. The morning was becoming warmer, and Phillippa allowed the leashed and bouncy Bitsy on the ground, where he sniffed at the dirt and the grass and eventually settled on Marcus's boots. Then Phillippa gave in to indulgence and relaxed her rigid posture enough to lean back against the bench as well.

"I might be more adept at knowing what I see if you tell me what I'm looking for," she said softly.

"Beg pardon?" His brows came down.

"Laurent," she stated, and then, knowing she was covering tricky territory, chose her next words with care. "If I knew what he looked like, what he sounds and acts like—you do suspect Laurent of being the maker of this mischief, correct?"

Marcus nodded, but added, "He in collusion with another, possibly, as you so cunningly pointed out the other night."

"Then tell me about him. Laurent. Nemeses likely know more about each other than anyone else, after all."

"I'd ask if that held true for you, but I fear the lengthy explanation of your hatred of Lady Jane and vice versa. No, Mrs.—Phillippa. You're right to ask. It's high time I told you what I suspect, if only as a part of your preparations."

He took a deep breath and readjusted himself on the bench, maybe so he wouldn't have to look at her, maybe so his hand would rest ever so close to hers on the wrought-iron beams. Even if neither were his aim, he achieved both.

"I cannot say if I know more about Laurent than anyone else; I certainly know more than most, though. And in point of fact, Lord Whitford's explanation of Laurent's upbringing is mostly true to what we know. Of course, we didn't learn the man's name until the pistols fell into British possession.

"He's a very refined man, but cold, too. He enjoys the finer things in life. I have no doubt he would be very taken with your"—Marcus waved his hand vaguely in her direction—"sophistication."

Phillippa shrugged. Naturally.

"He was born into aristocracy, but due to the Revolution had that legacy ripped away," Marcus continued. "He spent a certain amount of time in England, and I suspect, although I don't know it for a fact, that he can mimic an upper-class British accent cleanly. But to do so would be to wear the dirt of his enemy, so I doubt he employs it unless necessary.

"I know you think yourself familiar with mortal battle, considering your relationship with Lady Jane, but Phillippa, I beg you to heed me. Laurent is vicious. He will kill me, you, and anyone who gets in his way." Marcus reached out and touched her shoulder gently, but his hand shook from his restraint.

"Do you know what he looks like?" Phillippa asked, knowing that he should, given that the Blue Raven and Laurent's final battle had been face-to-face.

"Pale. Dark hair. Eyes that will look right through you," he responded dully, as if reciting from a textbook rather than his own experience.

He has to sound that way, Phillippa thought. It's the only way to survive the memories.

Phillippa wrenched her gaze away from his, and again took in the calming vista of the park in the morning. The man with the newspaper continued to read. The young gentlemen riding their horses had looped back and were again by the willow tree. Not one had any clue what they were discussing, what darkness lurked at the corners of their daily lives.

"He sounds rather like a vampire." Phillippa shivered, but Marcus made no reply. "I'm due at your brother's," Phillippa said abruptly, shocking Marcus back to the present.

"My brother's?"

"Mariah invited me to help organize donations for the orphanage, and I thought since I was forced out of my comfortable bed this morning in any case . . ."

That earned her a smile, albeit a reluctant one.

"You are being remarkably accommodating this morning," he said. "It's faintly disturbing."

She shot him her sauciest grin. He removed his hand from her shoulder, the cool air falling between them, cracking their brief cocoon in two. Phillippa stood and picked up Bitsy, who had taken to curling himself at Marcus's feet and vibrating there. The moment Phillippa stood, her driver and manservant snapped to attention and readied the carriage for her.

"I wish you a pleasant morning then, Mrs. Benning," Marcus said, seeming to want to say more but hesitating. "Thank you for meeting me."

"It was my pleasure. You should take care of your eye," she said, again restraining herself from reaching up and touching it.

"And you should take care of vampires," he replied with a smile, a small amount of his flippant humor come back to play, as he took her hand and leaned over it.

"Oh, you mean like that one?" she replied innocently.

"Which one?"

She indicated a man who stood behind him, about thirty yards away, pointedly not staring at the pair of them. He was pale, rail thin, as if he'd risen from his deathbed, and he leaned on a gold-headed cane. And yet despite that, he stood with compact fury. Icy eyes stared down the length of the Serpentine, and his hair was so black it shone blue in the morning sunlight.

"Maybe I should invite him to the Benning Ball; he'd certainly fit the dark and mysterious theme," she mused aloud. "He'd make good atmosphere if nothing else—unless, of course, he's the French spy."

Marcus turned and took in the man, whose nonchalance made him conspicuous, and Marcus went so rigid, Phillippa could feel it through their joined hands. Then, when he turned back to Phillippa, his body was still a single tense cord, but his tone was jovial, light. Too light.

"He fits the description of a vampire, certainly, but it's not Laurent. Remember, Phillippa, know, don't guess." And then he kissed her hand and let it go. And she went to her carriage.

But as Phillippa climbed into the phateon and gave directions for Lady Worth's, she noticed that Marcus's eyes did not follow her. He had again turned to look in the direction of where the man with the cane had stood, his brows drawn down, his fists at his side.

But the man with the cane had vanished. There was no one there.

Sixteen

MARCUS took the long way home from the park, the one that took the majority of the day and bisected the city, meandering and doubling back while he ran errands at his bootmaker, his bank, even stopping at a greengrocer and purchasing three oranges, earning suspicious looks for his gentlemanly garb from those in more common attire. It was the rare gentleman who bought his own oranges.

But that small purchase allowed him to pause and made anyone who might be following him pause, also. Marcus forced himself to keep at a reasonable pace. He forced himself to not take corners and alleyways that beckoned as a confusing route for his surreptitious tail, if there was one. He hadn't yet seen anything out of the common way, not a glimpse, not a shadow, but since that morning, the short hairs on the back of his neck stood at rigid attention. His scalp prickled with awareness, and Marcus knew—he *knew*—he was being watched.

But whether or not he was under surveillance, whether or not his steps were being traced, Marcus eventually had to take those inevitable steps home.

The sun was low in the sky, lending a brass glow to everything it touched, reflecting off the windows of his bachelor's lodgings as he climbed the steps. Marcus took rooms at a gentlemen's boardinghouse off of Leicester Square and was happy enough to pay double to be the ground floor's only occupant. Oh, he could have taken rooms at a hotel and made use of their superior amenities, including a kitchen, but he liked his lodgings. They allowed him a little privacy and afforded him a little protection.

His chambers were modest but all that a bachelor required; a sitting room, study, and bedchamber, comfortably furnished, attended to weekly by a lady who was engaged by the landlord to clean the entire house. And after she was properly vetted, he was happy enough to let her dust away—everything except his study, of course. That was kept locked with two different kinds of bolts.

Or at least, it was supposed to be.

The study door was closed, everything seemed as it should, except for the tumbler of the second set of locks. It was fractionally off its vertical alignment. Marcus approached it cautiously, quietly, every step across the wooden floor threatening to squeak under his weight. He had reached for the door handle, he turned his hand—

When suddenly, from behind him, he saw it.

A brief shadow, a flicker outside his apartment's front door.

Silently, quick as a cat in the night, Marcus moved from the study door across the hall. The shadow twitched under the door again. Marcus felt under his coat for the pistol that was strapped to his side.

Silently, he counted to three, then wrenched the door open.

"Oh, thank goodness. Mr. Worth, could you help me with these boxes?"

The reedy voice of Leslie Farmapple rang out—or at least Marcus though it was Leslie. It was difficult to tell, hidden as he was underneath a pile of nearly unmanageable boxes in his arms, which wobbled as he shifted his balance.

"Leslie, is that you?"

"Yes, Mr. Worth," was the muffled reply. "Please, assist me, if you would!"

"Oh, of course! But what are all these boxes?"

"These," a flushed and harried Leslie said as Marcus took a box off the top of the pile, "are the contents of your desk. Mr. Crawley noticed it was still in disarray, so Sterling insisted it be cleaned out and delivered to you."

"There was no need, Leslie. I would have gotten them myself," Marcus said, his glance falling back across the hall to the study door. Strangely, nothing looked amiss from this light.

Leslie did not notice (or could not see) Marcus's preoccupation, and as such, staggered past him into the flat's hallway. "Yes, well, I think Sterling rather hoped to avoid that possibility," Leslie said grumpily as he dropped the boxes on the hallway floor with a thud. "I knew you had a remarkable amount of mess," he said disapprovingly, "but really, you could have tried some decipherable system of management."

"Yes, Leslie." Marcus sighed. "But it hardly matters now, doesn't it?"

Leslie flushed, chagrined. "Just so you know . . ." He hesitated, looked about him, and started again. "Just so you know, I think Fieldstone gave you a bit of a bad brush. Seemed hastily done."

Marcus just shook his head. "Perhaps it was too long overdue. But thank you, Leslie. And I'm sorry I never kept my desk neat enough for your liking."

Leslie smiled ruefully. "Yes, well, I doubt a messy desk would have won or lost us a war. Good day, Mr. Worth." He tipped his hat. "I don't know if we should meet again. But I hope so."

"Good day, Leslie." Marcus extended his hand, somewhat shocking the secretary, who cautiously shook it. "I'm certain we shall."

As Leslie Farmapple let himself of out the building and into the falling evening, Marcus shut his front door and turned back to his quiet apartments.

And was immediately slammed up against the wall.

"I," growled a cold and raspy voice, "am going to kill you."

He clutched a gold-headed, polished black cane as the fists that dug into Marcus's coat and shirtfront pressed hard white knuckles into his shoulders, pinning his arms to his sides.

But not his legs.

Marcus kicked out, his boot connecting with the black-haired man's shin just hard enough to loosen that man's footing. Marcus took advantage, leveraging his strength to push back, firing himself off the wall, forcing the man backward, marching him across the hall and pining him against the study door.

"Not a terribly fond greeting," Marcus hissed.

The man from the park sneered back at him. "You meddling fool," he bit out before he landed a series of short quick blows to Marcus's left side, the only place his arms could reach. Marcus responded by pressing his assailant harder into the wall, slamming him back.

"You don't want to play fair? Fine." Marcus grunted as he reached down and pressed hard against the man's thigh, feeling the scar that he knew was there.

The dark-haired man turned even paler as he cried out in pain. Marcus let him free as he slumped to the floor.

"That . . . hurt . . ." he said from the floor, his breath coming back to him slowly.

"You hit me in my wounds, I'll hit you in yours," Marcus replied, standing back and folding his arms across his chest.

"Mine's fresher. Graham would kill you if he saw you pull such a dirty trick."

"Yes, well, Graham's not here. And you're supposed to be in the country."

"What happened to your eye?" the man asked, peering up at Marcus.

"Nothing worthy of note," Marcus replied truthfully. "I got boxed by a pimp in Whitechapel."

"Tsk, tsk, Marcus, you used to have better taste."

"I was doing research, Byrne." He said sardonically, as he bent down and offered his hand. "Come on. You look like you could use some tea."

"I'd like an explanation better—such as why I'm hearing reports of the Blue Raven running around town," he growled, his cold voice condemning now, his black-winged eyebrows painted with fury.

Marcus sighed. "That might require more than tea."

And as such, Marcus escorted Byrne Worth, Marcus's second-eldest brother—and incidentally, the Blue Raven—into his small, messy study.

An explanation, indeed.

Marcus and Byrne had been a team, almost from the moment of Marcus's birth. Graham, their eldest brother, was already seven when Byrne came along, and quite grown-up, he would not hesitate to tell people then. Graham observed such a superior air with his baby brother that Byrne could not consider him a companion. But Marcus, just two years younger, fit the bill nicely.

Byrne had been born with the dramatic good looks of jet black hair—hair so black it shone blue—and piercing ice blue eyes, along with a cynicism that played well with his thirst for adventure. Marcus had been the wrangly, scroungy one, in adolescence too tall to be used to his body, and nothing at all piercing about his open, good-humored demeanor.

One could suppose that such differences of looks and temperament would hold a pair of brothers apart, but in fact, they were generally glued together, able to read each other's thoughts with a high degree of accuracy, and an unbreakable bond of trust.

When one was having trouble with mathematics, it was natural that he would seek assistance from the other.

When one decided to purchase a commission, it was natural that the other would, too.

And when Byrne became a spy, it was natural that Marcus became his field contact, the person who gathered and sorted all of his information, discovered where and for what he'd be needed next.

Of course, that wasn't the original plan. Both Marcus and Byrne had been commissioned to the Seventeenth Regiment of His Majesty's army, whose movements during the long war with France had ranged from the Loire Valley, to over the Pyrenees and into Spain. And it was in Spain that Marcus and Byrne intercepted their first enemy missive.

It hadn't been difficult, really. The little Spaniard was barely more than a boy, running around the village. But when Byrne and Marcus saw him pick up a dirty piece of parchment from a table in a pub and glance suspiciously around to see if he was being watched, Byrne decided to follow. And as such, Marcus followed Byrne.

It was Byrne who stole into the derelict mansion that the boy snuck into and who came away with the piece of paper and information on who was there, for it was Byrne's dark hair, then-tan complexion, and passable Spanish that allowed him to momentarily pass as a fellow countryman to anyone who he might encounter. But it was Marcus who was able to decipher the information and tell their battalion commander exactly what it meant, which resulted in saving the lives of nearly every man in the regiment.

And that's how they succeeded. When the Home Office got wind of their exploits, they were reassigned their commissions, this time, to be working directly for the War Department. It didn't change much in how they went about their days; they were still with the Seventeenth Regiment, using its movements as a mask for theirs.

Byrne, for one, was having the time of his life, poking his nose into things, embedding himself for weeks at a time in little villages (his Spanish improved, and his French had always been impeccable), gleaning scraps of information that he brought back to Marcus, who put the sometimes inscrutable puzzle together. They, especially after Marcus took a short knife in his side, began to define their roles more cleanly: Byrne the man of action, and Marcus the man of thought.

It was difficult to say who invented the Blue Raven persona: Marcus or Byrne. But the reason why was easier to answer: They'd been asked to.

Marcus had been sent back to London in the winter of 1812 for some weeks to recuperate from his wound. There, while he was bored out of his mind and interred with Graham and his new bride Mariah, Marcus was asked by the Home Office to write up reports of some of his and Byrne's adventures, to give the War Department and Parliament some idea as to the progress on the Continent. Unwilling to commit his or his brother's name to the pages of an official document, Marcus, playing on his brother's name and looks, assigned him an alias: the Blue Raven. He wrote in as official a tone as he could manage, but actions have a way of overcoming the constraints of vocabulary, and the official reports read something like very dry adventure stories.

Imagine Marcus's surprise when, over his morning breakfast, he opened the *Times* and discovered one of his reports, printed in whole.

In subsequent days, it was followed by another, and another.

The response had been ecstatic: 1812 had not been an easy year; two wars were being fought, and fatigue was settling over the public. The Blue Raven had a way of keeping the population from despair. Just the name in print set tongues wagging, which the government translated into flag-waving and bond-buying.

When Marcus returned to the front and to Byrne, the stories continued in the press: some close to true, and some so obviously fabricated that when a months-old newspaper found its way to their eyes, Byrne and Marcus would laugh themselves silly over it.

They had never told Graham. Graham had succeeded their father to the title by the age of seventeen, and soon his condescending demeanor became fact. He was worried sick when both brothers took commissions. If he had known that one was the notorious Blue Raven and the other his inventor, he would have gone mad. So it was Byrne and Marcus's secret. It became a thread in the fabric that held them together.

Byrne had never, in all their years as brothers and as partners, doubted Marcus: his intentions, his information, or his strength of purpose.

Until now.

"Fieldstone was right to fire you; you've gone mad." Byrne grunted as he refilled his glass from the flask Marcus kept in his study desk. Marcus shook his head slowly. Even to his own ears, the story of his suspicions and subsequent actions that he had just finished telling his brother was on the far side of ridiculous, but he had hoped that Byrne, at least, would not have doubted him.

"How many times have I been wrong, Byrne?" Marcus asked pointedly. "How many? Out of all the information I ever collected or sifted through, I can only recall being wrong once, and that was when you ended up in a dairy field in the middle of Belgium, which actually saved you from walking into a sniper's nest." Marcus downed his own brandy.

Byrne shot his brother a chilling look.

"I didn't say you were wrong, Marcus, I said you've gone mad," he replied. "You confided your suspicions to Fieldstone—within earshot of a civilian?"

Marcus had the grace to look sheepish.

"And," Byrne continued, his aggravation adding bitter juice to his rising voice, "you have since enlisted that civilian in your schemes? And who is this civilian, one might ask—not a man of learning or of trade, not even a person of discretion. No, you decided to involve the bright, gay, light-headed Phillippa Benning!"

Marcus couldn't fault his brother's thunderous look. It must have been a somewhat rude awakening to be holed up at one's cottage in the Lake District, only to be assaulted by the rumor that you were actually running around London dockside.

For indeed, a rumor had snaked its way out from London proper, reaching any ear willing to listen. Maybe it was Johnny Dicks turning up dead. Maybe it was the black feathers raining down at the Whitford Banquet. Maybe it was the blue and black invitations Phillippa had circulated, promising intrigue and secrets revealed at the Benning Ball, but somehow, someway, the words "the Blue Raven" were being whispered on the breeze throughout England.

And as for Byrne, so pale, so cynical, and so damned tired, the notion of his resurrection set his expression to black.

Especially considering how close he was hovering at the edge of existence.

Byrne had not returned from the wars the same brash young man he had been upon leaving for them. To Marcus's mind, the moment he began to notice a change was the moment he returned to the regiment, having recovered from the stab wound in his side. Byrne had become more protective. Oh, he still laughed, he still had his normal flair, but it was as if he had realized that in the thrill of his escapades, people could get hurt. But the blackness descended like a curtain once the ruthless specter of Laurent came into their lives.

Marcus had thought that with the end of the war and the subsequent end of Laurent, Byrne would return to his old self. Instead, the bullet that Marcus had had to pull out of his brother's leg ripped through more than bone and muscle. The wound had never fully healed, and it left Byrne in constant pain and constantly seeking ways to alleviate it.

The lowest point was when, after having been missing for three days, Marcus pulled Byrne out of an opium den on the south side of the Thames, barely breathing, wasted away to almost nothing.

They kept him home for three weeks before Byrne threatened to go stark raving mad. It was then decided that Byrne, having inherited a cottage in the Lake District from a Great-aunt Lowe, would go to the country to recuperate, removing him from the vices and addictions that were consuming him.

But given Byrne's current skeletal appearance, Marcus feared the months of solitude had only heightened his demons.

"Why are you doing this?" Byrne's voice cracked and raged. "Why are you tearing into these old wounds—for a woman? A blond, empty-headed piece of vanity like Phillippa Benning."

"You're being exceedingly unfair to someone you haven't met. However," Marcus continued, staving off what he was certain would be a caustic reply from his brother, "the evidence is there. Fieldstone refused to see it. Hell, everyone refused to see it. Except her."

"She's using you. Actually, she's using *me*, because she's using you thinking that you're me. And *dammit*, Marcus," Byrne yelled, his anger finally catching up to him, "why didn't you send for me? Why did you take this on yourself?"

"Because you're not well," Marcus stated quietly.

"Bloody right, I'm not well, but it's not your place to do this! Its not your job—"

"Not my job!?" Marcus exploded, oversetting a small table in his anger. "Then, tell me, *brother*, what was I supposed to do? You were hurt—and lost. And suddenly, this man, this *thing* that was supposed to be buried in salted earth is back. If not my job, whose job is it? It can't be you. Last time it nearly killed you—"

"Maybe it should have!" Byrne yelled back, rising swiftly.

Marcus froze.

Indeed, Byrne had come back from the war a changed man. But this . . . this was something altogether different.

"Byrne," Marcus breathed his brother's name. But Byrne shook it off, letting that road remain untraveled.

"I'm still here. I'm the one who has to face this—whatever it is."

"Not alone. You've never had to face it alone."

"I did that day!" Byrne replied, sinking into his chair. "I had to walk the length of that little village alone. I went into that inn alone. And, acting on information *you gave me*, I stood five feet away from Laurent, and I shot him. I killed him, and I plucked the pistol from his hand. And now you tell me he is still alive!"

"I know it seems impossible—"

"It is impossible." Byrne rose, too anxious to stay still, and began pacing the length of the study, his cane offering small assistance. "He spoke with me. He knew who I was. He expected me. He was Laurent."

Marcus knew why this one death haunted his brother. Because, in all the battles they had fought, in all the times they had fired their pistols to save their own lives, this was the only time they had committed murder.

The war had been over for nearly a fortnight. Surrenders had been made and accepted. But Laurent, he still ran free.

The man had been a particularly bloodthirsty kind of evil. He had no compunction in killing an informant once the information was in hand, even when restraining said informant would have allowed ample time for his escape. He taunted Byrne and Marcus, sneering whispers about plucking and serving ravens to his Emperor. And he slaughtered those who got in his way.

And so when, before they could board a ship for home, a scrap of information had reached Marcus about a man matching Laurent's description, holed up in a fish's fin, Marcus and Byrne had decided that it was for the good of two nations that this lead was pursued.

And while it was Byrne who walked that road, who shot that pistol, it was Marcus who led him to it. And it was Marcus who found his brother, unconscious from blood loss, sheltered under a dinghy beached onshore, as the tide crept in.

Marcus had wanted Laurent dead and was satisfied that he was—up until the moment that Johnny Dicks told him otherwise.

"I meant to spare you this," Marcus said quietly, watching his brother continue to pace.

"Yes." His brother's voice dripped with disdain. "It's so much easier to seduce Mrs. Benning without the actual Blue Raven around."

"That's not what this is about." Marcus's voice became low and cold.

"Are you certain of that? You looked rather cozy this morning, and from what I hear, she's not one to allow someone like you to cozy up to her. Without incentive."

"She," Marcus said emphatically, "actually came up with a plan. *She* has allowed me entrée into a world that would have found me out had I gone undercover to infiltrate it. *She* actually has a brain, with a breadth of ability that would shock you. Her capacity for understanding what is important to this scheme is beyond yours, so I would be very careful what you say about Philippa Benning."

Marcus, in his rush to make his point clear, had come to hover over his brother. They stood toe-to-toe, but Marcus had always had the advantage of height. However, it was Byrne who in this instance had the advantage of understanding his brother.

A small smile turned at the corners of Byrne's mouth, as Marcus, numb, slowly began to realize what he had just said—or not said.

"Marcus, you want to take a turn chasing that tail, be my guest, but don't drag me or the Blue Raven into it."

And with that, Byrne stood and headed toward the door.

"Unless you have a spare pallet here, I'm going to call on Graham and Mariah; they'll put me up."

His hand had reached the door handle when Marcus's next words stilled its movement.

"He left his mark at the Whitford Banquet."

Byrne turned slowly.

"His mark?"

"Laurent. He managed to slaughter a few dozen ravens in a pie and stole your pistols out of Whitford's gallery."

Byrne swore softly. "That bugger put the blasted things on display?"

"Did you expect him not to? They're the jewel of his collection," Marcus answered drily.

"I didn't expect anything. I never wanted to hear of the damn things again," Byrne mumbled. Then, after what Marcus considered to be a significant pause, Byrne asked, "And Fieldstone still ignores you?"

Marcus shot a glance over to the boxes Leslie had dropped off not too long ago, residing on top of his disorganized and yet in order desk. "As you see," he replied.

Byrne sighed deeply. "What is the next event on this list?"

Marcus felt the tension that had knotted his stomach slip away. He managed to hold in his sigh of relief.

"The Hampshires' Racing Party," he answered evenly.

"And your Mrs. Benning has arranged admission for us?"

"No," Marcus replied, causing Byrne to look up. "She has arranged an invitation for me. But I'm certain it can be expanded to include you."

Byrne paused for a moment, leaned back against the door, contemplative. Marcus took the opportunity to make his final appeal.

"You have to trust me, Byrne," he intoned seriously. "I'm right about this."

"You're not infallible," Byrne retorted. "You *think* it's Laurent, because he called me a pigeon. You don't *know.* You think the Security section is involved—because of . . . of wax and paper, for God's sake! But you certainly don't know. You can't think, Marcus, you have to know. You told me that."

"I'm well aware," Marcus replied.

Byrne sighed, began rolling his cane between his hand. "All right," he conceded. "The Racing Party—I can try to sneak in as an underbutler or a waiter—houses always take on extra staff for large parties."

"You can barely stand," Marcus argued.

"I'm going," Byrne commanded. "If you're right, we'll find

out, but if you're wrong, I'd know it, and I can go back to my cottage in peace."

So that was it. Byrne didn't believe him. He thought he was paranoid, or worse, using the Blue Raven to seduce a woman, nothing more. The fracture that existed between the once inseparable brothers cracked deeper.

"Fine," Marcus conceded, "but you'll never pass as a servant with that cane." He regarded his brother keenly. "Why not go as yourself? We'll see about securing you an invitation." And then, off his brother's look, "You're in London society. You're far more likely to run into someone you know."

Byrne smiled ruefully. "I haven't gone out as myself in years."

Marcus's grin mirrored his brother's. "Give it a chance. Who knows? Could be your best disguise yet."

Byrne weighed his options. "I'm not dancing," he warned.

"I'll send out a decree to that effect." Marcus joined his brother at the door.

"Come on, I'll go over to Graham's with you. Keep Mariah from smothering you immediately." He gave Byrne a slap on the shoulder, but Byrne remained still.

"Marcus," Byrne ventured, his hesitation marking his fear of what he was about to say. "If Laurent is still alive—and I'm not saying he is—but if he's still alive, you've been wrong twice."

Seventeen

LORD and Lady Hampshire, oddly enough, did not reside in Hampshire.

Their family seat was near Waltham Abbey, in Essex, a comfortable drive from the hustle and bustle of London. They kept a lovely house in town, of course, as Lord Hampshire was active in the House of Lords, but he enjoyed his weekends at Hampshire House, where he had converted a run-down tenant farm into the foremost horse breeding program in the country, the largest outside of Newmarket, Britain's racing hub. Indeed, Lord Hampshire enjoyed his weekends of leisure, spending time hauling hay, mucking stalls, pretending his only cares were the state of his stables and the breeding of his horses. However, upon Lord Hampshire's marriage, he found his weekends considerably altered.

Lady Hampshire was, and always had been, a social creature. Her husband knew this before he married her but thought that her youthful vivacity would calm once she was settled with children.

It did not.

Lady Hampshire loved London, her friends, her life. However, she also loved her husband dearly, and he her, and the two grumbled profusely about sleeping without the soft snores of the other close by. Therefore, when Lord Hampshire went to Hampshire House in Waltham Abbey, his wife accompanied him.

And generally several of her closest friends accompanied her.

It began innocently enough. Lady Hampshire would tell her husband, earlier in the week, that she thought her friend Mrs. Such-and-Such could do with a spell in the country. "Her color, you see," she would say, and Lord Hampshire would be so touched by his wife's concern for her friend, he would offer that she accompany them to Hampshire House that weekend. But by the time the coach was rigged for the three-hour drive, four other friends had voiced their need for country air, and suddenly an entire entourage of coaches and servants were following the Hampshires out of town on Friday and back into town the following Monday.

This pattern repeated itself all throughout the Season until Lord Hampshire finally put his foot down. His weekend retreats had become a noisy traveling circus! His household was overturned weekly! His household store of jams and jellies was nearly depleted! His stables, which housed prizewinning breeding stock, horses commissioned by His Majesty's cavalry, had become so confused by the preponderance of new people gadding about, they were skittish at the sounds of approaching carriage wheels! If his wife couldn't bear to be without her friends for one weekend, then he would go to Hampshire House alone!

After a miserable weekend spent apart, Lord and Lady Hampshire struck a compromise. There would be peace back at Hampshire House, and she would be limited to inviting people to one weekend per Season.

But what a weekend it would be.

Combining their two great loves, horses and society, the Hampshires' Racing Party began. Lady Hampshire narrowed down her closest hundred or so friends to invite to a weekend of sport, competition, and delights. It was just enough time to rejuvenate away from the dirt and grime of the city, but short enough so no one would be in danger of missing anything. Lord Hampshire, in turn, constructed a massive racing pavilion on their land, as grand as Ascot, with Palladian villas surrounding the track. Other private breeding farms were invited to try out their stock, but it was Lord Hampshire's unequaled stables that tended to rule the day.

Soon enough the Hampshires' Racing Party took on a sort of cachet as the pre-Newmarket racing event. There were no purses or prizes, but if your horse did well on Lord Hampshire's track, its odds for taking the thousand guineas on the Rowley Mile improved greatly.

The house was flooded with visitors starting on Friday evening, with the races themselves occurring on Saturday from first light to sundown. At luncheon, some of the guests were invited to compete in their own races: three-legged, riding backwards, any foolishness that could be wagered on and laughed over. If some ladies or gentlemen were not as horse-mad as the Hampshires or many of their guests, they were not allowed to be bored—oh no. There was an unending array of daylight delights afforded them, from gossip to tea to croquet to bowling. Hampshire House was fronted by a small lake for those who enjoyed fishing, and a large hedge maze had been constructed in the rear, losing several young giggling maidens annually, who had to be rescued by their beaux.

But 'twas when Saturday night fell that the Hampshires' Racing Party earned its fantastic reputation.

Fireworks were imported from the best warehouses in China designed to light the sky in equine shapes. Feasts of the local farmers' rustic cuisine graced the table. There was dancing, of course, in a ballroom grander in scale than many people's London residences. Three separate orchestras were hired to play, so there would be no end to the music or the night. And with literally a hundred places to hide in the house and on the grounds, merrymaking and mischief ensued in no small measure.

Which was one of the many things that worried Marcus.

He and Byrne pulled up in Graham's carriage (Mariah would not hear of them riding out on horseback especially with Byrne's injury) to the warm, redbrick manor, built among the neat, clean lines of Georgian architecture, just as the summer sun dipped below the horizon. They were already exhausted by the nearly hour-long wait it took for their carriage to reach the front of the line.

"This is madness," Byrne grumbled under his breath, "we should have just snuck in as servants."

"Your leg's a dead giveaway," Marcus countered diplomatically.

"I could handle walking without a cane for a few days . . ." Byrne argued.

"And then be required to walk with one for the rest of your life? You're a bigger idiot than I took you for. Besides," he continued before Byrne could snap back, "too many people here already know me."

"Thanks to Mrs. Benning," Byrne replied irritably, his frown replaced by a scowl.

"Does it go against your principles as a spy to walk in the front door?" Marcus asked. "Sometimes its best to hide in plain sight, you know."

But Byrne simply deepened his black look as the carriage door was pulled open by a liveried footman. Byrne disembarked, leaning heavily on his cane, taking deep gulps of air into his skeletal frame.

It had been a year, Marcus thought. Physically, he should be whole by now.

Only one small trunk of clothes between them, it was quickly taken by another footman up into the house, as yet another footman directed their driver to the carriage house and stables.

"There must be five hundred people here, counting the staff," Byrne surmised.

"Counting all the racers, their breeders, their jockeys, and the locals that will come to watch tomorrow, I'd put it closer to a thousand," Marcus revised, as they stepped into the grand main foyer.

Hampshire House was a truly impressive structure, fluted marble columns flanking the entryway, leading into a rose marble hall, whose ceiling stretched to the second story. The cold stone surface of the walls was relieved only by a score of paintings, each depicting horses either grazing contentedly in the field or running like the wind. Horse-mad, indeed, Marcus thought, as he stepped closer to one particular painting that depicted two rather, er, amorous beasts in either a fight for their lives or a different kind of tussle altogether.

The grand staircase was the centerpiece of the room and currently occupied by no fewer than two dozen bodies, either carting luggage up the stairs or processing grandly down it. One of the downward procession, a lady of middle years with a wide smile, greeted Marcus upon spying him.

"Mr. Worth!" Lady Hampshire said in surprisingly calm tones. Amid the chaos that surrounded her, she was calm and collected, reveling in the bustle of her own creation.

Marcus turned and bowed smartly to their hostess. "Lady Hampshire. A pleasure. May I introduce my brother, Byrne?"

"Mr. Worth," she said turning to Byrne, eyeing his pallor, "very pleased to meet you. I've been told you recently returned from the country."

"Yes, only to find my brother heading for it. Thank you for accommodating me at such short notice."

But their pleasantries were interrupted by the arrival of another carriage, with occupants far more prestigious than Marcus and his brother, causing Lady Hampshire to gracefully excuse herself to greet the newly arrived.

Turning toward the stairs, they began their ascent, only to be stopped by Mrs. Tottendale.

"Finally," that good lady said. "I've been waiting for all this time; now I can go join everyone else in the parlor."

"Waiting for us, ma'am?" Byrne inquired, his voice cold and

sharp. Marcus could see that Byrne's sense of danger had spiked upon being greeted thusly, his entire body tensing for fight or flight. He inserted himself in between his brother and Totty.

"Byrne, this is Mrs. Tottendale, companion to Mrs. Benning," Marcus said calmly, his eyes never leaving his brother's face.

"No, not you." Totty said, by way of reply. "I've been sent to tell the girls when *that one* arrived."

She flung a long, bony hand in the direction of the entryway, where Lady Hampshire and the Marquis of Broughton were laughing gaily over some flippant remark of his. Marcus's eyes narrowed, as he felt his body tense in annoyance. The smarmy git, he thought. Too polished by half, he told himself, Phillippa would have nothing to do, nothing to work on with him.

"You'd think I was some sort of servant girl," Totty continued, oblivious to the effect of her remarks, "seeing as how I was dispatched like a spy in the night, simply to report back to my betters."

"Mrs. Tottendale," Byrne replied, coming to the aid of his suddenly mute brother, "no one would ever dare mistake you for a servant." He bowed over her hand.

"Hmph. Or a girl for that matter," she finished for him, earning a clipped smile from Byrne. Totty turned to go, only to be called back by Marcus, who had calmed his pulse enough to speak.

"Mrs. Tottendale, would you be so good as to let Mrs. Benning know that we have arrived as well?"

"No need for that," Totty replied. "She spied your carriage in the drive over a half hour ago."

Indeed, Phillippa had spied the Worth family carriage as it turned into the drive. She had been able to do this because for the preceding three hours, she had done nothing but chatter with the ladies in the main salon, keeping up conversation while keeping her eyes glued to the large glazed windows and the slow inch of traffic up to the main doors.

It had not gone unnoticed.

"Phillippa, you simply must tear your gaze away from the windows," Nora said, placing down her teacup. And then, loudly, for the benefit of the rest of the room, "The Marquis of Broughton will be here soon enough."

Phillippa had to smother her surprise. Nora thought all this time she had been holding vigil for Broughton, and in truth she had nearly forgotten about him.

The rest of the ladies in the room sent up a wave of titters, causing Phillippa to blush. Luckily, she did this most becomingly. It was no secret that every day for the past week, Broughton had come to call at Phillippa's house. He did this, of course, during calling hours and was never alone with her, but his marked attentiveness was noticed by the foremost gossips of the Ton.

Nora, now in a hush to her friend, whispered, "I sent Totty as a lookout; she'll let us know when he arrives." Then, handing a tray of biscuits to Phillippa, Nora shot her friend a smirk. "Lady Jane and her father are not set to arrive until tomorrow morning; you'll have Broughton to yourself all evening."

If this was meant to make Phillippa calmer, it did not have that effect. Phillippa might be persuaded of Broughton's preference for her, if only she was not aware of the fact that every day this week, after he had finished calling on her, he repaired directly to call upon Lady Jane. As such, if she were to win against the lovely Lady Jane and secure him, Broughton might expect that tonight she make good on her innuendos.

But Phillippa's mind was far more occupied with Marcus Worth and the danger that lurked here at this party. Oh, how could no one else see it?

The Whitford Banquet had been the talk of everywhere for a week now. Did no one fear a reprisal of the same calamity here at the Hampshires' Racing Party? For her part, Phillippa wished for nothing more than to search Lady Hampshire's rooms and discover the guest list, seeing if she could put together any suspicious persons with those who were at the Whitford Banquet.

As it was, she was simply keeping her eyes open, cataloguing every carriage that came up the drive, every face that met her eye.

But she only discovered people she already knew.

This changed almost immediately.

An hour after Totty returned to the salon, breathlessly reaching for her favorite "strong" tea and announcing the arrival of the Marquis of Broughton to the assembled ladies, causing no few looks to be thrown her way, the ladies joined the gentlemen in the main parlor (not to be confused with the second parlor, the blue parlor, any of the sitting rooms, or the ladies' salon) to await the call to dine.

Tonight was only Friday; it was meant to be a quiet evening, with supper and cards and some small musical amusements, as the racing began very early the next morning. As such, it was an informal meal, men forgoing their silk knee breeches for plainer satin, and ladies only wearing their second-best diamond necklaces.

Phillippa entered the main parlor to her usual acclaim, immediately began searching the room for Marcus, and found him chatting in low tones with . . .

Could it be?

He had the dark hair, so black it shone blue. He had the pale countenance and the cane. But what was the man from the park that day doing with Marcus?

"Mrs. Benning," Marcus said, as she floated toward them. "May I introduce my brother, Byrne."

A twinge of shock flitted down her spine. "Your brother."

"Yes," the dark haired man, Marcus's brother, replied. "I understand I have you to thank for the invitation." He bowed sharply, leaning on his cane.

"You . . . you have me at some disadvantage, I'm afraid. When Mar—Mr. Worth told me his brother had expressed an interest in coming to the Racing Party, I assumed he meant Lord Worth and Mariah."

Marcus cleared his throat. "Byrne is my second eldest brother, ma'am. He—"

"He was in the park that morning," Phillippa finished for him.

"You'll have to excuse him for that; he'd come all the way from the country just that day. He . . . he . . ."

". . . didn't expect to see you with Marcus," Byrne curtly finished for him, letting his eyes roam the rest of the room, as if he had better things to do than converse with her.

Phillippa felt her hackles rise. What did he mean by that? That she was not good enough to be seen with his brother or vice versa? Either was an insult, and neither suited her temper today. But luckily, at that moment, supper was announced, and since Broughton had not come down yet, Phillippa allowed Marcus to escort her into the dining room. His brother trailed behind, off in his own little world.

"Marcus," Phillippa took the opportunity to whisper, "I have kept my eyes open for anyone new, and I have seen nothing. Of course, I have not been belowstairs . . ." She looked down briefly at his hand and placed hers in the crook of his arm. "This place is massive; he could be hiding anywhere," she continued. "The stables, the hedge maze, the forecourt, the hunting box . . ."

"We—Byrne and I—will search tonight, once everyone's asleep, but I doubt anything will occur before tomorrow."

To Phillippa's mind, Byrne could barely hold himself upright, let alone patrol, but she let it go.

"Why tomorrow?"

"Because that's when there will be the most commotion, and at the party, I'm assuming many people will be drinking and letting their guards down in that respect," he whispered back, leaning his head down to her ear. She could feel his breath on her neck, stirring the soft tendrils that danced at its nape.

She looked behind her and caught Byrne's eye, regarding them intently.

"Marcus," she breathed, her heart pounding, "your brother Byrne. Can he be trusted?"

"Implicitly." Marcus returned immediately, slightly affronted tones to his voice.

"What I mean is, does he know about"—she pitched her voice even lower, barely more than mouthing the words—"the Blue Raven?"

Marcus looked at her for a moment, his eye catching hers for the briefest of seconds. "Yes," he replied, "he's the only one who does."

❧

Dinner was a gay affair for those who had no worries beyond wagering on what horse would win the three-year-old race tomorrow or what frock would look best in the morning sunlight at the racing pavilion. But for the three at the table who had other worries, dinner was slow torture, a dance of controlled movements to keep one from going mad.

Phillippa, while her concerns were likely the largest, had the most controlled mask, used as she was to hiding her emotions in society. She had been seated across from Broughton, who deigned to arrive just in time for the first course. But his lateness was forgiven as fashionable as soon as he flashed his smile at the hostess and turned his soulful eyes to Phillippa. He really did have very smooth manners, she thought to herself, as he folded his superior physique gracefully into his chair. A slow wink came to his eye, and in spite of her mind racing on other far more serious subjects, Phillippa could not help the smile that came to her lips. He was like a boy, she thought, all roguish charm and confidence. But while her dinner partner was all charm and smiles, her conversation faltered slightly, trying to categorize everyone around the table.

Mrs. Hurston, her turban, and Thomas Hurston, her son, both of whom would never have anything to do with foreign politics.

Lord and Lady Overton, who, if memory served, lived in Greece for two years some time ago; could they have sympathizer leanings?

The Quayles, the Finches, Lord and Lady Huffington, who had brought their friend Mr. Crawley, Lord Sterling and Penny, along with the Dunninghams, the Clovers . . . all of them people she was acquainted with, people she could not suspect!

Unfortunately, as Marcus was seated as far from her as mathematically possible, there was no one with whom she could share her concerns, and therefore, her discomposure did not go unnoticed.

"Mrs. Benning?" Broughton whispered from across the table. "Are you quite well?"

"Hm? Oh, my lord, of course I'm well. I simply was trying to recall . . . what the name of that particular tie you're wearing is called."

"This?" he lazily fingered his cravat and its multitude of knots, meant to look haphazard, but actually quite complicated. "It's called the Dove's Feather. See how it folds like the vanes of a feather? I invented it."

"Well that's very smart of you." She smiled at him, letting a little heat into her gaze. "But what if your cravat is not white? What if your necktie is blue, or orange, or black?"

He smiled back at her, the heat in his gaze matching her own. "Well, if its blue, we shall call it the Bluebird. If it is orange, the Oriole." She wrinkled her nose at that, causing him to laugh. "And if it is black, the Crow."

"Oh no, not the Crow!" Nora spoke from two seats down. "Call it the Raven. It's far more romantic."

Broughton shot a smile to Nora, declaring, "For you, Miss De Regis, the Raven it is. But I warn you, I hold the patent. No one will ever know the secret to the Raven."

Phillippa couldn't help it; she shot a look down the table, finding Marcus's gaze on hers.

No, no one ever would know the secret to the Raven.

Except her, she thought with a warm thrill.

Until the Benning Ball, that is. The moment that thought crossed her mind, that warmth left her. She was to reveal the secret of the Blue Raven; it was going to be her shining moment; her history would be written.

So why did the thought no longer excite her mind the way it once did?

Her face must have reflected her unusual apprehension, because Marcus suddenly gave a small quirk of his brow, concern shadowing his features. Immediately, Phillippa put her smile back on and refused to think in such a melancholy fashion. Really, it likely did her features no good to be caught thinking.

And as such, she turned her attention back to Broughton and to the comfort of frivolity.

Upon exiting the dining room, leaving the men to their port, the women repaired again to the main parlor, leaving Phillippa in a quandary. She knew what Broughton was expecting of her. He had been sending her heated looks and pointed conversation all evening. His eyes had followed her form like a lion hunting its prey as she exited the room. However, her heart, which should not have entered into the equation, was suddenly forestalling her assignation with Broughton. It was not her emotions, she told herself; it was some other small feeling entirely: if Marcus and Byrne were going to search the premises that evening, she'd be damned if she was going to let them go alone.

So she needed some excuse to retire early—and alone. Illness was the easiest, and the one with a foundation already laid.

For the next twenty minutes, Phillippa acted unfocused, fractured. And it had not gone unnoticed that she had been discomfited at dinner.

"Darling, are you quite well?" Totty asked, her gaze suspicious over the rim of her glass.

Lady Hampshire had decided that there would be some music

that evening, and until the gentlemen emerged from their masculine conversation, she allowed the younger ladies to practice their pianoforte and vocal exercises in the drawing room. Therefore, Totty had to raise her voice a bit above normal to be heard. And Phillippa had to raise her voice back.

"Totty, I'm afraid I've a bit of a headache—" she began, interrupted by Totty's nodding.

"God, yes, terribly loud in here. Can't understand anyone with the caterwauling going on." Unfortunately, just before Totty said "caterwauling," the cacophony came to an abrupt halt, causing no small amount of embarrassment for Totty, and Miss Louisa Dunningham and Miss Penny Sterling, who were the creators of the noise, and, of course, everyone in between.

Phillippa caught a slight smirk from Nora, as Louisa and Penny began to awkwardly pack up their music. With a disapproving frown at Nora, Phillippa said, a bit lower now, although their conversation became the focus of everyone, "No, it isn't that. In fact, I found the music rather lovely, soothing in its way. No, I'm afraid, the, ah, travel from this morning has finally worn me out. I'll take my leave."

Penny and Louisa, after letting out visible sighs of relief, returned to their music. And Phillippa, assisted by Totty and Nora, excused themselves from the room.

"Phillippa, how could you!" Nora exclaimed as soon as they were out in the hall. "There's nothing as dreadfully dull as a debutante bent on musical display; you told me so yourself!"

"Quite right, Nora," Phillippa said patiently, "and if it had been anyone other than Louisa Dunningham, I would have let it be, but truth be told, she is a very accomplished soprano."

"Well," Nora, hemmed, knowing fully of Phillippa's rightness but unwilling to admit to it.

"I should hate to ruin her confidence on that score, don't you agree, Totty?" Phillippa asked, turning to her astonished companion.

"I . . . I suppose."

"But you're off to bed; I'm the one that will have to listen to her!" Nora wailed.

"Nora, not everyone has the advantage of your beauty and talents," Phillippa said, a hint of impatience in her voice. "Louisa Dunningham needs all the accomplishments she can muster to catch a husband."

Nora, satisfied with that explanation and the compliments to herself, returned to her smiling, mischievous countenance. "Oh well, I suppose I can stand Louisa and Penny for another hour or so."

"Excellent. Now, before you return to your mother, I must ask something of you: Keep Broughton engaged this evening. He will be most disappointed when he discovers I've retired."

But Nora looked at her queerly. "Phillippa, do you honestly think Broughton will remain downstairs with the likes of Louisa and Penny when he know you're upstairs waiting for him?"

Phillippa blinked at her friend. "Waiting for him? I'm not, I will not—"

But Nora silenced her with a twinkling eye and a shake of her head. "Oh, Phillippa, everyone knows that your excuse to leave was just an excuse. I'll bet you a shilling the Marquis of Broughton does not wait ten minutes to come and knock on your door."

And with that and a knowing smile (although, really, when did Nora De Regis become so worldly as to portray knowing smiles?) Nora turned and flounced back to the drawing room, a giggle escaping her as she disappeared from sight.

And Phillippa, far from escaping her situation, realized she stepped deeper into it.

Marcus had never been one for sitting around with the gentlemen after dinner. In his mind, the practice originally allowed gentlemen to discuss business without rudely causing half the room's population to be bewildered by the complexities of their conversation. That said, since gentlemen these days rarely had anything to do with business, the mind-set of most the gentlemen present was, since they were free to do so, vulgarity must be indulged in. As if gentlemen of leisure would ever lack for clubs, gaming establishments, boxing matches, athletic pursuits, pubs, and Parliament, where such manners were allowed and encouraged. But nay, since they were without ladies for as long as they desired, they were within their rights to get foxed and be free with their thoughts.

Too free, in some cases.

"And then I said . . ." Mr. Standen, a portly and florid man, slurred from the other end of the table, "that if the cheeky little skirt wasn't going to give me a toss, I didn't give a toss for her, and I left her on the side of the road!"

Those enough in their cups to find the notion funny laughed uproariously. Those whose tastes were more moderate found nothing witty in Mr. Standen's speech beyond his sentence structure, and studiously looked bemused. Marcus was one of the latter party. But he was much surprised to discover that Byrne was one of the former.

It had not escaped Marcus's notice through the course of dinner just how much wine and how little food Byrne was consuming. Marcus knew Byrne could hold his drink, in general, as long as he didn't hold quite so much of it. He had always been careful.

"Don't you think that's enough?" Marcus whispered to his brother as Byrne signaled the waitstaff for another glass of port. Byrne just shot his brother a look, his eyes bright and shining, his face flushed with drink.

"I'm . . . I'm just faking it," Byrne whispered, a bit too loudly. "Luring the crowd into a false sense of ser . . . security."

Marcus's mouth set tighter. "I've seen you 'faking it' Byrne. This doesn't pass."

Byrne simply returned his mouth to his port and his unfocused mind to the table's conversation.

"Mystique is going to take it this year, I'll wager you five to one," Lord Hampshire was saying to Sterling on his left. "She's the best of this set of threes. Never seen such power in my life. Wish she was of breeding age a decade ago; the war effort could have used her bloodstock."

If Marcus's mind pinched upon Hampshire's words, Byrne's either did not or he ignored it.

"But what about Pretty Lady?" Sterling replied. "I'm laying odds she's going to take a bite out of Mystique in the mile if she gets close enough."

Marcus knew Hampshire was horse-mad; it was the whole point of this gathering, after all. But in all his time working under Sterling, he had no notion that the man knew anything about horses.

"Byrne," Marcus whispered to his brother, "Sterling doesn't follow races, does he?"

But Byrne just shrugged. "Dunno. Dunno anything 'bout anyone anymore."

This was a fair point. How could Byrne, who had been recuperating in the country for the past year and who had been on the Continent for a few before that, have any notion as to the intricate details of Society's life?

Marcus made a mental note to ask Phillippa. She would know.

Just as his mind flashed on the delightful Mrs. Benning, coincidentally enough, so did the conversation.

"I know another pretty lady ready to take a bite out of someone," Thomas Hurston spoke up, causing the young bucks that surrounded him to begin chortling and slapping Broughton on the back.

Broughton, meanwhile, smirked arrogantly as he held up a hand. "I am a gentlemen and, therefore, will keep my conquests to myself." But anyone could see that the gleam in his eyes invited commentary.

This was met with a chorus of boos from his cronies, who immediately took Broughton up on his silent offer.

"Come on, Broughton!"

"You can't leave us with nothing!"

"She's the ultimate conquest. I heard she's had her legs closed since Benning kicked off!"

"Ripe for the plucking. She's been playing you hot and cold for weeks!"

Marcus did his best to keep his blood from rising too high. After all, young idiots conjectured about females all the time, and Marcus had done his fair share back when he was a young idiot.

"You know she must be gagging for it! She's probably wetter'n the Thames," one young idiot added.

Lord Hampshire had his mouth dropped open like a fish, shocked beyond speech that this is what his table had devolved into. Marcus caught his eye, as Hampshire shook his head. Sterling was also without speech, but that could have been because he was laughing too hard.

Marcus reflected that perhaps this gentlemanly conversation had gone on long enough.

And given the time, the situation, and the stakes at play at this weekend party, Marcus cooled the blood in his ears with one simple phrase, as old as time: *Don't get mad, get even.*

He leaned over and whispered into his brother's ear, "Byrne, give me the vial that's in your coat pocket."

Byrne's gaze shot to his, clear for the first time all evening. "How'd you know about that?"

"Because I know. How many drops make you sleep?" Marcus asked, his face giving away nothing to the raucous crowd, as he palmed the vial from his brother.

Byrne was silent a moment. "Two or three. Maybe four."

It was a deft switch, an easy thing for a master spy like Byrne. Unfortunately, Marcus didn't trust Byrne's hands that evening and had to make the switch himself. It was successful, if a little less clean than he would have liked, but the alcohol consumed by everyone that evening made him easily overlooked. An attribute he had always found to his advantage.

As the quips and comments continued about the various attributes Mrs. Benning and others of her set laid claim to, the Marquis of Broughton finally put an end to the ribaldry by holding up his hands in a gesture of defeat.

"All I can say, gentlemen," he drawled nonchalantly, "is that there are some great advantages to courting a widow."

A steady stream of guffaws and "hear, hears" erupted from the crowd of young bucks, clapping each other on the back.

"A toast then!" Marcus boomed out over the crowd, rising to his feet. All fell silent. Raising his glass in the air, he continued, his eyes never straying from Broughton's face.

"To courting widows," he said, his jaw set, his hand steady.

Marcus knew the moment that Broughton recognized him. Not as Marcus Worth, third son, but as Marcus Worth, recent favorite of Phillippa Benning and a rival for her attention and affections. Even through the haze of alcohol, Broughton kept his gaze sharp. His cronies, having fallen silent, watched for his reaction. Broughton's jaw twitched into that lazy, dangerous smile that had so many ladies swooning. He rose to his feet, graceful, confident, swaggering. Raising his newly filled glass, Broughton matched its height to Marcus's.

"To courting widows," he replied and drank deep.

Eighteen

"IT'S just me; don't look so disappointed."

Marcus Worth winked at Phillippa as she peeked out from behind the door of her bedchamber.

In truth, Phillippa was tired, irate, and sleep-deprived. It was three in the morning, and believe it or not, this was the first time someone had knocked on her door! She had been abed since ten, and wholly expecting to being forced to have Totty give a paltry excuse to Broughton when he came with his amorous intentions. Which never occurred. Eventually, Totty had fallen asleep, but Phillippa's stomach remained in knots. Half of her mind was relieved, but the other half—really, did Broughton think her repulsive?

Perhaps her cry of illness was based in truth.

"Can I come in?" Marcus smiled at her, his voice giving nothing away, but she knew he was worried that the longer he stood out in the hall, the greater the chances were he would be recognized. He held a short candle, but in the darkness of the hall, it might as well have been a beacon.

"Can't," she replied, and at his quizzical frown, she continued. "Totty fell asleep in here—on the settee."

"I need to speak with you. Should we, er, find another room?" Marcus asked, a faint blush spreading across his cheek, just detectable in the darkness.

"I told you, Totty can sleep through a battlefield—but just in case, we'll go to her room. It's just next door." She said and, slipping out the door, grabbed his hand and tiptoed quickly to the room adjacent to hers.

The chamber was dark, and Phillippa groped for a moment to find a candlestick that Marcus could light. Finding one on the sideboard, she brought it to him, his hand enveloping hers, holding it steady, as he leaned the unlit taper into the flame.

Really, could she be blamed if she stepped a little closer to him?

But as soon as the candles were lit, the room relieved of its total darkness, the moment passed them by.

Marcus placed the candles on the small table next to a chair set up by the low fire, and Phillippa remembered again that she was tired and irritable and not exactly coiffed and clothed to her best advantage in the middle of the night.

"You should wear your hair like that always," Marcus commented, falling into his lopsided grin, tugging at the long rope of braid hanging down her back.

"I was asleep, I'll have you know," she swatted his hand away.

"No you weren't," he retorted. "You answered the door a bare three seconds after I knocked. Were you up waiting for me?"

"No," she replied coolly.

"Were you up waiting for anyone else?" he asked, raising a brow quizzically.

Silence descended on the room, as Phillippa's throat went dry and her gaze shot to his. "Of—of course not," she managed, "if I was waiting for someone, do you think I'd be dressed like this?"

Phillippa twirled in her plain white cambric nightdress, lacking in all ruffs and furls or anything feminine and alluring. The neck was high but wide and kept falling off her shoulder in a ragamuffin fashion. Her robe was a deep periwinkle but just as unadorned. No one could say she was dressed to impress.

But for some strange reason, Marcus was staring.

It made her acutely uncomfortable. As if he was looking through the clothes, and . . .

"Marcus," she said, jolting him out of his reverie, "it's the middle of the night. What do you want?"

The question hung in the air between them, and just for a moment, their eyes met. And for that moment, she wasn't tired and irritable, she wasn't in her plain nightclothes, she was being pulled forward by an invisible string toward him. Heat surrounded them, infused them, and she could see that heat in his eyes.

But only for a moment.

"I want you—" he said, his voice strangled, and so he cleared his throat and started again. "I want you to—Do you recall the exercise I asked you to do in the park?"

The tension that had awoken her skin, her spine, her fingertips left the air. Of course, she thought, deflated, he hadn't come to her for . . . for *that*. He was Marcus Worth. Aside from one incident for which he had been roundly scolded, he had expressed no interest in her beyond her connections to society and, however strange it seemed, her brain.

Between Marcus's lack of interest and Broughton not showing up at her door that evening, her ego was taking a tremendous beating.

Was this what it felt like to not be pretty? How very unpleasant.

"The memory exercise, you mean?" she replied. He nodded, to which she replied, gamely, "No, I don't recall that at all."

He smiled at her approvingly. "Very funny. If you ever fall on hard times, you can take up work as a court jester."

"What about the exercise, Marcus?" she said tiredly, which he must have noticed, because he grabbed a shawl that had been thrown over a stuffed armchair in front of the smouldering fire and wrapped it around her shoulders, bidding her to sit.

"I'm sorry, you are exhausted. I'll make this quick." He pulled over the spindly chair from the escritoire and folded himself down into it.

"I've been trying to get the best lay of this place as possible, but it's massive, there are a million things our adversary could be after, and just as many places to hide, so I need you to keep your eyes open."

"For what? For Laurent?"

"I want you to keep track of who is here and where they are. The minute you don't recognize someone, come and tell me. And tomorrow, at the evening festivities, if someone is *not* there who you think should be, I need to know."

A daunting task, Phillippa thought as she swallowed nervously. Almost too daunting. "But what if I miss someone or something? I'm not a professional like you—"

But he silenced her with a wry smile and a shake of his head. "You have a mind like a steel trap, when it suits your purpose."

"Can't . . . can't we enlist your brother to assist us? You did say he knows about you."

Marcus looked askance for a moment, his brows coming together in a knot. "Of course, my brother will be . . . assisting. I just don't know how much."

"Because of . . . his leg?" she asked, trying to guess his thoughts. Obviously, something about Byrne had Marcus worried, but she doubted it was as simple as his physical capabilities.

But Marcus jumped at the opportunity she afforded. "Yes, because of his leg. It's an injury he sustained, er, helping the Blue Raven on the Continent, and . . . he's not completely healed."

"I'm sorry, I don't mean to pry—" Phillippa began.

"Yes, you do," Marcus countered, but his smile told her to continue.

"Your brother, Byrne—he looks . . ."

"Like death warmed over?"

"Unhealthy," she supplied diplomatically. "Surely it would be wise to let him rest. Has a doctor examined him?"

Marcus guffawed at that, causing Phillippa to lean forward and shush him.

"Yes, he's been seen by doctors. And yes, he should be resting, attempting to heal, but he refuses. And I'd rather him not be in town by himself. Besides, he knows I could never stop him. Or protect him."

Marcus hung his head in his hands at this admission, and for the first time, Phillippa saw just how tired Marcus was, too.

Not just by the evening, as his head had not yet touched a pillow either, but by the whole endeavor. By the strains of a life lived in secret and the trouble it caused for those around him.

Gently she reached out, smoothed her hand over his head. It was a gesture of comfort, of support. He leaned into her hand, taking her caresses as offered. Her forehead came to meet his.

His head came up, and he met her eyes.

There it was again. That heat. It held them both frozen for a minute, a century.

And then Marcus leaned forward, his breath, mingling with hers, warm against her cheek. Unconsciously, she licked her lips. She saw his gaze flick to her tongue, his eyes going black.

And if he would lean just that much closer, Phillippa would not be the one to stop him.

But he didn't.

He pulled back, just barely, keeping her in his trance, as he spoke, his voice husky and low.

"Phillippa, I . . ."

"Yes," she said, not knowing the question, but willing that to be her answer.

"I . . . wanted to ask you about your husband."

"My husband?" she pulled back, confused, breaking the spell that surrounded them.

"I—I was given to understand that you are very devoted to his memory."

"Marcus, please don't ask me about my husband," she said, the exhaustion again taking hold of her body.

"It's just—if you were so devoted to him—and I know nothing of the man—but why Broughton?"

Phillippa stared at Marcus, as he stumbled on.

"Why let him into your life? Are . . . are they similar men?"

Phillippa leaned back in her chair, setting herself away from him. She lifted her jaw and cast a cold glare. The message was clear. How dare he? How *dare* he question this part of her life? And to think she had just moments ago been so willing to lean into him, to caress him, to let him . . .

"Marcus," she repeated, her voice ice, "do not ask me about my husband."

After holding her gaze a beat, he nodded, defeated.

"Come," he said, standing. "You should be in your bed. And I should be in mine."

As he ushered her to the door, Phillippa could only fleetingly think that, had he kept his questions to himself, they would be otherwise.

But the morning came—as it often does in the summer in the country—despicably cheerful, sunny, and crisp. And this day found a good portion of the Ton, who had little to no interest in seeing the sun rise in their regular life, awake and alert with the excitement of what was to come.

The Hampshires' racing pavilion was a rarity on a private estate. Most breeding farms had spacious fields for cross-country running, along with a practice track, but their horses were taken to the races. The Hampshires' breeding program was so vast and superior, they had no qualms about bringing the races to them.

The pavilion itself was a white oak construction, built with all the comforts of a formal parlor, but with a much more pointed view. Lord Hampshire was a generous man, fitting the pavilion with bench seating for the local townsfolk, as they enjoyed wagering their pennies as much as the gentlemen enjoyed wagering pounds. And Lady Hampshire was just as generous to her friends, having designed boxes removed from the local townsfolk, outfitted with every possible convenience, from working fireplaces for those cold mornings, to cushioned settees for the small canine friend, to a bellpull to call a servant to cater to the smallest request.

By nine in the morning, the first of the races had begun, those that had not arrived at the party the night before trickled in, and the servants served hot breakfast and tea to the ladies and gentlemen in those highly comfortable boxes.

By one in the afternoon, the three-year-olds had taken the stage, the entire Ton now firmly in residence. The races kept the guests enthralled, and the refreshments kept them enthusiastic as Lord Hampshire trotted out his stable's prized Thoroughbreds. There was conversation to the right of them about lineages and lines. There was conversation to the left about the packed English dirt the beasts did their mortal challenge on. But Marcus and Byrne found their conversation far less equestrian.

They had come out to stand among the crowds gathered at the edge of the racing track. Many other gentlemen had, in their enthusiasm, left the ladies in the boxes and come to see the horseflesh up close. Most had begun to divest themselves of their jackets in the heat and excitement of the day, including Marcus. But Byrne burrowed and shivered in his overcoat.

"A lovely bit of breeding, I won't deny," Byrne was saying, hiding his pale face from the sun in the high collar of his coat. "But I wouldn't gamble so much on her."

Marcus set his jaw tighter. "If I didn't know any better, I'd say you weren't speaking about the races. Now," he continued, steering the conversation back to what was at hand, "Fieldstone just arrived, as did Lord Whitford—he was the unfortunate host of the banquet, if you recall—Sterling is here, has been since last night, of course, but he didn't emerge from his rooms last night."

"How do you know? Did you keep watch all night?" Byrne asked with a sneer.

"I placed a hair in his doorjamb. It would have fallen if he had opened the door. I passed his door at six this morning, and the hair was still in place." It was a simple trick, one Byrne had taught him, and as such he couldn't fault its logic.

"Oh, then where were you last night?" Byrne inquired, false innocence. "I didn't hear you come in."

In order to ease the crush of guests, Byrne had agreed to stay in Marcus's room, giving up the quarters that Phillippa had set aside for Mariah and Graham. This earned him unending gratitude and only one small glance from their hostess. If Lady Hampshire thought Phillippa had a potential lover in Marcus Worth, it simply meant he would be coming to her room, not the other way around. Besides, everyone knew that the Marquis of Broughton was her real conquest.

As Byrne was more than willing to remind him.

"You might have been with Mrs. Benning, since everyone knows that she found herself suspiciously without her bed partner last night," he said maliciously.

For indeed, that seemed to be the main source of gossip among the guests that day. Phillippa had cried a headache and retired early. Broughton stayed in the drawing room all of three minutes after the gentlemen joined the ladies, to retire as well, he stated (or slurred, depending upon honesty). Those without knowledge of the contents of Broughton's toasting beverage speculated with glee as to why the social world's two most celebrated and attractive members would retire so very early.

Imagine those gossipers' disappointment when Broughton's valet whispered to the underbutler, who told the cook, who told the upstairs maids, who told all of the other guests' valets and ladies' maids that the Marquis of Broughton had done nothing more scandalous than fall asleep before his shoes hit the floor!

And that the lady, having waited up well past three, finally gave up and went to bed herself. (Phillippa's maid was either a heavy sleeper, or more discreet than Broughton's valet. Very likely both.)

But whatever the gossip, Marcus was determined to ignore it and his brother, focusing on the work.

"I was searching the house and grounds," Marcus replied tightly.

"Did you find anything?"

"No, this place is entirely too large to contain by myself."

"That's what you have me for," Byrne quipped.

"Do I? Tell me, how useful do you find yourself passed out drunk before eleven?" Marcus spat coldy.

"My leg was hurting," Byrne replied defensively.

"So you medicate it with a vat of wine?"

"At least I got some sleep. Which is of a great deal more use than stalking Mrs. Benning and drugging her lover."

"Dammit, Byrne!" Marcus spat, shocking not only his brother, but several of the gentlemen around them. "I thought you might believe me," he whispered, after prying eyes and ears had turned away. "I thought, you of all people, had perceived the seriousness of the situation."

Byrne's jaw was set, his face cold and immobile in the offending sunlight.

"Can't you feel it?" Marcus continued. "There is something going on here. He—Laurent—is here somewhere. And I may not fully understand what he's planning, but it's not a damn tea party."

Marcus knew that Byrne could feel it. He had to. His instincts, however rusted by time and addled by laudanum and alcohol, were too good. It wasn't anything overt. No one in a black cloak, twirling a mustache while acting in a shady manner. It was more a sense of things being slightly off. A different face in the crowd, looking around too nonchalantly. A water barrel placed to one side, just barely out of alignment with the other water barrels for the horses.

Marcus had already inspected those barrels, already tried to memorize that different face, but still the cold, tense air—palpable to some, ignored by most—clung to the day's proceedings.

Every time the racers came round the track, every time the crowd erupted into cheers, it was another tick of the clock. It wasn't the who or what that had Marcus on edge. It was the when.

And try as he might to deny it, Marcus knew Byrne felt it, too.

"Even if I could tell that something was going to occur," his brother finally said, "how am I supposed to take these circumstances seriously, when you are not?"

Marcus turned in shock to Byrne. "Not . . . not taking it seriously?" he sputtered. "Byrne, I'm the only one who ever has! How dare you—"

"I saw you." Byrne interrupted. "At supper, last night. Before, too. You couldn't keep your eyes off her."

Marcus went still. "Phillippa is . . . she's not . . ."

"You're mad for her. You compromised your entire mission to slip your rival for her affections a sleeping draught. I wanted to believe you, when you said she was invaluable to your plans. But you can't be serious about catching Laurent as long as you are using the circumstances to get Phillippa Benning into bed."

Marcus set his jaw tight. "I wouldn't do that."

"No?" Byrne replied. "Then where were you last night? You didn't spend the whole time patrolling the grounds. You cleared your path, are you telling me you *didn't* go see her?"

Marcus couldn't deny this. And maybe it was the fact that it was Byrne speaking, maybe it was the draining effort involved in keeping his eyes trained for mischief on absolutely no sleep, but Marcus couldn't deny the sense that was being made, either.

Because the content of their conversation last night had hardly been about the weather. It had hardly been about Laurent either.

And all he kept thinking about was the answer to his question he had not received. About how close her skin had been to his and how keeping her close, touching her, having her hand in his hair felt so very, very right. And then he had stupidly asked her about her husband, about Broughton, and he had, in that moment, forgotten his purpose.

Phillippa Benning was an asset, a brilliant one. Her connections, her gift of memory. But last night, she had also proved herself to be a liability. To him.

"Nothing happened last night," Marcus said finally to a waiting Byrne.

Byrne simply patted Marcus on the shoulder. "You need to sleep," he said. "I'll keep my eyes on Sterling, or Fieldstone, or Crawley, and whoever else comes by."

Marcus met Byrne's eyes and saw the resolution, the purpose.

"I won't disappoint you," Byrne said, seriously. "I promise."

Phillippa saw Marcus leave the pavilion's grounds through her opera glasses from the comfort of her box.

She had been holding court with Nora on the settee to her left, and Bitsy on the cushion to her right. Totty was at the front of the box, racing enthusiast that she was, delighted in the day's activities. And everyone who was anyone, including the hostess Lady Hampshire, had stopped in during the day to pay their respects and gossip endlessly. It was a delightful affair, the day glorious, and the races amusing. Phillippa should be all that was comfortable, and yet she found herself remarkably agitated, nervously folding and unfolding her hands.

Currently, Phillippa was entertaining Miss Penny Sterling, much to Nora's dismay. But Phillippa promised Marcus she'd cultivate the child—and besides, Penny was delightful, if unremarkably so.

"And Sir Ridgeway then asked if he could have another dance, but my father much prefers Mr. Crawley to him, but Sir Ridgeway is so very kind. Mrs. Benning, what do you think I should do?" Penny looked at Phillippa hopefully. Since Totty had done Phillippa the great service of steering Louisa and Mrs. Dunningham toward the balustrade to watch the races, Penny took the opportunity to seek motherly guidance from Phillippa. That Phillippa was only four years Penny's elder did not faze her.

"Tell me dear, what are your objections to Mr. Crawley?" Phillippa asked.

"I have none, not really," she said. "He works with my father, he calls often. But he's not Sir Reginald Ridgeway."

"Well. Sir Reginald is a good friend and a consummate gentleman," Phillippa purred. "Feel free to dance with him twice, but only if you also dance twice with Mr. Crawley. We can't let any of the men think you favor them over another, can we?"

"Of course not!" Penny replied instantly. Then, "Er, why not?"

"Because then they'll think they have you and no longer try to catch you."

"Oh," Penny said, a confused scowl taking over her features. "But Papa says I should make men think I love them, and that way I'll get married faster."

"Faster?" Phillippa asked. Lord help the child whose font of marital advice is her father.

"Yes, Papa says he cannot take the idea of escorting me out another Season. Apparently it's a trying thing."

Or it was an expensive thing. And judging by Penny's clothes, money could be of the essence in the Sterling household.

"Well, one way to make men love you is to dress to best advantage," Phillippa broached. She heard Nora snort behind her but ignored it.

"Absolutely," Penny agreed. "I studied the ladies' journals for months before my debut, and I picked out this color myself. What do you think?" She held out a length of her skirt, a puce shade of twill fabric. The shade was likely intended to capture the bit of violet in Penny's eyes, but it failed miserably.

Maybe funds were not the difficulty, Phillippa thought grimly, but Penny's taste. No seventeen-year-old girl in her first Season should be given complete reign over her own wardrobe. And with a disconnected mother and a bewildered father, it seemed like that had occurred.

Humming a noncommital reply, Phillippa was saved from further comment by Mrs. Dunningham spotting a friend in the crowds, forcing the girls to take their leave.

Phillippa resolved silently to call on Madame Le Trois on Penny's behalf immediately upon their return to London, as she bade the ladies adieu and relaxed back into the sofa cushions. However, her eyes were still alert and her hands were still twisting nervously in her lap.

This did not go unnoticed, although its cause was given a different source.

"Good heavens, Phillippa, darling, leave off, you'll twist your handkerchief into a ball," Totty remarked, as her eyes followed the horses through the turn.

She finally stood, excusing herself from the settee where the surrounding crowd was becoming stifling, and joined Totty at the front of the box. Nora, not to be left out, followed.

"It's no secret why she's nervous," Nora muttered under her breath.

"Hmm?" Phillippa replied, and then seeing the damage she had indeed caused to her square of fine linen, promptly stopped abusing the poor object. "What do you mean, Nora? What have I to be nervous about?"

"Anticipation, of course," Nora replied, and then, at a whisper, so the chattering ladies behind them wouldn't hear. "Since Broughton disappointed you last night, you have another full day of anticipation until . . ."

Phillippa turned her gaze away from the spot where Marcus Worth had stood, and let go of her questions as to where he could have gone—the final races were about to begin—to look questioningly at her diminutive friend. Nora's gaze shone bright and hopeful.

"Nora, what on earth are you talking about?" Phillippa inquired.

Nora blushed awkwardly and continued. "You . . . and Broughton. In all the books, the anticipation is often excruciating, until the moment of—"

"You are no longer allowed to read such books," Phillippa declared disdainfully. "Obviously they've rotted your mind."

"You're the one who gave them to me—"

But Totty's attention was captured as well. "Miss Nora, are you asking Phillippa what I think you're asking?"

"But we all know it, Philly. You must be worried." Nora frowned.

"About what?"

"About Broughton. Did he reject you? Is he still interested in you? Because a man choosing sleep over . . . is that normal? I hope you didn't do something wrong—offend him in some way?"

Phillippa, not for the first time, wished she hadn't made Nora quite so sophisticated and that her mother hadn't passively allowed it.

"He hasn't come to your box yet," Nora said, eyeing Broughton and his cronies cheering at the edge of the track. "Mrs. Dunningham was asking what happened, as was Lady Plessy, and Lord Draye . . ."

Phillippa could only blink for a moment. Out of all the things she had racing through her brain, this was the most annoying, because it was the least important. Who cared if people speculated about her sleeping situation? She was Phillippa Benning, for heaven's sake; she was used to it. But something about the way Nora questioned her allure—and that not only had Broughton fallen asleep and not come to her room, but the man who did she had found herself leaning into and caressing—and then he had the temerity to question her about her husband!

Add to that a madman running around somewhere, and Phillippa's head was suddenly too full of conflicting thoughts. She had to remove herself before she became, God forbid, candid.

". . . and now that Lady Jane's here—but never mind that, you'll reel him in tonight, and Lady Jane will become a distant memory," Nora rambled as Phillippa audibly sucked in her breath.

"I need some air," she said, excusing herself from a concerned Totty and a blinking Nora. As she turned for the door, Phillippa heard Nora ask Totty if she'd said something wrong, but by the time Totty replied, Phillippa and Bitsy were out the door.

There were people everywhere; there really was no escaping them. But as long as those people did not speak to her, Phillippa was well-situated to walk and breathe and think as she pleased.

Strangely, most of her thoughts were on Marcus.

Was it her imagination, or had he changed recently?

She did not know him very well, true, but what she did know was that he had an easygoing manner, a quick sense of humor, and an openness you wouldn't expect from someone who spent their life keeping secrets.

However, in the past few days, he'd become shuttered. She thought she could pinpoint it to around the time his brother arrived. A worrisome individual, Mr. Byrne Worth. He seemed shadowed, and not in that alluring way described in all the gothic novels, which the right woman with a loving heart could fix and make well again. Honestly, who had time for such things? No, he was shadowed in a way that made him cold, and it made Phillippa very, very worried for Marcus. Because, brother or no, what if Marcus trusted him, to his (and her) detriment?

She pivoted up the path sharply, a dark scowl masking her pretty features. Oh, why was her mind so involved by Marcus Worth? She shouldn't be thinking of him in such a personal way. They were merely using each other. Colleagues, in a roundabout sense. So what if her memory of their one and only kiss had been enhanced with time? So what if her hands had an unnatural affinity for his person? His hand, his hair, wherever she was allowed to place them, there they went. So what if her dreams had recently begun to feature said person's hands? And eyes? And form? It was Broughton who was her object . . . wasn't he?

But Broughton hadn't shown.

Last night, she had been so tired of waiting for Broughton, a man whom she intended to reject, it was terribly peevish to find she would not have the opportunity of doing so. But to have people questioning if he still wanted her! Well, it offended every sensibility! She was of a mind to march into the middle of that pavilion and—

"Mrs. Benning!" A masculine voice called, "Lovely to see you!"

She had been wandering in a determined circle, blindly. Little did she realize she had circled over to where Lady Jane Cummings and her father, the Duke of Rayne, were coming up the path.

The Duke was a man of later middle years, with a middle paunch to match. His hair had gone white in the past few years, no doubt from the strain of losing his beloved wife. He had always been a genial fellow about town but must have collected some dust in his head since then, for never in the past would he have made the mistake of calling a greeting to his daughter's declared enemy.

"Your Grace," Phillippa said on a curtsy, keeping her composure. Lady Jane dipped as well, if a little shallowly. However, this went unnoticed by her father, who clamped his hand over Phillippa's.

"You've grown up so nice and tall. How long's it been? Three years? Four? And how's your husband?"

Both ladies looked shocked, as Lady Jane turned to the Duke. "Father, I think—"

"Yes, yes, I know, I'll let you catch up with your friend. I'm desperate to see the races myself." And with a wink and a pat on Bitsy's head, the Duke left Lady Jane to face Phillippa on her own.

The ladies could only stare.

Bitsy had the good sense to contain his growls.

Lady Jane broke the silence first. "I apologize for my father," she said stiffly.

"Is he all right?" Phillippa asked quietly.

"Of course he is," Lady Jane snapped, and then, with a little more grace, "Thank you for inquiry."

She moved to go past and catch up with her father but turned back instead, catching Phillippa by surprise.

"Do you think you'll win now?" Lady Jane asked, as she brought a haughty sneer to her lips.

"Win?" Phillippa echoed, bewildered.

"Do you think if you let Broughton into your bed tonight, it will get him to offer for you? Don't you know that men only want what they can't have?"

"Is that what you think?" Phillippa replied coolly.

"Rumor has it you put the man to sleep." Lady Jane sneered. "You're not the only one who can play deep, but unlike you, I play to win."

And with that, Lady Jane turned on her heel and stalked off after her father, leaving Phillippa's mouth open and her mind thunderously dark. She let out a deep breath, trying to let her anger go with it, but no one ever got her back up like Jane Cummings. This might take a lot of breathing.

The sun had dipped past the treetops by the time Phillippa looked up from her wander and her deep breathing, and she did not immediately recognize her surroundings. She'd been too much in her head: the fast rush of anger, the cool blue of regret, the mad flush of confusion. All had blinded her to her whereabouts, which was somewhere in the vicinity of the pavilion, as she could still hear the alternating groans and cheers from the crowd.

Suddenly, the soft sound of nickering broke through the air, and Phillippa whirled around and saw, much to her relief, that she was at Lord Hampshire's stables. A massive structure, white-washed to match the pavilion, no doubt, it had to house scores of Lord Hampshire's best stock.

The structure seemed devoid of any presence of humans; the stable lads who had drawn the short straw and were supposed to be watching the stock must have snuck over to the races to watch Mystique win the three-year-old finals, she thought. The horses looked none the worse for a lack of supervision, however, and since the day was so temperate, the outer stable doors were open, allowing the horses within to enjoy the sweet air. There was a long row of beautiful horses, their faces turned to Phillippa and Bitsy. Scanning the long row, they found that the nickering in question had come from a glorious black mare, whose appearance apparently belied a sweet disposition.

"Oh! Aren't you lovely!" Phillippa gasped aloud. "Admittedly, I'm no judge of horseflesh"—in truth, she cared little about the beasts beyond that their coats matched her carriage—"but you must be the pride of the stables."

Bitsy had the upper paw in this instance, for unlike his owner, he was a prime judge of horseflesh. And indeed, he happily wriggled free of Phillippa's embrace and trotted over to the black beast's stall, rose up on his hind legs, and greeted her.

Phillippa trod carefully over to the horse, who was looking at Bitsy in bemusement, careful not to get her Madame Le Trois silk flounced skirts muddy from the stable dirt.

"Would you like a bit of hay?" Phillippa asked, as she picked a handful out of the bundle at the stall's door.

The black beast took it eagerly, licking Phillippa's hand with her sticky tongue for more.

"Ew!" Phillippa cried. "That is quite enough"—a quick glance at the top of the stall gave her the beast's name—"Letty. Your manners are quite deplorable. You would eat Bitsy if I offered her to you, wouldn't you?"

At that, Bitsy stopped preening for Letty and cowered behind Phillippa.

Phillippa was about to laugh out loud—for the first time that day—when behind Letty, through the stall, into the interior of the stable, she saw someone move.

She would have thought nothing of it if she hadn't recognized the paunch and whispy blond hair of Lord Sterling.

Ducking down quickly, Phillippa hid her body beneath Letty's half door, muddy skirts be damned. But try as she might to hear anything, she couldn't from her current crouched position.

Slowly, she brought her head up, inching her eyes above the door. There she was greeted by Letty's long, wet nose.

"Drat it all!" she whispered. "Letty, move!"

After a gentle shove, Letty obliged her, affording Phillippa a view of Lord Sterling and someone else.

It was someone she didn't recognize. She couldn't see much of him, for much of him was blocked by Sterling's girth and height. But she saw a slight frame, light hair. Blond? Maybe light brown? He was in a brown coat—broadcloth, she guessed, but she couldn't be sure—and a straw hat that marked him as one of the local farmers. She was unfamiliar with most of the locals, but she made an educated guess that Lord Sterling, whose country estate was far to the north, would be unfamiliar as well. Was this truly a local farmer, or was it someone who merely presented himself as such to get into the Hampshire Races?

The stranger turned to the side; he had a satchel on his back. He and Lord Sterling spoke in low voices, and Phillippa would be damned if she could hear anything above a low murmur. Should she move closer? But how and where? Oh, if only Marcus were here!

Frustrated, Phillippa kept her efforts focused on watching the man she didn't know. Memorizing what features she could see and his movements. In fact, she was so intent on the stranger, she almost didn't catch it when Lord Sterling unloaded the satchel from the stranger's back, and after a moment or two of rummaging inside, he walked to the left and—

Suddenly, Phillippa was once again assaulted by the cold wet of Letty's nose.

"Letty!" Phillippa whispered furiously. Her view was blocked; she had lost sight of her quarry. "Letty, move!" she said again, pushing against the black beast's neck.

But Letty did not wish to move. And since this was the second time the forthright blond woman had felt it necessary to push against her, she decided to make her point vocally.

Letty danced back, whinnying high as she did.

Phillippa ducked down low, beneath the half door of Letty's stall again, praying fervently that the noise would go on unregarded. After all, Letty was a known resident of these stables; it was perfectly within her rights to neigh and prance.

She remained motionless, grasping a wiggling Bitsy tight in her arms, barely daring to breathe.

Five seconds passed.

Then another ten.

Slowly, Phillippa exhaled, and then, loosening her grip on Bitsy, dared to bring her head above the stall door's line.

The figures were farther away now, close to the main doors of the stables. Backlit as they were by the afternoon sun, Phillippa could barely tell which figure was Lord Sterling and which was the stranger. They were still speaking, but there was no hope of hearing anything. Maybe she could follow them once they left, "accidentally" meet Lord Sterling on a path, and get a good look at his friend so she would have something to say to Marcus.

Just then, Bitsy, who had heretofore been far too silent, took the opportunity afforded by his recently reinflated lungs, and barked.

And Phillippa saw the two heads turn in unison toward her.

She ducked quickly, but to no avail.

"Who's there?" she recognized the booming tenor of Lord Sterling's voice. Then a shuffling of feet on hay and the creak of the stable doors.

Not a moment to lose, Phillippa picked up Bitsy and dashed around the corner of the building. Holding the dog tight again, she used a hand to muzzle her precious Bitsy and dove behind a row of water barrels lined up next to the stables, kept cool in the shade of a chestnut tree and the shadow of the structure. She was thin, she could fit. Her only hope was that the stout Lord Sterling wouldn't think to look there.

She lay on the ground, the wet, packed earth behind those barrels, one hand muzzling Bitsy, the other muzzling herself. She willed her breath to slow down from the deep gasps that followed quick movement. But as she heard the footfalls of two men, she stopped breathing altogether.

"I'm telling you I saw someone," Lord Sterling said, his voice alarmingly close to Phillippa's hiding place.

There was a pause, a muffled shuffling of feet, a wariness prickling across Phillippa's skin.

Those footsteps were getting closer.

Then, a voice she didn't recognize. And, it turned out, a voice of reason.

"Come on," the stranger said, "you'll be missed."

The footsteps started to recede. Still, it was an eon before Philipa felt safe enough to move. When she did, inching her head up from behind the barrels, and seeing only the long, retreating forms of Lord Sterling and the stranger, she breathed a heartfelt sigh of relief.

Once the men moved beyond the horizon, she got up off the ground.

And then she moved with all possible speed, one desperate thought running constantly through her head.

She had to find Marcus.

Of course, she had to change her dress first.

Well, the Grecian-style Madame Le Trois walking dress was in total disrepair; she simply could *not* appear in public like that without raising questions about what she had been doing and seriously damaging her reputation.

She snuck into the Hampshires' manor using the servants' entrance and was immediately ushered to her room using a back passage that deposited her almost directly to her door. After a quick look in the mirror, she discovered that not only was her dress in a state, but so was her hair. Even with her ladies' maid working with all possible speed, she still was not presentable for nearly three-quarters of an hour.

By then, Phillippa's imagination was running wild. Who was the stranger? What had been in the satchel? If Marcus was right, and Lord Sterling was involved, why?

The minute her maid finished the final touches on her hair, she shot out of the chair and was out the door.

She had spied Marcus walking away from the races, but to where? Where was she to start?

His rooms, she thought, were as good a place as any.

Hampshire House was, for all its modern remodeling, constructed in the Elizabethan era, and therefore as a tribute to the Virgin Queen had been built in the shape of a capital *E*. Bedrooms lined the second and third floors of the outside prongs—the east and west wing, respectively—while family rooms filled the middle prong and state rooms (including the formal dining room and ballroom) occupied the long, connecting spine of the house.

Phillippa's rooms were in the east wing. Marcus's rooms she knew were in the west. Although where in the west wing was a bit of a mystery.

Simple enough, she told herself. The house was built on easy lines to follow, and once she was in the west wing, she would . . . well, she would figure out that part when she came to it.

But as Phillippa walked briskly through the corridors, turning left here and right there, she quickly found herself lost in the maze.

"Where on earth . . ." she said to herself as she put her hands on her hips and began retracing her steps.

Doubling back through the rich mahogany hallways, Phillippa was counting off doors when she heard a clipped, bored voice.

"My brother says your memory is faultless—but apparently not your sense of direction?"

At the end of the empty corridor stood Byrne Worth, leaning heavily on his cane. The setting sun streamed through a nearby window, turning his black hair to flame, but still his sunken face and compressed mouth bespoke nothing but contempt.

"Coming or going?" he asked, clipping short his words as if he had no time to be bothered with her.

"I'm looking for your brother, Mr. Worth," she replied, her tone as imperious as she could manage. And Phillippa Benning could manage imperious very well indeed. "Pray, have you seen him?"

"Not for a few hours," Byrne drawled, an eyebrow going up as he spoke. "He told me he was going to lie down for a while." Byrne motioned to a nearby doorway. "He was up late last night, you see."

Phillippa shot Byrne a frostbitten smile, as she made for the door he had indicated. But despite the need for a cane, Byrne Worth proved he could move when he needed to, taking two quick steps and then blocking the door with the silver-headed cane.

"You wouldn't wish to disturb him, I'm certain," Byrne said.

Phillippa looked Byrne dead in the eye as she spoke. "I need to speak to him."

"Is it important?"

His voice had dropped the clipped coldness, just barely, letting Phillippa see the concern that was there. But only for a moment.

"You can tell me, I'll let Marcus know," Byrne continued, his voice cool as steel again.

She could. She could tell Byrne, it was an option. But did she dare risk it? Marcus said he knew about the Blue Raven, and for whatever fracture had occurred between the brothers, it was obvious that Marcus trusted him. But she knew implicitly that Byrne did not trust her. More to the point, she got the strangest sense that he didn't even like her, let alone respect her. Would he believe her when she told him what she saw?

Before she could come up with an answer to her dilemma, her dilemma was unceremoniously interrupted.

"I say, Phillippa, where have you been? I've been looking for you everywhere."

Turning around, she saw Broughton and a few of his cronies at the end of the hall, the races having ended for the day, obviously.

Turning back to Byrne, she saw the smallest, cruelest smile pass over his countenance.

"Or are you just playing a mean game?" he whispered. Then, with a clipped bow, he disappeared into the room he had just barred her from, closing the door in her face.

Recovering quickly, Phillippa whirled around and with a saucy smile, greeted Broughton.

"I've been looking for you, of course." Honey dripped from her words.

She watched as Broughton's friends shot him smirks, as they disappeared into their own chambers. Broughton came up to her, took her hand.

She looked up into that deliciously wicked face, the blond hair and tanned skin gleaming with the exertions of a day spent outdoors.

Mr. Byrne Worth thought her capable of playing a mean game. Well, truth be told, she was. And the Marquis of Broughton was about to find out how mean. She had a score to settle with him and a sparring match to win.

They had business to discuss.

At dinner that evening, Broughton sulked. And moped. And sent her looks of hot anticipation. And then sulked some more. Well, after he had made her wait up all night for the privilege of not being called upon (whether or not he was a welcome guest), now it was his turn.

As he escorted her back to her room that afternoon so she could prepare for supper, Broughton had broached the subject everyone else had discussed except them.

"I must apologize for last night," he said in his affected, lazy drawl.

"Must you?" Phillippa asked innocently.

"Yes. I don't know what happened—it must have been the wine—but I got to the stairs, and I nearly fell asleep there. It was all I could do to get to my room."

"Was it?"

"Yes, and I know you were waiting for me," he began to tug at his collar. Obviously he was not used to his charms failing.

"Was I?" Phillippa cocked her head to one side.

"Phillippa, don't be cruel," Broughton pleaded. He took a breath and allowed his charming smile to return full force. "But tonight, I won't disappoint you."

"You won't?"

"I assure you, I am exceedingly well-rested." He drew his hand under her chin at that, delicately lifting her face to his. He smiled down at her, and Phillippa had to admit he was the most handsome man of her acquaintance, but she was struck by just how many teeth Broughton had. Surely more than normal. "Just wait until I knock on your door tonight."

"No, Phillip," she said, smiling into his eyes. They maneuvered down the hall so slowly, she was certain they drew eyes, but her voice was pitched so sweetly, no one would know what she spoke of.

"No?" he echoed.

"I find that I don't like to be kept waiting. And according to what you said, *you* kept me waiting all night."

Broughton's brow furrowed. "But you said we'd have *hours* to ourselves this weekend—"

"Really, Phillip, I don't remember making any promises."

They were at her door now and came to a stop. She took a step closer to him. "But there will be hours tonight when no one will be watching us. However, I will not wait for you to knock on my door."

"But—"

"You will have to wait for me to knock on yours."

That toothy grin returned in full force. He *was* exceptionally good-looking. It struck her every time he smiled. And it was so nice that she was able to control him so effortlessly. Really, the poor man had thought he'd won, when he asked, "What time?"

"What time?" she repeated.

"What time will you knock on my door?"

"Heavens, I haven't decided if I'm going to." And with a smile, she slipped into her room, shutting the door in his shocked face with a laugh.

It was the most fun she'd had this whole weekend. And seeing Broughton tortured, working through her challenge, while eating supper was the second.

Indeed, Phillippa found herself rather discomfited that night at the dining table. Even the sight of Lady Jane, seated to Broughton's left, trying and failing utterly to engage his attentions could not bring a smile to Phillippa's face.

And she couldn't fault the food, oh no! Lady Hampshire's cook had pulled out all the stops, the prize birds having been killed and dressed for the occasion, the sauces a delight, the trifles lighter than air.

But it was impossible to eat, to focus on conversation, nay, to focus on anything other than the fact that she had yet to tell Marcus about what she saw at the stables.

Once she and Broughton finished their meeting, Phillippa had to rush to bathe and dress again, this time for the evening's festivities. Not knowing what lay ahead that evening, she did not rightly know how to dress. She went through several options before she chose her most sturdy dancing slippers and another of her Madame Le Trois commissions with skirts voluminous enough for pockets, a devastatingly decadent cream satin with silver thread. She was already setting a fashion. More than one young lady sported a wider skirt that evening—all because of Phillippa's desire for pockets!

She now stuffed those pockets with a bit of candle, a few coins, even Totty's little sewing kit. Who knew what she would need? But all this preparation came with a price, and by the time she came downstairs, everyone was already heading into the dining room. Broughton, good boy that he was, had duly waited for her, in order to escort her in, forcing Nora, in a quick whisper, to eat her earlier words about Phillippa having "done something wrong."

Once seated, Phillippa had hoped to be near enough to Marcus to engage him in whispered conversation. But she had not taken the time to butter up the hostess to her advantage, because she found herself not only at almost the other end of the table from Marcus but seated directly next to Lord Sterling!

She tried everything. She tried a discreet cough, an overly loud laugh to catch Marcus's eye, but to no avail. . . . Hell, she would have attempted engaging him in a game of charades if she, firstly, could do so without anyone else noticing, and secondly, didn't hate charades. . . . She didn't think he was ignoring her, though after she was so rudely abrupt to him last evening, he had every right to. No, instead she hoped that since he had left off his spectacles for the evening, it was possible that at this distance, she was nothing more than a large blur.

By the time the dessert courses were being served, Phillippa was a nervous wreck. She tried attending her conversation to Lord Sterling, but he said nothing more incendiary than to comment on the food or ask her advice on his daughter's prospects.

As the host and hostess rose from the table, Phillippa was on her feet, too. And Broughton abandoned Lady Jane to take Phillippa's arm.

Luckily, since dancing and entertainments had been arranged, the practice of the ladies excusing themselves from the men was abandoned for the evening, as the party moved with laughter and gaiety toward the ballroom.

Trying to walk with dignity when desperately trying to reach someone is no easy task. Doing it in a cream silk ball gown embroidered with silver thread and silk dancing slippers while being escorted out by a sulky marquis didn't assist matters.

"I hope my conduct so far this evening meets with your approval," Broughton sneered under his breath, causing Phillippa to smile somewhat viciously.

"You are the consummate gentleman. You aren't trying to sway my decision, by any chance?"

Broughton's eyes flashed as they maneuvered with equal parts grace and speed through the flowing crowd. "Unabashedly," Broughton said.

"Phillip." She smiled, stepping into him, placing her hand on his chest, as they were crushed together by the wave of young people, eager to join the dance. "You do know how to soothe a girl's wounded ego."

Phillippa and Broughton finally managed to pass through the hall and into the center of the festivites. Unfortunately, Marcus was so far ahead of them that by the time she had reached the grand ballroom, bedecked in rich autumnal silks and a full orchestra playing a minuet at the far end, he had already taken his dinner partner, Nora, to the floor.

"Oh, drat it all," she said, standing on tiptoes to watch Marcus take Nora through a turn. She had been so attentive to him during dinner, hadn't she? Phillippa's face turned red at recalling how every time she looked over at Marcus, Nora was there, laughing at some unheard comment, artlessly grazing his hand with hers. And now she had him taking the floor with her! And on top of it all, he looked to be enjoying it!

Was it just her, or did Marcus look ridiculously handsome that evening? His afternoon of rest had obviously done him good, his hair grown out of its fashionable cut just slightly enough to make it stylish, his clothing impeccable. She had noticed more than one lady, including Nora, give him an approving once-over, and at least one man. Marcus was well on his way to being accepted by the highest echelons of the Ton as one of them. Soon, he wouldn't need her anymore.

A startling thought, which Phillippa refused to allow more than a second in her mind. She had more important matters to attend to. Namely, getting to Marcus and finally speaking to the wretched man!

"I'm afraid I must abandon you," Broughton said, as he brought her hand to his lips. "I promised a dance to Lady Jane earlier, and I'd just as soon get it over with."

"Fine," Phillippa said distractedly.

"You're not . . . angry?" Broughton asked quizzically.

"No, go ahead," Phillippa waved him away, all the while keeping her eye on Marcus and Nora.

"But, Phillippa—why?"

Remembering her game, Phillippa shot Broughton a bewitching smile. "Because I know you'll be back right after."

Broughton scowled and stalked off. Perhaps she was having too much fun leading him by a string, she thought, as she waited patiently for the minuet to end. He was likely to chafe against the binds.

However, she could not worry about that now. The average dozen or so gentlemen had asked to step out with her for this dance, but she declined them all, claiming it was to late to join in the first dance. Slowly, she wedged her way through the young ladies and gentlemen, the matron mamas and their patient husbands, who lined the edge of the dance floor. The ballroom was wide in the way of most Tudor grand halls, but not up to modern standards and therefore, to fit two lines of dancers, the rest of the attendants were squeezed mercilessly to the sides of the long hall. And given Lady Hampshire's penchant for company, the Hampshire Ballroom was all but at a standstill. But Phillippa, intent on her course, did not allow difficulties such as other people to stand in her way.

As annoying as it had been to see Nora dancing (gracelessly, to her mind) with Marcus, Phillippa knew that there was an advantage to the situation. When requested to do so, Nora would hand over her dance partner without too many questions.

And that's exactly what she did.

"Nora, do you mind if I have a word with Mr. Worth?" Phillippa asked, after greeting her friend, as the last strains of the minuet fell away, and the guests' applause rose.

Nora, with a quick quirk of her head, smiled and said, "By all means. But I see the Marquis of Broughton over there, escorting Lady Jane to the floor."

Phillippa smiled at Marcus, then took Nora's arm and pulled her slightly away.

"Nora, I just need a moment," Phillippa said in a soothing but unquestioning tone. But Nora was never one to remain wholly questionless.

"Phillippa, what are you doing?" Nora whispered furtively. "Broughton is dancing with Lady Jane, and you only want to speak to Mr. Worth? I know he's your 'project' or some such thing, but honestly, I sat next to him all through dinner, and he was most dreadfully dull –didn't once compliment my dress or my hair. I don't know what you see in him."

"No, you wouldn't," Phillippa countered.

Nora, flinched back, shocked. Phillippa was a little shocked herself, so rarely did the undressed truth pass her lips. But she held her ground. And Nora, once recovered, stood hers.

"Broughton is being *very* attentive to Lady Jane. And if you're not careful, you're going to lose him."

A quick glance told Phillippa that Nora was right. Broughton was pulling out all the stops to flirt with Jane, an obvious ploy to engage her jealousy. Phillippa drew herself up to her full height and stepped closer to her friend. "It may not look it, but Broughton is well in hand. He'll be fine without me for a few moments. And I have to speak to Mr. Worth. Nora," she said, softening her speech, "please, Thomas Hurston has been desolate all evening; you're the only person here who can make him smile."

Nora wrinkled her nose, shooting a glace first toward Thomas Hurston, then quickly, furtively, toward the Marquis of Broughton.

"Fine," she said, as she flounced away. "But don't say I didn't warn you."

Duly warned, Phillippa thought and turned back to Marcus.

He had dreamed of her, of course. His slumber that afternoon was marked by fevered memories of what it had been like to taste her, to touch her. The way that simple nightgown had fallen off her shoulder. Then his memory began to entwine with his imagination, and the idea of his skin pressed against her flushed breasts, bare stomach, that jointure of all earthly delights . . .

Needless to say, he slept much longer than he had intended.

Because, upon waking, he was forced to remember that she had rejected him last night.

Again.

And it sat in his stomach like a lump of cold lead.

Byrne mentioned he'd run into Phillippa in the hall, that she was with Broughton at the time. And to see the way Broughton stared at her mournfully through dinner, escorted her solicitously, was basically a pet on her lead, made him all the more infuriated. To think that Phillippa preferred that—

Marcus sighed. Byrne was right. He had lost sight of what he was here for. It was a mutual exchange. He used her for her social contacts; she used him for the Benning Ball. Somewhere in the middle, his head had gotten muddled, and he began thinking she might actually care for him. That was just foolish. Especially considering that he was supposed to be on his guard that night.

His brother had shown his face at dinner, but as soon as the dancing and revelry began, he disappeared. They had decided that since Marcus was quickly becoming a face in the Ton, his face had to be seen, at least for a little while. Meanwhile, Byrne took up a post at the far end of the room, his cane serving as the perfect excuse to avoid dancing, and also closest to the door that, as Marcus had discovered last evening, led to a staircase to Lord Hampshire's private library, where he kept his safe.

Marcus had intended to dance a few times before approaching Phillippa. Be casual and at ease when he did so. He did not expect her to immediately come up to him.

"Mrs. Benning," Marcus said on a bow. She curtsied perfunctorily in return, before bursting into speech.

"Marcus—Mr. Worth, I've been trying to find you for ages—"

"Really? I'm not that hard to find. I was in the dining room, if you recall."

"I meant, I've been trying to *speak* to you for ages. This afternoon, I—"

"I was hoping to speak to you, too," he interrupted her. "I didn't think the dance floor was the best place to do it, but . . . Last night, I was rude and had no right to tread on your priva—"

"Marcus, I don't care about that. For the love of God, I saw Sterling with a stranger this afternoon!"

That gave him pause.

The music had started again, the dancers moving through a quadrille with verve, and pressing Marcus and Phillippa farther into those lined on the sides.

He sought out his brother's eyes across the room and found them. Willing Byrne to understand the situation, he was afforded a raised eyebrow and a short nod, acknowledging that he would stay at his post. Marcus nodded back.

"Come on," he said. Grabbing her gloved hand, he pulled her through the laughing dancers, dodging raised arms and double steps as they made their way to the main entrance to the ballroom.

"Marcus—" Phillippa cried as she trotted to keep up with his long gait. "Everyone will see!"

"The quickest way out is through," he replied, glancing at her over his shoulder. She was holding up her skirts with one hand and clasping his with the other. The flush of exertion made her eyes glow, and Marcus had to snap his head back around to keep from stopping altogether.

Once they had cleared the ballroom (turning no small number of heads as they did so), Marcus wound his way to the front of the house, finding a piece of statuary—in the shape of a rearing thoroughbred, of course—to afford them a small amount of privacy.

"Now," Marcus said, turning to face her, "you saw Sterling."

"And a stranger," she added breathlessly.

"And a stranger—at the races?" he inquired.

"No, during the races, at the main stables. The stranger—he was dressed like a farmer, but I don't think he was a farmer, because why would Sterling be alone with a farmer?" she said, spewing forth the pent-up story with a pace that marked it as something other than human speech. "And his accent—I heard him speak with an English accent, but you told me Laurent could mimic it . . . They were alone, you see. The stable lads must have gone to watch the main race, and it was just me and Bitsy and Letty, and then they were there and then I had to hide and my Madame Le Trois got so muddy, it's completely ruined, and I know she'll never make me another one—"

At this point, Marcus decided that for Phillippa to tell him what she wanted to, she would simply have to stop talking.

Quickly but gently, Marcus stepped closer to Phillippa, placed one hand on her waist and the other across her mouth.

Her large blue eyes sought his, questioning. He met her gaze, calm, and (he hoped) reassuring. "Take a deep breath," he told her, and she did so, her lips moving against his hand. "Now, exhale," he instructed, and warm, moist air met his palm.

"Good," he soothed, removing his hand as he did so. "Now, they were at the stables?"

She nodded.

"During the races?"

"Yes, and the stables were empty." She kept her voice modulated, serene.

"You're certain it was Sterling?"

"Well, of course! He was wearing that mill gray coat and buff trousers and the top hat that is two inches too tall for his frame—"

"That will do," Marcus interrupted, before she could get carried away again. He took another deep breath. She took the hint and inhaled deeply as well. "Can you describe the stranger?" Marcus asked, not allowing any anticipation to enter his voice.

"He . . . had light hair. A thin frame. I didn't get a good look at his face," she looked thoughtful for a moment. "He was dressed like the local farmers. A straw hat, he had a satchel on his back—oh, Marcus! The satchel!"

Her grip tightened on his hand as her eyes went wide. "They heard me, but they didn't see me. I went to hide, and then, I saw them walking off, and the satchel—he didn't have it when he left!"

The main stables—of course. If the satchel was left behind on purpose, it could be . . .

"When will the fireworks start?" he asked abruptly.

"Ah, probably midnight—within the hour," she replied, perplexed.

"Phillippa," he pulled her to him, gripped her shoulders. "I'm going to the stables. Stay here, tell Byrne where I've gone and to keep an eye on Sterling."

"What?" she cried. "No, I'm coming with you."

"Phillippa, it could be dangerous," he countered, his thumb massaging the fine silk of her dress.

"Marcus, I know, and believe me, I'd rather not walk straight into danger, but the main stables—they're massive. You'll never find the satchel in the dark without me."

He moved his hand to caress her neck, her jawline. "That's a chance I'm willing to take." And he turned away.

Of course, Phillippa Benning wasn't one to leave well enough alone. Catching up to him as he headed out the front doors of the

Hampshires' manor house, he discovered a strong grip latched to his wrist.

"Rotten luck, Mr. Worth," Phillippa said, catching up to him. "You're not rid of me that easily."

Marcus knew he had a choice. He could escort her back the ballroom and force Totty or Broughton to take hold of her. He could take her upstairs and lock her in her room. But truth be told, he didn't have the time to waste for the former, and he highly suspected that if he attempted the latter, he'd lock himself in with her. And knowing his options were limited, Marcus did the only thing he could.

He prayed.

"God save me from meddlesome females," he said, rolling his eyes heavenward, and took off for the main stables, Phillippa keeping pace beside him.

It was over a mile of winding path to the main stables from the manor house, and the quickest way to get there was through the rear, past the fountained gardens, beyond the twelve-foot-tall hedge maze that had grown since the Stuart era. Several couples had sought the cool night air of the grounds as opposed to the oppressive heat of the ballroom, and knowing this was a possibility, Lady Hampshire had thoughtfully lit the gardens and hedge maze with sconces, allowing the illusion of respectability but really casting only darker shadows than before.

Marcus and Phillippa skirted the edge of the gardens, keeping out of the light and out of other couples' way as much as possible. They avoided the hedge maze and its amorous occupants altogether by cutting through the paddocks, Marcus quick to point out the animals' leavings to the careful-stepping Phillippa.

"Just over that rise," Phillippa whispered, her voice barely above the hum of the party, faded in the distance. "And then it should be to the right."

Marcus followed Phillippa's directions, took them over another paddock fence on the rise of the hill, and then discovered the Hampshires' main stables.

Phillippa was right; they were massive, Marcus thought, and he squeezed her hand as they made their way to the structure.

"It houses all Lord Hampshire's best horseflesh," Phillippa said, reading his thoughts, "when they're not racing, or outfitting a brigade, that is. He has room for over a hundred."

As they crept closer to the building, Phillippa drew his attention to a number of water barrels lined up against the building. "I hid behind those when they came looking for me."

Marcus eyed the barrels and the tiny space between them and the building.

"You wedged yourself in there?" he asked, incredulous.

She drew herself up, as if affronted. "I'm quite slender, you know. I can fit in a number of small spaces."

"Yes," he grinned, "like already occupied sarcophagi."

She punched him weakly on the shoulder for that but smiled. He grinned down at her, and for a moment, he forgot his purpose.

Damn, he thought, shaking it off and moving silently around the building to the main door, every time she smiled at him, he lost his focus. And that could not happen. Certainly not now.

The stable door was unlocked, but pushing it in was a frightening experience, the hinges squeaking with every inch. Once he had it wide enough to accommodate his long frame, he slipped through. Phillippa followed, and after some silent debate, they left the door open to facilitate their escape and avoid squeaking.

Two long rows of stalls, housing the finest in English horseflesh, lined the long building. No light came from the tack room or the rafters, where the stableboys kept their cots. Since fireworks were expected, and their chores done for the day, obviously they went out to watch. Marcus worried that one or two might have stayed behind, but no one emerged as Phillippa and Marcus made their way into the darkened stables.

"All right," Marcus whispered, turning to Phillippa. "Where were they standing?"

She made to move down the row, but something had him stopping her, taking her arm and holding her still.

He pressed a finger to his lips, urging her silent and then listening to the night air, silent except for a few snores from the building's tenants.

Nothing.

He was about to release her, when suddenly, he heard a creak issue from the stable doors, the crunch of booted feet on fresh hay. And Marcus did the only thing he could think of. He took Phillippa and ran toward the far end of the stables. There, he threw her into a shadowed corner, pushed her up against a wall, and hid as much of her distinctively dressed body as he could with his own.

He heard the feminine giggle before Phillippa did, he was certain. It was matched by an amorous tenor, who spoke low, in a working-class accent.

"George said the lads would be watchin' the pretty lights from the field, so we are all alone."

The girl giggled again. "Gor, I've been waitin' to get you to mi'self all this weekend . . ."

Marcus heard their footsteps coming closer, their breathless murmurs. He had to find the device. These two servants couldn't be here. And he could think of only one way to get them to leave.

Phillippa's hand was resting gently on his shoulder, her body pressed against the length of his. Her eyes sought out his in the dark, locking on with a question as she listened to the approaching couple.

And that fight that had been twisting through his body for days, weeks, was finally lost.

"Forgive me," he mouthed in silence, as his lips descended to hers.

Nineteen

HEAT. It drugged him, lured him. She drugged him. When his mouth met hers, she opened to him immediately, as if she, too, had been thinking of this.

Dreaming of this.

His tongue slid tantalizingly over her lips, beyond the barrier of her teeth to mate with hers. The moment they touched, every nerve of his body dazzled awake. She let out the softest sigh, as if she were drifting down from the sky and more than happy about it. Urging him forward.

His mind knew that he was taking advantage of the situation. But the blood coursing through his veins did not care.

He pressed her back into the corner, his hand coming up to embrace her head, caress the skin at the nape of her neck—*oh, that skin*—the other hand at her waist, kneading her soft flesh, working its way up, to cup her breast, graze the hardened peak of her nipple.

She squealed at this intimate touch, but pressed into his hand, begged for more. And he was more than willing to give it.

As his thigh nudged its way between her legs, his thumb dipped below her scandalously low neckline, brushing against the nubbed evidence of her arousal.

At that, she broke the kiss, gasping. Marcus moved his mouth to her neck, her ear, her collarbone, murmuring his adoration against her skin. Clasped as she was against him, holding onto him for dear life, he was lost to all other thought, all other sounds.

It must have been Phillippa's gasps, the little breathless sighs that clouded his mind, that drew the attention of the other occupants of the stables. The girl spoke first.

"What was—oh," she cried, her footfalls stopping short. Marcus broke off his attentions from Phillippa's earlobe to glare menacingly over his shoulder. There he met the eyes of the young man, giving silent warning to stay away. He nudged Phillippa a little farther into the shadows, praying that she was hidden enough to not be recognized.

The young footman—as his unbuttoned uniform informed him to be—apparently was wise enough to leave trysting gentry alone and quickly tugged at his ladylove's hand.

"Come on, Sal," he said, hiding the smirk in his voice. "I know a better spot for us, under the old oak tree."

As he pulled her away, Marcus could hear the rushed whispers between the two. But Marcus didn't care what they gossiped about. As soon as their footsteps fell away and the squeak of the stable door signaled their exit, he turned to look back at Phillippa.

Her lips were swollen and reddened from his assault. Her cheeks flushed, and her eyes shining bright in the darkness. She looked up at him expectantly, waiting. For him to move toward her, or to move away?

Then she glanced down and saw that his hand was still perched at her breast, his fingers still nestled inside her gown, idly toying with her pebbled nipple. Her eyes flew to his face, as he immediately withdrew his hand into the cold air, removing the other from the warmth of her shoulder.

Slowly, she untwined herself from him, unlaced her fingers from his hair, let go of his shoulder. But they kept their bodies still, and Marcus, his blood humming, kept her pressed into the dark corner.

"I'm sorry," he rasped, his eyes searching her face.

"Don't . . . don't be," she replied, her voice husky, shaky.

"It was the only thing I could think of—to get rid of them," he whispered.

She nodded.

"You can slap me now, if you want. As is customary."

She blushed profusely at that and managed a small smile. "No, I, uh—I think I'll hold it in account, if necessary."

"As you like." He grinned and finally, painfully, moved his body away from hers.

And, after a quick glance at his trousers, he sent up a silent prayer of thanks for the dark.

As he walked away, looking around the quiet stables, still, but for the occasional snort and sleepy whinny, the cold air acted as an unyielding reminder of his purpose there. Of what they were looking for.

Damn. Damn, damn, damn, damn, damn.

She had gotten into his head.

But worse than that, he suspected she had gotten into his heart.

"Come on," he snapped, his voice harsher than strictly necessary, but it was the only way in his mind to reestablish his course. "You insisted on coming along, now show me where Sterling and this stranger were standing."

Phillippa's knees were shaky. The wall was holding her up. And her body, her body sang from having been pressed and molded so perfectly to his. And once he left, it cried out for his return. It was unfair, this sharp reaction she had to him. It was delicious.

But then his voice became clipped and cold—a great deal like his brother's—and it was as sobering as freezing water to the face.

Obviously he was used to kissing women to get out of difficult situations. It was another day of work for him.

Fine. She gathered her strength and strode out of the corner. She brushed past Marcus as she moved farther down the row, stopping at a stall labeled Letty.

"I was crouched on the outside of the building, here." Then she moved briskly back toward the front doors, just about in the center of the row. "I saw through the stall, and they came, and stopped about here, and rifled through the satchel."

Marcus nodded, then immediately joined her, and began rummaging around the hay and straw that layered the packed earth of the stable floor.

"It'll be small," he mumbled, "otherwise, the stable lads would have found it."

Phillippa joined him in rummaging, however delicately.

It was quiet for several minutes, the silence pounding down on her. Her mind turned unerringly back to the darkened corner, the way his hands caressed her, enveloped her, and she could not let it.

"Marcus," she finally said, breaking through her own thoughts, and apparently his, because he turned around, startled. "Can we—can you talk about something? Anything?"

"Certainly," he replied, pulling himself back on his heels, resigned. "What would you like me to talk about?"

"You could—you could tell me what we're looking for," she ventured, hoping that this would keep her mind, their minds, occupied.

Marcus seemed to consider this. He moved to another stall, began rummaging there before he started speaking.

"At the Whitford Banquet," he said in a whisper, "they caused a distraction and then stole something from the house, while everyone was in a panic."

"I recall," Phillippa replied, toeing back some hay with her delicate slipper. Stables, even the best, were smelly places. "They stole your pistols."

"No, they stole documents, too," Marcus corrected. "Designs for a new kind of pin barrel firing rifle; Whitford was still building the prototype. The design was to be sold to His Majesty's army, which would have made Whitford a lot of money, not to mention given Britain an advantage on the field."

"What does this have to do with whatever we're looking for?" she asked.

Marcus grunted as he lifted a hay bale to look underneath it. Nothing. "Guns were Whitford's pride and joy, not to mention his own particular brand of patriotism. What is Hampshire's?"

She didn't even have to think it over. "His horses; he lent half his stock to the war effort during the Hundred Days." Phillippa gave a small gasp of shock, causing Marcus to look up. "You think Laurent means to steal the horses?"

Marcus shook his head. "I don't think even Laurent could manage that. But he could destroy Hampshire's breeding program. I think in this instance, the distraction and the purpose will be met with one blow."

Phillippa nodded, catching on. "We're looking for . . . for some kind of incendiary device, aren't we?" she asked, a drop of fear pitching her voice.

Marcus nodded. "It's only a guess. Laurent in the past has experimented with chemicals. I've done a little study myself, but I'm no man of science."

Phillippa felt all the blood drain from her face, her heart beginning to beat double time. Panicking. Her legs gave out from under her, and she lowered herself to sit on the bale of hay Marcus had just put down.

He obviously noticed her pallor and irregular breathing, because he moved to kneel in front of her, took her by the shoulders, and held her at arm's length. "Phillippa, I could be wrong. . . . But if I'm not . . . I'll stay and look. You go back to the house; tell Byrne where I am—"

She shook her head. "I'm not leaving you here."

"Phillippa—"

"Marcus, no, I can't; you could die—"

He could have argued. He could have threatened, cajoled, throttled her. Instead, he stared. At her knees.

Even for Marcus, this was strange. Phillippa was about to ask him if she had a tear in her gown at knee level, but then he took hold of her legs.

"Marcus, what are you—" But her unfinished question was answered when he swung her legs to the side and began examining a small break, a crevice in the bale on which she was seated.

Phillippa stood watching as Marcus reached into the hay bale, almost up to his elbow. She leaned down, crouched beside him, as he rummaged around and pulled out—

Well, Phillippa didn't really know what it was.

It looked like the innards of a clock, small, it fit neatly into Marcus's hand, with a vial attached, enclosing some kind of yellowy bit of wax. A tiny hammer was held in place by a taut wire. The whole thing ticked, winding down.

"I think—that its phosphorus," Marcus said, examing the device closely.

"The smelly stuff that makes fireworks flash?" Phillippa asked, and received a quick nod of approval in return.

"It reacts to the air, burns bright white." Marcus delicately touched the hammer on the tension wire. "Phillippa," he said, his brow furrowed in intense concentration, "I need you to step away from me now."

Phillippa did as she was told, taking cautious, measured steps back, all the while keeping her eyes on what Marcus was doing. The ticking of the device was becoming slower, the spaces in between stretching further apart, echoing in the dark of the stables.

Marcus delicately reached into the device and took hold of the tiny hammer. Gingerly, and with aching precision, he held his breath, closed his eyes, and broke the hammer off.

And nothing happened.

Phillippa tiptoed back to Marcus's side and placed a hand on his shoulder as he exhaled in relief.

"Wind up the gears, and it ticks down," he said, staring at the device, "like a clockwork toy. Once the time runs out, the hammer breaks the glass, exposing the phosphorus to the air, igniting it."

"But it's so small; surely it can't burn this whole place down." Phillippa replied, her eyes narrowing.

"Yes, but stuck in the middle of the bale, it would send the whole thing up, and then fire would spread, and voilà: a burning stable." Marcus said, standing.

"And they wound it eight hours in advance?" she asked.

"I doubt it, someone was here just before we were."

No, Phillippa thought. It was too simple, too easy that they found it. And the device was so small, ridiculous to have kept it in so large a satchel. Do men know nothing of how to execute fashion usefully?

"Marcus," Phillippa said, grabbing his arm, "the satchel—it was bigger than this. I mean it was fuller."

Marcus stared down into her eyes for a moment; then together, they looked down the length of the stables.

In front of every stall was a bale of straw, laid out to replace the muck from the stalls in the morning. And at the far end of the structure, piled to rafters, were bales enough to keep the stalls clean for the next month.

Phillippa gulped, as Marcus turned his gaze to the device in his hand. "How many?" he asked her.

"How many what?" she replied, her eyes flickering with alarming speed from one bale, to another, to another.

"How many devices do you think were in that bag?" he asked.

"I don't know," she replied.

"Phillippa!" he commanded.

"I don't know!" she cried, turning her mind back to that afternoon, back to the stranger and the satchel on his back.

"A half dozen, maybe?" she answered hopefully. "Marcus we can find them, I know it. You start on that end, and I'll start on this one."

Unfortunately, her faith in their device-finding abilities was not to be tested. For at that moment, in the distance, the whine and pop of that evening's main event sounded through the night.

The fireworks had begun.

"Too late," Marcus said, and Phillippa heard the soft pop of breaking glass, as the dry-as-kindling bale to their left began to at first smoke and then burst into flame.

Twenty

"GET down!" Marcus yelled, putting his arms around Phillippa's shoulders and ducking. Another bale burst into flame, then another. One up in the rafters. Marcus glanced over his shoulder, and saw what he feared; the neat stack of bales leaking smoke. The whole pile would be on fire in a matter of moments.

It all happened so fast. The pop of distant fireworks died as whinnying Thoroughbreds began to snort and scream, rearing as the flames began to spread. Phillippa clung to Marcus's waist like a lifeline, pulling him toward the stable doors.

"We have to get out of here!" she cried from under his arm.

Marcus was quick to agree.

As fire seemed to spread with abandon underfoot, and burning straw began to fall from the rafters, Marcus and Phillippa covered their mouths and made their way to the stable door and ran out into the cold, sweet air.

As Marcus took a deep breath, clearing his head of the chemical-tainted smoke that had just begun to assault his lungs, Phillippa wasted no time in running back to the stables.

"Wait, what are you doing?" Marcus said as he ran after her.

"The horses! We have to get them out!" she yelled as he caught her about the waist.

"You can't go back in there," he argued, and when she pulled against his embrace, he stilled her. "The stalls—do they have exterior doors?"

She nodded through tears, and they took off for the side of the building, which was now emitting noxious smoke and ominous light.

As Marcus pulled open the first latch of the exterior stalls and led out a frantic mare, Phillippa, having realized that the two of them were not going to be enough to get all the horses out, cried out into the glowing night. "Oy! Fire! The stables are on fire! Help! Fire!"

The air remained still. Until suddenly, they heard from the other side of a hill an answering cry of, "We're coming! We're coming!" and a dozen boys, ranging in age from eight to fifteen, ran over the rise.

Immediately the eldest boy, who must have been head stable lad, commanded, "Billy, Frankie, run to the house, get help!" and the remaining ten split into groups on either side of the building, pulling open the exterior doors of the stalls, freeing the frightened and bucking occupants.

As they worked, more people, alerted by the quick-of-foot stable lads and Phillippa's yelling, began to join them, some working on the stall doors, some taking the water barrels that had once served as Phillippa's hiding place and putting them to use.

Marcus moved to the next stall and the next, working with as much speed as possible, when Phillippa's urgent voice drew his attention.

"Marcus," she said breathlessly, pulling at his sleeve, "I think that's the man I saw—the stranger."

She pointed toward a figure silhouetted at the top of the hill, about a hundred feet away, next to a tree, watching the chaos of the fire. It was impossible to make out his features in the dark at that distance, but occasional flashes from overhead fireworks and the fire of the stables was enough to highlight his frame and light-colored hair.

He must have realized he'd been spotted, because the man—Phillippa's stranger—took off like a bullet, disappearing behind the rise of the hill.

Marcus hesitated only a moment. Then he abandoned the stables to the crowd that had begun to gather and took off after the man.

A cry of "Wait for me!" echoed behind him, as Phillippa joined in the footrace.

Phillippa, when she put her mind to it, could move surprisingly fast. Marcus, however, was faster, and he was not about to obey her dictate and wait for her. His objective was to catch the man who moved with lightning speed across the paddocks and back toward the house.

Even in the dark, it was easy to keep his eyes on the man. He was the only one moving away from the stables; everyone else they passed was moving toward them. Marcus's long legs ate up the ground with remarkable speed. Closing the distance between them, Marcus was within a few dozen feet of his quarry when the stranger took a sharp turn and disappeared into the Hampshires' reknowned hedge maze.

"Damn it!" Marcus spat, as Phillippa came up behind him, gasping for breath. The maze had a twelve-foot wall of thick boxwood hedge and three other ways in and out; they couldn't post a sentry at each entrance. The only way to keep track of the man was to follow him in. That was the best and perhaps the only chance they'd have to catch him. "Come on," he said, grabbing Phillippa's hand as they plunged into the maze's dark recesses.

Marcus started to the left, as he had seen the stranger do. But from there, he could only follow his instincts. A right, a left, another left. He was certain they were within feet of the stranger; he followed the sound of shuffling feet and concentrated on the panicked puffs of breathing he could hear under the ongoing fireworks spectacular.

They passed a few other couples frolicking in the maze, playing hide-and-seek. Either they didn't know about the disaster going on at the stables, or they used it to their advantage. But their giggles and breathless laughter floated eerily over the hedges and unfortunately masked the stranger's movements, momentarily confusing Marcus. He pressed on, following, following . . .

But when he tried to take another corner, he was held by Phillippa, pulling him in the other direction.

"He went this way," she said in a whisper.

"No, he went this way," Marcus replied.

"We just came from over there; we went in a big circle. I recognize that hedge!"

"Its all the same hedge!" he argued. Then, "You're sure?"

"Four lefts take us back to where we started," she replied, exasperated. "If he's trying to get out, he had to go this way."

Marcus looked to the left, then the right. And for once, he allowed Phillippa to guide him.

She moved with certainty, cutting through the maze with the knowledge of one who'd mapped its secrets before, from previous weekend parties. She cut right, then another right, then led them down a straight path to what must have been near to the heart of the maze, when at the end of the row, Marcus saw the figure in the dark. And the glint of metal in his hand.

Marcus pulled Phillippa to him, threw her into the hedge, and covered her body with his own before the shot rang out. He felt her body freeze against his. And time held them there.

Have to move.

Have to move *now*.

Together they reversed course, running as fast as they could back the way they came, before another shot could rend the air.

Sprinting, they turned the corner, then another, retraced their steps. Phillippa outran Marcus this time, fear lighting her movements and pain slowing his. But she never let go of his hand. Until, on another turn, she ran directly into someone else.

"Omph!" Phillippa cried, as she and the lady were both flattened to the ground.

"Hey!" came a familiar voice, and as she looked up, Marcus recognized that it belonged to Lady Jane Cummings.

Both ladies regained their feet, Lady Jane regarding Phillippa with a sneer. "What do you think you're doing?" Lady Jane harrumphed. "How dare you assault me! And what are you doing with Mr. Worth? What kind of game—"

But her accusations were to go unspoken, for at that moment, another shot came from behind them.

"Jane, get down!" Phillippa cried, tackling her archenemy to the floor. Marcus ducked. The bullet whizzed over their heads, penetrating the hedge and landing there.

"Move!" Marcus cried, taking Phillippa's hand and dragging both her and Lady Jane around the corner.

As they all regained their feet, Lady Jane cried, "Someone's shooting at you!"

"We know!" Phillippa replied.

"Phillippa, who's shooting at you?" Her voice was bordering on hysteria, and Marcus's strength was sapping from him. They were someplace he didn't recognize. Someplace . . . lost . . .

Phillippa took charge, grabbing Lady Jane's arm and saying, "We need to get out of here. Do you know the way?"

Jane, pale and frightened, nodded immediately. "I found the way out three times already. We have to go . . . this way." And as she moved briskly in that direction, Phillippa and Marcus followed.

Quick turns, panicked glances over their shoulders, Marcus was led along by the two women. From pursuer to pursued, they moved quickly to their destination, and finally he saw the lights from the house.

Marcus nearly cried in relief, for as they breached the exit of the hedge maze, finding themselves at the far end of Lady Hampshire's fountain garden, they were greeted by the sight of crowds of people, watching either the fireworks burst into intricate shapes, or the haze of bright yellow light on the sky that was the stables.

Either way, their adversary could not fire into a crowd.

Phillippa and Lady Jane nodded to each other, assumed faces of composure that belied their mussed appearances, as they began to edge their way into the mass of people.

Marcus would have laughed, if he'd had the ability. But he didn't. And as he, Phillippa, and conspicuously in front of them, Lady Jane, crossed the threshold from the gardens into the house, his knees gave out on him.

The bullet in his shoulder had finally sapped his strength.

"Marcus?" Phillippa whispered as he slumped against her shoulder. His weight leaned into her, and she brought her hand to his face, maneuvered him to meet her eyes. He was foggy, unfocused, but when he found her gaze, he locked on, as if his life depended on it.

Then she saw the blood.

Her hand had brushed against the dark wool covering his far shoulder, and when she drew it back, her once cream glove was smeared with a bright rusty red, wet and sticky.

"Marcus!" she cried, losing all sense of secrecy, examining his arm as his body fell against hers. The wool of his dark coat was punctured, a small hole dug deep into the back of his muscular right shoulder.

"Jane!" Phillippa called out, drawing her attention. Lady Jane turned, her face still schooled in an impassive mask. However, when she saw Phillippa's distress, her eyes widened in shock.

Phillippa could only thank God for medium-scale disasters. For on an average day, Lady Jane Cummings coming to Mrs. Phillippa Benning's aid would be gossiped about immediately.

But since this was no ordinary day, it went largely unnoticed by those people headed out of the house to watch the various spectacles.

"He's shot," Phillippa said in a whisper, as Lady Jane went even paler.

"Oh my God! We have to tell Lord Hampshire. We have to call the magistrate!"

"No!" Phillippa ejaculated. "Jane, we can't tell anyone! No one, do you understand?" When Jane nodded slowly, Phillippa continued. "Can you find his brother? He'll know what to do."

"Who?"

"His brother, Byrne. He's got dark hair, pale complexion, a cane."

Marcus lifted his head from Phillippa's shoulder, fighting for consciousness, mumbling. "He was in the ballroom."

"I'm going to take Marcus to his chamber; have Byrne meet us there," Phillippa commanded, and then, before Lady Jane could turn and leave, "Jane, this is serious. No one can know."

She nodded, then disappeared into the crowd, moving determinedly toward the ballroom.

Marcus's long weight pushed against Phillippa's side as he spoke into her ear. "Can you trust her?"

It was a risk, she knew. They were trusting her worst enemy with their biggest secret. But Jane had been so cool under pressure, getting them out of the maze. And a decade ago, Phillippa had trusted Jane with every secret and vice versa.

But, this was not ten years ago. She and Jane were different people now. How different, was the material question.

Refusing to acknowledge her mixed feelings, Phillippa simply blew out a breath and smiled encouragingly. "We'll have to." Then, once she saw him nod limply, she forced his eyes to her face.

"We have to move now," she said.

There were fewer people coming out of the ballroom now, heading toward the garden, but they had been observed enough to raise a few eyebrows. The dark wool of Marcus's coat camouflaged the most obvious clue to his injury, and most attendants of the party were too happily intoxicated or self-involved to pay him much mind.

But if he should fall to the floor unconscious, that would change, and quickly.

"Come on," Phillippa urged, willing Marcus to take the next step. Slowly they crossed the hall and found the staircase leading up to the west wing. Phillippa held him up, but Marcus, resolute and determined as he was, still stumbled once when ascending the stairs.

"Too much wine," Phillippa smiled as an excuse to Mrs. Biddington, as they passed her on the stairs. Mrs. Biddington was luckily so rarely in the company of the Incomparable Mrs. Benning that she willingly accepted this explanation, nodded blindly, and hurried down the stairs.

By the time they reached Marcus's room, his complexion was beyond pale. But he kept moving forward, determined, taking the next step, and the next, and the next, until he was finally at his bedchamber.

She saw him hesitate at the door. "Come," Phillippa murmured, "let's get you to bed."

But Marcus shook his head, the faintest particle of a smile crossing his face before resuming its stark, intense demeanor. "Check . . . check the room. I have to. Make sure—it's safe."

Marcus reached for the doorknob, but his hand shook so violently as he did, Phillippa squealed and stilled his hand with her own. "I'll do it," she said. "Wait here."

He looked as if he might veto her, but Phillippa was brooking no arguments right now. Before he could stop her, she transferred Marcus's weight from her side to the doorframe and slid inside.

The bedchamber was dark, neat. No disturbance had taken place there. Not knowing exactly the best way to check a room for potential enemies, Phillippa quickly searched the best hiding places. She threw open the wardrobe, checked under the bed, in the valet's antechamber. Nothing.

Throwing open the bedchamber door, she found that Marcus, fighting the black sleep of unconsciousness, was not alone.

Byrne and Lady Jane had arrived.

"You left him in the hall?" Byrne whispered coldly as he wrapped his brother's uninjured side around his shoulders, walking him into the room.

"Byrne, its all right," Marcus said woozily.

"He . . . he told me to check the room," Phillippa said defensively, as she guided them in.

"And?" Byrne shot back.

"And nothing; it's safe."

Byrne grunted in reply, easing Marcus onto the bed. Sitting seemed to help, as the extertion he had lent to walking could now be concentrated on breathing, color returning slightly to his cheeks. She sat down next to him on the bed, holding him up as Byrne inspected the hole in Marcus's shoulder. "No exit wound. And the bullet's deep."

"I know," Marcus said on a laugh, which quickly turned into a grimace of pain.

"Marcus," Byrne said, his voice soaked in regret, "I should've—I'm sorry I didn't—"

"We'll do the 'I told you so' later," Marcus gritted. "Right now, would you be so kind as to get the bullet out of my shoulder?"

"Should I call for a doctor?" Lady Jane said from the other side of the room.

"No!" Marcus, Phillippa, and Byrne cried together.

Marcus looked to Phillippa, cocked one eyebrow rakishly, nodded in Jane's direction.

Phillippa got the message, and went to Lady Jane's side. "Jane, can you help us? We'll need, um, fresh water, and . . ." Unable to think of other necessary supplies, she turned to Marcus and Byrne.

"Linens, lots of them. Ointment, whatever you can find," Marcus supplied.

"And brandy," Byrne finished.

"Phillippa," Jane said, pitching her voice low, "please let me call for a doctor. I can't go scouring through a strange house looking for things like that, I'll be caught."

"Says the girl who single-handedly raided the kitchens of Mrs. Humphrey's School to throw a tea party at midnight when we were ten." Phillippa countered, earning a challenging smile from Lady Jane.

Phillippa took a step closer to her archenemy, dropped her voice to a whisper. "Please, Jane." And then Phillippa said the words she knew she would come to regret, but had to be laid bare. "I'll be in your debt."

A sparkle of mischievousness lit Jane's eyes as she nodded, turned around, and flounced out of the room.

After closing the door behind her, Phillippa skittered back to Marcus's side, where Byrne was assisting him in removing his fine wool formal evening coat.

Marcus hissed through his teeth as the bloodied sleeve was pulled down, revealing his linen shirt, which was once stark white, the whole arm and back now a violent red, plastered to his body.

"He's lost a lot of blood," Phillippa said gravely.

"He's going to lose a lot more when we dig the bullet out of his shoulder," Byrne answered.

"But, you know what you're doing, right?" she worried. "You've done this before?"

"Actually," Marcus replied, "I've done it to him. I suspect he's looking forward to his payback."

Byrne snorted a chuckle, then turned serious. "Now tell me who did this," he said, turning his intense gaze to Phillippa.

"I . . . I don't know," Phillippa stuttered a reply. "I'd never met him; I don't know his name."

"Describe him." Byrne ordered, and Phillippa obliged.

"Smaller, thin, maybe ten stone at most. This afternoon he was dressed like a farmer, straw hat, dun-colored trousers—terribly rough twill, I'm certain"—she paused when Byrne cleared his throat impatiently—"but this evening," she continued, "I . . . I couldn't see what he was wearing. Dark colors. Maybe evening dress."

"Maybe?" Byrne questioned harshly.

"Maybe not," she conceded.

"Byrne, it was him." Marcus spoke up. "He had the pistols."

"Good." Byrne nodded, pacing, as he took this all in. Then, "Do you think there's a chance he's still here?"

Marcus remained still for a moment, then nodded his head.

"Where?" Byrne responded, his jaw set.

"He could . . . if he wanted something in the house, he'd be searching right now . . . but I think he went back to blend into the mayhem at the stables. Crawled back into whatever disguise he'd assumed."

Byrne, stopped pacing and drummed his fingers on the head of his cane. "Time is of the essence," he said.

"But what about Marcus?" Phillippa cried. "He needs your help."

A look passed between the two brothers, an unspoken communication.

"It's your shoulder. Are you sure?" Byrne asked.

"Yes," Marcus answered seriously. "We'll be fine."

Byrne shot a quick glance toward Phillippa, his eyes narrowing in honest appraisal. "I'll save my payback for another time."

And then he hobbled out the door, leaving Phillippa alone with Marcus.

"He's . . . he's not going to take the bullet out?" she asked dazedly.

"No," Marcus replied. "You are."

Shock coursed through her system as Phillippa felt her legs go unsteady for the first time all evening.

"Did you say . . . did you say what I think you said?"

"Yes," his voice was resolute.

Oh God.

"Let's get to work." He sighed, adjusting his seat on the bed. "First things first. I need you to take off my shirt."

She could do this, Phillippa decided. Doctors do this kind of thing all the time. Midwives birth children, for heaven's sake. Compared to that, pulling one little bullet out of his shoulder would be akin to removing a splinter. Her experience with blood was limited, but when Alistair lay dying, she had managed to soothe his brow, keep him cool . . .

She could do this. She would not cower in fear. She would simply have to approach it in an efficient, businesslike manner.

With a silent prayer heavenward, Phillippa moved to him and plucked at the knot of his cravat, opening it with relatively steady fingers.

Marcus let out a sigh of relief as she removed the offending article and tossed it on the bed.

"That thing . . . has been choking me all night," he said, using his good arm to free the small buttons at his collar, breathing deeply.

"Can't be easy running after a villain in a cravat," Phillippa conceded, as she concentrated on easing open the long row of tiny buttons down the front of his shirt.

"Among other things," Marcus countered, his eyebrow shooting up in a decidedly rakish fashion.

As Phillippa freed the last of the buttons, she pushed the cloth off his good shoulder, her hands grazing over his muscled chest and shoulder. So much for the businesslike demeanor, Phillippa thought, as she felt her face going hot.

She could feel his gaze on her face, watching her every action and reaction, so she set her mouth in a thin line and carried on. She freed his good arm from the sleeve, and then, maneuvering around behind him, transferred her attentions to the bloodied shoulder, the sight of which seemed to grow in her vision, everything else receding into nothing.

This would prove more difficult.

She must have been staring at it for some time, because Marcus broke into her thoughts, saying, "Phillippa, listen to me."

She did, focusing only on his voice. Amazingly, it was steady and calm, even though sweat dripped from his skin as he fought to keep the pain at bay.

"Just be as gentle as you can; it will be fine," he said soothingly.

Phillippa gulped hard, nodded. "It will be fine," she repeated under her breath, as she eased the sticky, wet cloth off his skin. "It will be fine, it will be fine, it will be fine . . ."

Then, amazingly, she had the sleeve pulled past the wrist, and the thing was done.

He smiled at her, his warm brown gaze fuzzy but comforting. "Good girl."

She moved back onto the bed, kneeling behind him. Unfortunately, the removal of the shirt only highlighted the size of the hole, and now that the cloth was gone, the oozing blood became more readily apparent. The hole was high in the shoulder, angled upward. She thought his shoulder blade must certainly be fractured at least, but if the gunman had aimed a few inches lower, the ball would be in his lungs. The wound must have hurt dreadfully, for even the smallest twitch of his muscles expelled more fluid.

Her breathing must have become unsteady, because Marcus reached behind him with his free hand, took hold of hers, and pulled her to face him.

"Phillippa—no, no, darling, look at me. *It's just me.* Now, I'm going to tell you what to do. Can you handle that?"

She focused her attention on his face. His voice was calm, yes, but his eyes, they held the first color of worry behind the rich brown. She had to do this. She had to be strong for him. She would not let him see her fail.

"Handle it?" she repeated in her most imperious, superior tone. "I am Phillippa Benning. I can handle anything."

He leaned in and kissed her forehead. It was not the passionate devouring she had known from him. It was proud and soothing. It gave her strength.

Once he released her, she drew back, put her hands on her hips. "Now what do we do first?"

However, that question was not to be answered, as a knock at the door startled them both.

Phillippa moved quickly, went to the door's keyhole.

"It's Lady Jane," Phillippa said, opening the door and admitting said lady, who's arms overflowed with her findings.

"I found the linen closet and a bottle of brandy," she said as Phillippa helped her unload the goods from her arms. "And a jug of water. I couldn't find any ointment because I had no idea what I was looking for, and I couldn't ask my ladies' maid, because she'd wonder why I needed it and I had no idea what to tell her."

"Good Lord, Jane, surely you could have thought of a lie for her." Phillippa explained as if to a child. "Couldn't you have just told her you stubbed your foot or some such thing?"

"No, I *surely* could not!" Lady Jane expostulated, putting her nose in the air. "Not everyone lies as easily as you, Phillippa. I am an *honest* individual."

"Well, I am so sorry to have offended your delicate sensibilities," Phillippa snipped, "but in all the chasing and running away from a madman, and Marcus—Mr. Worth—getting shot, I sillily relied on your cunning and guile. I do beg your pardon."

"Well, I shall not beg yours," Lady Jane sneered back, her eyes beginning to glisten. "You've always been like this, thinking everyone and everything can fall into your line—"

"I have not! You're the one who—"

"Ladies," Marcus said from his position on the bed. "Could we continue this later?"

Phillippa felt her face go hot as she took a step back from Jane. It was unfortunate that they simply could not stop arguing, but for her part, Phillippa decided to blame the stressful circumstances.

She took hold of the water jug and the linens, brought them to the small table beside the bed. Jane grabbed the flask of brandy, following.

"Where's your brother?" she asked, as she handed the flask to him.

"He . . . he went to get something." Phillippa covered, meeting Marcus's eye.

The room went still for a moment, as if everyone was uncertain of what to do. Then Jane, who seemed to have been remarkably mesmerized by the sight of Marcus's unclothed chest, shifted her gaze to Phillippa and gave her a frank appraisal.

"You need a new dress," she stated.

Phillippa looked down at her once-lovely cream and silver Madame Le Trois, the hem now dirty, the satin crushed, and blood smeared on her sleeve and skirts from having supported Marcus up the stairs.

"Yes, thank you, I'm aware." Phillippa said coolly. "Luckily, I'm a favorite of Madame Le Trois."

"No," Jane snitted back, "I mean, if you ever want to leave this room without causing a riot, you'll need a new dress."

"Oh." Jane was right, of course. Her appearance must be shocking, to say the least. But as worried as she had been about Marcus's circumstances, she had not thought about her own.

"I'll go get you one," Jane broke into her thoughts and moved to the door.

"Wait," Phillippa said, as Jane's hand was on the latch, "one of your dresses?"

"Never fear," she smiled, "it'll be one I haven't worn—this weekend."

And she disappeared back into the hall.

"Well," Marcus said, his voice breaking the silence, "shall we continue?"

"We . . . we *truly* aren't going to wait for your brother to return?" Phillippa asked hesitantly.

Marcus shook his head. "He might not be back until daybreak. We have the supplies. I'll talk you through it."

Linens were torn into strips. Fresh water was poured out into a bowl. Scissors from Totty's kit were laid out on the bedside table. A pair of pincers were obtained from Marcus's supplies. Brandy. All placed precisely for Phillippa's ease of use.

First, she cleaned the area around the wound, flushed it with water, dried it with a piece of linen. Then at his command, she fetched over a candle to light her work.

"Hold it up to the wound," he said, "can you see anything?"

She peered inside the hole, inside him, making out little beyond the punctured flesh. Then, "I see—I see a bit of metal," she said, spying the small gray shine of reflected light from deep within.

"That's good," he said. "Can you reach it?"

"Reach it?" she repeated. "You want me to try to . . . to touch it?"

"With the pincers, Phillippa," he smiled, his voice only slightly strained.

"Right," she replied, rolling her eyes at her own foolishness and, placing the candle down, she fetched the long, thin metal tongs from the table.

Now all she had to do was stick the pincers into his shoulder and draw out the bullet. The only problem being how badly her hands were shaking.

She tried a deep, calming breath. She tried a swig of brandy, as did Marcus. It helped a little, enough so Phillippa repositioned herself at his shoulder and steadied herself.

However, the upward angle of the wound made access less than simple.

"I think this might be easier if you were to lie down."

He nodded limply. Slowly, gently, Phillippa helped ease him onto the bed, onto his stomach.

She shifted him as well as she could to facilitate his comfort. And in doing so, she noticed the jagged scar in his side. Her finger traced it gently, reverently.

Marcus turned his head to the side. "Stabbed. Long time ago."

She nodded, lifted her hand.

"It's time to do this," he said. She brought the candle as close as possible, crouched on the bed beside him, and resolutely inserted the pincers.

She moved slowly, not wanting to cause any unnecessary pain, but unfortunately, the brandy and breathing had not been enough to hold her hand completely still.

"Can you do me a favor?" Marcus asked through his teeth. "Can you prattle on about something?"

"Certainly," Phillippa replied, her voice unnaturally high. "What would you like me to prattle about?"

"You could," he paused to take a few breaths, "tell me why you and Lady Jane don't get on."

She felt the pincers hit the solid surface of the bullet.

"That's not easy to explain," Phillippa replied, trying like the devil to not push against the bullet, causing it to go deeper.

"That, or you could tell me about your marriage," Marcus challenged. At her lack of a reply, he continued, "You're fishing around my shoulder for a chunk of metal. Lady Jane or Alistair Benning. Your choice."

Phillippa sighed, exasperated. "I'd rather discuss most anything else. I'd discuss Broughton if you'd asked."

Marcus chuckled weakly at that. "Did you know that if you married him, you'd be Phillip and Phillippa?"

She smiled ruefully. "The thought had crossed my mind," she admitted.

"You know you're too good for him, don't you?"

"I know several people who would tell you I'm no good whatsoever," she retorted with cheer, as the pincers grazed the side of the wound, causing Marcus to wince in pain.

She wished he would yell. She wished he would cry out, but even though his breaths came hard, sweat coated his taut skin, and his voice was strained, he held himself in. He was being so strong. The only thing he asked of her was that she prattle on, the only thing that might keep his mind off the pain she was putting him through. And at that moment, the decision she made was easy.

She decided to let him in.

"My marriage to Alistair Benning," she began, "was very short." She felt him tense, then go still. As she managed to maneuver the prongs of the pincers around the sides of the bullet, she continued. "I was in my first Season, and he was very impressive. He was, in fact, the man of my dreams: ancient name, elite Ton, handsome, charming. He swept me off my feet."

"You were young and in love," Marcus said.

"I was young, yes," she said, gently pulling the pincers out, "and I certainly thought I was in love. We were to sail to Venice for our honeymoon. But on the ship, a yacht given to us by my father, the whole crew came down with a fever. Five days into the voyage, Alistair died."

"And you've . . . mourned him ever since?" Marcus asked.

"For a time, yes. I mourned the man of my dreams." Suddenly, he gave a sharp gasp, as the pincers, bullet intact, were withdrawn from the hole in his shoulder. Exhaling her nerves, she dropped the small ball of iron and pincers on the table and pressed a strip of linen against the wound, again bleeding profusely.

"And then?" he asked, after he steadied his breathing.

"Then" she answered, "I discovered who he really was."

For a brief moment, she considered telling him about how she had mourned the loss of Alistair, of their life together, for the first month. Then, tired of being coddled and pitied by her family, she had decided to move into the ancient Benning House on Grosvenor Square, which, since Alistair was the last of the line, she inherited. She found out soon enough, she inherited an empty house; the facade was the only thing kept up for appearances. And then the creditors began to knock. Luckily, they did so at the servants' entrance, allowing her to preserve her dignity, and the lie of his solvency. Publicly, she preserved the lie of Alistair's love. Lovelorn widows were so much more appealing than angry ones.

She almost told Marcus all of this—this story, which she had confided to no one else.

Almost.

"And that," she concluded, "is the story of my marriage."

And that was all she was willing to say.

Twenty-one

EXHAUSTION came quickly. And so did the fever.

All his energy had been so focused on talking her through the process of removing the bullet, when it was done, his will drained away.

She pressed the linen into his wound, pressure helping to stanch the bleeding. Helping him to sit up again, she wound his crushed cravat around his body, holding the linens in place and applying much needed pressure. His shoulder was throbbing mercilessly, he would have killed for a drop of Byrne's laudanum. But his head could not be muddled, at least, not to the blissful extent that those precious drops would allow, so he settled for a swig of brandy from the flask on the beside table.

She moved with efficency now, all of her nerves gone. After all, for her, the worst part of the ordeal was over. Of course, for him, it had just begun.

She murmured soothing words, nothing phrases, the simple melody of a nursery rhyme, as she ran a cool cloth over his forehead, his neck, his chest. He was too tired and too grateful for her ministrations to stop them. His skin was growing hot now, the expected fever coming on, the real danger in any battle.

Phillippa eased him back down onto the bed, on his stomach, and ran the cool, wet cloth on his back in long strokes.

Why had she chosen to tell him about her husband? Twenty-four hours ago, it was staunchly forbidden, the subject that shut her down, forced him from the room. But today, she had chosen to tell him that, contrary to popular belief, she had been disappointed in love. That wall that she had erected around her heart had shown the smallest crack.

He could only think of two possible reasons for such a revelation. First, that her relationship with Lady Jane was so black, so terrifying that she would not reveal it to anyone. He doubted this, if only because, as hard and proud and bright as she was, she was not cold. Not really. And neither was Lady Jane, in his limited experience.

The second option was that, for whatever reason, she had wanted him to know. She wanted to let him into that part of her life, that part that was unknown to anyone else. That possibly, he, not Broughton nor any of her other beautiful suitors, could be the one to dismantle that wall.

A thrilling thought—but also a frightening one.

For, as his mind drifted to warm blackness, the sweet undertow of sleep calling to him, he kept harkening back to that moment when he saw that flash of metal in the maze, and covered her body with his in the veriest nick of time.

She was not safe with him.

He could not be the one to break down the wall around her heart.

Because that bullet could have just as easily pierced it.

He fell into slumber quickly, fitfully. Phillippa tried her best to keep him cool, using up over half the jug of water in the attempt. It simply would not do to have him die, she told herself. It would require explanations to their hosts and the magistrate that she was unprepared to give. And besides, she needed him alive for the Benning Ball! That was the whole reason she was so diligent in her ministrations, she resolved. The only reason.

Phillippa was well-versed in making small adjustments to the truth for the sake of society, but when it was just her and just Marcus in a room alone together, the lies she told herself began to fall flat.

Something had changed. The when and the where of it she could not place, but at some point, she began to care deeply for Marcus Worth. Unassuming Marcus Worth!

It was the double life he led, surely. The dashing Blue Raven, his exploits and expertise. The danger that lurked around every corner. Although she had to admit that, having been a party to that danger, its excitement was not nearly all that it was cracked up to be. But it was the alluring secret that drew her to him, she was convinced, that made his acceptable countenance positively mouthwatering. Not his kindness or amiability. Not his humor or his faith in her abilities. Those were all well and good, but it would never do for Phillippa Benning to be brought to a heel because of the mundane day-to-day. By someone, well, average.

And Marcus Worth, as the Blue Raven, would never be average.

Her ruminations were interrupted by a discreet knock on the door. Seeing that Marcus had stilled and was resting comfortably, she went to the door, ushering in Lady Jane.

"I have a dress—" Lady Jane began, but Phillippa brought one finger to her own lips. She then indicated Marcus's slumbering form before Lady Jane could continue, but at a much lower pitch.

"I also managed to scratch my arm and procure some ointment," Jane finished, handing over a small pot of browning cream, and showing off a long, thin, red line on her arm.

"How'd you do that?" Phillippa asked.

"Just my fingernail; I have very sensitive skin, you know."

"Yes," Phillippa remarked, "you freckly redheads are positively cursed with it. But, Jane," she continued before Jane could snipe back, "you didn't have to do that."

"Oh, I didn't. I told my ladies' maid you did it in a fit of jealousy," Jane smiled wickedly.

Phillippa shot Jane a look as she put the jar down on the dresser, the dress on a nearby chair. Under the dress was a small pile of linens, unnecessary, considering the massive amount Jane had brought them earlier.

"More linens?" she asked.

"Oh, those aren't for him; they're for you."

"For me?"

"To fill out the top of the dress. You've always been the lesser of us in that area."

Phillippa smiled ruefully. "You're having fun, aren't you?"

"Just a little," Jane replied. Then, with a glance to the bed, "Will he be all right?"

Phillippa followed her gaze, saw that Marcus had rejected the covers, and his long, lithe back was exposed to view. She went to the bed, pulled the sheet back over him. "I think so. I hope so. I don't know much about this sort of thing."

"As well you shouldn't," Jane replied. "Who among us knows how to treat a bullet wound?"

"He does," Phillipa replied, with a nod to the sleeping Marcus. "He talked me through it."

Phillippa smoothed a hand over his brown hair, pushed a lock away from his fevered skin. She must have gotten lost in staring at him, because Lady Jane had to clear her throat to get her attention.

"Well, I should be back in bed by now; the party deteriorated after the stables were put out."

"Oh! The fire at the stables! Was anyone hurt?" Phillippa asked.

"A stableboy or two got singed." She shrugged. "They saved the horses. The building's a charred ruin, however."

Phillippa walked Jane to the door, one question hanging in the air. As Jane put her hand on the door's latch, Phillippa decided it was worth the gamble to ask it.

"Jane. Earlier, Marcus—Mr. Worth—asked me why you and I were . . . at odds."

Jane's eyes became cool. "And what did you tell him?"

"I told him it was difficult to explain," Phillippa replied.

"It is difficult," Jane agreed.

"Can . . . can you explain it?" Phillippa asked.

Jane kept her eyes on Phillippa's, as her jaw worked it over. "Lots of little reasons, I suppose. None of them big enough to merit this conversation," she concluded frostily. "Don't worry about the dress; you can discard it when you're done, I shan't wear it again."

And with that, their roles rightfully returned to the antagonistic places they had held for so long, Phillippa bade Lady Jane good night, and closed the door.

Marcus awoke at daybreak, his throat parched, his body crying out for relief from the heat of his fever. He was weak, yes, but his mind was there. He was not lost in some fevered dream. He knew this because Phillippa was not there, as she had been, in his mind, all through the night, his body wrapped around hers, their skin melded into one flesh.

Instead, he was greeted by Byrne.

"Good morning," Byrne said. "How do you feel?"

"Like cow dung," Marcus replied. "I need sleep."

"Yes, but first, we need to get you out of this house," Byrne said, as he threw assorted shirts and bloody linens into a valise. "And we need to do it without letting anyone know you've been injured."

Byrne was right, of course. The party ended today, and everyone would be piling into their carriages to go back to the city. He could not cry illness, because that would alert everyone, and especially Sterling (if he was helping Laurent as suspected) that he was injured. No, Marcus had to get up and walk out of this room, through the house, and into the carriage as if nothing had happened.

"Your fever's a bit less," Byrne remarked, placing a cool hand on Marcus's forehead.

"Where's Phillippa?" Marcus asked, looking around the room.

"I got back a few hours ago. I sent her to bed. She was successful with the bullet, I see." Byrne indicated the small lump of iron left on the bedside table. Marcus's eyes fell on the chair across the room, where Phillippa's once-beautiful dress lay, bloody and torn and dirty, as Byrne continued. "And I have to admit, she had a cooler head under the circumstances than I would have expected."

"Yes, she's a bloody rock," Marcus grunted, as he forced himself up to a sitting position. And for the first time, he noticed Byrne's condition.

"You look terrible."

Indeed, Byrne was pale, far paler than usual, and his eyes were deep hollows of bleakness. The hand that gripped his cane so tightly shook with the effort. "My leg is killing me," Byrne snapped. "Besides, you don't look so well yourself."

Marcus suspected that in an effort to keep on his adversary's trail, Byrne had forgone the usual dose of laudanum that he had grown to rely on like a second cane. Had it gotten so bad that he could not make it through one day without the stuff?

But Marcus was in no condition to pursue it now.

"All right," he sighed, "let's do this."

Two invalids, one known, one unknown, made there way out the door and into the hall, their bags having been sent down with a footman just ten minutes before. They had stuffed every article that had suffered some stain of blood that they could find into their trunks, including the linens, the sheets, and Phillippa's dress.

Marcus had, with Byrne's assistance, improved his appearance as much as possible, and hopefully his pallor and bleary focus could be attributed to the punishments for overindulgence. And considering the early hour, surely there would be only a handful of guests milling about. They had only to make it down the hall, down the stairs, and out the door.

Unfortunately, one of those guests milling about was Lord Hampshire, who had cornered a half-asleep Lord Sterling, and a concerned-looking Crawley at the top of the stairs.

Sterling looked as if he had been dragged out of his bed; Hampshire looked as if he had never entered his. No wonder, too, what with his party ending in the catastrophic demise of his prized stables. Crawley was dressed for the day but wore the expression of someone who had acquired little sleep.

"The stock was saved, thank the heavens," Lord Hampshire was ranting, "but if you think I'm not going to bring this up at the next assembly, or to your departmental superiors, you've gone mad!"

"Now, Bernard, it was an accident; it had to be." Sterling yawned, placating.

"This," Hampshire shook a piece of parchment in his hand at Sterling, "is no accident!"

"Sir, Lord Hampshire is right to be concerned, especially considering—" Crawley interrupted, but then turned.

It was then that the gentlemen realized they were not alone on the stairs, as both Hampshire and Sterling turned together to see Marcus, supported by Byrne, approaching.

"Perhaps we should discuss this later," Marcus could hear Sterling murmur. But Lord Hampshire was too invested and would have none of it.

"Ah! Mr. Worth, and uh, Mr. Worth! You're both army men," Hampshire began, intent on convincing the newest arrivals of his point. "After the affairs of last night, this was found tacked to my front door."

He shoved the parchment under Marcus's and Byrne's noses. Marcus, without his glasses and rather unsteady, forced himself to focus on the paper. It was strategically singed at the edges, and scrawled in the middle was this simple phrase, "*Vive la France.*"

Rather direct, in Marcus's mind.

"Who found it?" Marcus asked, his voice weak and thready.

"I did," Crawley piped up. "Surely this means something. Mr. Worth, you and I worked together a long time; this note is terribly provoking—"

Byrne took up the burden of conversation. "I rather think it's a prank. After all, that business at the Whitford affair—he blamed the French for that, too, didn't he?"

"Exactly! It's as if they want us to invade again and beat their French asses back to the Mediterranean!" Lord Hampshire spat.

"Bernard, just because we are used to them being our enemy, doesn't mean they are any longer," Sterling reasoned. "I've not had enough sleep myself," he said, and then, with a pointed look to the Worths, Marcus in particular, "and by looking at the two of you, I'd say you could use another few hours yourself."

"We could," Marcus managed to agree. "I did have a glass too much fun last evening." He forced himself to give his most rakish smile. "But it will have to wait until we get to London."

"Are you sure that's wise? Mr. Marcus, you in particular look the worse for wear," Sterling said as he peered at them with surprisingly bright eyes.

"Our brother expects us," Byrne concurred, "and our sister-in-law will have our heads if we're not on time."

Then, with painful, perfect bows, Marcus and Byrne proceeded down the stairs.

It took all the control in Marcus's body to keep his balance and not reach out for the assistance of the handrail. He knew eyes were on him, and he knew that he had to be perfect. He heard

Hampshire continue to argue his point, saying that he would discover who did this, and if it really was the French, he would use all his influence in the House of Lords to bring about their punishment. Lord Sterling said nothing, and Marcus could feel his intent gaze burning a hole in the back of his head.

He tried to concentrate on the words, felt their importance, another piece of the puzzle falling into place. If he was right, was it really so simple?

But such contemplation would have to wait. Hampshire's voice faded away, and Marcus went through the door of the house to the crisp, cool brightness of morning. He climbed with all possible grace into the carriage that waited just at the doors and collapsed with exhaustion on the seat. And as the horseshoes clip-clopped along the gravel drive, blissful blackness claimed him once again.

The next few days were rather blurry. Marcus and Byrne went to Marcus's bachelor quarters, assiduously avoiding Graham and Mariah's (well, really Mariah's) summonses to Worth House, which came almost hourly. Byrne finally managed to put her off with one dinner and a penned excuse from Marcus, saying he had a previous engagement. Whether or not Mariah interpreted that previous engagement to be with one Mrs. Benning, her not-so-secret hope for her brother-in-law's happiness, she did not let on. However, she also stopped her constant requests for Marcus's company.

Marcus, for his part, was not so comfortably ensconced. The doctor, a discreet man they had met trying to save soldiers' limbs and lives in the Seventeenth Regiment, had changed his dressing, applied a gunpowder poultice, and prescribed rest. But once the fever broke in cool waves, Marcus did not want to rest. His bedding itched. His shoulder ached. He pushed himself to stay conscious as long as possible. In the first few days, it was never more than a few hours at a time.

But he was determined to use those hours.

Byrne would leave the house at night. Where he went, Marcus did not know, nor did Byrne choose to confide in him. He could have been tracking down leads, hunting for Laurent along the dockside, tracing his footsteps.

Or he could be drunk or worse, dulling the pain of his leg, of his existence.

Marcus didn't know if his getting shot had shocked his brother into sobriety or sent him spiraling further. When he came home one morning, almost a week after the shooting, his stench strongly suggested the latter.

He must have been surprised to see Marcus sitting in the study, behind his desk, sorting through papers, but he made no mention of it.

Marcus looked up as Byrne entered, bearing a box from the market.

"Breakfast," he grunted, laying the box on the table. In it were oranges, cheese, cold meats, and bread. A bottle of milk. Since there was no cook or kitchen in Marcus's bachelor quarters, he, like most gentlemen, scrounged food from his club or Graham and Mariah's, but he did keep a cupboard with stock necessities. Unfortunately, the small larder had become quite depleted in the past five days of bedrest.

"Thanks," Marcus replied, as he tore off a hunk of bread. "Where'd you get it?"

"Market day in Covent Garden," he answered. "You should be in bed."

"There's work to be done," Marcus shot back.

"Not for you." Byrne hobbled over to the seat he had taken to occupying. "I have been out there, you know, looking for him, trying to find a hint, a clue of anything. But there're no leads. It's like he doesn't exist. And there's no damn reason for these things happening."

Marcus held up a piece of paper. "I think there is."

It was the list—the list of society parties that had led Marcus on this not-so-merry chase for the past few weeks. "Why target these events?" he asked.

"Because they are hosted by people known for their patriotism," Byrne guessed.

"No, they're not." Marcus countered. "The next two events on the list, the Gold Ball at Regent's Park and the Benning Ball—no particular patriotism there. I think we have to divide this list in half." Marcus proceeded to tear the paper in twain, flat across the middle.

"Oy!" Byrne said, "That's evidence."

But Marcus didn't even spare him a look over the top of his glasses. "The first two, the Whitford Banquet and the Hampshires' Racing Party," he began, "those two are heavily patriotic, but more than that, they profited greatly from the war."

Byrne's brow furrowed, as he took the first half of the list. "True. Whitford's arms manufacturing and Hampshire's stud and stables were heavy suppliers to the army's needs."

"And their businesses have slowed since the end of the war."

"But not completely. For God's sake, we still have France under occupation; guns and horses will always be in demand," Byrne argued. "Besides, if Laurent meant to damage the British Army by going after Whitford and Hampshire's contributions, he seems to have fallen short."

"Exactly!" Marcus exclaimed. "What's he done? He stole a pair of guns and some schematics. He burned down a barn. Its not as if there aren't hundreds of other private stables that supply the army, and its not as if Whitford's schematics can't be replicated. Laurent's actions are more of a nuisance than a disturbance."

"He also shot you," Byrne drawled.

But Marcus dismissed this with a wave of his hand. "I got in his way," he said, rising. "He went after Whitford and Hampshire because they are positioned to raise a fuss. Both are influential members of Society. Hampshire's vocal in the House of Lords.

Annoy them, and it's to their benefit to raise the level of anti-French rhetoric in Parliament."

And with that, Marcus moved quickly around the desk and pulled out a copy of the day's *Times*, finding the article he searched for and handing it to Byrne.

> *The incident at Lord Hampshire's famed Racing Party this past weekend was marked by what Lord Hampshire himself called, "a Frog-legged dig at solid British enterprise." He claims the unfortunate fire was orchestrated by French agents, authorized by the French government.*
>
> *Lord Fieldstone, head of His Majesty's War Department, issued no statement negating such claims, as he did with Lord Whitford's recent similar accusation regarding his botched affair. Rumblings within the hallowed halls of Whitehall are that Lord Fieldstone is taking this accusation more seriously, especially since the dissolution of the French Parliament by their Prime Minister, the Duc de Richelieu.*

"Read the society pages, and you'll find that French expatriates are being given the cut direct," Marcus said, indicating the next page. "This anti-French sentiment is infecting the Ton, and soon the middle class and servants will follow, until all they need is one incident, and we'll be back at war."

"But *why*?" Byrne sighed. "I'm tired. This whole situation makes me tired. I have to imagine most everyone else in this country is bloody tired of war."

"But some people make their money from war," Marcus argued. "And they miss it . . . All I have to do is figure out which person was making enough money off the war to want to start it again."

"You suspect Sterling," Byrne said, flipping the paper over, skimming the society pages.

"Yes," Marcus replied. "But I'd need more solid evidence than just my suspicions. He was at both parties, but so were Crawley, Fieldstone, a hundred other people."

"Yes, but he was in the stables." Byrne looked down, then back up. "You could ask Mrs. Benning about his financial portfolio. I'd wager she knows more than his accountant."

"No." Marcus replied sharply, not looking up from his desk.

Byrne glanced up from the *Times*. "I know things went pear-shaped this weekend, but I will admit she kept her head. And she has a decent memory; you were right about that. She's proven useful, Marcus."

"I said no," Marcus repeated. Seeing that his brother was not going to take that for an answer, he sighed, took off his spectacles, and rubbed his tired eyes. "This situation has proven far too dangerous, as my shoulder can attest. I'm not involving her any further."

Byrne seemed to want to reply, but he thought better of it. He took his cane, started rolling it between his hands, contemplating.

"What's the other half of the list?"

"Hmm?" Marcus looked up from his desk.

"The Gold Ball at Regent's Park and the Benning Ball. What do they have to do with anything?"

"I . . . I don't know." Marcus replied. "I just know that they are the most anticipated events of the Season."

"Well, the Gold Ball is sponsored by the Crown. One assumes that security there would be tight."

"But I don't think it is," Marcus argued. "It's a masquerade, held outdoors. Even with the Palace Guard on hand to protect the Regent, how secure could the place be?" Marcus rubbed his chin thoughtfully. Wait. Could it be . . . ? "That's it."

Byrne ceased rolling his cane between his hands.

"They're going to do something while the Prince is there," Marcus explained, coming to his feet. "The sentiment being what it is, and Prinny being who he is, if something were to happen, he'd *demand* war."

"Wonderful. What are they going to do?" Byrne asked.

That stilled Marcus.

"And who are *they*?" he continued. "Who is Laurent conspiring with?"

But Marcus just shook his head. "No, who has Laurent been hired by?" Quickly he moved from behind his desk to his bedchamber door. Throwing it open, he went immediately to the wardrobe, started pulling out his most worn, most common clothes.

"What are you doing?" Byrne asked as he hobbled in behind his brother.

"Going back to the beginning," Marcus answered as he struggled to pull on a pair of serviceable brown trousers. "Johnny Dicks had a friend. He said she was with him the night he acquired the list. She might know something."

"And you haven't questioned her yet?" Byrne asked incredulously.

"She disappeared when Johnny Dicks was killed. I went to the pub—the Bull and Whisker—but Marty Wilkins—you remember him, from the Seventeenth?—he said the girl—Meggie, I believe—went into hiding when she heard about Johnny. No one I'd talked to had seen her. Now that some time has passed"—Marcus went about pulling on his boots—"maybe I can get a different answer."

"No." Byrne said softly.

"What?"

"You're not going." Byrne replied.

"I feel fine," Marcus replied. "In fact, if you keep me cooped up in here much longer, I'll go mad."

"Raise your arm over your head." Byrne commanded.

Marcus obliged him, but not without forcing himself to hide a wince of pain.

"You may feel right enough, but you don't think your face is already recognized in the Bull and Whisker? I'll go track Meggie down."

"But Byrne—" Marcus said. He was cut short by his brother's pleading look.

"Let me do this, please!" Byrne asked him, pleaded with his eyes. "It's one thing I can do."

Marcus paused in his movements. All this time, he had never considered that Byrne might feel marginalized by his actions.

For in the intervening year, not only had Byrne moved away from Marcus, began holding himself in, became distant, but Marcus realized that he had moved away, too. He was running his own investigation, had been pursuing it single-mindedly. The fraternity that had marked their relationship the whole of their lives had suffered a rift. Their previous roles had been abandoned, and maybe his brother was lost without it.

"Maybe you're right," Marcus conceded. "I have a pile of papers to sort through; I could use a nap. Besides, you're the Blue Raven. You're the one who has to save the day."

Byrne nodded. He turned to the door, looked out into the study to the pile of work on Marcus's desk. It was a reasonable excuse, the pile of papers. It would do.

"I'll get a change of clothes," Byrne replied and moved to where he had stowed his valise in Marcus's wardrobe.

"I'll start . . . writing a letter," Marcus replied, and moved to the next room to his desk.

He sat down, took a piece of fresh paper in hand, and laid it in front of him. After a moment, Byrne yelled through the open door.

"Is it to Mrs. Benning?" Byrne asked across the rooms.

"No. Why?" Marcus inquired.

"I just thought," Byrne said as he emerged from the bedroom, cloaked in dirty trousers, muddy boots, and a patch-worn greatcoat, his posture stooped and gnarled. He completed the picture with a brown bottle in his hand and a dusty cap that covered his dark hair and eyes. "You said she was to be no longer involved, correct?"

Marcus's eyebrow shot up.

"Does she know it?" he asked.

Phillippa entered Worth House nearly shaking.

Was he here? It had been almost a full week now, and she hadn't heard from him. She had no way of knowing if he had survived his wound or succumbed to it, and she had no way of inquiring. She could only hope that when Mariah issued her usual invitation to one of her dinner parties that Marcus would be there, too.

He must have recovered by now. He must have. But what if the fever had taken hold and weakened his body? What if . . . No, she would not allow herself to think that way, she scolded herself as she crossed the threshold with Totty, Nora, and Nora's mother at her side, a bright and easy smile painted on her lips.

"Phillippa, why are we here?" Nora inquired in a low voice.

"Because one has to eat dinner somewhere," Phillippa replied serenely. "Besides, I've grown fond of Lady Worth."

"I know that her charity is your new pet project, but Lady Worth—ugh. I don't know how you can stand it."

"Now, now, that is unkind," Phillippa scolded, prompting Lady De Regis to give her leading daughter a look of reproval as well. "I think you'll find Lady Worth's manners without fault." And better than yours, Phillippa thought, but on that subject she kept her mouth shut.

"I trust there will be young gentlemen here for my Nora," Lady De Regis said, adding her quota to the day's conversation.

"Oh yes," Totty piped up, "if nothing else, Lord Worth has two brothers, both unmarried."

"Yes, a gimp and a bookish string bean who hangs after Phillippa's every word," Nora grumbled.

"Nora!" Phillippa exclaimed. She took her friend by the arm, as she would a child. When did Nora became so biting? And when had it happened that she herself stopped cultivating such wit?

"Oh, come on, Philly," Nora replied. "When did you become such a stick-in-the-mud? A month ago you would have said the exact same thing."

It was true. She was becoming a stick-in-the-mud. And somehow she didn't mind it.

It must have been when she began her partnership with Marcus. More than a partnership, really . . . He confided in her things no one else was privy to, like his aversion to firearms and haircuts, and he was unfailingly kind and gentle. How his sense of chivalry and his sense of humor were intertwined. And he knew more about her than she had ever let anyone else know. He wasn't just her partner in crime.

He was her friend.

And she was near to tears for word of that friend's good health.

But she would be damned if she let it show, she chastised herself as she was greeted warmly by Mariah upon entering the drawing room.

"Phillippa!" Mariah cried. "How lovely to see you!"

Phillippa was pleased to note that Mariah had taken her advice against plum-colored lace and instead wore a gown in warm russet tones.

"Mariah," she replied, kissing her hostess on the cheek. "I've brought some friends for you to sway to your cause. May I introduce Lady De Regis and her daughter Nora? And of course you know Mrs. Tottendale."

Curtsies were exchanged, murmured pleasantries. Phillippa could not help but scan the room, looking for a tall form, a happy smile, a reflection of spectacles. But, even as the room was far more crowded than at Phillippa's first dinner party, due to Mariah's charity being the latest cause célèbre, it did not contain the one single person Phillippa had hoped to seek out.

As if she could hear Phillippa's thoughts, Lady De Regis gave them voice. "I understand you have some brothers-in-law, Lady

Worth." Lady De Regis did not often feel it necessary to hide her intentions—a husband for her daughter—through vague speech. She and Lady Worth would get on well. "Are they here this evening?" she continued, scanning the room.

"I'm afraid not," Mariah answered. "Young men, you know, I can hardly nail them down for a weekly family supper."

"They're . . . they're not here?" Phillippa asked somewhat dazed. "Either of them?"

Mariah regarded Phillippa somewhat queerly. "Unfortunately not. I haven't seen Marcus since before last weekend. Byrne we managed to get to dinner once, but other than that . . ."

Realizing they stood with company, Phillippa shot Totty a look, silently begging assistance.

Totty took up her assignment with ease, taking Lady De Regis by the arm and pointing out that there were refreshments available. Nora, of course, had already flitted to a group of gentlemen on the other side of the room. If none of her beaux were here, it seemed that she would practice on their fathers.

"Mariah," Phillippa began, then cleared her throat, and began again. "I have not seen Marcus in the past week, either."

"Really?" Mariah asked, alarmed. "But I beg your pardon, I was given the impression that he was . . . in your company, at least some of the time."

"I'm sure you've noticed that Marcus and I have become friends. I doubt he'd go out of town without you hearing of it."

"I agree. And I do not doubt his affection for you. Far from it."

Phillippa blushed at such frank speaking from Mariah, but her purpose was too important to waste the conversation on Mariah's hopes. "I do hope Marcus—and of course Byrne—are not in any trouble," Phillippa posited hesitantly.

Mariah looked around the room and then, taking Phillippa by the arm, gently guided her to a far corner. "Marcus and Byrne were both in the army during the war, as I'm sure you know," she said, and Phillippa nodded. "There were great gaps of time when we didn't hear from them at all. What Graham and I decided was that no news was good news. Perhaps Marcus has retained some of his secretive ways. That's all."

Phillippa took a moment to digest this. "No news is good news," she repeated.

"Precisely," Mariah answered with a smile false enough so Phillippa could feel it. "I'm sure they're fine. However, if you felt it necessary to write him, or send someone round to check on him, I would be more than happy to give you Marcus's address."

"Yes," Phillippa replied instantly, "I could go and—I mean, I could *send* a servant to go and check on him."

Then as the bell rang for supper, both women, their hearts beating rapidly, were escorted to the dining room.

It was arduous sitting through another of Lady Worth's charity dinners, but for an entirely different reason this time. Mariah acquitted herself nicely, having taken several cues from Phillippa over the intervening weeks on ladylike persuasion versus lecturing. She only mentioned Jackie, Jeffy, etc., once, and that was when asked how her pupils got on at the school. No, Phillippa was counting the minutes to the supper's end so she could execute her escape.

Which she did, once the ladies excused themselves with all possible grace.

She could not feign illness, for that would draw scrutiny to Mariah's excellently prepared food. Nor could she pretend to rip her skirt, because, quite honestly, how many times was she going to use that excuse?

No, instead she utilized a butler, a small card, and a pencil.

Instructing the butler to hand the card to Mariah in exactly five minutes, she allowed herself to sink into conversation with Mrs. Hurston, who had for once left the godforsaken turban at home. Although, now that Phillippa saw Mrs. Hurston's uncovered head, she saw the use in such an object. If a product of age was that your hair thinned a bit, Mrs. Hurston was a hundred and forty. The wisps that existed were puffed and curled as much as possible, but in the future maybe Phillippa would be less exacting as to an older lady's head covering.

In precisely five minutes, Mariah was handed the card, and after scanning it, she quickly exclaimed, "Oh no!"

All heads turned her way. "Phillippa, my dear, I'm afraid there has been an incident at your home."

"At my home?" Phillippa quickly took the piece of paper.

"Apparently some rabble tried to get in by breaking a window," Mariah supplied to the eager crowd.

"How horrid!" "My goodness, is nothing safe?" "Its those Frenchies, I know it," was the general hue and cry from the twittering ladies.

"Its likely someone trying to discover the secret to the Benning Ball." The mention of which set the room to a titter. "Mariah, I'm afraid you must excuse me, I should go speak to my housekeeper, and the constable."

"Yes, of course," Mariah replied, rising as Phillippa did. Kissing her on the cheek, she whispered into Phillippa's ear, "Brava, by the bye."

Totty rose to join her, as did Nora and Lady De Regis. However, the latter were met by protests.

"Oh no, Nora, Lady De Regis, you should stay; I should hate for my evening to sour yours," Phillippa supplied, gesturing them back to their seats.

"But we all came in your carriage, Phillippa," Nora said, only a slight strain to her voice.

"Its quite all right, my dear," Mrs. Hurston spoke up. "You're going to the Blackwells' card party next, correct? Well, I've the barouche."

Thus settled, Nora and Lady De Regis returned to their seats, and Phillippa and Totty headed out the door.

Once ensconced in her carriage, trotting along at a surprising pace for the fashionable neighborhoods of London at this time of night, Phillippa turned to Totty. "Darling, I'm going to ask you a favor. I'm going to drop you off at the house." Totty looked as if she were going to ask a question, prompting Phillippa to continue, "And you're not going to ask me any questions about it. Oh, and if you could, break a window. A cheap one, on a low floor, around the back."

Totty eyed Phillippa suspiciously. "No need for me to ask questions. I'm not blind, you know," she said. "Or stupid. I've seen where you're headed, long before you did."

Phillippa met Totty's gaze. It was clear, cool, almost sober. It always surprised her how much Totty knew. Perhaps it shouldn't.

Phillippa squeezed Totty's hand as the driver pulled up in front of Benning House. As the footman opened the carriage door and escorted Totty down, Phillippa called after her friend. "Totty?"

She turned.

"Thank you." Phillippa smiled.

Totty dismissed this with a wave. "Young people always think they've stumbled across something new when they fall in love." She dropped the footman's hand, and began looking around the ground. "Ah, here we are," she said, as she picked up a large rock decoratively lining the walkway to the house. "Ta-ta!" she cried, and she disappeared around the back of the house.

Leaving Phillippa pale with shock, she wondered what Totty meant by love, and why her heart was beating so queerly, when the carriage pulled away into the dark night.

Marcus Worth had not the foresight to know that a guest would be arriving at his door that evening, and as such, he had determined to go to bed and store his strength for when Byrne returned, hopefully with Miss Meggie, or at least some word as to her whereabouts.

But not until he finished his letter to Phillippa.

He had started it a dozen times, each time escalating in insufficiency, awkwardness, and rambling. His most recent effort was the worst.

"Dear Mrs. Benning"—they all started in this way—"thank

you for your assistance when last we met, it was most kind." Kind. She pulled a bullet out of his shoulder and he called it kind? Utterly ridiculous. "However, I feel your assistance in the future would be unwise, considering the circumstances of said assistance." He really needed a different euphemism for *assistance*. "And as such, feel that your assistance will no longer be required. Therefore, such occasions in the future when next we meet, we should not assist each other . . ."

It devolved from there. Marcus rubbed his tired eyes. He should go to bed. He should go outside. He should do anything other than sit in this purgatory, writing away the person he ached for.

But it had to be done. The situation had become too dangerous. Surely, she would recognize that. In spite of her penchant for frippery, she was an eminently practical woman. She could arrange dinner parties with the same skillful ease that she chased dangerous villains through hedge mazes. She could memorize the entire attendance of Almack's and their wardrobes. She was utterly amazing.

And he was in love with her.

And there was no way they could be together, he knew, as he rose to his bare feet and began pacing his study like a caged animal.

Forget that she had responded to his kiss in the stables, twining herself around him like ivy. Forget, too, that he had allowed her to continue her mistaken assumption about his secret identity or lack thereof. Forget, once more, her single-minded pursuit of that jackass, the Marquis of Broughton. The truth was, Phillippa Benning existed on an entirely different plane than he did. And as soon as their association ended, she would go back to hers and he to his.

Therefore, best to end their association before one or the other of them ended up dead.

He seated himself at the desk again, crumpled up his last attempt, and took a fresh sheet of paper from the pile. He pushed his spectacles back up his nose, serious, intent.

The quill dripped a dot of ink on the page as he paused, willing himself to begin.

The dot was destined to be the only mark on that page. For in that moment, in the pause after determination and before movement, there was a knock on his front door.

Placing his quill back in the well, he stood, moved around his mess of discarded papers into the foyer, and wrenched open the door.

It was threatening rain. The slight drizzle clung to her cape, giving her an otherworldy radiance. But she did not smile at him; she did not reach out to him. She merely stared at him with those large blue eyes, taking in his whole form.

"Hello," Phillippa finally said, her voice soft and worn.

"Hello," he responded. As her gaze traveled down his torso, Marcus became suddenly aware that he wore trousers, the bandages around his shoulder, an opened dressing robe, and nothing else. "What are you doing here?" he blurted out, which brought her eyes back to his face.

"May I . . . may I come in?" she asked, a nervous smile trembling on her lips.

He contemplated his options, and standing on the doorstep with Phillippa outside while rain began to pelt them was not one. And so, every nerve in his body aware of her presence, he stood back and allowed her entry.

"Thank you," she said, as she passed by him and moved into the study, where the fire was lit. She seemed to steady herself by the fire, as she warmed her gloved hands. Marcus stayed by the study door, still. Waiting for her to move.

"What are you doing here?" he asked again, gently this time, his words sliding over the quiet room like smoke.

"I was . . . I wanted to make sure you were in good health," she stammered as she turned to him. "I hadn't heard word of you in almost a week, and I didn't know . . . if you were all right."

"I'm fine. You shouldn't have worried," he said, crossing his arms over his chest.

"I shouldn't have worried!" she cried, almost laughing. "Marcus the last time I saw you, you were in and out of conciousness—and then in the morning, you just left! And a week goes by, and I hear no word, no small notice of your state. You could have been dead, for all I knew!"

"I'm *fine*." Marcus gritted back at her. "And I thank you for your past assistance, but from here on out, my well-being should not be a concern of yours."

"How can I help but be concerned?" she said as her eyes welled up with tears. "Marcus, I thought . . . I thought we were friends."

"We had a business arrangement—and I'm calling an end to it," he said coldly.

She stilled, her body listing, as if the slightest touch could knock her over.

"You . . . you can call an end to whatever you like," she finally said, her chin going up in her superior way. "But it doesn't mean I wouldn't still be concerned about your welfare. I know too much. For God's sake, Marcus, you were shot—"

"And it could have just as easily been you!" he exclaimed, coming off the wall as he did, coming toward her. "That bullet could have hit you, wounded you, killed you, as easily as it did me. I can't have you involved any longer. You weren't supposed to be in this deep in the first place. No, you were supposed to get me invited to parties, that's all. Instead, you end up chasing evil men—men who will *hurt* you if they get the chance—and dodging bullets!" He was vaguely aware that he was ranting, pacing, yelling. But he didn't care. This is what he had in him to say, and it broke forth from the dam with powerful force.

"You are no longer allowed in this. You are no longer to come within a hundred feet of me," he commanded. He watched as she nodded, a single tear falling down her cheek. "If you see me walking down the street, you turn and walk the other way. Are we clear?"

She nodded again. His breaths came heavily, marking the silence like ticks of a clock.

"Phillippa," he finally asked, his voice steadier, "what are you still doing here?"

She met his eyes, and he saw it. That moment. That pause between determination and movement, between decision and action.

Then she crossed the room and kissed him.

Twenty-two

There was no hesitation. There was no question. There was no stalling, no what-ifs, no protests, no objections. There was only Phillippa and Marcus and what burned between them.

When Phillippa crossed the room, Marcus enveloped her in his embrace, devoured her with his mouth. It was what he wanted. What he needed. And he would not fight it any longer.

His hands came up to frame her face, dove into her perfectly coiffed hair, upsetting all manner of hairpins and jeweled clips. They bounced on the study's wooden floor, scattered underneath the desk, lost forever. Phillippa pressed her body into his as her hands came up to his face, played over the whorls of his ears, traced the length of his sideburns. She broke off his kiss briefly, momentarily bewildering him. But she simply slid the spectacles from his nose and tossed them onto his desk. Then she found his mouth again, their tongues dancing to a rhythm they knew instinctually.

Marcus could not get enough of her. He pulled her closer, tighter, his arms wrapping around, begging for skin to touch. The heavy cloak that folded around her fell to the floor with one easy tug on the cord that brushed her throat.

She was dressed for an evening out in one of her fluttery silk things that draped against her and did nothing to hide the swell of flesh here, the rise of her hip there. He reached out, took her hips, gently ground his knuckles into her sides as he pressed her up against the evidence of his need. And she pressed herself closer. He broke his mouth from hers, moved his attentions to the slender length of her neck and the delicate pulse that beat just behind her ear. Feeling that rapid beat against his breath made his heart race faster. And hearing her soft sigh made him voracious.

As for Phillippa, she found Marcus's dressing robe completely unnecessary, and she slid her hands under the soft fleece, pushing it off his smooth, strong shoulders. But her hands stopped there, and her whole body stilled.

"Your shoulder . . ." she whispered in the firelight, causing him to drag his head up from her throat.

Her hand skimmed the edge of his bandage, the dressing that wrapped across his chest, holding the linens in place.

"It's fine." He said looking into her eyes, dropping his arms to allow his robe to fall to the floor next to her cloak. Then, one hand massaging the back of her neck, he returned his attentions to that irresistible pulse behind her ear.

"You're sure?" she asked, her voice strained.

"Here," he said, "I'll prove it to you." Then, with a quick kiss on her mouth, he linked her arms around his neck, bent down, and picked her up.

"Oh my," she breathed. He carried her like she weighed no more than a piece of paper, but as carefully as if she were the most treasured thing in the universe.

"Told you," he said, grinning at her in the darkness. He moved quickly with her in his arms, crossing the study to another door, nudging it open with his foot.

"It doesn't hurt?" she asked, her hand lacing into his hair.

"Nothing hurts when you're here," he answered, and they crossed the threshold into the bedchamber.

He had a fire burning low in the hearth, but otherwise the room was dark. Marcus placed Phillippa gently on the edge of the bed. He kissed her gently, deeply, then moved away.

"What . . . what are you doing?" Phillippa asked, the slightest tinge of nerves coloring her voice.

"Lighting some candles," he replied, as he struck a flint, the spark flaring to life in the dark. "I want to see you." He lit a candelabra by the door, another by the bed. Phillippa swallowed silently to herself. This was real, it seemed. As much as her body ached for him, as much as her blood sang to be with him, she still had that small dot of fear creeping into her mind.

When Marcus turned back to her, he held for a moment, stopped and stared, a silly, lopsided grin playing across his mouth.

"What?" she asked, his smile making her smile.

"Nothing," he said, his grin full force now. "I was just thinking that this will be very, very different from when you were last in my bed."

She blushed, her eyes roaming about the room, her gloved hands folding on her lap, propriety being her default position. He noticed this quickly, for he came over and knelt before her. He took her hands from her lap and, his eyes never straying from hers, deftly flicked open the buttons at her wrists, tugged the soft fabric down her elbows, off her hands. He kissed the back of each hand, then their palms. Then he laced his fingers in hers, rose up, and kissed her mouth.

Her slippers came off as she slid back on the bed, Marcus following, pursuing, his mouth never leaving hers. He laid her back across the pillows, fanned out the full length of her hair. The sleeve of her gown drooped, her delicious shoulder exposed to his hungry eye. Marcus suddenly realized that he had never seen Phillippa as less than proper. Even when she was in a sarcophagus, she was coiffed to perfection (if dusty). Now she was tumbled, in disarray, her lips swollen from his kisses, her shoes and gloves free. She was wanton. And she was all his.

This sudden knowledge made him powerful, greedy. With a wicked grin, Marcus took advantage of her gown's loose bodice, pushing the other tiny cap sleeve down her shoulder. Then, with aching tenderness, he worked the rest of the bodice down, allowing her breasts to spring free.

The cool air hit her like a thousand pinpricks of shock. Her small, pink nipples puckered upon exposure, as she swiftly sucked in her breath. His hand came up to cover her left breast, his thumb and forefinger teasing the stiffened peak.

Oh, that hand. She did have an uncommon fondness for it.

She leaned into his attentions, as his mouth broke from hers, and he kissed his way down her neck, over her collarbone, to the crest of her right breast, kissing her there, his teeth grazing across that terribly sensitive spot.

Such were Marcus's skills that she didn't even notice when his free hand began creeping up her leg, fingering the ties to her stockings. It was only when his clever hand had deftly removed the tie, and it crept still further that the dot of fear in her belly began to grow, and she froze again.

Marcus felt it the minute she began to withdraw from him. But this was too precious to lose. Gently, he stilled his attentions but did not move his hands from their hard-won positions.

"What's wrong?" he whispered.

"Nothing," she said, her voice merely a whisper, and a shaky one at that.

He lifted his head from her breast and sought her eyes. It was only then that he saw the shine to them, tears threatening to fall.

He lifted himself away from her, forced himself to roll to one side, propped up on one elbow.

"We don't have to do this, you know," he said, and as much as it killed him to say it, he meant it.

"No!" she cried, her hand reaching out to touch his chest. "I want to, desperately," she said with a blushing smile, causing him to smile ruefully. "It's just . . . I'm just . . ."

"You're nervous," he concluded softly.

"I . . . I haven't done this in while," she began, her eyes steady not on his face but on her hand as it drifted softly to and fro over his chest. "And that was only my husband, and he wasn't . . . it wasn't . . ."

"Sweetheart," he whispered, his hand stilling hers, holding it against his heart. She could feel the rapid, steady beats, the life flowing through him. "Look at me."

She met his eyes and saw there only tenderness.

"It's just me," he said.

And she knew. She knew everything would be all right. It was just him. And just her. There was no judge nor jury here. Marcus would not despise her for lacking the sophistication she so ruthlessly cultivated in society. For once, she could be herself. Nervous, silly, shy, bold, happy: Whatever she happened to be, he would match her.

"It's just you," she replied, relaxation sliding over her in waves. "And it's just me."

With his easy nod, she took his body and pulled him back on top of her, relishing his weight.

Her newfound freedom to act as she pleased, to take as she pleased, made Phillippa bold. She delighted in running her hands over the muscles in his arms, the varied planes of his back, the thin scar on his side. While he returned his attentions to her breasts, she reached down and cupped his buttocks, pressing him against her. Her legs twined around his, letting their most private areas touch, with only layers of cloth between them.

The necessity of those layers of cloth was debatable to Phillippa.

Reaching between them, she found the buttons to the fly of his trousers, fumbling them open.

Now it was Marcus's turn to go still.

He quickly grabbed her hand, just as she was about to graze the smooth length of his shaft, which, he knew, would have spelled disaster.

"Hold on a minute," he said his voice strained with the effort.

"Why?" she asked with a naughty lilt. "After all, it's just you."

Trust her to throw his words so skillfully back at him, he thought ruefully.

"And I want to see you," she continued, her voice low and silky.

"Yes," he replied, burying his forehead in her shoulder, "but if you do that, this will be over before we begin." He lifted his head, kissed her deeply, and brought her hand up from dangerous territory. "And I want you to enjoy this."

"But I am enjoying this!" she cried, causing him to cock his eyebrow.

"Trust me, you're not." But then a wicked fire lit his eyes. "But don't worry, you will."

And then, with one deft movement, Marcus sat Phillippa up, pulled her gown and shift over her head, and exposed her completely.

Naked except for her stockings, Phillippa desperately wanted to cross her arms over her breasts, burrow under the sheets. But Marcus wouldn't allow it. He held her arms wide and looked his fill. The way his eyes raked over her, caressed her, took her in, sent a spiral of awareness low in her belly, spreading warmth. Gently, he laid her back down, their tongues mating as the feeling of his skin on hers set every nerve on fire. Slowly, he let his hand slide down the soft length of her torso and cup her mound. She rose to greet him, indulging in that wicked pressure that made her head swim.

She made a soft noise, spurring a relieved Marcus onward. He had no claims to being a lothario, so well-practiced in the art of love as to be bored. No, his attention was very much held. But while his experience was not expansive, what he'd had was education enough to know that lovemaking was not about his pleasure; it was about hers.

And so with as much grace as he could remember, he worked his fingers into her slick wetness, slowly mimicking the motions his manhood yearned to make, while his thumb found and teased, tortured, tormented the tiny bead hiding at the front of her sex.

Surely, this dizzying sensation that Phillippa felt was not normal. Surely, the pulsing of her body, the sensitivity she felt all over and one place in particular meant something was wrong. But good Lord, she did not care. Moans soaked through whispers, and all she wanted was whatever she was struggling toward and Marcus's hand—that diabolically clever hand, caressing her, urging her forward, filling her with need—to take her there.

Suddenly, she felt her body fall over the edge, and she cried out, her breath coming in short, jagged bursts. She radiated energy, warmth, the crash of wave after wave of pleasure causing her to clutch tightly to Marcus's body, to grasp his thighs with hers.

Marcus held her as she came, his cheek pressed right against hers, her cries nearly causing him to lose all control. Only his trousers saved him, and thoughts of boring, basic military maneuvers. It was the most marvelous sight he'd ever witnessed. He grinned against her cheek, kissed her temple, her eyes, as her shudders began to subside.

He held her there for almost a minute as she stilled, and then with a grin, she began to giggle.

"What's so funny?" he asked, his grin matching her own.

"I finally understand," she laughed, "why people make such a fuss over this."

Her easy laughter had him chuckling with her. "I know you must think me silly," she continued, but he cut her off with a deep, drawing kiss.

"I think," he finally said, after he had managed to render them both a bit breathless, "that you've never been more beautiful." He wrapped her in his arms and pulled her on top of him.

This time, when his hands went to remove her stockings, she did not stop him; instead, she relished his touch, her skin still vibrating from the pleasure he had given so freely. And this time, when her hand went to the buttons of his trousers, he did not stop her, instead letting her work his trousers free of his hips and legs. He let her pull him free and guide him into her.

"It's just me," he said, when Phillippa didn't say anything for a few seconds.

A slow smile spread across her face. "I don't think there's anything 'just' about you," she said, raising her hips and then settling back down onto him again, a torturous, agonizing slide down his shaft.

It was all Marcus could do to not crash into her right then. Grabbing her hips, he rolled her onto her back, rolling with her.

"Phillippa, darling," he whispered, threading his fingers through her hair, worshipping her face with featherlight kisses, "I need you."

"I need you, too." She opened herself up to him, her thighs rising to his flanks, wrapping around him, as he slid deeper into her.

This was different than the pleasure he had given her before, she thought. It was heady, this fullness. With every push, with every plunge, he stoked the flames of her desire. And with every moan, with light caresses of her hands, she brought him closer to the edge. He wanted to fight it. He wanted to hold himself away from her, still have her and be able to resist her all at once.

But it was no use.

"It's just me," she whispered in his ear, as she clung to his body, that now-familiar tingle growing, urging, pulling her from deep within.

That was all it took. Those three little words. He could feel himself breaking within her, so, reaching between them, he found her nub and sent her soaring.

"It's just me," he replied, as she shattered around him. Marcus let out a shout and, holding her tight, joined her in the fall.

They lay still, cocooned within the sheets, wrapped around each other. To move would ruin the perfect quiet, dissolve the contact they each craved.

Marcus could feel her heart beating beneath his, as his mind began to clear of the bewitchment she had cast over him. God, she felt good. If he never left this bed, it would be too soon. She was everything and the only thing. He nuzzled her ear, taking in that scent of her that felt so much like coming home.

Light fingers ran up and down his back languidly, as she placed tiny kisses on his collarbone, his neck. And suddenly Marcus felt panic.

"I'm crushing you. I'm sorry," he lifted his weight from her, the cold air rushing cruelly into the void.

"Don't you dare leave," she whispered, pulling him back down to her. He grinned into her hair, happy that she was as unwilling to quit their contact as he.

"In the spirit of compromise, then," he breathed into her ear, as he rolled onto his side, taking her with him. She giggled girlishly as he tucked the sheets around her backside, his hand coming to rest there appreciatively.

"I had a feeling you'd be good at this." She smiled. "Those clever hands," she remarked, as said hands began roaming over the rounded flesh, hitching her leg up higher around his.

"You shouldn't sell yourself short. I find your talents most remarkable." He grinned back at her, capturing her ear between his teeth, grazing her neck.

"Yes, but for once, it is you who are the one with the reputation to uphold," she answered.

"I am?" Marcus queried, his eyebrow coming up.

"They say the Blue Raven is an expert lover, stealing a lady's virtue and secrets at the same time."

Marcus froze in his movements, lifted his hand away from her side. "Phillippa, love," he began, pulling back to look at her, "I should tell you—"

"That the reports of your deeds are exaggerated?" she finished for him. "I know, you told me before. But in terms of your *prowess*, I am happy to confirm the reports in their entirety." Marcus could feel himself blushing at this laudable ovation of his efforts, as she continued. "And truth be told, I'd be terribly jealous if I thought you'd made love to hundreds of ladies like you have me."

"Phillippa, it's never been like this for me, with anyone," Marcus said quickly, holding her gaze with his. "Do you understand? But I need you to know that—"

He was silenced again, this time with a long, chaste kiss that removed the words from his lips and filled his soul with light.

"I do understand," she whispered breathlessly and kissed him again.

He would tell her, he promised himself. He would. But right now there were no words. Right now there was only the room and the bed, their cocoon. The yearning they felt for each other, the grappling for fulfillment, and the long, dark night.

Hours passed, and Phillippa drifted to sleep easily, content. Marcus, meanwhile, lay awake, his mind at odds with itself.

On the one side, his heart soared at having the sleeping form of Phillippa Benning in his arms. Curled into a ball beside him, her juts and hollows fitted perfectly against his. She was what he had been dreaming about for weeks, and the reality was better than he could have ever imagined. He wanted to keep her there forever.

But the other part of his brain, the small, niggling conscience, knew that it would not keep her safe.

There was still the specter of danger that lurked outside the door. If Laurent and his associates knew Marcus was hunting him, then having Phillippa in his life meant she was an easy target.

And there was still the small notion of the lie—little really, insubstantial—that he had allowed her to believe him to be the Blue Raven.

Marcus eased his body away from hers, fought his guilt as she gave a small whimper in her sleep. He found his trousers in the dark and pulled them on. He needed to think, and he wasn't going to do that if he were lying next to Phillippa's soft, naked form.

He moved quietly into the study, easing the bedroom door shut behind him. Looking around the room, his eyes immediately fell on the cloak and dressing robe on the floor, rushing his mind back to how she had crossed the room and kissed him with such passion.

Well, he wasn't going to get any thinking done with those there either.

He grabbed his robe and shrugged it on, then gingerly took Phillippa's dark velvet cloak, folded it, and hung it behind the door, next to his hat. They looked nice together, he decided. They looked as if they belonged.

Marcus stoked up the dying fire, throwing some warmth into the room as the door opened behind him and, much to his surprise, Byrne entered, soaked to the skin and smiling.

"It is nasty weather out, brother," Byrne proclaimed as he stomped into the room, ridding his boots of watery mud.

"Shh!" Marcus said, his eyes flicking automatically to the bedchamber door.

"Why? Marcus, I have such news!" Byrne said as he rid himself of his wet cloak, resting it to dry on the fire grate.

"And I have, er, neighbors," Marcus replied, as he glanced quickly to the mantel clock above the hearth. "Its three o'clock in the morning."

"I know, I didn't expect to be successful so quickly either," Byrne slapped Marcus on the shoulder, causing him to grunt in pain. "Oh, sorry, forgot." Byrne gave him a quick grin, his enthusiasm unabated.

"You certainly seem in a good mood," Marcus drawled. He did seem rather bright-eyed and energetic, Marcus observed. The opiates his brother had developed a weakening fondness for tended to make him lazy, surly.

"I am. My leg hurts like the devil, though, so I'll make this short. When you're right, you're right, Marcus, that's all."

Excellent. Word games from a dripping-wet, pain-riddled, full-of-life drug addict. "What was I right about now?"

"That I, as the Blue Raven, would save the day," Byrne cheered. "I found Meggie."

That had Marcus sitting up straight. "You did? How?"

"It wasn't too difficult. All I did was drop a word in one person's ear, a coin in the hand of another. I told them I'd been her customer before, and that she pleased me. She'd been long enough in hiding, without money, that she was willing to service almost anyone."

"Charming. What did she say?"

Byrne leaned forward in his chair. "She not only saw the Frenchy, as she and Johnny Dicks called him, but she followed him, picked his pocket for the list."

Marcus leaned forward, too. "She could tell us which way he went."

"Better—Meggie said he got into a carriage with a crest on it. She said she'd be able to point it out if she saw it again."

Marcus was on his feet, pacing now. "She can't stay in Whitechapel. He found and killed Johnny Dicks; he'll find her, now that she came out of hiding to meet with you."

"Be calm, I've already hidden her again." Byrne replied, rolling his cane between his hands. The pain in his leg must be getting acute, Marcus knew. "I took her to Graham's. Mrs. Riddle, the housekeeper, always had a soft spot for me. Meggie said she'd done scullery work before, so she should be safe enough there, as long as she obeys my orders to not leave the house. I told you I could do this." Byrne grinned. "One of the Blue Raven's most formidable talents."

Marcus paced for a moment, considering the information given.

"We'll take her to the park tomorrow, closed carriage, and we'll see if she spies the crest," Byrne concluded, as his attention was caught by something on the floor.

"Its Sterling's crest; it has to be," Marcus said, rubbing his temples. "If she can confirm that, we may not have to wait until the Gold Ball to discover the next piece of the puzzle. We can go straight to Fieldstone. We won't have to use Phillippa and continue this ridiculous charade any longer, we can—what is it?" Marcus said as he noticed that Byrne's gaze was attuned to an object on the ground, glinting in the firelight. He leaned down and picked it up.

A hairpin.

Marcus held his breath, as Byrne turned the little twist of metal over and over again in his hand.

"Whose is this?" Byrne asked, and then, with a flick of a glance to the door, where Marcus had hung Phillippa's dark velvet cloak, "And whose is that?"

"They're mine," Phillippa said, her voice cool and clear from the bedchamber doorway.

Phillippa had awoken only a few minutes after Marcus had left the room. For a moment, she was confused as to her whereabouts, but then the memories flooded back, bringing blood to her cheeks. She lifted her head, confirmed that she was alone. But was she abandoned? No, she decided, she could hear voices from the room beyond.

Quickly she buried her face in the pillow again. Oh, the things they'd done! The things *she'd* done. Had she really been so wanton? So . . . brave? So open to a man?

But it wasn't any man. It was Marcus Worth. And she had a feeling that the other voice she heard in the room beyond was his brother Byrne.

Even though both she and Marcus were grown, independent adults, Phillippa's experience with trysts was minimal enough that she would still be deeply embarrassed to be caught in such an . . . indecorous state by a third party, let alone his brother.

Therefore, she untwined herself from the sheets with all possible speed and set about throwing on her gown, which was puddled on the floor.

Her stockings were more difficult to find, as Marcus had thrown them across the room. She found the first by the foot of the bed, its ribbon still in its loops. The other she eventually found right beside the door.

Bending down to pick it up, she paused in her movements when, quite by accident, her ear aligned with the keyhole, and she could hear the brothers perfectly.

"What was I right about now?" Marcus said, clearly impatient.

"That I, as the Blue Raven, would save the day," Byrne's voice said with glee.

What?

Phillippa remained crouched, her ear perked and waiting. They started talking about some girl named Meggie, a pickpocket who would help them track down Laurent—but Phillippa didn't care about any of that. All she could think was that Marcus did not correct him. Surely Byrne was only pretending, surely . . .

But then, he said it again.

"I told you I could do this—one of the Blue Raven's most formidable talents."

And then Phillippa's stomach dropped. Her mind raced back to their first encounters. In the sarcophagus, she'd heard him addressed as the Blue Raven—or did she? When she'd first told him what she "knew," he'd denied it, true, but then he let her go on believing it . . . and he agreed to their bargain. He agreed to be revealed as the Blue Raven at the Benning Ball. The world swam before her, and she didn't even realize she was twisting the stocking in her hand to the point of tearing it.

Slowly, she rose. Slowly, she turned the knob of the door, opened it the barest crack.

"We won't have to use Phillippa and continue this ridiculous charade . . ." she heard Marcus say as he paced, his back to her. If

Phillippa had felt tears forming behind her eyes, that one sentence dried them. She was part of a ridiculous charade, was she? Well, no longer.

She saw Byrne pick up one of her hairpins. Her cue to throw the door open wide.

"And whose is that?" he asked, indicating her cloak, hanging next to Marcus's hat.

"They're mine," she answered, barefooted, hair a tumbling mess, only one stocking on, but her head held high.

She walked right past stone-faced Marcus and extended her hand to Byrne.

"I'm sorry, I don't believe we've been formally introduced. I'm Mrs. Benning. You must be the Blue Raven."

Twenty-three

"I'M correct, am I not?" Phillippa said, her voice clear, passionless. Byrne raised his eyebrows at Marcus, as if asking what to do. Marcus couldn't respond. He had run out of answers.

Phillippa's gaze never strayed from Byrne's face, her hand remained outstretched, waiting.

"Yes," Marcus finally replied, "he is."

Phillippa dropped her hand, turned around, faced Marcus.

"Not you."

Marcus searched her face, found no sympathy, no recourse there. "Not me," he replied.

The room held silent, as time stretched on with each tick of the mantel clock. Byrne stood up and wordlessly excused himself from the room.

"I have to go," she finally said and brushed past him again, into the bedroom. He followed her, watched as she retrieved her shoes from the side of the bed.

"I would remind you that you approached me," he said, crossing his arms over his chest. "And I told you more than once that I was not who you thought I was."

"That," she huffed as she slipped the shoes on her feet, "is readily apparent now."

"Phillippa," he approached her now, took her gently by the arm. "It can't be that important, can it?"

But Phillippa wrenched her arm free. "What do you know about what's important to me? You lied to me. You used me."

"As if your intentions toward me were good and pure," he retorted.

"I *never* lied to you. I never involved you in some 'ridiculous charade,' " she retorted, marching past him into the study, retrieving her cloak.

"Oh, really? You never paraded me down Bond Street, treating me like your new pet?" he followed her, maneuvered so his back was to the main doors, effectively blocking her from leaving.

"That was part of *your* plan, not mine," she shot back, her prideful chin going up.

"You never paid me attention to make your beloved Broughton jealous?" Marcus sneered. "Face it, Phillippa, your entire life is a ridiculous charade."

Marcus knew that in that moment he had gone too far. He knew it before he felt the hard crack of her palm against his face. And he knew, too, that he deserved this slap that she had held in account. He deserved her scorn and the tears that he saw threatening to fall on her cheek.

"You don't come within one hundred feet of me, understood? You see me walking down the street, you turn and walk the other way." She shook angrily.

"If only for your own protection, yes," he answered, his hand massaging his stinging cheek. "But Phillippa, you have to know the truth—" But she shook her head.

"The truth is, you entered our bargain under false pretenses," she said, her voice wobbling. "And everything . . . everything that came after is false because of it."

"No," Marcus replied softly. "Everything that came after is the truest thing in the world. Because it's us." He lowered his hand, took her naked one—she hadn't been able to locate her gloves. "Phillippa, it's me. It's just me."

She withdrew her hand from his, her eyes shooting to his face. "That, Mr. Worth, seems to be the problem."

And with that, she slipped past him and out the door.

Marcus didn't know how long he stood there, alone, frozen. He just kept staring at the spot where Phillippa had stood before she maneuvered past him, an apparition now. His skin went cold, his eyes hard. She was gone. His mind knew it; his heart didn't want to accept it. But the memory of her cruel parting shot turned his vision black, and he threw a fist into the door, causing a spindly crunch as the thin pine of the door gave way, beginning to crack.

"Ow!" he grunted, stepping back from the door, shaking his hand free of the pain.

All right, so, hitting a solid object with his fist was not a solution. But for a single moment, it wasn't his heart that was hurting. He turned around, examined the room. The piles of balled-up paper on the floor, a dozen attempts at writing the letter that would remove Phillippa from his life. "Thank you for your assistance," they said. Ruthlessly, he began picking up those thanks and throwing them into the grate. If he'd wanted to get rid of her, well, he more than succeeded, and it was without formality or sentiment.

As he was pitching the balls of paper into the grate, watching them curl, burn, disappear into the air, the door creaked on its hinges, admitting Byrne.

"Don't worry," Marcus said, his eyes never leaving the fire, "she's gone."

Byrne's gaze flicked to the door, which bore fractures from Marcus's burst of anger. "Are you all right?" he asked, gingerly taking a step into the room.

Marcus flexed his hand. "It's fine, see?"

Byrne took another step into the room, quietly shutting the door behind him. "Marcus, are you all right?"

Marcus threw the last of his unworthy letters into the fire, watched it as the edges caught flame. "I'm fine," he repeated. With a rueful, cynical smile, he looked up from the fire. "It worked. She's gone."

❧

When Phillippa arrived home, she was in no mood to hear the cries of distress from her housekeeper that someone had broken a window. She also didn't give a damn that she woke up half the household to accommodate her need for a bath immediately. She was uncaring about how her appearance—hair disheveled, missing stocking, missing gloves—set her lady's maid into a tizzy of deep concern coupled with salacious conjecture. What she did know, once she was comfortably ensconced in her large, copper tub, steaming-hot water helping to clear her mind, was that she had been made a fool of.

And Phillippa Benning despised being played for a fool.

The only other time she had been taken in was when Alistair successfully hid his financial straits from her, before their marriage. That he had also fooled her father, who had made inquires into his situation, had done nothing to balm her wound. The rude shock of discovering his house empty of any furnishings, the creditors knocking ceaselessly on her door, the dawning understanding that her husband had not married her for love or even affection—that was nothing compared to this.

Maybe because, even though he had been discovered as poor and a liar, Alistair had still been Haute Ton. His breeding had been impeccable, his family name ancient and illustrious. Even the lack of a title hadn't tarnished his eligibility. No one would ever scoff at her aligning herself with Alistair. She was able to maintain her pride.

But Marcus Worth? Every day of their acquaintance, she had

believed him to be something he wasn't. And he let her. He let her think him more than a third son, more than a clerk in the War Department. More than a nobody.

She had skipped happily astray from her position in the world, entertaining his sister-in-law's earnestness, losing her lead with Broughton, hell, even being kind to Lady Jane!—all because of him.

She dunked her head under the water, letting it fill her ears, muffling any noise, separating herself from the world as entirely as she could.

When she surfaced, she took a deep breath and pushed the water out of her eyes that might have been mistaken for tears.

Phillippa Benning didn't feel sorry for herself. Phillippa Benning didn't agonize over past mistakes.

No, instead, Phillippa Benning decided to return with a vengeance.

It started with a new wardrobe. Well, one couldn't reclaim her throne in society without the proper clothing, now could one? The next morning, Phillippa, Bitsy in her arms, called Totty down for breakfast and insisted that they visit Madame Le Trois immediately. If Totty wondered about Phillippa's authoritative demeanor, especially given that she had last seen the girl headed out to visit Mr. Worth, it was not vocalized. She simply called for her morning concoction from Leighton and mentally arranged her day according to Phillippa's demands.

Madame Le Trois was set to work at once on gowns, day dresses, pelisses, underthings, and stockings that did not have one iota of practicality about them. No more cambric, no more wide, fluid skirts, and absolutely no more pockets. Instead, Phillippa insisted on the lightest chiffon and silks, cut against her frame to leave very little ease of movement and just enough to the imagination. The necklines and back lines were scandalously low, the colors provoctive, and the entire thing outrageously expensive.

But it made Phillippa feel good, rediscovering a little bit of her power.

Once her wardrobe (and a few spontaneous pieces for Bitsy) was redone, Phillippa embarked on a mission to regain any footing she might have lost. And her first stop was with Broughton.

She found him in the park, taking his brilliant pure white mare, Rebecca, through her paces. Rebecca matched Broughton in terms of breeding and haughtiness, so understandably, Phillippa's carriage, pulled by beautiful matched bays, received a decided snub from man and horse alike.

"Oh, Phillip, how can you be so cruel?" Phillippa laughed.

"How can I be so cruel?" Broughton replied, an eyebrow going up.

"Yes, after I waited for you." Phillippa reached into her pocket, and pulled out a cube of sugar and enticed Rebecca to come closer. Proud as she was, Rebecca did eye the sugar cube once or twice before turning away. "I waited for you to call on me for a week. At the Hampshires, I was going to come to your room," she lied, but fortunately, she lied very well. "I truly was, but with the fire and the panic, I . . . I became so scared. All I wanted to do was apologize, but I couldn't very well call on you, could I?" She lowered her lashes here, bit her lip, the picture of disappointed love. "So I waited for you to call on me. And we both know how peevish waiting makes me."

By now Broughton had loosened the lead on Rebecca, allowing that regal creature to take the steps forward to meet Phillippa's hand. She let out a lovely peal of laughter as Rebecca's wet, rough tongue licked her hand, and then the mare nickered for more.

"Careful," Broughton said. "You're going to spoil her."

She let her eyes, shining pure innocence, meet his. "So you'll forgive me?"

Broughton shrugged. "To be fair, it was a confusing night. I ended up in the bloody hedge maze, got separated from my, er, friends, and went in circles for hours."

"I think we should start over." She extended her hand. "Mrs. Benning. How do you do?"

He looked at her outreached hand. Then gingerly took it.

"Broughton," he offered.

"Very pleased to meet you. Would you care to come call, Lord Broughton?" she maneuvered. "Tomorrow?"

"For tea?" Broughton scoffed.

She didn't make any promises to him. She didn't offer to let him call much later or to stay long past tea or to meet him in any dark, secluded place. She didn't have it in her to make a promise she knew she wasn't ready to keep. Her need for revenge did not go that far. Instead, she smiled at him, looked him up and down. Then she called out, "Driver!" and the whip sent the matched bays to a trot, and she pulled away, leaving Broughton bewildered and smiling. And leaving Phillippa back in control of the game.

If, when leaving the park, after nodding hello to all and sundry, she saw the Worth carriage, which contained Marcus and a wide-bonneted woman, she did not comment on it. Nor did she stop. She simply moved along, her eyes fixed straight ahead.

From this point on, Phillippa threw herself back into being the Infamous Phillippa Benning with relish, attending round after round of parties and routs that rivaled even the gayest of the Prince Regent's celebrated court. She went to the opera and there sent up such gales of laughter at the act breaks, speaking with the fawning Lord Draye, that she inevitably attracted more people to her box. She danced for hours on end at any number of parties, and when that gathering came to an end, she sought another. She became the lifeblood of every Ton event, going to musicales, card parties, and literary salons at an alarming rate. She made her opinion known, saying that Mrs. Archibald's latest gothic wasn't up to snuff, while Miss Austen's work struck her as provincial. She was kind enough to not cut Mrs. Hurston for wearing a turban again, but she felt it necessary to comment on the woman's penchant for awful feathers in her coiffure. And everyone was once again in Phillippa Benning's thrall.

Broughton did call on her for tea, and every tea for days. As did Nora, Lady Jersey, Princess Esterhazy, and every eligible young buck in London. When Penny Sterling called with Louisa Dunningham, Phillippa was polite but remote. She let it be known that she was merely tolerating their presence, not encouraging it, a feat achieved by the barest of conversation and on more worldy subjects than Penny and Louisa could hope to keep up with. When they left, after a spare half hour in Phillippa's pink drawing room, Nora and Broughton were reduced to fits of giggles.

"Oh, Phillippa!" Nora cried once she caught her breath. "How wicked you are! I thought Penny Sterling was going to cry when you called her embroidered reticule déclassé!"

"As if that missish little thing even knows what déclassé means," Broughton agreed. "I must say, Phillippa, I do enjoy your teas; you have a way of making them remarkably entertaining."

Phillippa smiled at this, let her finger graze Broughton's as she handed him a refreshed cup of tea, a new blend from India, which she despised but knew Broughton was quite taken with.

"But I don't understand why you'd claim them as acquaintances in the first place," Broughton inquired, after a long sip.

Phillippa gave an elegant little shrug. "I thought perhaps Miss Sterling and Miss Dunningham could be cultivated into interesting young women. Apparently I was wrong."

This sent Broughton and Nora into another series of snickers. If Phillippa felt the smallest twinge of regret at her cruelty, if she thought that maybe Totty, who sat across the room silently sipping her spiked tea, might have sent her a disapproving look, she did not let it bother her for long. For Broughton drew her attention, proposing a picnic lunch tomorrow if the weather allowed, and forcing her out of her head and back into the life she knew.

Penny Sterling and Louisa Dunningham were not the only ones to feel the sting of Phillippa's tongue. Indeed, she knew that the simplest way to devastate someone was to not say anything at all.

She used this principle to great effect twice: once in a rather expected way, and the second time, devastatingly.

Phillippa's recent uptick in social activity meant that she could not avoid the people she planned to entirely, for sooner or later, they would be run into. Such was the case when she bumped directly into Lady Jane Cummings in the overcrowded hallway of Lady Charlbury's decided crush.

Phillippa was flanked by Nora, Lady Jane by one of her little entourage. The circumstances of the party were such that Phillippa and Lady Jane blocked traffic as they stared each other up and down.

Then Lady Jane did the most surprising thing. Disobeying all rules of their pact of mutual loathing, she lowered herself into as decent a curtsy as she could manage in the tight space, and murmured, "Good evening, Phillippa."

However, if Lady Jane Cummings thought that she was going to get a civil response from Phillippa Benning, she was proven wrong. For with the simplest flick of an eyebrow, Phillippa put up her chin and slid past Lady Jane in the thick crowd.

A cut direct, as seen by everyone in that crowded hall, it quickly lit up the gossips with purpose, spreading the tale to all assembled. Lady Jane reportedly bore it with a simple shrug, a wry twist of her lips. Later, in the ladies' retiring room, after having been asked why she said anything at all to Phillippa Benning, given their well-documented hatred of each other, Lady Jane answered, "I'd heard a rumor that she'd changed. Obviously, it was wrong."

When this news reached Phillippa, she was unmoved. Mostly because she was busy preparing for another night out.

It was a Friday, the day before the Gold Ball at Regent's Park. Phillippa sat at her dressing table, having her hair put up into hundreds of tiny curls, each defined by a seed pearl pin, when Totty came in, wearing her favorite dark blue evening gown and silk paisley shawl.

"Phillippa dear, do you think I could get away with wearing

this to the Worths' again? I know I wore it last week, but my currant gown is being mended, and the lilac has mud on it still from Broughton's ridiculous picnic."

Phillippa kept her eyes focused on her lady's maid's work as she answered, "Don't fret, Totty, we're not going to the Worths' dinner party. The blue will do."

Totty crossed the room in three quick strides. "Not going? But we're expected, I sent out the acceptance last week myself."

"Come now, Totty, don't tell me you're disappointed. You dislike going to Mariah Worth's odious dinners as much as I do."

"I'm not disappointed; I'm surprised," Totty replied. Then, proceeding cautiously, "May I ask why the sudden change?"

Phillippa's lady's maid applied the final touches to her coiffure, releasing Phillippa to stand and cross to the bed, where her gloves lay waiting. "I'm just terribly bored by the whole thing. As I was telling Mrs. Hurston a few nights ago, it's simply too earnest an evening for my taste, and the lady quite agreed. We're to Vauxhall tonight instead! Broughton took a box for supper."

"You told Mrs. Hurston," Totty raised her eyebrows. "Phillippa, did you, erm, did you inform Lady Worth of your change of plan?"

Phillippa paused in her motions, infinitesimally. She had intended to write Mariah, she had. But she didn't know what to say. She had a feeling that Mariah, of all people, would see through her skin and find the true cause of her actions, and that was something she could not bear. And so she left off writing the note until the next day, and then the next. And now it was too late.

"Mariah is a very intelligent woman," Phillippa replied. "She'll understand."

At Worth House that evening, Mariah Worth waited patiently in the salon for her guests to arrive. Her husband waited beside her. This time a fortnight ago had been the highlight of her year; the place had been packed to the rafters with interesting, influential people, all of whom were willing to fund her orphanage. Since Phillippa Benning's involvement, Mariah decided to build an entirely new wing on the school, and she was excited to show her friend the plans the architect had drawn up.

However, as the clock struck the hour, and only a paltry few people arrived, Mariah had to face the facts: No one of any influence was coming, least of all Phillippa.

She smiled as best she could through the dinner, listening to meager gossip about how Phillippa Benning was going to all the best parties in town, and how she was seen in the company of the Marquis of Broughton several times this week. Only when Phillippa was described as gushing about going to Vauxhall with the Marquis that evening, did Mariah's smile falter. But if she'd learned anything from her association of with Mrs. Benning, it was how to carry through any awkward situation, and as such, she changed the subject happily to Jackie, Jeffy, and all their friends, and away from her own disappointment.

That night, when lying in bed, Graham Worth held his wife tight in his arms, and said, "Don't worry, pet. She's a cruel, evil thing, and Marcus would be well rid of her."

"But she's not," Mariah answered. "I think she's been hurt." What she did not say was that she suspected Marcus to be the cause—and hopefully, the cure.

The next day, Saturday, Phillippa had a great deal of things to do. First of all, she had to sleep. That night was the Gold Ball, and she was not going to be caught yawning halfway through. Indeed, last year, Lady Hertford yawned, an insult that nearly caused Prinny to exclude her from his private box. Only the crème de la crème of the assembled were ever invited into the Prince's private box, an opulent room full of the best food, music, and people. This year, Phillippa was determined to be invited, and with Broughton at her side, she could do it.

After sleep was gained, she had to bathe and powder and pull and press herself into being the most exquisite version of Phillippa Benning imaginable. This had absolutely nothing to do with the fact that Marcus Worth would be attending this evening's festivities, she told herself. Or at least, she knew he would try to. Phillippa was not certain if they had been invited, but since it was well-known that he was no longer a favorite of hers, she had reason to doubt it.

No, her need to look absolutely stunning had nothing to do with Marcus Worth. Instead, she had decided that tonight, she would give Broughton what he'd waited so long for.

It would be fairly easy, she figured. Lying in his bed, maybe she'd be able to wash Marcus out of her mind. She didn't expect to enjoy it, but maybe she'd find some comfort in it. And besides, Broughton had displayed enormous patience with her. Day after day of teas, picnics, playing her gallant at every party. And if she was going to win him, securing forever her throne in society, this was the next step.

So why did she feel such dread?

Phillippa's musings and toilette were interrupted suddenly, when a maid knocked on the door, entered, and handed her a card.

"*Mr. Worth*," was all it said.

Her heart skipped a beat, her stomach plummeted. "He's here?" she asked, "Now?" When the maid nodded a frantic yes, Phillippa leaped out of her chair and commanded, "Hand me a gown—any gown! Oh no, not that one," and proceeded to throw her room into a tizzy to get her dressed and downstairs.

A record fourteen minutes later, Phillippa, dressed in a slinky gown of robin's egg blue, her hair swiftly brought up in an elegant chignon, opened the door to her pink drawing room and saw . . .

Byrne Worth, sitting on the sofa, rolling his cane between his hands.

"Oh," Phillippa said, too surprised to stop herself.

"Mrs. Benning," Byrne said, not bothering to stand, causing Phillippa's eyebrow to rise involuntarily. But she said nothing, crossed the room, and seated herself in the Louis XIV chair opposite.

"Mr. Worth," she replied, her tone as haughty as possible.

"You're a right bitch, you know that, Mrs. Benning?" Byrne said evenly, his voice cool as ice.

Shocked as she was at such language, Phillippa's eyes narrowed appreciatively. "I see we're not standing on ceremony."

"Whether or not Marcus deserves your childish bit of spite, I sincerely doubt Mariah does."

Phillippa shifted slightly in her seat. "I do regret it if your sister-in-law's feelings were injured, but I—"

However, Byrne waved her paltry excuses away. "Mariah's made of sterner stuff than you take her for. In fact, according to Graham, she's more concerned about your feelings; she thinks your heart's been broken."

Phillippa fought to keep her face an impassive mask. "And I suppose you told them I had no heart?" she replied.

Byrne smiled meanly, and changed the subject. "Tell me, Mrs. Benning, are you still planning on revealing the identity of the Blue Raven at your Ball?"

Phillippa shrugged. "Unfortunately, I didn't strike my bargain with the actual Blue Raven, which creates a bit of an ethical dilemma for me."

"Well, while you debate the ethics of revealing a military secret, I have a few things for you to bear in mind." Byrne stood a little shakily. Phillippa noticed for the first time that his gaze was startlingly focused, sharpened by pain. He had forgone his medicine for tonight's work.

"The Blue Raven," he said, leaning heavily on his cane, "is an invention. While recovering from a stab wound to the side, my brother was asked to write up some of *our* assignments, analyze their success and failure, and somehow they ended up in the papers." Byrne paused, forcing her to digest his words. "I say *our*, because ninety percent of the work—research, decryption—was done by Marcus. The reports that reached the papers were beyond exaggerated. Some just made up entirely." Byrne looked down at his cane; involuntarily, his breath hitched before he continued. "Real war is hard. I—the Blue Raven—didn't exist without Marcus. He saved our entire regiment's lives, and my life, more times than I deserve."

Lowering her eyes before Bynre could see their distinct shine, Phillippa replied, "If . . . if that's true, why didn't Marcus tell me that himself?"

Byrne shrugged. "Because he doesn't need the approval of the world. Unlike some."

Phillippa let that sink in for a moment, as Byrne continued. "And since you've . . . returned to your element, I say he's far better off without you."

Phillippa's head came up at that. "He lied to me," she said softly, resolutely.

"Some madman's trying to start a war, and I'm a laudanum-addicted cripple," Byrne replied. "Would you have helped Marcus otherwise?"

Byrne turned around, picked up a packet that had been sitting next to him. "This is for you," he said, and once handing it to her, bowed stiffly and walked to the door.

Phillippa turned the packet over in her hand before whirling around, saying, "Wait!"

Byrne stopped with his hand on the doorknob.

"Um," Phillippa began, "are . . . did you receive—I mean, I don't know if I can get you invitations to the Gold Ball anymore. I'm sorry. How . . . how do you intend to get in?"

Byrne's eyebrow went up. "We'll manage." And before Phillippa could argue or demand details, Byrne was out the door.

Phillippa turned the brown oilskin packet over in her hands once and once again. It was thick, stuffed with something soft. She tore the paper open, exposing a piece of paper and a pair of elbow-length gloves.

Her gloves.

She could feel her eyes welling up as she unfurled the long

white pieces of fabric. But the tears didn't fall until the dozen or so tiny jeweled hairpins that had been wrapped in the gloves rained to the ground.

He returned them. He'd excised her from his house, from his heart. She held the gloves to her mouth to hold back the sobs, but then she inhaled Marcus's scent, which had insidiously soaked into the fabric, having been with him for a week.

She threw the gloves aside, and sobbing, knelt to retrieve the hairpins that had scattered on the thick rug. There, on her knees, she saw that the packet had yielded one other thing from its contents, which had fluttered to the floor with the wrapping.

A letter.

"Phillippa"—it began, and she could hear her name on his lips, pressing on her heart—"contained are articles belonging to you. I believe I found them all. I know I have no right to ask anything of you, but I must beg a personal favor: Do not attend the Gold Ball tonight. For your own well-being and my soundness of mind. I consider it highly unlikely, however, that you will humor this request. If that is the case, I can only ask that you do your best to avoid trouble. Stay with Mrs. Tottendale, stay safe. And if you cannot avoid it, then run."

It was signed, "Yours—Marcus."

Phillippa read the note three times before she managed, with shaking hands, to fold it up again. Then she rose to her feet, resolute. She had a ball to dress for.

Twenty-four

REGENT'S Park, located on the northern edge of the city, was not a part of town often frequented by the Ton elite. They tended to stay south of Oxford Street, near their beloved Hyde Park, St. James's, Pall Mall, and the like. However, since 1811, when the Prince Regent had taken over the lease on the hunting grounds formerly known as Marylebone Park, he had commissioned famed architect John Nash to restructure the entire park (not to mention several streets and blocks of London) in a style pleasing and glorifying to his reign. And maybe a summer house or two.

The park's reconstruction was nowhere near complete, but in an effort to keep up public enthusiasm for his ambitious, expensive projects (and perhaps lease some of the fifty-plus manor houses intended to be built in the park as a means of financing the reconstruction), the Prince opened the park once a year for the Gold Ball, an evening of dinner, dancing, and entertainments unparalleled by the finest hostesses in London.

As it was called the Gold Ball, it's no surprise gold was the predominant color. A pavilion was erected beside the central Prince of Wales Circus, outfitted with thousands of yards of gold-threaded Indian silks, golden and crystal chandeliers hung from the caves, and millions of gold-dipped candles that reflected off the gold-laquered dance floor like a lake of fire. The pavilion boasted private boxes that functioned as separate rooms, decorated in sumptuous style. The dancing and merriment spilled out into the park, along torchlit paths, and it was not uncommon to find gold-dressed Earls and Viscountesses wandering lost in the park come morning, having had, of course, the time of their lives.

No one turned down an invitation to the Gold Ball at Regent's Park. Even the Duke of Wellington, whose ambivilence toward the spendthrift Prince was well-known in discreet circles, would be there. Whether he would follow the fashion and take leave of his conservative formal black attire and wear shades of gold provided much speculation. Had Phillippa weighed in, she would have likely wagered against it. Wellington was a friend of her father's, and even though he was a fine dresser, a suit of gold might be too much, even for him. But she didn't have the time or inclination to ponder the Duke's choice of evening garments. Her mind was irrevocably focused on other matters.

Where was he? Phillippa and Totty had endured the long line of carriages, the long line to be announced and received, and now, the stirring, whirling masses on the hectare-sized dance floor. With Marcus's height, she thought that even though most everyone was wearing the same color and had been supplied with gold masks, she would be able to spot him.

But she'd been at the party a full half hour and had not seen him.

"Drat it all!" she said aloud, startling Totty, who stood beside her, nearly oversetting the drink handed to her by a gold-liveried footman.

"Whatever's the problem dear?" Totty replied, steadying her drink so it didn't spill, before taking a sip.

"I . . . haven't spotted, er, Broughton, is all," Phillippa answered, eyeing Totty's drink.

"Well, go and look for him; he's likely with his cronies at the card tables. I've a mind to wander into the dining area, see what goodies are being served."

Phillippa squeezed her fan tightly, hiding her nerves. "Oh no, I'd much rather stay with you." With a final glance at Totty's hand, she asked, "Totty, darling, would you do me a favor? Could you make that your last drink of the evening?"

Totty looked at Phillippa as if she had lost her mind.

"Its just that"—and here, Phillippa decided to forgo artifice and spill out her concerns—"I am afraid something is going to happen this evening, and I need you to have your wits about you."

Totty took one step closer to Phillippa, then without a glance, placed her glass on a passing footman's tray. "What's going to happen tonight?" she asked seriously.

"I don't know," Phillippa answered, "but if you would be so good as to keep an eye out for Marcus Worth—"

"Phillippa, you made quite certain this past week that he would not be invited."

"I know, but I still think he's here."

"How?" Totty replied. "They didn't let anyone past the entrance to the park without an invitation! And there are the Prince's guards—"

"I don't know how, but he's here." She took a deep breath, sighed. "Somewhere, he's here."

"Of course he's here," a deep voice said from behind Phillippa as a hand snaked to her waist. "I wouldn't miss this party for the world."

She knew it was Broughton the moment he touched her. Not because he inspired any stirring of feeling, but because he did not.

"Hello!" Phillippa replied, perhaps a bit too brightly, but she was rewarded with a smile from Broughton. He did look his ravishing best, gold silk coat and waistcoat, the puff of white at his throat marked only by a large gold pin with his family crest on it.

"Hello to you, too," he responded with a growl. Perhaps he was trying to be alluring, provocative. Too bad Phillippa could only find such posturing tiresome right now.

"Hello as well!" Nora piped up from behind Broughton, wedging her way into the group. "Phillippa, we've been looking for you everywhere. You'll never guess what we just saw!"

"It was rather astounding, in fact: Miss Sterling, hiding behind a bit of shrubbery," Broughton drawled, mischief in his eyes.

"She was wearing copper! Can you imagine? Her dressmaker must have run out of gold!"

"Indeed?" Phillippa asked, swallowing her pity for poor Penny Sterling. She knew she should have guided her to Madame Le Trois, but—

"You were so right to cut her when you did!" Nora continued blithely.

"Truly, the child's a mess." Broughton continued, taking two glasses of champagne off a tray brought by a footman and handing one to Phillippa. "Now, I must claim the next dance with you. Phillippa?"

But Phillippa wasn't paying attention. Instead, her eyes were fixed on the champagne-serving footman.

He stooped a little as he walked, a trifle bowlegged. He wore the mask, the gold uniform, the gold-dusted hair of all the footmen lining the floor, but it was his eyes—those warm, kind brown eyes staring through the mask—that held her. Everything else in the pavilion dropped away.

It's just me, he mouthed, and held a finger to his lips.

"Phillippa? Phillippa," Broughton was saying, and then, following her line of sight to the footman who stood behind him, addressed the footman callously. "You're done here, aren't you? Sod off then." Once Marcus took a discreet step back, Broughton turned his attention back to Phillippa. "The waltz has begun . . . Shall we?"

All Phillippa wanted to do was stay there, speak to Marcus. But with the expectant eyes of Broughton and Nora upon her, her options were limited.

"I . . . I can't abandon Totty." She smiled.

"Of course you can, child," Totty replied, "I'll wait here for you."

"Of course you can, she says," Broughton added, his impatience beginning to show. "As if you need your companion's permission."

Broughton was right, of course, if a little cruel. She was her own woman, she didn't need Totty's permission. But she'd intended to stay by her side that night. She flicked a glance to Totty, then, discreetly, to Marcus, who hung back against one of the pavilion's decorated supportive pillars. She would be on the dance floor. She would be safe from trouble there, surely.

"Yes, Phillip, I'd love to dance with you," Phillippa smiled, causing Broughton's petulant grimace to break into a smile. She handed her drink to Totty, took his arm, and as Nora's next dance partner came to fetch her, the pair of couples took the floor.

Marcus stood stock-still as Phillippa and Broughton took the floor, his stomach doing nastly little flip-flops as he watched them twirl away. He wasn't surprised that she had ignored his request to not attend the party. By all accounts, one could be on their deathbed and still feel it necessary to attend the Gold Ball. But what did surprise him was that she had looked at him kindly.

He did not expect kindness from Phillippa Benning. Tales of her exploits this past week had burned his ears. She could teach a master class in English snobbery. So why did she look at him as if she had been waiting for him, and only him?

Then again, maybe she had just been startled.

As Marcus mused over these things, he was unaware that someone had gingerly maneuvered from the dance floor's sideline and come to stand next to him at his post.

"Unless Laurent is dancing with Mrs. Benning, you're staring in the wrong direction."

A gnarled old man leaning heavily on a cane stood beside him, whistling through his teeth as he spoke. His moth-eaten, gold-spun clothing was possibly fashionable fifty years ago, but certainly no longer. However, as Baron Fortesque, no one questioned the balding, warted, liver-spotted old man's right to be there. Besides, most everyone else was having too good a time to notice that the old man had an improbably full, if dirty, set of teeth.

"Do you think she got the package I sent?" Marcus asked, bowing to serve Byrne's stooped frame a glass of champagne, which he downed in one gulp, playing to character.

"Of course she did. Didn't stop her coming, though, did it?" Byrne muttered, in a hacking, wheezing voice. Marcus wondered briefly how much of his brother's disassociated demeanor was artifice.

"No, but she was reluctant to leave Mrs. Tottendale's side. Maybe she's trying to stay out of trouble." *For me,* he thought.

"Well, the old bat is right there, drink in hand as usual." Byrne commented, nodding toward Totty, who stood calmly at the edge of the dancing. "Marcus, we have work to do."

Marcus nodded, and then, with one last glance out to the most beautiful couple on the dance floor, he turned away.

So, if half of that couple sought the eyes of one particular footman, he wasn't there to see. And if Totty raised a brow and discreetly shot a look back to the same bowlegged footman and the old man, neither of them noticed.

Phillippa knew that she and Broughton were drawing attention. The flimsy half masks did little to hide their identities, and the two of them were so well-known that their figures could be picked out at a distance. She knew what everyone was saying, too: that they were charmingly coupled, that they looked marvelous together. But Phillippa's delight in being the cause of everyone's whispers and smiles was marred by the fact that she was scouring the crowd, looking for something, anything. Keeping her eyes open.

"You keep staring over my shoulder instead of at me, I'll become quite cross," Broughton remarked, as he took her through a turn.

Phillippa's gaze immediately returned to Broughton's. "Oh, I . . . I just saw the Duke of Wellington, look." She pointed to the edge of the structure, where Wellington (who sported a waistcoat of gold; everything else was stark, formal evening dress) was surrounded by fawning ladies and gentlemen alike. Phillippa couldn't be sure, she squinted a bit, but . . . was that Lord Sterling speaking with the Duke?

"Phillippa, what on earth are you doing *gawking*?" Broughton sniffed. "So unbecoming. The man's no better than you or me."

Phillippa's brow furrowed. "Actually . . ."

"War hero or not, his title is bestowed," Broughton scoffed, as if it was a shocking secret.

Phillippa smiled at Broughton and deftly changed the subject. "I'm terrible, I know. But I see interesting people, and I simply have to look at them. When I spy the Prince Regent, I promise not to ignore you and gawk too horribly."

Broughton gave out a bark of laughter, drawing many approving eyes toward the apparently happy couple.

"Certainly you've met the Prince before?" Broughton asked.

"I was presented, but only for a moment," Phillippa answered.

"Well then, let's make sure he remembers you this time." As the music ended, he guided her to far side of the pavilion, where the Prince Regent and his entourage were holding court.

She kept her head up as they moved through the crowd, her heart thudding the entire time. Part of her was desperate to go with Broughton and make their bows to the Prince. But the other part of her kept wary. She glanced back at the man she thought could be Sterling speaking with Wellington. They were engrossed in conversation. She twisted her head, trying to spot Totty, but to no avail. She did lock eyes briefly with Nora, who grinned at her ecstatically.

"Phillip, really, should we?" she asked hesitantly.

"Of course," he sang jovially. "I've played at the Prince's table several times; he'll not be offended by my approach . . . and since you're with me . . ."

This was likely true. It was a festive atmosphere, and the attendees all peers. The rules of court relaxed further with every glass of champagne. But still, some measure of responsibility must be retained.

"Very well, but at least let me go and tell Totty where I've gone."

But it was too late. Broughton suddenly came to a stop and dropped to a deep court bow, revealing to Phillippa that they stood directly before the Prince Regent. He was greeted by the Prince with a bored, "Broughton. Come to lose more money to me?"

Broughton gave an alarmingly high laugh. "If Your Highness is playing, I would be honored to oblige. But I forget my manners. This is Mrs.—"

"Benning, I know. I daresy all of London does," the Prince finished for him, suddenly deeply interested in his fingernails.

Phillippa gave her most elegant curtsy. "Your Highness is too kind," she said demurely. "The Ball is masterful," she complimented, "a resounding success."

"You approve, then?" The Prince lifted an eyebrow. "I'm given to understand that your approval is hard-won and exacting."

She could have enthused that the party was perfect, not a candlestick out of place. But the Prince did not seem interested in her answer, which made her decide to make it interesting.

"Actually, I find the linens a touch too peach in color."

That brought the Prince's head up from his fingernails, and

Broughton shot her an outraged glance. But she held firm, meeting the Prince's eyes with an innocent smirk painted on her lips. "But everything else passes inspection."

The shocked Prince Regent stared blankly at her for a moment before letting out a great bark of laughter, drawing no small number of eyes to them.

Just then, an aide to the Prince came over and whispered in his ear. "Ah, it seems there are some vittles ready to be served in my box," he reported. And the Prince was fond of his vittles. "Would you care to join me? That is, if Mrs. Benning can bring herself to eat from peach-colored linens."

Hidden relief washed over her as she smiled. "I'll do my best."

The Prince led the way up to his box, Phillippa and Broughton behind him. Oh, she had done it! She had been invited to the Prince's box! Oh, Lady Jane would be eaten with jealousy—everyone would. In the midst of her heart-pounding thrill, Phillippa had almost forgotten about the impending danger she knew swirled around them, about the havoc wreaked and the man Marcus chased.

Until, of course, that man shouldered past her.

He was headed in the opposite direction and, in the great crush of the Gold Ball pavilion, brushed against her side. He wore the same gold half mask as everyone else, and the same gold attire, but still, she knew. She knew it was the same man that she had seen in farmer's clothes, in the Hampshire stables. His hair was sandy-colored and balding in the back, something she hadn't taken note of before. But his posture, his walk, was exactly the same.

She stretched and turned as she walked, peering over her shoulder, marking his progress. The man wedged his way through the crowd quickly, landing at the spot where Sterling and Wellington had once stood. They had been there only a moment ago, but now they were nowhere to be seen, and the man looked as perplexed by this as Phillippa was. He looked to the left, then to the right, then behind him, out into the park. Then, before Phillippa could blink, he glanced discreetly over his shoulder, and stepped out into the night.

Oh Lord, what was she to do? Phillippa came to a halt and began to look around frantically. Where was Marcus? Where was Totty? She had to tell someone. She had to follow that man before he disappeared completely.

"Phillippa?" Broughton asked, stopping beside her. "Come along; the Prince is waiting."

"Phillip," she stuttered, "I have to go . . . go and speak to—to someone."

"Not with the Prince waiting, you don't." He took her elbow and began to guide her into the narrow, canopied space that led to the Royal Box.

She looked down at the hand holding her elbow, then back up at Broughton's face. It was hard and cold. "I apologize, but this is important."

"More important than this? More important than me? Phillippa, you can't go anywhere. What are you thinking?"

She didn't know what she was thinking, but she knew that if she didn't follow that man, he would disappear forever. She met Broughton's eyes, matching ice with ice. "Make my excuses to the Prince, if you would."

She wretched her arm free. Broughton's face became very hot as he leaned into her, his voice a harsh whisper. "That's all you are, Mrs. Benning. Excuses."

He made a smart bow, turned on his heel, and walked away.

Phillippa did not regret disappointing Broughton. And she had no time to regret standing up the Prince. With all possible haste, she walked lightly back to the main floor of the pavilion and ducked her way through the crowd, past an oblivious Nora and a dancing Lady Jane. She craned her neck, looking for Totty, looking for Marcus. Once she reached the spot where the man had stood, she peered into the dark recesses of the park beyond.

The pathways were lit with torches. The immediate areas were planted, in the full lush bloom of late summer/early autumn. But beyond the Prince of Wales Circus were rolling plains, gardens not yet planted, and lakes dug but not yet filled. At the edge of the path, a dividing line between the cultivated land and the wildness beyond, Phillippa saw him.

It was an incredibly stupid idea. Hell, it was absolute insanity. But she scanned the crowd once more, looking into the faces of every footman she saw, and still could not find Marcus among them. And once the man slipped out past that line, he would be gone forever.

Her heart thudded in her chest like mad as she took that first step down into the gardens.

"You're a complete idiot, Philly," she whispered to herself and moved into the shadows.

It wasn't as hard as she thought it would be to stay within sight of the man and to stay unnoticed. Several revelers passed her, completely toshed, weaving their way down the paths and through the gardens. But they paid her no mind, intent as she was on her goal. She would simply stay a good number of yards away from him, out of sight, discover where he was headed, and then turn back for Marcus and safety. But with every step in this direction, Marcus and the safety of the pavilion were a step farther away.

He turned right suddenly; she turned with him. She managed to keep things between them, a rosebush, a sycamore tree. Her gold and ivory beaded dress was made to be eye-catching, and she could only breathe a sigh of relief when they moved into a grove of oak trees, beyond the torchlit pathways. She ducked behind a tree, crouched next to some thorny undergrowth. She was less visible here, which was lucky, because she had more than one pair of eyes to hide from.

The man she had followed was standing with two other men, deep in conversation.

"You said we'd have some sport, cause some trouble. I never signed on for killing," said the man Phillippa recognized as Lord Sterling.

"What do you think war is?" spoke a man Phillippa didn't recognize, his speech colored by a French accent.

"One moment, if you please," the shorter man, whom Phillippa had followed, spoke conciliatorily. He took Sterling aside a step or two, far enough for the illusion of privacy.

"Unfortunately, what we've done so far has only caused grumbling resentment, and we need something big to jolt people into action," he reasoned. "Surely you can see that."

"But not the Duke! Dammit, the man's a hero."

"Sacrifices have to be made," the Frenchman said.

"You keep out of this," Sterling snipped. "He's not your country's hero."

"Lord Sterling, if you please," the shorter man snapped, causing Sterling to quiet, pouting like a recalcitrant child.

Phillippa guessed that the Frenchman was Laurent; he had to be. His voice sent chills of dread down her spine. But who was the other man, then? The one she followed? The one who seemed to be in charge? He had removed his half mask. She had to get closer to him, had to get a good look at his face.

She must've stepped on a twig or rustled a branch. Suddenly all three heads came up and swiveled in her direction. Each of the men drew out weapons. The Frenchman, a gleaming silver pistol from his side; Sterling a razor-honed dagger; the other man, a penknife, blunted but deadly.

Phillippa didn't breathe, didn't blink. She stayed absolutely still.

The three men paused, alert, their ears scanning for another sound, another rustle.

And they were granted one.

A squirrel hopped out of the underbrush, looked at the three men for a moment, then scampered up a tree.

They relaxed their frames, pocketed their weapons. Phillippa would have sighed in relief, if she could have chanced the sigh. Instead, she watched as Laurent circled the other two men, his languid movements not concealing the controlled anger of his frame.

"It does not matter; the opportunity has been missed tonight," Laurent said as he passed Sterling, prodding him on the shoulder. "*He* missed it."

"I . . ." Sterling replied, his voice becoming queerly high.

"He let your Duke go."

"It doesn't mean he can't get him back," the shorter man said. "The ball will go on for hours yet. Of the three of us, he is the only one who can speak to Wellington without causing suspicion, *mon ami.*"

"*Non.* He is too weak." Laurent circled again, his hands behind his back.

"Now, just a minute," Sterling argued. "The man had to greet other people. Dammit, my daughter is here; I have to get back to her."

Sterling tried to move past Laurent, but the Frenchman was quicker, blocking his path.

"Move aside," Sterling commanded shakily.

Laurent just smiled, a predatory gleam of teeth in the dark.

"Move aside, you damned Frog, or I will—" Sterling reached to his side for his dagger but found nothing there.

He looked up, shocked, as Laurent waggled Sterling's silver-handled dagger in his face.

"Damn you both, then," Sterling said, right before Laurent elegantly swiped the razor-sharp blade through the air.

A curtain of blood dropped from the thin line in Sterling's neck. He fell to his knees, all strength flowing out of him in a red river. He crumpled to the ground, his head turned so that his pale eyes met Phillippa's in the dark. And she saw the moment his life left him.

She must have made a noise. Gasped, cried, screamed. Their heads came up, their knives drawn. They looked in her direction. And this time, they found her.

Run. Run now.

Phillippa took off like a jackrabbit, her feet carrying her toward the glow of the pavilion in the distance. She just had to move, just had to get there, find Marcus. She heard the rip of her too-binding skirt on a thorny bush. She felt the pulsating, pounding of the feet of the men behind her. She would never outrun them; they were gaining on her. She opened her mouth to scream, to draw some attention to herself, but a hand clamped over her mouth as she did.

It was the shorter man, the Englishman, who pulled her to the ground. He climbed on top of her in the dirt, holding her down with his penknife to her throat.

"Who is it?" the Frenchman asked casually, as the other pulled at her mask, ripping it aside.

"Mrs. Benning . . ." the man on top of her said. "Well, well, well . . ."

"*Non.* It is the sparrow that belongs to the pigeon. She must have recognized you." The Frenchman grinned. "I'll take her with me."

"Are you sure?" the shorter man asked, who, even this close, Phillippa did not recognize. She stared into his face, forced herself to memorize his features. "But she saw—"

Phillippa refused to lie there for this any longer. Using all the strength she had, she made a fist and aimed directly for the shorter man's throat.

He recoiled in pain, dropping the penknife. She kicked him off of her and struggled to get up, to get away. But it was no use.

She felt the solid thud of the pistol's handle on the back of her head. The ground came up to meet her, and the world went black.

"This was not in the plan." The Englishman said, over the prone body of one Mrs. Phillippa Benning. "Neither was killing Sterling," he admonished.

Laurent shrugged. "He was a—how you say?—liability. He would have broken."

"I must go, lest I be discovered." He nudged the delectable Mrs. Benning's side with his shoe. She was out cold. "What are you going to do with her?" he asked, hiding the worry in his voice. Phillippa Benning was well-known and as well-loved as she was hated. Her disappearance would draw attention.

But Laurent just smiled. "You and I part here, I think," he said.

To argue would only have drawn the madman's ire, so the Englishman nodded and carefully retraced his steps, back to where Sterling lay, his blood no longer flowing. He swiftly rifled through the dead man's pockets, took his pocket watch, snuffbox, and any coin he had. Make it look like a bloodthirsty cutpurse. He refused to acknowledge that his hands were shaking, that Laurent's cold-bloodness scared him beyond reason. He was more than happy to remove himself from that man for the rest of the evening.

The rest of his life, if he had any luck in the matter.

Twenty-five

Arabella Arbuthnot Tottendale, affectionately known as Totty, was not an excitable woman. One could not live with Phillippa Benning and be excitable—unless one wanted to live with constant heart palpitations. Indeed, Totty had married, borne a child, had the misfortune of burying him, and then many years later buried her husband next to her son. She blamed none, brought no hue and cry, as she accepted these circumstances as facts of life. She, in fact, was generally happy, sociable, and catty—but in the most pleasant of ways. To worry Totty was akin to shaking a mountain: rare but possible, and only caused by the greatest of distress.

So the fact that Totty was becoming deeply alarmed by Phillippa's continued absence should have raised some alarms itself.

And Marcus Worth, who had damnedably lost sight of Sterling a half hour before, was already on high alert. When he saw Totty scanning the pavilion, peeking into its alcoves, it was the final straw. He wound through the crowd to her side.

"What's wrong?" he asked, coming away from his post, carrying a tray of champagne with him.

Totty kept looking wildly around before her eyes settled on Marcus's tall frame. "Thank God—I can't find Phillippa."

Fear coursed through Marcus's body. Phillippa missing . . . and Sterling . . . He gripped Totty's elbow, guided her to the side of the room. "Are you sure?"

Totty favored him with a look generally reserved for the mentally addled. "Of course I'm sure. She told me—she made me promise—that I'd stay with her this evening. But I can't find her now."

Taking a deep breath, Marcus urged Totty to do the same. "When was the last time you saw her?" he finally inquired.

"When she went to dance with Broughton, I went to the ladies' retiring room. I thought she wouldn't miss me. Oh, I fear the worst, Mr. Worth. She'd been acting so odd of late, especially after your brother called this afternoon—"

"Wait. Byrne called on her this afternoon? Mrs. Tottendale, slow down, I don't understand."

Totty, in her frustration, knocked the tray of champagne out of Marcus's hand, causing a loud clatter and broken glasses, not to mention a great deal of attention to come their way. "I'm not drunk. She made me promise not to drink."

"All right," he soothed, holding up his hands in a gesture of compliance. "She went to dance with Broughton, and you haven't seen her since."

"Yes, and I've looked everywhere. She's not at the banquet. She's not on the dance floor. She's not in the card room."

"Totty?" Nora's voice broke through the crowd. "Is everything all right?"

"I can't find Phillippa," Totty said, turning to the young lady. "I've looked everywhere."

"Don't worry," Nora patted Totty's hand in a condescending manner, "I know where she is. Totty dear, shall we get you a new glass of champagne?"

"Where is she?" Marcus asked, drawing Nora's eyes to him. She looked at him with utter distaste.

"You should grab a pan and clean up this mess," she said sneeringly, dismissing him without another glance. When he didn't move, she was forced to look up at him once more, this time, seeing past the livery and half mask.

"Oh, you're . . . you're that Mr. Worth. Couldn't wrangle an invitation?" she taunted. "Phillippa told me about you; she said you followed her around like a puppy, that your slavering devotion has become more and more bothersome. Well, you won't have the opportunity to bother her tonight. She is in the Prince's private box—with the Marquis of Broughton."

Totty seemed unsure whether or not to believe this. Marcus wished he could. But the fact that Sterling had eluded him at the same time as Phillippa's disappearance was still too large a coincidence.

"Are you certain?" Marcus asked.

"I'm going to call the guard over for you," Nora said, her eyes narrowing.

"Are you certain?" he gritted through his teeth, towering over the diminutive Nora.

But Nora replied with a laugh. "I saw her myself." She turned, and announced to the whole room, "Phillippa Benning is with the Marquis of Broughton in the Prince's box."

"No, she's not," came a voice from the depths of the crowd. People shuffled to the sides, admitting Lady Jane Cummings to the fore.

"Well, of course, you would say something like that." Nora scoffed. "You wouldn't want everyone to know that Phillippa has won Broughton."

Lady Jane sent Nora a withering look. She glided past her and moved to stand directly in front of Marcus. "I saw Phillippa go out into the park. She was following a man."

"Lord Sterling is missing, too," he grumbled under his breath.

"Oh, for heaven's sake, this is ridiculous. Guard! Guard!" Nora cried, drawing only more attention to their situation, not any particular guards.

Lady Jane rightly ignored Nora's remarks. "It was not Broughton. I did not recognize the man."

Marcus looked from Totty to Lady Jane and back again. "Show me where," he commanded Lady Jane. Then, to Totty, "Locate my brother, Byrne. He's disguised as an old man."

"At the card tables." Lady Jane finished for him. At Marcus's astonished look, she shrugged, "I spotted him earlier and figured you two were up to some trouble."

The three moved quickly, leaving Nora outraged among broken champagne glasses and bemused guests. She shook quietly with rage, as a gentlemanly hand landed on her shoulder.

"Miss De Regis?" Lord Fieldstone said. Having overheard the child yelling for guards, he had moved across the room as quickly as his portly frame allowed, finding her alone among broken crystal. "Is there something going on?"

Nora looked up into that good gentleman's face, spite and fire shooting from her eyes. "Yes, Lord Fieldstone, there is! Marcus Worth and, apparently, his brother have gate-crashed the Ball! And they have taken off after Phillippa, even though there is no way Phillippa followed a strange man into the woods—because she just wouldn't! Not with Broughton at her heel!"

Fieldstone, beyond having to deal with the politics of his office, was a man of young family. Reggie, his eldest, was only ten. So he was, in many ways, used to the peculiarly involved ramblings of children and knew the best way to coax the whole story out of them.

"My dear," he said in his kindest, most paternal tone, "you have obviously suffered a great wrong."

Nora nodded, her eyes becoming huge.

"Don't worry, we'll right it. But I think it best if you start at the beginning."

It did not take long to find the body. Lady Jane took them to the spot where she had seen Phillippa disappear into the gardens, and

Marcus had followed the paths until the paths were no more. Byrne hobbled at his heels, Totty and Lady Jane behind him. When they spotted the grove of trees, Marcus's instincts took over, and he headed for them.

"Byrne," Marcus called out from the center of the grove. "Keep the ladies back."

"Too late," Byrne drawled, coming to stand next to his brother over the pale, bloodied form of Lord Sterling. They heard the gasps from Totty and Lady Jane. Byrne looked over his shoulder, met Lady Jane's eyes, saw her clasping Totty to her protectively. "Jane, take Mrs. Tottendale back to the party, and tell them what we've discovered."

Jane nodded and guided the still gasping Totty back the way they came.

"He's dead." Byrne said, as Marcus knelt beside the body.

"And his killers long gone." Marcus mused. There were footprints in the soft soil, more than one set. "There were two men; they turned on Sterling."

"Not just Laurent," Byrne surmised.

Marcus squinted, focused only on those footprints. "They ran . . . this way." He stood and followed the footprints to a thorny bit of underbrush and then past it, back toward the pavilion.

He found a patch of material, caught on a rosebush. He then found the scene of a struggle, and his mind went black.

They chased her. They caught her. And when he found them, they would die.

But how?

"Dammit," Marcus breathed. "Sterling was our only lead. How are we to find them now?" he stood and began to pace. "How am I going to find her, Byrne? Laurent will show no mercy; he will hurt Phillippa. Before he kills her, he will—"

But before he could succumb completely to his black thoughts, Byrne came up and delivered a much-needed knock to Marcus's temple, felling him to his knees.

"Take a deep breath, little brother," Byrne said, as the stars cleared from Marcus's eyes. "You need to think; its what you're good at. Now, you were right about Sterling. But obviously, he wasn't the only one. Who could it be?"

But Marcus wasn't focusing on his brother's voice. He was focused on the tiny glint of metal he saw underneath the shrubbery. He reached for it: a dulled, well-used penknife.

"Marcus!" Byrne's voice penetrated his thoughts. "Who do you think? Crawley? Someone else from the War Department?"

"Yes," Marcus answered, turning the knife over in his hand. "And I think I know who."

Phillippa had the worst hangover of her life. At least, she supposed it was a hangover: the same dull throbs shooting down to the base of her neck, the same darkly blurred vision, mouth of cotton, and sore muscles. But all too soon she realized the sore muscles were from tight bindings at her wrists, ankles, and across her midsection. The mouth of cotton was actually a gag. And the dark blurriness of her vision was due to a sack of some kind, placed unceremoniously over her head.

Certainly her hair was a complete mess. But that was the least of her worries, as suddenly the memory of what she had seen and whom she had run from flooded back.

She brought her head up, began to struggle at her bindings. But it was no use. She was tied to a deeply uncomfortable chair, her wrists firmly secured to the solid wooden arms, her feet bound together and tied to the chair legs. She couldn't move more than her fingers and toes.

Her movements drew attention, and she froze as she heard footsteps, felt the close breath of her captor on her cheek.

Unceremoniously, the sack was ripped from her head, leaving Phillippa blinking up at her captor.

"*Bon soir,*" the Frenchman said, grinning like a jungle cat about to play with its food. "You are awake. *Bon.*"

It seemed a good idea to scream like mad. Unfortunately, the gag remained firmly in place, severely muting and garbling any sound that she could make, and she only strained herself into hoarseness.

"Ah, ah, ah," he said. "I'm afraid that strip of linen will have to stay in place. I have neighbors, you see. It would be *très* rude to disturb them."

For the first time Phillippa allowed herself to look about the room, take stock of her surroundings. It was a sparsely furnished room but of good quality, with moldings and fresh wallpaper. There were candles on almost every surface, but the drapes were heavy, so no light escaped. What furnishings there were she recognized as French, a Louis Quinze settee, a Sun King inlay on a side table. But what interested Phillippa most was the wall she was facing. Tacked up on it were dozens and dozens of maps and drawings. Different sections of London, the layout of a grand house, the streets of Brighton, the hold of a ship. All of his plans, right before her.

She took in the wall as he leaned his lithe frame against the chair, infiltrating Phillippa's space, forcing her to pull away as far as she could—which was not much. He fingered a curl of her hair at her brow. "So lovely, you are. But allow me to introduce myself. We will be spending so much time together."

He stood up, rounded to stand in front of her, and gave her a proper French court bow. "*Je m'appelle le Comte de Laurent aux Villeurs*. Or, at least, I was once."

She raised an eyebrow.

"My lands were taken from me, as were my parents, during the Revolution. I was but a boy, reduced to becoming Laurent. That is how you know me, *non?* That is how the pigeon knows me."

She cocked her head to one side, questioning.

"Your beloved Blue Raven." Laurent's eyes narrowed. "There is no need for you to introduce yourself. You are Madame Benning, the ladybird of the pigeon." Phillippa shook her head, frightened, but honest. She was not the Blue Raven's lady—technically.

But Laurent just laughed. "Do not deny it. I am not as stupid as my partners. I saw you in the maze, a beacon of sunlight in the dark. Once I discovered who you were, I followed you. But you never led me to him. He kept his distance from you." Laurent sent her an appraising glance. "God knows how. But tonight, you were caught doing your master's bidding. He endangered you stupidly. And it will be his downfall."

Phillippa objected roundly to the idea of being mastered by anyone, but was of course unable to voice this objection. Laurent straightened, began to walk back and forth lazily, pontificating. "When we began, I did not expect the pigeon to trace my plans so quickly. It was unfortunate luck. But he has certainly made this enterprise so much more interesting."

Laurent came to her then, his long, thin finger drawing a line up Phillippa's throat, fingering her chin. "He will come for you, you know. The only reason you live is so he can watch you die."

Phillippa wanted to ask what made him think that Marcus would find her. What made him think that if he did, he would not be the one to fall. But the man seemed to blindly believe that he would face his archenemy tonight. And he relished it. His madness was beginning to show.

It was amazing how focused Phillippa's mind became in those moments. She surveyed Laurent's form, spotting a dirk in his boot, a dagger at his side. Those silver pistols were likely under his coat. She examined the room and saw that it had only one exit and entrance. Once Marcus entered, there would be no escape. What furniture there was could easily conceal a weapon: a knife in the settee cushions, a pistol in a flowerpot. And only Laurent would know they were there. They were on his grounds. He had the advantage.

Phillippa prayed that Marcus did not find her. Not tonight. Not when he would be walking into such circumstances. But if he did, she would have to be ready. And so, while Laurent kept pacing, his eyes on the clock, Phillippa began to plan.

Getting into Whitehall at night was a fairly simple task. If one did not have access, one simply had to sneak past the armed gates, the sentries posted on every entrance, break in through a window, navigate the corridors without being seen by the night watch patrolling the halls with candlesticks and clubs, and pick the lock of one's destination.

Luckily, when they reached the door of the Security section of the War Department, it was already unlocked.

And Leslie Farmapple was inside.

He was in Sterling's private office. The safe in the corner was open and emptied of all valuables. They watched as Leslie ransacked his desk, abandoning all order and neatness in his rush.

"That's not up to your usual standard, Leslie," Marcus drawled.

The short, tweedy man looked up but did not pause in his movements. "Mr. Worth, and er, Mr. Worth," he stammered nervously, his voice surprisingly hoarse. "I . . . I was just tidying up—as you see, Lord Sterling can never find anything."

Marcus came forward slowly and placed the penknife on the desk in front of Leslie. "You dropped something," he said quietly, holding his gaze.

Leslie stopped moving. He stared at the penknife for whole seconds, before he gave a small, nervous laugh. "I can explain," he said and lunged for the knife.

But Marcus was quicker. The moment Leslie's hand reached the table, he grabbed his wrist, pulled him forward, his head slamming onto the desk.

"Ow!" Leslie yelled. "Guards! Guards!" but his voice was not strong enough. Marcus quickly rounded the desk and, pulling Leslie upright, threw his fist directly into that man's right eye.

"That's the second time tonight someone has tried to call the guard on me." Marcus sneered, landing a punch this time to the left side of his face. "Go ahead, Leslie, call them again. And we'll discuss with them how you betrayed your country by falling in league with our enemies." He threw another punch, and another, each a sickening crunch and thud of bone breaking flesh, Leslie falling to the floor, his arms no longer able to protect himself from the blows. "We can talk about how you slit Sterling's throat when he no longer proved useful."

"No!" Leslie managed to croak out. "Laurent—he did that." Marcus paused. Leslie gasped for air, blood running from his nose and mouth. "He's insane. He killed Sterling. He took Mrs. Benning—"

Marcus grabbed Leslie by the collar and dragged him up, pinning him back against a wall. "Where?" he growled.

"I . . . I don't know . . ." Leslie whimpered. "He took her. I just wanted to get away before he killed me, too. I was going to get my papers, my money, and run. My mother would understand, I'd send her a note . . ." His rambling stopped when a pistol, held by a steel-eyed Byrne was slowly cocked against his temple.

"What my brother meant to say was, if you want to live past this minute, you'd best start guessing where Laurent would take Mrs. Benning."

"I don't know. I mean, I think he has rooms in Weymouth Street, I . . . I had him followed there once, but, but I don't know for sure. Please don't kill me, my poor mother would be alone . . ."

Marcus slowly released Leslie, letting his feet touch the floor again. "We're not going to kill you, Leslie. But if one hair on Phillippa Benning's head is harmed, you'll wish we had. Understood?"

Leslie nodded silently, his entire body quivering in fear. Marcus took him by the shoulder, and Byrne kept his pistol trained on Leslie's head as they escorted him out of Sterling's office. "Good." He said. "Let's go. And you can explain yourself on the way."

"It was the money, you see." Leslie said, as the carriage rumbled along to Weymouth Street, an address close to the entrance of Regent's Park. "There's so much more money to be made from war than from peace. Surely you can understand that."

Leslie kept talking, filling the carriage with his plots and plans. Marcus guessed that the pistol Byrne kept trained on him was facilitating Leslie's honesty.

"So, you were going to sell the Whitford rifle designs to the French?" Marcus asked.

"And the English," he said defensively.

"What about the Hampshire stables? There are dozens of breeding farms that supply the military."

"And the ones I'm invested in stand to make a great deal more money with a full-scale conflict than merely the occupation."

"But it wasn't just that, was it? Hampshire's positioned in the House of Lords to sway several votes if he argues to escalate a conflict," Marcus confirmed, leaning forward on his knees.

Leslie nodded, eyeing Byrne's pistol. "That thing could go off, you know; this carriage is not sprung very well," he whined.

Byrne remained silent, his hand frighteningly steady.

"A chance you'll have to take, I'm afraid." Marcus answered for him.

Leslie leveled his gaze at Marcus, considering. "I thought once about asking you to join us, you know."

"Me? Why?"

"Its funny"—he smiled—"but since the war ended, you had been desperately looking for some threat, some little thing to investigate. You were almost as bored as I was," he reflected. "It is rigorously difficult to be without purpose, is it not?"

Marcus almost lunged across the carriage to strangle Leslie, but he held himself back. "Bored? You were *bored*, and so when Sterling approached you—"

But Leslie laughed at this. "You think Lord Sterling approached me? Sterling couldn't lace his shoes without me." He leaned forward now, his eyes black beads of anger. "I brought Sterling in—used his 'superior' breeding and social connections to get into the necessary events. He needed the money, too. Turns out someone's been blackmailing him about his relationship with Crawley." Leslie smiled wickedly.

"But Laurent—he's more than either of you could handle," Byrne replied coldly.

Leslie did not reply.

The carriage turned the corner onto Weymouth Street and slowed.

"So what was the plan for tonight? Disrupt the ball so the Prince would get involved?" Marcus asked, pulling back the carriage curtains with a finger, looking for the number they had been given.

"At first, but then it was decided drastic action was needed." Leslie's cool smile chilled the carriage, as they rumbled to a halt. "It was this one," he said, looking up at a quiet, cloaked building. "He's going to kill you both."

Byrne reached out with his free hand, choking Leslie with a viselike grip. He clawed at Byrne's hand, but to no avail. "You've never been on a battlefield, have you? Don't worry, when the bullets start flying, we'll make sure you are in the middle of the action."

Byrne released Leslie, allowing him to sputter to catch his breath.

Marcus looked at his brother, saw his cold, steel resolve. He was back on those battlefields, focused only on cutting down the enemy. Back in that little seaside town, facing his enemy one last time.

"Let's go," he said brusquely, opening the door of the carriage.

The clock ticked by second after agonizing second. Laurent checked his pocket watch more than once, making certain the two matched. Phillippa wished she could scratch her nose. She wished she could stand up and stretch. But she had to keep in her mind everything she could see, everything she needed to do. She had shifted her chair as best she could, using Laurent's preoccupation to edge closer to the sideboard. She was about to shift herself again, when suddenly, Laurent stood and went to the window. He nudged back the curtain ever so slightly, peering out into the darkness. After a moment, he frowned and threw the curtain back into place.

"Looking for someone?"

Laurent whipped around, drawing the pistol from his back and aiming it squarely at Phillippa's temple. Upon turning, he found Marcus at the door, holding a knife to the neck of the man Phillippa recognized as being the shorter man she'd followed at the party. He was swollen and bruising around the eyes now and, Phillippa was pleased to note, the throat.

Marcus's hands were bloodied but otherwise unharmed. He met her gaze, his eyes asking if she was all right. She nodded ever so slightly, her whole body torn between sweet relief at seeing him and fear for what was to come.

Laurent smiled, every muscle in his body tensed in anticipation. "You found the penknife, I see? And followed it to Monsieur Farmapple."

"I'm sorry Laurent, he made me tell him where you lived, I . . ." he stammered, Marcus shutting him up by applying the slightest pressure to the knife.

"*Oui*, Leslie. And I let you follow me that day, so you would tell him." Laurent examined Marcus, crouched behind Leslie. "I caught sight of you in the maze. You crouched behind your woman then, as you hide now."

"Come now, Laurent, how about a trade. Your friend for my friend." Marcus offered, slight amusement in his voice.

Laurent laughed at that. "Go ahead, kill him. But you won't mind if I save her for later, do you? I want to enjoy her first."

Marcus lost all humor, moving inch by painful inch farther into the room. "Touch her, and you die."

"Touch her?" Laurent taunted. "You mean like this?" He let the barrel of the gun nuzzle her cheek, push aside a wisp of her hair. "You are weak, pigeon. You can do nothing."

"Don't bet on it," came a hard voice from behind the curtain.

Laurent swiveled around. Byrne stood there, having entered from the window, his pistol leveled squarely between Laurent's eyes.

Laurent narrowed his eyes, called over his shoulder. "You brought a friend, pigeon! Care to tell me whom I'm going to be killing?"

"Oh, I'll introduce myself," Byrne replied, taking a step into the room. "Byrne Worth. The Blue Raven."

Laurent's face registered shock. "Then who . . . ?"

"He's nobody," Byrne said quickly. "My associate."

"They're brothers," Leslie piped up, before Marcus held the knife tighter still to his throat.

"Your brother?" Laurent looked amused. "Fitting. Well, my dear," he said to Phillippa, "it seems you are no longer nearly as useful as previously thought. Pity."

Phillippa could see his finger on the trigger, and she saw the moment before it was pulled.

Now.

Phillippa threw all her weight to one side, rocking her to the side, knocking her into the side table on her way down. The gun went off right before she hit the ground.

After that, several things happened at once, and quickly.

She had aimed as best she could and managed to knock some of the candles off the table, one of them rolling close to her wrist. She maneuvered herself closer to the burning flame, as she watched Leslie break Marcus's hold on him, withdrawing a short knife from a nearby vase. (She *knew* that was a good hiding place! Mr. Farmapple must have guessed as much as well.) Leslie swung out and tried to cut at Marcus, Marcus deflecting with his own short blade.

Behind her, Laurent tossed the fired pistol aside, bull running into Byrne, causing his shot to go wide. They struggled, fists landing, as Laurent reached into his boot and withdrew a dagger. Byrne rolled as Laurent tried to land the dagger in his flesh, finding his cane in the process.

No one seemed to notice that one of the candles had rolled to the heavy curtains.

After nearly scalding her hand, Phillippa managed to burn through the rope at her wrist sufficiently to break free. She worked quickly, freeing her other hand and then her mouth.

Meanwhile, Marcus had managed to knock the blade free from Leslie's hand and knocked him to the floor in the process. He looked about him, noticed the smoke, and then Phillippa.

"Look out," she cried, and Marcus turned just in time to deflect Leslie's blade with his right forearm, unfortunately ending with the dagger sunk into his arm. Leslie, deprived of his weapon, looked wildly about for some other means of fighting, as Marcus landed left hook after left hook into the man's face. Thud after thud, he beat him down until he was no longer moving, just twitching. Then Marcus reeled back and turned his attention to Phillippa.

"Your arm," she cried, as he pulled Leslie's blade free.

"Its fine," he grumbled. "We have to get out of here before we burn to cinders."

Together, they sawed at the ropes binding her legs and her torso, freeing her from the chair. Marcus pulled her to her feet, as painful pricks rushed down her numbed limbs, waking them up. The fire from the curtains was spreading to the walls and furniture now, the room was filling with black, toxic smoke, infiltrating Phillippa's lungs and eyes. She coughed, great hacking things that felled her to her knees. She could barely see as Marcus dragged her toward the door. As they reached the door, she looked over her shoulder, only to see black smoke, red fire, and Byrne and Laurent struggling against each other in the flames.

They had to keep moving, Marcus knew. He had to get her out. He pulled Phillippa, stumbling, nearly unconscious, out of the room, down the stairs to the outside. Surprisingly, in the mere minutes since they had entered the building, a crowd had gathered. The other tenants of the Weymouth Street house stood gathered in their nightclothes. Some were organizing buckets of water; some were knocking on doors, sending alarms up and down the street.

But what was most surprising was that Lord Fieldstone, in his gold finery, surrounded by members of the palace guard, stood with a bruised and bloody Leslie.

"That's him!" Leslie cried, pointing to Marcus. "That's the man who tried to kill me. he . . . he's in league with the French spy Laurent! He killed Lord Sterling!"

Damn. In his desperation to get Phillippa out, he hadn't noticed that Leslie was not lying on the floor where he had left him. Marcus tensed in anger, and felt Phillippa shake her head no at his side, but when she opened her mouth to speak, no sound came out.

"He's mad, I tell you!" Leslie continued. "Lord Fieldstone, he's been planning this for weeks. I discovered his plot, I tried to stop him, but—"

Lord Fieldstone held up his hand. "Guards," he ordered, pointing to Leslie. "Arrest this man."

"What? No! No, its him, I tell you!" But Leslie's cries went unheeded, as the palace guard collapsed upon him. Fieldstone stepped forward, toward Marcus.

"We could see the fire from the party. I should have taken your suspicions more seriously all those weeks ago. I apologize. But when Miss De Regis told me you had chased after Mrs. Benning, I knew something was wrong. Then Lady Jane Cummings told me about your wounding at the Hampshire event, and finding Sterling's body, and I—"

As happy as he was to hear this mea culpa, Marcus had no time for it. "Can you look after her?" he asked, nodding toward Phillippa. Phillippa looked up at him wildly as Lord Fieldstone answered, "Yes, of course. But Worth, you . . . you can't be thinking of going back in there. The whole thing is going to come down in a matter of minutes!"

"I have to," he answered simply. Marcus had a feeling—he knew his brother, and he feared his intentions. Phillippa clung to Marcus's neck, buried her head in his chest. "Darling," he said, untwining her arms from around his neck. "I'll be right back." He looked into her eyes, brimming with frantic tears. "I promise."

With that, he tore himself away, grabbing a blanket from one of the onlookers as he hurled himself back into the inferno.

He threw the blanket over his head, favoring his left arm as he cautiously moved up the stairs, now weakened by the spreading fire. An old, rickety building like this caught fire as easily as tinder. He made it to the top of the stairs, just before they gave way entirely, trapping him on the second floor. But he would worry about that on the way down. He made his way past falling debris and pushed his way into the room where Byrne and Laurent still struggled.

They didn't notice him. They were too intent on killing each other. They rolled along the floor, narrowly missing a burning couch, the flaming remains of Phillippa's chair. Laurent swung a dagger, Byrne swiped at it with his cane. Both men gained their feet. The Frenchman, unsteady on his feet, lunged forward, only to have his dagger knocked out of his hand by Byrne's cane.

Laurent weaved, a stupid grin on his face. "We are done with this nonsense, *oui*?" Byrne didn't respond. "Luckily, I still have one pistol left," he sneered, reaching underneath his coat, patting his side, and then patting again, frantically. Nothing was there.

"Looking for this?" Byrne replied, holding up the second silver-handled pistol. Laurent let out a tired, desperate laugh, raising his hands in a gesture of defeat. "You think by killing me, you'll stop us? There are far more of us than you think."

"I don't care. I just want to know one thing." Byrne cocked the pistol. "Who was it I killed last year at the inn?"

Laurent's smile disappeared. "I had a brother once, too," he answered. Then, after a moment, "I don't suppose we could work something out? As gentlemen."

"No," Byrne replied. "I'm tired of being a gentleman."

The gunshot barely made a sound in the crackling of the inferno. Red spread across Laurent's chest, as he dropped to his knees. He fell forward, slumped over on his side like a sleeping child.

Byrne threw the gun to the side and fell to his knees beside him.

And didn't move.

If Marcus hadn't seen the final moments, he would have thought Byrne dead. But not yet.

Marcus crossed the room, beams cracking under his weight. "Byrne!" he yelled. Byrne's head snapped up. "Byrne, this place is about to fall—we have to get out of here."

"I'm done, Marcus," Byrne said, his voice resigned, defeated.

"No, you're not," Marcus yelled back. "Come on, let's go!" He pulled at Byrne's arm, to no avail.

"No," Byrne grunted, dragging his arm back.

"Byrne, come on!" he said, using all his strength to pull his brother's skeletal frame up off the ground, to his feet.

"Why?" Byrne yelled back, his eyes meeting Marcus's, pleading for an answer, for a reason.

"Because if you die here, I die with you," Marcus answered. "I'm not leaving you. Do you want my death on you, too?"

Byrne slowly shook his head no. Before he could argue further, Marcus wrapped his arm around his brother, drapping him under the blanket. "The stairs are gone," he said, "We'll have to use the window."

Byrne nodded, and they made their way to the window, where Byrne had managed to climb some vines on the wall, gaining entrance. The vines were long gone now, but they were only on the second floor.

And so, brother looked at brother, and they made a running leap.

Phillippa couldn't think. She could only look at the fire that consumed the house where she had been held captive. Marcus was in there. How was he going to get out? The entire structure was engulfed. Men with pails of water, coming from who knows where, threw the contents of the buckets on the flames, a futile effort. Fire marshals had arrived by now, pouring bags of sand onto the flames, along with Totty, Lady Jane, and half the Ton, all gold-clad, all running from the Gold Ball, music still audible in the distance. Totty held Phillippa's hand as she kept her eyes trained on the building. There was still no sign of Marcus.

Suddenly, a gasp arose from the crowd, as two blanketed figures came flying out of the second-story window.

They landed with hard thuds, rolling into the street. Phillippa broke free from Lord Fieldstone and Totty, running for the figures. They wobbled to their feet.

"Are you all right?" she could hear Marcus say.

"Yes," Byrne croaked, his voice raw from smoke.

She reached them, throwing herself into Marcus's arms. "You came back," she rasped. And then, she couldn't help it, the tears began to flow in earnest. "Marcus, I'm so sorry, I was so stupid, I should have never followed that man—" But there, her voice gave out. Marcus held her close, kissed her eyes, her wet cheeks.

"You're not hurt?" he asked gruffly. She shook her head no.

She saw, as Marcus glanced over at Byrne, something passing between them. But before she could ask about it, Totty and Lord Fieldstone had caught up to them.

"Mr. Worth!" Totty exclaimed. "Thank God you're all right. Thank you, thank you, you brought my Phillippa back to me!"

"Mrs. Tottendale, could you do me the great favor of taking Phillippa home?" he asked, smoothing his hands over her hair.

Totty murmured that of course she would take care of her, but Phillippa objected, shook her head. "I . . ." *I want to stay with you,* she tried to say, but her voice had completely abandoned her.

"Shh," Marcus replied, kissing her forehead. "I have some things to take care of." His glance shot unconsciously toward Byrne, who was wrapped in a blanket, being shuffled about by

Lord Fieldstone. He shifted his gaze back to hers, his eyes softening. "Don't worry, I'll be along."

She looked at him solemnly, gauging whether his words were a comfort or a promise. Then she allowed Totty to take her by the hand and guide her away.

His words had been a promise. That night, long after Phillippa had fallen into fitful sleep, he slipped in through the gardens and crept into her house, into her bedchamber. She felt his warm, strong arms surround her, holding her as she slept. She woke up groggily, only to feel a gentle kiss on her lips. "Shhh . . ." Marcus whispered. "Sleep now."

So she snuggled into his embrace, and knowing she was safe, she slept deeply, peacefully.

But when she woke in the morning, he was gone.

Twenty-six

Upon opening her eyes, Phillippa, deeply confused as to her whereabouts, was greeted by the unusual sight of Mariah Worth, sitting by her bed.

"Good morning," Mariah said cheerfully. She was wearing visiting attire, a smart teal costume with an adorable hat perched on her head that Phillippa would have admired if she hadn't been so startled.

"Tell me, Mrs. Benning, do you have any sisters?" Mariah asked, sipping a cup of tea from the tray at her elbow.

Bewildered, Phillippa shook her head no.

"Neither have I. I have six brothers, mind you, likely why I'm so good at running herd over Graham's family," Mariah continued blithely, "but I have to imagine that this is something sisters would do: Wake each other up in the morning, bearing tea. Take care of each other."

Phillippa suddenly remembered how she got where she was and scanned the room, but she found its only male occupant was

Bitsy, who hopped up on the bed, turned thrice, and settled into the covers beside her. "Marcus . . ." she managed to croak out, her voice a harsh whisper.

"Don't try to speak," Mariah soothed, standing to smooth Phillippa's hair. "Marcus told us of your ordeal last night, and I must say you are either incredibly foolish or incredibly brave—I like to think the latter." She smiled. "Well, I came right over. You need some rest, and I'm here to make sure you get it."

"But—the Ball . . . Totty . . ." Phillippa rasped again, her throat a raw length of fire.

"Mrs. Tottendale quite agrees with me," Mariah said in a tone that brooked no argument. "She's downstairs arranging all the flowers that have arrived and fending off all your callers—until you're ready. As for the Benning Ball, its over a week away, is it not?"

Phillippa nodded and truly hoped she had time to add Mariah to the guest list without her knowing she was ever off it.

"If you like, I can help you with the preparations . . . but if not, I understand. I do not have nearly your good taste—"

Phillippa immediately shook her head, croaking, "No, you—can help."

Mariah gave a relieved smile, and patted Phillippa on the hand. Phillippa, for her part, was not used to ceding control in most situations, and certainly not over something as large as the Benning Ball. But because she was so awfully tired, because she could still feel the frightening heat of of those flames, she felt almost thankful that Mariah had come to help. She felt cared for.

"Now, the doctor has been sent for—just as a precaution. Why don't you sleep until her gets here?" Mariah said softly.

"Mariah, I'm sorry—"

But Mariah simply cut her off. "What on earth for?" she stated, tucking the sheets around Phillippa again.

For being cruel. For considering herself above anyone else. For not recognizing a good friend when she saw it.

But instead of straining her voice with an explanation Mariah didn't want to hear, Phillippa simply smiled in her exaustion, and whispered, "Thank you."

"Its what friends do," Mariah replied with a wink.

Four days passed.

Four long, arduous days, and no word either of or from Marcus. The doctor had visited. He promised that Phillippa would be fine, her throat sore from inhaling so much smoke, and prescribed quantities of honeyed tea and a minimum of conversation.

Phillippa let Mariah and Totty mother her, the former forcing tea down her gullet and the latter fluffing her pillows as she brought in food to be sampled and chosen for the Ball. Phillippa still had no idea what she was going to do for her Ball's main event, but she was happy to have Mariah assist in the small details. Indeed, it was rare for Phillippa to be fussed over in this manner; her own mother was not the fussing kind. It was curious. It was vaguely annoying. But more than anything, it was comforting.

Flowers were delivered by the cartload from every conceivable personage. They filled the parlors, drawing rooms, breakfast room, and hallways. Callers, too, a few of which might even have cared about Phillippa's welfare. Nora visited exactly once, her mother in tow. She had never been very adept at handling serious matters, a quality that made her a scathing society gossip but not particularly selfless. Mrs. Hurston came by, too, surprising Phillippa with her tears and useful suggestions for throat-soothing medicines. Totty and Mariah sat by her side as well-wishers, gossips, and the plain morbidly curious paraded by, each fawning over Phillippa, seeking her attention.

If she wasn't so tired, so anxious, she'd be preening.

Half of society turned up at her doorstep; the other half left cards. All except the one she wished most to see.

Phillippa concluded he must have important affairs of state to deal with, debriefing by Fieldstone and the like. He would not stay away forever, surely. She would wait for him to send word, to call. She would do so with perfect patience, she decided.

That is, until she received one last visitor.

"I must say, Phillippa, you are the topic of everyone's conversation," Broughton said, upon taking his seat on the pink settee in Phillippa's front drawing room. It was late in the afternoon—so late, in fact, that the rest of Phillippa's callers had left to prepare for their various evenings out. Phillippa suspected Broughton had chosen the hour specifically. He wanted them to be alone.

"If you hadn't already been the Queen of Society, you are now," he said, lazily crossing his legs at the ankles, perfectly at his ease. "Everyone is saying you saved Wellington's life or some such thing. I will say, however, that now that I know you've been helping the Crown, it explains your behavior so much better."

"My behavior?" Phillippa asked evenly, stroking Bitsy, who had insisted on staying in the room for this conversation. Her throat was much recovered now, although the doctor still felt it best that she speak as little as possible.

"Running all over the place. Keeping me stepping high, trying to figure out when you'd next deign to meet with me." Broughton leveled a look at her. "I must say, I did not like it."

Ah, so he had come to give her notice. Take his leave. Well, Phillippa supposed she deserved it. She did lead him a merry dance.

But then Broughton stood, paced in a manner she assumed was meant to be authoritative. "But I find what I like less is the idea of you in danger. So I have come to the decision that you should marry me."

Phillippa blinked. Even Bitsy began paying attention.

"I had thought we might develop the kind of relationship where we each retain a measure of freedom. But I'll have to marry sometime, and it might as well be to the most celebrated heroine of the Ton." He came and leaned against her pink Louis XIV chair, forcing her to look up at him. "Someone has to keep you safe, Phillippa. Someone should be taking care of you."

Broughton, his planned speech finished, stood before her expectantly.

"I . . . I don't know what to say," Phillippa replied honestly.

"Say yes, of course!" He smiled. "We are perfectly matched, you and I. Think of the headlines, Phillippa. Think of the wedding we'll have; it'll be talked about for decades." He came to sit beside her. "Think of the gorgeous little brats you'll have; a dynasty to establish. And think of how comfortable and merry you'll be."

Phillippa could have laughed. If this offer came two months ago, one month ago, she would have been ecstatic. Everything she'd ever wanted: society permanently at her feet, the most eligible bachelor in London signing up to be her husband. Juicy gossip, gay parties, forever and ever, ad infinitum. The problem was, of course, she didn't want it anymore.

"Phillip," she said, turning to him, "is . . . is that all?"

Confusion furrowed his brow. "What else is there?" he asked, smiling nervously.

Phillippa smiled back at him, patted his hand. "Thank you for your offer, Phillip; it is most generous of you."

"Yes, I know."

"But," she continued, rising from her seat, "I want different things now."

"What do you want, Phillippa? I'll buy you anything you please." Broughton smiled.

Phillippa sighed. "I want to be loved. Not kept. I'm not meant to be kept." She shot a look out the window, an eyebrow going up, "And I refuse to be kept waiting any longer for what I want."

And then, with no other explanation to the handsome, somewhat flat man beside her, she rose and walked out the door.

"What do you suppose this could be?" Lord Fieldstone asked, holding up a charred fragment of paper.

Marcus examined the black-edged flake with an exhausted sigh. He was going cross-eyed on this, reconstructing the surviving bits of paper and schematics pulled out of the remains of Laurent's flat. They had pushed six of the desks in the main room of the Security section of the War Department together, affording enough room for the laying out of what had been salvaged.

Which wasn't much.

Marcus stood with Fieldstone, a heart-hardened Crawley, and any other members of the Security section that could be found and recalled to active duty, piecing together the mystery of Laurent's cryptic remarks about his "other friends within London," and their plans for the future.

The only member of the Security section in good standing not in the room was Byrne. He had decided to go back to the country. Once Phillippa had left Weymouth Street, Marcus dragged Byrne to Graham's, where he informed their older brother of the entire story.

Needless to say, Graham had been concerned. Byrne remained silent throughout, and then, once Marcus reached the end of the story, said, "You pulled me out, and I wanted to curse you for it. But I didn't die for a reason." As Graham and Marcus put him into the carriage for the long ride to the Lake District, he had made a promise to try to be stronger than his needs, to rejoin life someday. But it was a long road back to humanity, and Byrne had traveled far in the other direction. He said he had to walk it alone.

Turning his mind from Byrne, Marcus inevitably landed on the subject that had infiltrated his mind so completely. *She* was ever present.

Where was she now? Was she entertaining friends, was she eating supper with Totty and the ever-helpful Mariah? Was she out dancing with Broughton? These dastardly thoughts seeped in wherever a pause existed. She was back in her right world, he told himself, and he in his. So he refused to be tortured by his own mind. He had come back into his work immediately, with Lord Fieldstone's earnest support, and begun digging through Leslie's desk, yielding little, and the remains of the burned house, yielding less. He had to find something, some information on the other underground operations. A new lead, a new place for his mind to go.

And in time, maybe he would stop thinking of her every second. Maybe one day, he'd not think of her at all. And once she no longer meant anything to him, she'd no longer be in danger. She'd be truly and completely safe.

And he'd be able to sleep at night for knowing it.

"Worth," Lord Fieldstone cleared his throat, snapping him back to the present.

"Yes, sorry," he said, squinting again at the charred bit of paper. "Perhaps it's an architectural drawing. See how these lines—at least I think they're lines—intersect here?"

"No, Worth," Fieldstone interrupted, elbowing Marcus to bring his head up. Fieldstone indicated the door. "You have a visitor."

He knew it was her before his eyes met hers.

She held up her hand in a nervous sort of wave and lowered it awkwardly. "It's just me," Phillippa said, her gaze never leaving his. The room held still, as if any movement would shatter the space.

Then Fieldstone cleared his throat and started forward with a smart bow. "Mrs. Benning, I'm pleased to see you looking so well. May I ask, er, how you got past the guards?"

Phillippa gave that effortless, elegant shrug of hers. "I'm Phillippa Benning," she said plainly, without conceit.

"Right," Lord Fieldstone said. "I'll, ah, just go have a word with them. Worth, why don't you show the lady to your office? The rest of you, continue . . . continuing." And with that delicate bit of maneuvering, Fieldstone took his leave and went down the hall, and after a short moment, the rest of the room followed instructions and resumed their activites.

Marcus led Phillippa to the back office, where Sterling had once watched over them all. It was filled with boxes, some being packed, some being emptied. One of Marcus's exercises of the past four days had been moving Sterling out and moving himself in. Officially, the story was that Sterling had died an innocent bystander, but Marcus knew otherwise and wanted to eradicate the traitor as thoroughly as possible.

"Your office?" Phillippa asked, once Marcus closed the door, and after weighing propriety against privacy, lowered the blinds.

"I've, ah, been promoted," he said, running his hand over his hair.

"Congratulations," she said. Then, after a moment, "How's your arm?"

"Fine." He held up his right arm. She could see the bandage peeking out from his sleeve.

She nodded. After another pause, she said, "Broughton came to see me."

He held his breath for what she would say next.

"He proposed."

All the strength left him, and he leaned casually against his desk for support. "I suppose congratulations are in order for you as well."

She folded her arms over her chest, cocked her head to one side. "If you think that, you're a bigger moron than I took you for."

Marcus's head came up. He opened his mouth to speak, but no words came. He couldn't think of any. But it didn't matter, because Phillippa wasn't about to let him get a word in.

"Four days, Marcus!" she yelled. "It's been four bloody days! And you couldn't come to call? You couldn't write a note, make sure I was well, or let me know where you went that night?"

"I . . . I had work to do. Important work. Besides," he grumbled, "Mariah was there, and she let me know—"

"Oh, so you sent your sister-in-law as a substitute? I adore Mariah, but Marcus—"

"Phillippa, you can't be here," he tried to interject, stop her ranting, but she cut him off with a prodding finger to the chest, pushing him back into his chair.

"I have come here with one question, Mr. Worth, and you will answer it honestly."

"Just one?" he asked, an eyebrow going up.

"Just one," she intoned. "And then, if you want me to, I'll go."

"All right."

She leaned her hip against the desk, effectively blocking his escape.

"Do you love me?" Her voice was clear as she met his eyes.

He would have leaped up then, taken her into his arms, if he could. But he knew he couldn't. He shouldn't.

"That's not a fair question," he hedged.

"What's unfair about it? It's a simple yes or no question. Do you love me?"

"Its unfair because . . . because you know the answer."

"Aha!" she triumphed, a smirk coming to her face. "Do I? Because you save me in the hedge maze, you push me away, you make love to me, you save me from the fire, and then you push me away again! And since somewhere in the midst of all that, I fell wholly and devastatingly in love with you, you'll forgive me if I'm somewhat confused on the subject."

"Phillippa—" Marcus sighed.

"Do you love me?" she pressed.

"Stop—" he warned, rising from his seat.

"Do you love me?"

"Yes!" he finally exclaimed, unable to hold it in any longer. "Yes, I love you. I'm completely mad about you. Are you happy now?"

He grabbed her then, as he'd ached to, as every nerve in his body told him to. He pressed her body against his, against the desk, and kissed her silly.

Her arms snaked around his neck; her mouth tore at his. But this was indulgence. As soon as she sighed, that tiny happy sigh that sent a shot of lust down his spine, he put her at arm's length.

"But that's why I can't have you near me, Phillippa." He gave in to temptation, lightly caressing her neck as he spoke. "Don't you understand? I got you involved in this mess. Me, playacting the hero? It nearly got you killed. *I* nearly got you killed—and I couldn't stand it, Phillippa, I couldn't—"

"But you saved me," she soothed in a whisper. "You're the one who saved me." She closed the space between them, placed her hand on his heart. "You can't keep me at arm's length simply because you think it keeps you or me safer. I won't accept it."

He looked into her eyes then and saw stern determination.

"I promise"—her eyes twinkled mischeviously—"if it's the only way, I will find some means of getting kidnapped or shot at every other week until you realize you'll be far better off with me by your side than out of your sight." She stood on her tiptoes, kissed him gently. And suddenly, a light went on in his head. She loved him. A weight lifted from his chest, and his blood began to hum with joy.

He accepted the inevitable, and it made him happy.

"I didn't think you'd want me," he admitted. Her eyes were shining, and it made his heart full. "I lied to you. And then, after the fire, I thought you would be better off without me." Seeing her curious expression, he stuttered, "Its only logical; you are Phillippa Benning."

"Marcus, your logic is ridiculous." She smiled at him and kissed him again.

So involved they became in their activity, that neither Marcus nor Phillippa heard the knock at the door, or Lord Fieldstone stick his head in.

"Worth, I, uh—oh," Fieldstone said, as Marcus and Phillippa broke apart like guilty schoolchildren.

"Worth," a blushing Fieldstone continued, "when you have a moment, we should really get back to this; the Prime Minister is going to want a report tomorrow about what information we recovered from the ashes."

"Ashes? You mean from Laurent's flat?" At their nod, she cocked a brow. "I don't suppose any of that wall of maps survived."

Fieldstone's mustache twitched. "Wall of maps?"

"Yes," she replied, "there were dozens of them. I stared at the silly things for a half hour, waiting for Marcus to arrive."

Marcus smiled. "You don't happen to remember . . ."

"Don't be silly; of course I do." She went to the door, where Fieldstone stood blinking, passing him on her way into the main room. "Let's see, there was one of Buckingham House, it looked multileveled, including the sewers that ran by it. There was one of Kentshire, Dilby, oh, there was one of the Thames and the Regent's Canal; it had these little *X*s on it, I could probably show you where, if you got me another map, or—"

But Phillippa found herself unable to speak further, as a resounding smack was placed on her lips by a flushed and grateful Fieldstone.

"Mr. Worth, get Mrs. Benning a chair. Get her anything she asks for!" Fieldstone whooped and then started ordering the room about, sending men out for maps of Dilby, Kentshire, the Thames, and Regent's Canal.

"Anything I ask for?" Her eyebrow went up, a plan forming behind her eyes.

"Anything you want." He smiled warily.

"Mr. Marcus Worth, I do hope you don't come to regret that."

Epilogue

FIVE days of massive planning and replanning later, the Benning Ball was in full swing. While speculation had been that she might have to postpone or cancel, Mariah's help had proved a godsend, and Phillippa was not one to let a little thing like being kidnapped get in the way of being the most celebrated hostess in London. And now that she had her main event back in place, she would be.

As she told Marcus several times, a bargain was a bargain was a bargain.

The house was bedecked in midnight blue drapes, silver candles casting an eerie glow. All the guests were given black domino masks and heavy velvet cloaks at the door, masking identities and the normally bright colors of evening gowns in luscious darkness. Eerie music in minor chords set the tone, and mirrors had been placed in every conceivable corner, heightening the dramatic spirit.

"Are you ready?" Phillippa whispered in the dark from the balcony above the ballroom. She peeked through the dark curtains, saw Totty holding Bitsy as she chatted with the beturbanded Mrs. Hurston.

She saw Lady Jane dancing gracefully with the younger son of a Duke.

She saw Louisa Dunningham with her mother, listless without her friend Penny. Miss Sterling was now in mourning for her father. At least she would never know of his complicity and always think of the man as a decent, loving parent. She would be safe in that lie.

Looking farther down the hall, Phillippa could see Nora dancing with Broughton in a manner most forward for an unmarried lady. Broughton didn't seem to mind. Nora was welcome to try her hand with him. Who knows? Given Lady Jane's lack of interest, Nora may have a chance.

And finally, Phillippa saw Mariah standing next to Graham as she cornered the Duke of Wellington. She was pointing out the various decorations and wall hangings she had taken part in choosing, obviously proud of her work, as she should be. And Wellington, for his part, looked politely enthused.

Phillippa smiled, as she ducked back behind the curtain and turned around. "I said, are you ready?"

"Is this absolutely necessary?" Marcus asked, pulling at his collar.

Phillippa simply rolled her eyes. "I promised them a show. Besides, a bargain is a bargain—"

"Is a bargain, I know," Marcus sighed. "I'm just not used to being . . . put on display."

"You'll be brilliant." She squeezed his hand and, with an easy smile, ducked through the curtains, leaving him nervous in the wings.

She nodded to the musicians, who upon the signal stood and trumpeted a fanfare. The room went quiet, and all eyes fell upon Phillippa.

"Ladies and gentlemen," she began, happy to find her voice

steady. "I would like to thank you all for coming—such wonderful friends and honored guests." She took a deep breath before continuing. "But there is one guest in particular I should like to single out."

A titter went through the crowd. Was it true? Could it be?

"Our guest of honor. I know there has been a great deal of speculation about his identity. There seems to be a mystery to solve. So let's dispense with the nonsense, shall we?"

"Yes, please!" came a voice from the crowd, eliciting chuckles, including from Phillippa.

"Ladies and gentlemen, I should like to introduce you to my husband, Marcus Worth."

A gasp went through the crowd, and Marcus stepped through the curtain. He waved nervously and came and held Phillippa's hand.

"We were married this afternoon," he said to the awed guests. "You are not, in fact, at the Benning Ball. You are instead at the Worth wedding reception."

Then, in perfect time, servants released dozens and dozens of cords, dropping the heavy dark blue drapery and revealing bowers of roses, white satin runners, and a feast fit for a King.

As a wave of applause ran through the crowd, growing, thundering, Marcus took Phillippa in his arms and kissed her soundly. A cheer rose up, and the musicians struck up a lively reel. Cloaks and masks fell away as men and women took to the floor, revealing their true selves.

"Now, that wasn't so hard, was it, Mr. Worth?" Phillippa asked, breathless.

"It was arduous, Mrs. Worth." Marcus smiled. "You'd best make it up to me with a dance."

He held out his hand and, since her hand had such a curious fondness for his, she took it, and he lead the way down from the balcony and through the crowd to the dance floor.

They danced every dance, their hands apart from each other

only as long as the dance necessitated, and when they moved about the room to speak with friends, their hands entwined completely.

Most wished them well, happy to see them so joyfully coupled. Admittedly, there were some people agog with disbelief that *she* would choose *him*, and *he* would choose *her*. But such people were few and far between. And even they, once they saw the newlywed couple that night, could not dispute that they had never seen a better-matched pair.

Marcus and Phillippa couldn't agree more.

Keep reading for a preview of the next historical romance from Kate Noble

THE SUMMER OF YOU

Coming soon from Berkley Sensation!

LADY Jane Cummings, only daughter of the Duke of Rayne, second cousin twice removed of the Prince Regent, and most soughtafter ginger-haired, but unfreckled, dance partner of the Ton was in trouble.

And it was all Phillippa Benning's fault.

Or Phillippa Worth, as Jane supposed she must become accustomed to calling her recently reclaimed friend. But how long would that friendship last if Phillippa persisted in causing Jane such distress that she committed social blunders was undetermined.

For you see, Lady Jane had missed a step.

She could be mistaken for a statue in that moment, standing stock still in the center of Phillippa's great ballroom, which was festooned in bridal drapery and white silk bowers running between massive bouquets of summer roses in every color. Dancers, as colorful as the flowers, swirled around Jane, stepping with mirth and verve in time to the music, while Lady Jane's attention was caught and held by the alarming, familiar shock of hair she saw at the other end of the row, lazily scanning the dancers from the sidelines. Everyone who was anyone was celebrating Phillippa's recent conversion from Benning to Worth, i.e. her marriage. And being as this was London and it was the Ton and Phillippa being, well, Phillippa, she must have invited the entire catalogue of Debrett's to her wedding celebration. Oh, but how could she have invited *him*?

Jane was jolted out of her shock when a twirling debutante, doing her best with the tricky steps of the quadrille, bumped into her frozen form. Murmured apologies set off a ripple of whispers that Lady Jane, of all people, had taken a misstep when dancing. Jane quickly rejoined her partner, falling into the steps with hurried but well-practiced ease.

"Is everything all right?" Lord Turnbridge asked, in his reedy, if earnest, voice.

"Of course, my lord," she smiled prettily at him, causing his face to take on a decidedly berry shade. "I was simply . . . struck by the decorations on the fireplace mantle. Mrs. Worth has outdone herself."

Jane turned her eyes towards the far end of the room, where the gold and white silk-draped fireplace stood and where she last saw that blazing shock of hair, that tall, languid form. But this time, no such sight was presented. She turned her head back around, scanning the crowd behind Lord Turnbridge fervently, but to no avail. Drat it all, where had he gone?

Lucky for Lady Jane's sanity and Lord Turnbridge's ego, the music ended then, and she need no longer subject her dance partner to such inattentiveness. Instead, she smiled sweetly at him as he escorted her to the side of the room. Annoyingly, Lord Tunrbridge escorted her very slowly. Once there, he bowed tediously low—it was all Jane could do not to tap her foot with impatience. But finally he rose, and Jane performed the most perfunctory of curtsies before he turned away to find his next partner, presumably allowing Jane to be found by hers.

That is, if she had wanted to be found.

As quick as grace and the crush of people would allow, Jane moved through the crowd, ducking and weaving through the flow of traffic like a fish in a current.

She couldn't have imagined him, could she? Oh please, let her be suffering delusions. She imagined Jason. He couldn't be in London. He just couldn't. She'd only had a month—maybe six weeks—and now . . .

Jane ducked into a corridor that she hoped led to Phillippa's outrageously pink drawing room—really, if Jane and Phillippa had been speaking to each other at the time of her redecoration, Jane would have seriously attempted to steer Phillippa into a few more varied shades. It was in the Pink Room, however, that desserts were being served. There, overly plump matrons would be devouring sweets with a speed that would distress their laces come tomorrow, and Jane knew no sane eligible man would go near the room. (Those men who did cross the threshold of a room that pink quickly scampered away, either because of a lack of young female attention or the fervent enthusiasm of their mothers.) But alas, a left turn, and another left, and Jane quickly found herself nowhere near the Pink Room. Backtracking, Jane lifted a curtain she thought lead to the hallway.

Suffice it to say, it didn't.

"Jane!" Phillippa Worth, née Benning, cried, as she tore her lips away from those of her husband, who was kind enough to use his height to block her from view as she readjusted some clothing that had gone suspiciously awry. "Whatever are you doing?"

"I'm looking for a place to hide!" Jane whispered furiously, placing her hands on her hips.

"I apologize, Lady Jane," Marcus Worth said in his even, affable drawl, "but as you see, this alcove is occupied."

Jane shot him a rueful glance to which Marcus only smiled. "You've been married all of twelve hours, you can't wait another two until your wedding banquet is over?" Jane snorted at Phillippa.

Phillippa looked up at her husband, and he down at her, his easy grin apparently infectious.

"No."

"Don't suppose we can."

"Well you've got to," Jane replied, "because I am in a dreadful spot and it's all your fault!"

"Why?" Phillippa looked immediately concerned. "What have you done now?"

"I've done nothing," Jane scoffed. "'Tis your doing, and I demand that you fix it!"

"Me?" Phillippa replied, outraged. Then looking to Marcus, "Darling, you can't let her . . ."

"My dearest wife," Marcus interrupted, then, grinning, "I just love saying that. Ah—anyway," he continued, at said dearest wife's look, "if there is one thing I've learned during our brief courtship, its not to get in between the two of you when you squabble."

Phillippa looked like she was about to teach her new husband a very keen lesson about disagreeing with one's wife, but Jane had no time for such a segue. "How could you invite him?"

"Invite who?" Phillippa replied, immediately snapping back to the pertinent conversation.

"Jason!" Jane whispered in a rush, and watched a slight look of confusion mar Phillippa's brow.

"Jason? You mean your—" at Jane's nod, Phillippa expostulated. "But I didn't. I didn't even know he was in town. I would have added him to the guest list had I known, but—"

"You would have *added* him?" Jane expostulated.

"Well of course. He is, after all, a marquis." Phillippa replied blithely, but Jane threw up her hands.

"Did it never occur to you that I might not wish to see him?"

"So sorry," Phillippa sneered, "I haven't kept up with your preferences. Next time I'll plan my wedding celebration around *your* likes and dislikes, shall I?"

Before the conversation could further devolve into a spitting match, Marcus Worth luckily (and intelligently) intervened.

"Dearest," he said, putting a gentle hand on his wife's arm, before turning to her assailant. "Lady Jane, I take it you feel the need to make an expedient exit?" She nodded, and so he continued, "Did your father attend with you this evening?"

Jane shook her head. "He was feeling a little tired. Lady Charlbury was good enough to act as my chaperone this evening."

Even Phillippa raised her brows at that. Lady Charlbury was an interesting paradox: a widow of middle years, she ruled society through her friendships with the Lady Patronesses, but it was of late more and more difficult to get her to respond positively to an invitation. They had both been lucky enough to attend her fete earlier this season, but to have her attend Phillippa's!

"She's an old friend of my father's," Jane replied, with only the slightest braggadocio.

"Well, then my darling wife will go and tell her you had a headache, and we sent you home in our carriage," Marcus said, forcing the conversation back onto its rails, "and I will show Lady Jane the back way to the door."

Phillippa, nodded, agreeing to this scheme—in no small part, Jane was certain, because it afforded her the opportunity to be seen conversing with Lady Charlbury, who was impressive even by Phillippa's standards.

Phillippa leaned in, and gave her husband a not-so-quick peck on the lips. Then, once Jane stopped cringing, Marcus offered her his arm and lead her out of the alcove in the opposite direction of the flow of human traffic.

Marcus Worth neatly ducked and weaved his way through the crowd, managing to blend into the crowd so much that not a soul stopped him, or wished him well, or smiled in acknowledgement. Considering this was *his* wedding banquet, it was an astonishing feat. One that must have served him well in his covert role with the Home Office. It was rumoured he would be knighted for his services to the Crown, and no matter how much the public cajoled, Phillippa would not divulge specifics of said service. Which of course, made the gossip all the more rampant.

But of course, Jane was privy to the truth. She had witnessed Marcus and his brother Byrne in acts of heroics usually reserved for sensational novels.

"Turn here," Marcus's whisper interrupted her musings as he abruptly turned down an underlit servants' corridor.

It took Jane's eyes a moment to adjust, but when they did, she followed Marcus Worth's abominably long stride towards the kitchens.

"Right this way, Lady Jane," Marcus Worth said solicitously, carefully stooped in the low corridor—Phillippa had met and married perhaps the tallest man in London, outside of the circus. Lady Jane was just a hair shorter than the average female, and so to keep up with his leisurely stride, she was reduced to trotting.

Once in the kitchens, so rife with activity no one noticed the new master of the house and the daughter of a Duke wandering through, Marcus, after a quick word with one of the servants, guided her into a different corridor.

"This will take us to the butler's pantry, which is right beside the front door." Marcus informed her.

"Phillippa keeps her silver next to the front door?" Jane questioned. "Does she wish to invite burglary?"

But Marcus simply laughed at her snide remark. "No, the silver is kept in safer stores. We call it the butler's pantry because it keeps the butler, who has a habit of lying down in between answering the door."

Considering Marcus and Phillippa had been married mere hours, it was on the tip of Jane's tongue to ask not only how he became so familiar with the workings of this household but also with all its secret corridors. But Jane found it prudent to keep her mouth shut, especially since they had just breached the hidden door to the butler's pantry.

There was indeed a lack of silver, and in its stead a comfortable chair and blankets for either a terribly indulged or greatly beloved family retainer. A book on the chair completed the tableau, and Jane was tempted to peek at the title, but that would have necessitated moving, and the space was too tight for such allowances.

"Right through this door"—Marcus pointed in front of them—"and left out of the house. I believe you'll find a carriage waiting to convey you home at the top of the drive."

"Mr. Worth," Jane smiled at him, "you are a terribly useful sort."

Marcus, it seemed, decided to take that as a compliment, for after a moment he inclined his head with a smile.

"I am very glad Phillippa married you," she said, patting his arm, "and do hope you survive it."

At that, Marcus Worth threw back his head and barked with laughter. He opened the door in front of him, and escorted her out of the butler's pantry.

And since he was laughing, Jane simply had to join in. And so, as they laughed and came into the candlelight of the main foyer, they perhaps were less than attentive to who else could be in that general vicinity.

So the fist to Marcus's jaw came as a bit of a surprise.

Not that it actually connected. Marcus had alarmingly quick reflexes, and his extra height allowed him to narrowly avoid his attacker's reach. Jane smothered a scream, as Marcus caught the hands of his attacker and pinned them mercilessly behind his back. Then, attracting far too much attention from the festivities' attendants down the hall, he shoved the man face first against the door to the butler's pantry.

"For heaven's sake, Jason," Jane cried, as he squirmed beneath Marcus Worth's iron grip, his right cheek pressed against the wainscoting, "have you gone completely mad?"

"I take it this is the man you were so keen to avoid?" Marcus drawled.

"Yes, Mr. Worth, I'm so sor—"

"Oh shut it, Jane!" Jason spat out of the side of his mouth. Then, to Marcus, "Now, who are you and what the devil were you doing in that closet with my sister?!?"

Keep reading for a preview of the next historical romance by Donna MacMeans

THE SEDUCTION OF A DUKE

Coming Spring 2009 from Berkley Sensation!

Newport Beach, Rhode Island

WITH all the malice she could muster, Francesca Winthrop whacked the wooden croquet ball beneath her foot, sending her mother's ball careening across the manicured lawn, over the edge of the Newport cliffs, and possibly into the blue gray waters of the Atlantic Ocean. Pity, it wasn't her mother's head.

"Really, Francesca, that show of spirit was entirely unnecessary." Alva Winthrop signaled one of the dozen servants standing about for just such an occasion to search for her ball at the rocky base of the cliff, before feigning laughter for the benefit of the other society matriarchs watching the match. "Most women would be positively thrilled to learn they were about to marry a duke."

"Most women have at least met the man they are to marry, or had a say in the selection," Fran replied, careful to keep her voice low and her smile in place. *Never show emotion, or else risk the scorn that follows.* She'd been fed those words in infancy along with her pabulum. An only child, raised in a lonely edifice to enormous wealth, she learned her lessons well. A tear, a stutter in public earned her a slap across the face from her mother in private. Thus to the others in the game, Francesca Winthrop maintained a calm façade. Deep inside, however, she screamed her protest.

"I won't do this, Maman." She glanced away, bracing herself for her mother's anticipated reprimand. "I'm . . . I'm in love with someone else."

"Nonsense." Alva smoothed her hands over her white muslin skirts. "Love has little to do with the stewardship of great families. You've known since birth that your destiny was to bring a title to the Winthrops. With your father's money and your new husband's title, you'll be received into the best households on both continents."

"No, Maman, with the influence of your new son-in-law, *you'll* be the one received in those *best* households," Fran said, trying to ignore the stabbing pain caused by her mother's lack of consideration. Yet, it had always been that way. Her opinion in matters of her own future were . . . insignificant. Reality constricted her throat, making words difficult. "I shall be the one tied to a man I don't know and whom I don't love."

"We all make sacrifices, dear. You'll learn to adapt. He'll arrive in two days. We'll announce your engagement at the costume ball this Saturday."

Three days! Her mother had been planning that ball for two months, and Fran had been dreading it for at least as long. Now she would not only have to find the fortitude to face a room full of people but an unfamiliar fiancé as well. Dread, as hard and as solid as one of her painted croquet balls, fisted into a tight knot in her stomach.

Fran forced words past her constricted throat. They emerged in a harsh whisper, a testament to the unexpected blow dealt to her future. "Why now, Maman? You must have known of this earlier. Why not wait to tell me in private?"

Alva Winthrop stopped and turned, her glance stern and sharp. "Do try to aim for the wickets, dear. It's the winning that matters, not the course one takes to get there."

Fran stood paralyzed. For a moment, she contemplated hitting her bonus ball directly toward her mother's heel. The resulting injury might give her pause over the injury she was causing her daughter. In her saddened heart, however, she knew that it would be a worthless gesture. Her mother was impervious to another's concern.

Not only had her mother not asked about her love interest, she hadn't even acknowledged the difficulty and reluctance Fran had experienced in sharing that information. Obviously, her only daughter's personal desires were of less import than the advantageous placement of a croquet ball.

Fran gazed beyond the lawn to the familiar tranquil Atlantic. A few sails billowed in their escape from Narragansett Harbor. The Fall River steamer, a tiny spot on the deep blue horizon, chugged along on its daily foray between Newport and Long Island.

Facing the vast expanse of the ocean, even her father's gift of height failed to protect her from feeling small, insignificant, and utterly alone. Three days! What if she couldn't abide the Englishman? Her mother might not have cared about such things, but this was not her mother's life. She must take action. She must formulate a plan.

William Chambers, Marquess of Enon and most recently Duke of Bedford, sat beneath a potted palm in the eloquent parlor of the Fall River steamer anticipating imminent death. After all, death would put an end to the turbulent discord in his stomach, fueled by every rise and fall of the steamer's hull. The eight-day trip across the Atlantic Ocean had proved less than comfortable, but to add insult, he was ushered aboard this steamer with no time for recovery. His stomach rolled again, bringing the taste of bile to his throat. Could any woman, even one as rich as Midas, be worth this hell on water?

"Chambers. Chambers, old fellow, is that you?"

William forced one resistant eye open to focus on the opulent form of Henry Twiddlebody. Just when he thought he had sunk to the bottom of the barrel, life provided assurances in the form of Twiddlebodys of the further depths possible. Hesitant to move, for fear it would encourage the vile mixture in his innards to vacate its contained premises, William simply nodded to Henry. Unfortunately, the fool apparently assumed the gesture to be an invitation as he pulled a chair practically to William's knees.

"I say, old fellow, you're looking a bit green about the gills. I take it you've never held a commission in Her majesty's fleet, ey?"

Damnation! Trapped by a Twiddlebody and too ill to make an exit. Life couldn't get worse. William pressed his lips tightly together while the man chuckled at his own wit.

"I'm sorry to hear about the passing of your father, my boy. He was a good man." He looked askance at William, a smile tilting his lips under a full, wily mustache. "I guess I should be calling you 'Your Grace' now that you head up the estate."

William could almost feel what was coming next. Ever since he had discovered how his father had hopelessly squandered the family's estates with gambling debts, the most unsavory characters had found reason to approach him for an audience.

"I hadn't thought to see you this far from London, but it is fortunate indeed." Twiddlebody shifted his corpulent mass in the groaning chair to sidle closer to William's ear. "I hold some of your father's paper, you know. I wouldn't mention it normally, but as the old Duke has gone on to his just rewards, I thought perhaps you could redeem the marker. It's my missus, you see; she's been feeling poorly and—"

"Enough," William interrupted. "My solicitors have assured me all debts will be resolved shortly. I'm sure once you return to London, the matter will be settled."

Twiddlebody drew back, his eyes round with surprise. "You've uncovered some money then. I was led to believe . . ." His eyes narrowed and he leaned in closer, spewing a foul breath in William's face.

"Just what are you doing so far from home, Your Grace? You're not planning on ducking out of your father's responsibilities, are you?"

Anger bubbled up from William's gut, blacker than the poison churning in his innards. Perhaps his face reflected a bit of his fury, as Twiddlebody pulled back, a bit of horror reflected on his face as well.

"I apologize, Your Grace, I didn't mean to imply . . . I mean to say, there isn't a more honorable man in London than yourself, a gentleman in every sense of the word, a member of the Jockey Club, a man known for his charitable support. Even your father admitted as much. If you say the debt will be paid, then I'm as sure as I'm an Englishman that it will be."

If the steamer hadn't taken that moment to pitch suddenly to the left, William would have chanced his uncertain legs to carry him away from the insulting bugger. But if he stood, he was liable to be tossed into Twiddlebody's lap, a more demeaning hell he could not imagine.

"Which brings me back to the issue of why you've ventured out on the high seas," Twiddlebody continued. "You say there'll be sufficient funds to cover your father's . . . er . . . misfortunes." He hid his mouth beneath his hand as if in deep thought, which William believed was highly unlikely. "This steamer is headed to Newport, a known vacation spot for the rich, and away from New York City, the American business capital." Twiddlebody's eyes lit up, and he sat back, a grand smile spreading from ear to ear. "Why, you're going to catch yourself a wealthy bride, aren't you?"

He chuckled to himself while William plummeted into deep mortification. The heat in his face would be mixing with the aforementioned green to render a shade only his artist brother could fathom.

"Wait till I tell the missus," Twiddlebody prattled. "London's most eligible catch o' the day is hunting for a fat purse in America. Hearts will be breakin' back home, you can bank on that." He issued a hearty laugh as William lamented that his upholstered chair wasn't deep enough to swallow him whole. "You always were the responsible one. I had thought to present my markers to that younger brother of yours, but I'll take them to your solicitors first thing upon my return." Twiddlebody stood to take his leave, then shook his head. "Wait till I tell the missus."

William scowled at the thought of their father's debts being presented to Nicholas. Wouldn't he enjoy that? After all the years William had preached about obligation and responsibility to his black sheep brother, it would be more than humiliating to have men of Twiddlebody's ilk chasing after Nicholas in pursuit of payment for debts their father had incurred. Obviously William should have spent those years preaching to his father instead of Nicholas. Now that his brother had found his muse in that schoolteacher, his successes mocked William's competence as the head of the family. William's scowl deepened, just another item on a long list of his own shortcomings.

Not that he wasn't happy for his brother. Wasn't it William's actions that directly led to the discovery of Nicholas as a great artist? Of course his brother did not exactly appreciate his methods, nor did he appreciate his overtures to the schoolteacher. William grimaced. Naturally, he would not have suggested the things he had if he'd known about their relationship.

Still, Nicholas appeared quite content with his new respectable life, while maintaining a similar degree of respectability, in the face of his father's defaults, was costing William a small fortune. Only the threat of insolvency could have forced him to take this drastic measure. He had sworn never to remarry after his previous wife's death. However, thanks to the old Duke's lack of control, severe and even hurtful remedies had been required.

His fingers reached to rub a spot on his shoulder, a reminder of one of those hurtful remedies. If Deerfeld Abbey went on the auction block, proof of his family's ruination would be rampant. Even Nicholas would be drawn into the fray. William's pride as the oldest would not withstand that blow.

Thus he'd marry the woman suggested by his solicitors and keep the beggars from running off to Nicholas. After all, what did Twiddlebody call him? The responsible one? Was he being responsible marrying a stranger for the sake of her money, or was he merely being lazy? Was it honorable to sacrifice one's future happiness for the sake of the family, or was it foolish and lacking in respect? At one time, marriages arranged to enhance the family fortune were commonplace. Why then did this very circumstance make him feel lower than . . . a Twiddlebody?

The steamer mercifully docked before William could slip further into his maudlin thoughts. Although loathe to navigate the slightly swaying deck without benefit of a handrail, the lure of stationary dry land proved too much to ignore. He joined the crowd of men, women, and children funneling down the gangplank.

He searched the landscape before him. In New York, a gnarled old attorney had met him at the gangplank of the *Britannic* and rushed him to the Fall River steamer for the second leg of his voyage. Now, however, there didn't appear to be anyone—

"Your Grace?"

William turned sharply, a bit too sharply for his poor stomach to reconnoiter. He had a brief glimpse of a tall man in a white linen suit before he felt the blood rush from his head down to his toes.

"Whoa, steady there." The man grabbed his arm. "Take a moment to find your land legs."

It wasn't his legs that presented the problem, William thought glumly. Still, he preferred the stranger believe that misconception.

"Promise me that you aren't here to take me to another boat," William gasped.

The man laughed. "I have a rig tied up across the way. Once we collect your luggage—"

"I have no luggage," William interrupted, starting to feel human once again. "That is to say, I haven't any luggage here. There was some difficulty with unloading my trunk off the *Britannic.* My man stayed behind to ensure its safe arrival in Newport."

The man nodded. Now that William could focus on something other than his own discomfort, he could see the stranger wasn't much older than a student still at a university. He looked gangly, but comfortable in his white linen, far more comfortable than William felt in his frock coat and tails.

The stranger presented his hand. "Stephen Young, esquire. I've been sent by Whitby and Essex to welcome you to Newport, Your Grace."

William accepted the eager handshake, but grimaced. "'Your Grace' reminds me of my father." He neglected to add that the address reminded him as well of the unpleasant and dishonorable circumstances his father had left for William to resolve. "Perhaps we can dispatch with that particular address while I'm here? Perhaps we can pretend I'm just another American during my stay."

Stephen's glance suggested it would take more than a dropped title to allow him to pass as American; still the loss of the formalities felt good. As if all his difficulties could be so easily dispensed if he just declined the title. Life didn't work that way, but for a brief period of time he could pretend.

William, feeling stronger by the minute, took a good look at his surroundings. A bustling little seaport this was, though not with the industrial shipping that fouled the Cheapside of the Thames. If anything this port trafficked in people of various classes judging from their attire. The air held a wholesome freshness to it, more attune to the countryside than his familiar London. Indeed the hills and the trees reminded him of his brother's home in Yorkshire. Nicholas would approve of this place.

"This way, Your . . . sir."

William followed the young man to a simple one-horse rig and climbed aboard.

"Tell me, young squire," William teased, coaxing a smile to the boy's serious face. "How did you recognize me amongst all the other passengers?"

"Your clothes, sir."

"Ah yes," he frowned down at his trousers, "I suppose I do look a bit worse for wear. My man stayed behind in New York to escort my trunk once unloaded."

Confusion passed over the young man's face for a moment before it cleared. "No, sir, you look fine. A bit too fine, if I may say, for Newport, sir."

"Oh," William murmured, glancing about. Indeed, beyond the obvious laborers, the few men that passed by, and his young escort, all wore light linen suits better suited for the July heat than his frock coat and tails. He must stand out like a mule on a racetrack. "Then let's be off. And perhaps you can point out a suitable haberdashery along the way?"

The ride was short. Looking back toward the water, William felt he could just as easily have walked the short distance, if it had not been all uphill. His guide pulled the rig to the front of a grand hotel with a wide veranda on busy Bellevue Avenue. A sign proclaimed the establishment to be named the Ocean View.

Mr. Young prepared to hop out of the rig when William restrained him with a hand to his arm. "Tell me, squire, before you go, are you familiar with the purpose of my trip to Newport?"

The young man's smile lit up his fair features. "Of course, Whitby and Essex are handling the negotiations."

"I see . . ." William said, contemplating his next question. It really shouldn't matter. He would do his best by the wealthy American, as any honorable man might, and yet . . . He leaned forward, lowering his voice as befitting a discreet conversation.

"And do you know of the young woman to whom I find myself engaged?"

A wide smile blossomed on the younger man's face as he gazed beyond the horse's ears. "Frosty Franny? Everyone knows her and her honey."

The smile collapsed once he glimpsed William's scowl. A deep red darkened his features.

"I'm sorry, sir. That's just how the local papers refer to her. She's not really . . ." He cleared his throat. "Miss Winthrop, yes, sir, I know of her."

William nodded, his scowl still firmly in place. It was most disconcerting not knowing what his fiancée looked like. Alva Winthrop's letter advising of her daughter's availability had arrived at a most fortuitous moment. There had been no time for the exchange of photographs. Yet, this man's odious reference to her, attached to what he hoped was not some reference to her feminine virtues, made him wonder if he should not have waited a bit before embarking on this venture. The need for money was great, but great enough to be tied forever to a . . . a laughingstock? A woman had made a fool of him before. Once in a lifetime was enough.

"Everyone in Newport knows of Miss Winthrop," the man repeated, his tone sufficiently apologetic. "You are a lucky man to have secured her, sir."

He averted his gaze, thus William couldn't quite judge the honesty of that last proclamation. But as he studied Stephen's profile, the man squinted. "If I'm not mistaken"—he tilted his chin toward the opposite side of the street—"I believe there's your fiancée now."

"Where?" If William hadn't been raised on decorum in the way other young lads were raised on porridge, he would have pushed his escort aside to better view the women strolling beneath the elms that shaded the storefronts across the avenue. He bent forward, much to the protest of his still queasy stomach. "Which one?"

Stephen hopped from the rig, giving William a better view. He proceeded to tie the horse to the hotel's post.

"She's heading up the avenue toward the shops."

A tiny peal of a bell pulled William's glance across the avenue to the fancy gold lettering advertising a series of commercial establishments. A swaying bustle disappeared into the interior of one, while two other ladies approached the grouping.

"Which one?" William asked, wishing the two ladies would turn so he could see more than their profiles. Not receiving an answer, William slid across the seat and lowered himself to the street. Dodging the fashionable carriages, he dashed across the avenue in pursuit of the woman who would soon be his bride. If only he knew which woman that would be.

Silently cursing the tiny bell and awkward glances that announced her presence, Fran quickly slipped to the side of the tobacconist's front display of gaily painted cigar boxes so she could view the street without being seen. Ever since she had balked at her mother's proposal two days ago, spies in the form of her mother's matronly friends had watched her every move and hovered always within earshot. Fortunately she had anticipated such a turn of events and had taken measures to arrange for transport on the Fall River steamer without her mother's consent. Still, she needed to lose the two bloodhounds on her trail if her plan to reunite with Randolph was to succeed.

Mary, her maid, should have already secreted a bit of luggage with a few travel garments to the steamer's boarding ramp. If Fran could make it to the steamer undetected, she stood a chance of purchasing transatlantic passage to Germany without interference. From there she'd find Randolph. She wasn't sure how, but she felt confident that the love in her heart would lead to his door. They would marry and be forever free of her mother and her purchased Duke.

First, however, Mrs. Kravitz and her annoying daughter needed to continue up the boulevard, so she could exit unnoticed from this aromatic sanctuary. Fran inhaled the rich masculine scent of tobacco, letting a smile tease her lips. They would never think to look for her in this male bastion. If anything, Mrs. Kravitz would search for her in the millinery shop next door. Or better yet, continue down the avenue believing they would spot her around the next corner. Fran risked a glance toward the window.

Mrs. Kravitz hesitated outside the shop, near the painted wooden Indian, glancing up and down the street. Her daughter, Phoebe, cupped her hands on the glass window itself and peered in. Fran quickly pressed her spine to the wall to escape notice, holding her breath that they would continue on their way.

"Miss Winthrop, what a surprise to find you here. Are you purchasing something for your father, perhaps?"

Fran nearly jumped out of her corset. The gravelly-voiced proprietor stood close to her elbow. Too close, Fran thought, squelching the panic that such close proximity generated. However, with her own back pressed to the wall, there was no place to retreat. She placed a gloved finger to her lips, silencing the inquisitive man, then slowly shook her head.

He glanced toward the front window, his face relaxed into a smug expression. "I see. Is it Mrs. Kravitz you wish to avoid?" His lips twitched in a suppressed smile. "Or the unusually dressed gentleman?"

Gentleman? Her pulse picked up in surprise, but she maintained her outward calm. What gentleman?

Her glance slipped to the window. True to the proprietor's description, a man dressed in evening attire detained the two bloodhounds. He was handsome enough. Handsome, single, and wealthy, if Mrs. Kravitz's posturing with her daughter was any indication.

She raised her gaze to his eyes, dark blue intelligent eyes that missed nothing. Including her, she realized as his gaze shifted slightly, and he raised one dark brow in acknowledgment. Her heart pounding, she slid back against the wall. Oh, why did he have to intervene at this moment?

The whistle from the Fall River steamer rent the air, announcing its anticipated departure for Long Island. She was running out of time! She needed to be on that ship. She needed to find a way to Randolph, to the quiet, uncomplicated life of a barrister's wife.

"Miss Winthrop, are you sure there is nothing I can show you?" the persistent shopkeeper inquired. "I just received a new shipment of Turkish cigarettes? Perhaps your father would like a box of some Havanas?"

"Is there another exit from your store?" Fran asked. She tilted her head toward the window. "I don't wish to disturb the patrons at your front entrance."

"Why, yes," the proprietor replied cautiously. "We would have to go through the back storeroom, though. It's a bit dusty." He frowned down at her skirts. "We're not accustomed to fine ladies, like yourself, visiting our establishment. I'm afraid your beautiful skirts—"

"That is of little concern." Hope leapt to her throat. If she hurried, she still might make it. "Can you show me the way?"

She followed the man through a pair of curtains and wove her way around stacked wooden crates and wood shavings. A light covering of ash and dust mingled with brown flakes littering the floor. Mary would have a fit when she saw the state of her hems as a result of this quick detour, but no matter, that was of little import. Her guide reached the back door, opening it to a less traveled though much steeper Newport street. Fran ushered through. Once free of the establishment, she raced down the hill toward the port.

I'm coming, Randolph. I'm coming. Her hat slipped its moorings about midway down the hill and tumbled off to the side of the road. She lost one of her fine slippers, but continued in her madcap race. Slippers could always be replaced, but an opportunity to change the course of her future, less so. She approached the wharfmaster's building and foot traffic increased. She stopped short, her heartbeat pounding in her ears, her stays making breath difficult. All those people! Panic fueled her self-doubts. Could she do it? Could she plow through that crowd of strangers?

The steam whistle blasted two bursts, the warning signal that it was pulling away from the dock. Fran lifted her skirt so as not to trip and rushed toward the melee. She raced around the building and down to the ramp before she stopped, her chest heaving from the exertion, her hair long and loose from the loss of hairpins, her skin tingling from the assault of the wind, to see the steamer approaching Castle Rock on its departure from the bay.

"You're too late," Mary called amidst several pieces of luggage farther down the dock. "I tried to tell them, Miss Winthrop. I really did. But they left anyway. They said they couldn't wait and to try again next time."

Too late. The words stabbed her heart as tears burned her eyes. *Too late.* She could tell Mary that there wouldn't be a "next time." Once her mother heard tales of her reckless run through the heart of town to catch a boat that wouldn't wait, she would be locked in her room again. Her mother held no tolerance for public inappropriateness. She could tell Mary that this was her one shot at freedom and it had disappeared in a blue gray wake and a steam cloud trail. She could say many things if the lump in her throat wasn't squeezing the ability to talk right out of her. *Too late!* Her lip trembled.

"Miss Winthrop?" Mary approached, her eyes wide and her mouth twisted in a concerned moue. Her gaze swept from her untidy hair, past the twisted day dress to a bare toe poking through a rip in her stocking, visible beneath a dusty hem. Her voice dropped to a near whisper. "What happened to you?"

A vision of the overdressed stranger with a raised eyebrow and an intriguing smile slipped into her mind. He happened. He was responsible. And with whatever means she could find at her disposal, he would pay.